Praise for *Breed*

'A f... horror, chicly ghoulish, with ... ... on family values ... Above and beyond ... y count *Breed* has originality on its side; the ending is a true shocker. The book sets out to convey what it is like to be 'subject to the whip and rattle of unspeakable temptations.' And it does.'
New York Times

'Forget vampires, zombies and guys clad in hockey masks brandishing oversized machetes. Chase Novak unleashes truly scary literary horror villains in *Breed*: Mom and Dad . . . a thrill to read.'
USA Today

'An intelligent, dark thriller dense with paranoia, yielding creative anxiety, a genetically modified rollercoaster.'
New York Journal of Books

'A delightfully nauseating read . . . the perfect dark fairy tale for these times'
NPR.org

'A slice of shivering dread'
New York Daily News

'Smart and brutal, this joins the ranks of such elegant domestic shockers as Lionel Shriver's *We Need to Talk about Kevin* or John Ajvide Lindqvist's *Let the Right One In*'
Booklist

'A page-turner, classic yet original, filled with detail both subtle and unforgettable, unnerving in its mad logic and genuinely frightening.'
Richard Price, author of *Lush Life*

'An honest-to-goodness page-turner.'
Bookpage

'A creepy, bloody, hairy thrill ride.'
Entertainment Weekly

'The most elegantly skin-crawling, gut-churning novel I've read in years.'
Warren Ellis, author of *Gun Machine*

CHASE NOVAK

BREED

MULHOLLAND
BOOKS

HODDER

First published in Great Britain in 2012 by Mulholland Books
An imprint of Hodder & Stoughton
An Hachette UK company

First published in paperback in 2013

1

A CIP catalogue record for this title is available from the British Library

Paperback ISBN 978 1 444 73701 1
eBook ISBN 978 1 444 73700 4

Printed and bound by Clays Ltd, St Ives plc

Hodder & Stoughton policy is to use papers that are natural, renewable and
recyclable products and made from wood grown in sustainable forests. The
logging and manufacturing processes are expected to conform to the
environmental regulations of the country of origin.

Hodder & Stoughton Ltd
338 Euston Road
London NW1 3BH

www.hodder.co.uk

To Lynn

PART 1

Ye shall fear every man his mother,
and his father...

—Leviticus 19:3

PART 1

It's well known—part fact, part punch line—that people in New York think a great deal about real estate. In the case of Leslie Kramer, she actually was aware of the house Alex Twisden lived in before she had ever met him, or even knew his name. Leslie would often pass by the house on days she chose to walk to Gardenia Press, where, though single and childless herself, she edited children's books.

The house was a piece of pure old New York, built before taxes, before unions, back when the propertied classes had money for the finest stonework, the finest carpentry, and for a multitude of servants, including people to put straw in the streets so the wagon wheels of passing merchants would not clatter against the cobblestones. It was a four-story town house on East Sixty-Ninth Street, an often-photographed Federal-style dwelling made of pale salmon bricks, with windows that turned bursts of light into prismatic fans of color framed by pale green shutters.

It was one of the few residences on this block that had not been broken up into apartments, and the only house in the neighborhood owned by the same family since its construction. It was one of those places that seem immune to change, ever lovely, and ever redolent of privilege and the provenance that justifies the continuation of those privileges. The front of the house bore a polished brass plaque announcing the year of the house's construction, 1840. The window boxes were almost always in bloom, with snowdrops in the spring, and then with tulips, impatiens, geraniums, and various decorative cabbages, some of them so unusual and obscure that often passersby would stop on the sidewalk and wonder about them. The light post next to the eight-step porch was entwined with twinkling blue lights twelve months a year. Recycling was set out at the curb inside of cases that once held bottles of Château Beychevelle or Taittinger's.

Twisdens had been born and have died in these rooms. The first President Roosevelt dined there on several occasions and once famously played the ukulele and sang Cuban folk songs for a dinner party that included the mayor, the ambassador to the Court of St. James's, and a Russian ballerina who, it turned out, was embroiled in an affair with the host, Abraham Twisden. Twisdens who practiced law and medicine lived here, political Twisdens, bohemian Twisdens, drunken and idle Twisdens, one of whom lost the house in a card game on West Fourteenth Street, a debt that was nullified by the sudden death of the lucky winner, who turned out not to be so lucky after all.

Alex was raised in this house along with his sisters, Katherine and Cecile. Their world was this house, with its mahogany globes the size of cantaloupes on the newel posts of every stairway, with wedding-cake plaster on the ceilings, and wainscoting in the parlor and the library, and antique Persian carpets of red and purple and blue and gold on the wide plank floors, rugs knotted by little hands that had long since turned to dust.

Katherine lives now as a Buddhist nun in Thailand and has renounced the family; she has a brain tumor that has shortened her temper but seems not to be shortening her life. Cecile died at thirteen, of a staph infection following the removal of her appendix, and when their parents died in Corfu, in 1970, the house on Sixty-Ninth Street passed without contest directly to Alex.

In point of fact, it was the house that brought Alex and Leslie together in the first place. One drizzly spring morning, Alex noticed her stopped in front of his house, and he said, "Haven't I seen you before?"

"Oh, I like to stop here. It's on my way to work. And it's such a beautiful house."

"I'm afraid I'm its prisoner," Alex said. "I just don't like anyplace else in the world half so much."

"I can see why," Leslie said. The ends of her blunt-cut auburn hair touched the dark red, rain-spotted wool of her coat. She had the plain but lovely face of a pioneer; he could imagine her sitting at the back of a covered wagon, looking longingly east as her family headed west. Her eyes were bright green, and though she was smiling, there seemed something temperamental, easily wounded about her.

Alex, dressed for work in thousands of dollars' worth of English tailoring and, even in a more overtly social situation, tending toward the reticent, surprised himself by asking, "Would you be interested in seeing the inside?"

From there to courtship to wedding was a mere five months and it did not escape Leslie's attention that some people (well: many) thought of her as Alex Twisden's midlife trophy wife. Never mind that she loved him, and never mind that (of this she was certain) he loved her, and never mind that she was almost thirty (well: twenty-eight) and had an excellent (well: good) job at a great (well: up-and-coming) New York publishing company—the fact that she was seventeen years younger than Alex, and that he was wealthy and childless and probably (well: definitely) in the hunt for an heir, made Leslie a trophy wife, which, in the parlance of well-off Manhattanites, suggested she was practicing some high-end, socially sanctioned form of prostitution.

But now the shining trophy wife has a very significant ding in her. She has been trying to have a baby for three years, which is why she and Alex are currently sitting in the annex of Herald Church on West Ninetieth Street, a depressing, claustrophobic, smelly, badly lit, terrible, and depressing (yes, it is worth a second mention) basement in which they are attending the biweekly meeting of the Uptown Infertility Support Group. As Leslie looks around at the scuffed linoleum floors, the plasterboard walls, the strip lighting, and the metal folding chairs, she uncrosses and recrosses her legs and tries to read the expression on her husband's long, narrow, solemn face. But he is as unreadable here as he is when he rides the elevator to the top floor of the Erskine Building, where the venerable firm of Bailey, Twisden, Kaufman, and Chang go about their hushed business, a kind of law that seems to Leslie far closer to accountancy than to anything she has ever seen on TV. In TV law, lives hang in the balance, wrongs are redressed, and the system blindly gropes its way toward justice. At BTK&C, all that matters is the orderly transfer of property, and the golden rule seems to be "Don't ever touch the principal."

Neither Alex nor Leslie really wants or needs the psychological or moral support of other couples dealing with infertility. They attend because it is Alex's theory that these meetings, aside from being sobfests and weirdly twelve-steppy in their confessional nature, operate as a kind of clearinghouse for information about fertility treatments and fertility doctors. So far they have not met anyone who has done anything different from what Alex and Leslie have tried, often at the very same clinics, with the very same doctors, and even with the same kindhearted nurses. Tonight's meeting is particularly useless. Two of the nine couples in the group have already separated—infertility can wreak havoc on a marriage—yet both the husbands from these defunct unions continue not only to show up for meetings but to dominate the discussions. The Featherstones, a chubby, cheerful duo—he a second-grade teacher, she a pastry chef—want to share their fabulous news. Chelsea is, or at least *was,* pregnant, and even though she miscarried in the third week, both the Featherstones are ebullient, feeling they have their problem, if not defeated, then at least on the run, and they somehow induce the group to share their excitement. As the basement echoes with applause, Leslie pretends to look for something in her purse, and Alex simply sits there with his hands folded in his lap.

When she looks over at him he silently mouths the words *I love you.*

It's a balmy evening with the last tatters of daylight hanging pale gray and dark blue from the treetops of Central Park as Leslie and Alex walk home from the church basement on West Ninetieth Street to their town house on East Sixty-Ninth. For the hundredth time Leslie has asked him if he would have married her if he had known they were going to be cast into the medical hell of infertility, where the devils wear white and smell of hand sanitizer and think nothing of charging thousands upon thousands of dollars for failure, and in fact make you feel that the failure is not theirs but yours. And as always Alex has answered, "I believe that the day you consented to be my wife was the luckiest day of my life." These are the words he said the first time she tremulously posed the question, and now it is their private joke and solace for him to repeat the exact words each time the question is asked, and though the first time he said them Leslie responded with tears of relief, now the repetition makes her laugh—but the relief is still there, nevertheless.

They have, even without a child, so much to live for. They are healthy, they are in love, they are successful in their careers. Leslie was not raised poor, or to *be* poor, but the kind of material comfort that comes with marriage to Alex (whom she would have married even if he had been a mime or a bus driver) is beyond anything she had ever imagined for herself—though, of course, now she has grown accustomed to it. And Alex, though wealthy all his life, had always been surrounded by dour people lacking in charm, charisma, and sexual allure, and to be living with someone who appeals to him like a work of art and excites him sexually so that he feels half his age around her is beyond anything he had imagined for himself—though he, too, has grown accustomed to his good fortune.

Yet the good fortune of their lives is shadowed by an absence that, for all of its invisibility, casts a long cold shadow. When they are not avidly pursuing pregnancy, it seems that they are determinedly avoiding things that make them confront their childless state. They have become unreasonable even to themselves, most recently wasting opera tickets worth hundreds of dollars when to their dismay a new hipper-than-thou production of *Turandot* featured a children's chorus, all oohing and aahing behind the Principessa, causing them to flee, Alex leading the way, his eyes blazing with the fury of the betrayed, and Leslie following up the aisle, dragging her shawl behind her like an animal she had just killed.

Now they eschew opening nights and read the theater, movie, and opera reviews to make sure that they don't get their hearts broken by some display of beautiful children. But the wound of their unhappiness disfigures their life in other ways too. They find themselves seeing less and less of their friends who are parents. The Kaminskys, for example (he a cardiologist, she a lighting designer for the Public Theater), descended into a woe-is-me duet about their difficulties in getting their precious little Henry into a supposedly great preschool, one where presumably the juice boxes were infused with special elixirs that doubled the toddlers' IQs, and the Legos were specially devised in a top secret laboratory carved into the side of a mountain in Switzerland, and readings of *Goodnight Moon* included actual trips to the moon. Similarly, Leslie's colleague at Gardenia Press, Sheri McDougal, who looks like Greta Garbo and was the first openly gay woman from her little hamlet in Nova Scotia, now has a child sprouted from purchased sperm and, at dinner parties, actually sat the gorgeous little baby girl at the table and insisted guests make eye contact with her during conversation so Emily's brain could be stimulated and the little flame of her self-esteem could begin burning brightly.

Unless they were to move into one of those retirement communities—Seizure World, as Alex calls them—where they don't allow children beyond the gates, there is no way to live without seeing children. Even tonight, as Leslie and Alex walk through Central Park, it is poignant and disturbing to see children, some with their parents, some with nannies, some completely on their own. (Leslie and Alex have said that if they were to have a child they would never let him or her in the park on his own, or with a nanny.) But as the evening darkens toward night, the number of children suddenly decreases—they seem to fly away like the birds.

Yet as luck would have it, as soon as Leslie and Alex notice the absence of children, they come upon a father with his little two-year-old in a stroller. The father sits on a bench talking into his cell phone, one foot on the stroller as he pushes it back and forth, hoping to pacify his child. But the child—a wild-haired boy with dark eyebrows and bright red lips—begins to whimper and wave his hands, and the father, with a quick word or two, flips his phone shut and focuses his attention on his son.

"What are you saying, baby, huh, what's the fuss?"

The baby, distracted from his troubles by the sound of his father's cheerful voice, suddenly smiles.

The father takes the child's little asterisk of a hand and brings it to his lips and makes loud *yum yum yum* noises, as if devouring the finest delicacy. "Oooh, I could just eat you up," the father says, as if this were the most normal thing in the world and cannibalism of one's own child were the ultimate sign of affection.

The child shrieks. It could be hilarity; it could also be fear. And the father pretends to polish off one hand and now starts on the other.

Alex takes long strides, forcing Leslie to hurry just a little in order to keep up with him.

"I think that baby was scared," Leslie says.

"Yeah. Sounded it. There was something a little sick about the whole thing, wasn't there?"

"I know!" Leslie says. "My uncle James used to do this thing when he'd grab my nose and pretend to pull it off—and show me his thumb as if it were my nose. It totally freaked me out."

Alex drapes his arm over Leslie's shoulders. He knows that most of the pressure to conceive comes from him. He regrets it and he cannot help it. Once they have a child Leslie will be grateful.

"Maybe we need to reopen the conversation about adoption," Leslie says as a couple of bicyclists come zooming past them, with their spandex shorts and Martian helmets.

"I'm afraid I'm a little old-fashioned about these things," Alex says. Allowing people to shorten his name from Alexander to Alex and even calling himself Alex constitutes his principal concession to modern American life, and his intention is to hold the line on everything else. "I feel a responsibility. The Cranes and the Hillmans on my mother's side, and the Twisdens and Glomans on my father's side, have enjoyed extraordinary successes and given extraordinary public service for the last two hundred years, and that's just in America. I would like to continue that line. And Leslie, your family is nothing to sneeze at either. You have teachers, doctors, congressmen."

"I have a cousin who ran for Congress in 1998 in Ohio and had his ass handed to him."

"I know this is hard on you," Alex says, gathering her closer to him.

They have already tried all the time-tested ways of getting pregnant, and then went on to acupuncture, and from there to herbalists. It has been both their privilege and their misfortune that they have plenty of money to spend on treatments, and whereas many couples finally spend themselves out of the quest for fertility, Alex and Leslie have pressed on—and on and on. They have seen two hypnotists— one in Tribeca, whose breath smelled like rust, and the other in Los Angeles, who looked like a marionette come to life. They have spent time at the Whispering Sage Sanctuary in Clearwater, Florida, a so-called Ayurvedic health center, where a long weekend of Panchakarma therapies, yoga, and meditation was offered, and where all they got was a wrenched back for Alex and a touch of food poisoning for Leslie. They have consulted homeopaths and psychiatrists, and, though neither of them is particularly religious, they also went to a clinic called Answered Prayers, in which words and phrases such as *ectopic, ovarian cysts, endometriosis, polycystic ovarian syndrome, terato-zoospermia,* and *oopause* were bandied about but where it basically boiled down to readings of the New Testament and listening to sermons about opening yourself to the blessings of God. They fasted, they ate nothing but fruit, they had the cleanest colons in the world.

And they worried about their marriage. They had seen firsthand how the Baby Hunt doused the flames of romance, turning the joy of sex into the job of sex and making the body a source of failure rather than pleasure. But still they persisted—six different in vitro fertilizations, and a thorough investigation of the legal and psychological dangers of an egg donor or a sperm donor, or even a live person who could impregnate Leslie or whom Alex could impregnate, even though expensive technicians had already tested Leslie's eggs and Alex's sperm and as far as anyone could see they were just fine. Yet lightning would not strike; it was out there, but it was dry, distant lightning, just a little quiver of light in the lowering sky, with no rain to follow.

Tonight as they make their way through Central Park after the support-group meeting (what Alex calls the Fertilize-Her Society), with nothing to look forward to except a quiet dinner for two and, depending on Leslie's basal temperature, some sad copulation, Leslie and Alex see Jim and Jill Johnson walking their little Yorkshire terrier.

They had come to know the Johnsons, however slightly, through the Uptown Infertility Support Group, though it has been months since the Johnsons have been in attendance. The Johnsons are like them in many ways. Like Alex, Jim is significantly older than his wife; Jim, too, is a lawyer, though with a practice far less lucrative than

Alex's. Like Leslie, Jill is from the Midwest; Jill is a high school teacher and seems to envy Leslie, imagining her job as an editor at a publishing company to be full of glamour and excitement. Twice they all had drinks together after their group meeting, and once they even met for dinner. The dinner was not a success. Jill seemed to have some strange grievance against Leslie. She would say things like "Oh, it must feel strange for you being out with a poor little high school teacher."

"That's insane," Leslie had exclaimed, to Alex's delight.

Tonight, Jim Johnson is dressed in a dark brown leather jacket and a light brown beret. His hair is much too long. To Alex, he looks like one of those lawyers who imagine themselves champions of the underdogs but who are actually vain grandstanders, would-be gadflies, Sandinistas in three-piece suits. But the real sight to behold is Jill. Never particularly slender, she is immense. At first Alex thinks unhappiness and bad genes have made Jill obese, but he realizes she is pregnant, gloriously, radiantly, and, by the looks of it, quintupfully pregnant. New York City, some say, is the schadenfreude capital of the world—but for Alex and Leslie, seeing a formerly infertile couple pregnant gives them hope. The Johnsons have been trying to get pregnant for eleven years.

"So how did this happen?" Alex bursts out, pointing at Jill's belly.

"Alex," Leslie says, giving him a little shove.

"It's a reasonable question," he says, as if to her but really to them. "After all we've been through together? Come on, we're soldiers in the same battalion. Right? So what is it? A new diet, a new exercise, a new doctor?"

But the Johnsons are playing coy. "You know, the thing is," Jill says, "we tried so many things, in the end I'm not sure what the heck worked." Her voice is breathless; she sounds like what she is: a woman carrying fifty extra pounds.

Alex narrows his eyes at Jim, causing the father-to-be to shift his weight and his glance—he is the very definition of *shifty*.

"Well, if you have some great new doctor or something," Alex says, "I wish you'd tell us. We're really at the end of our rope. And, honestly, Jim, I think we have a right to know. At the very least—" Alex pokes Jim lightly in the stomach. "Professional courtesy, right?"

"We're actually not able to do that," Jim says. "It's complicated."

"Complicated?" Alex says, as if the word itself were absurd. "Try us."

"Oh, come on, Alex, we're fine," Leslie says. This is far from her idea of how to get information out of people—she would invite them over, serve them a brilliant meal with wonderful wine.

"I'll tell you what, old friend," Jim says to Alex, his smile as cold as a zipper. "With a young'un on the way, the mind turns to practical matters. Make me a partner in your law firm and I'll tell you exactly what we did to make this happen." Jim pats his wife's stomach while their little dog begins to yip impatiently.

The men's eyes lock. It is just now dawning on Alex that this meeting might not be a total coincidence. The Johnsons might well have known that he and Leslie would be coming out of Fertilize-Her at this time and crossing the park on their way to the Upper East Side. And as these thoughts form themselves in Alex's mind, Jim seems to be nodding his head as if to say *That's right, you're figuring it out.*

"I might see my way clear to offering you a position, but I'm certainly not able to offer a partnership," Alex says, with such seriousness that both of the women turn toward Jim, like people in a stadium watching a tennis match.

"I would need some guarantee that a partnership was at least possible."

"In the world of business, everything is possible," Alex says.

"All right, then," Jim says.

"It's a deal," Alex says. He extends his hand. Jim offers his own in return but slowly, suddenly shy. Alex further extends his own reach and seizes Jim's hand. It looks to Leslie like a big fish eating a small fish. "Come see me at nine o'clock tomorrow."

"I have an appointment at nine tomorrow," Jim says.

"Break it," Alex advises. Though he is ostensibly the supplicant in this matter, he has seized control of the situation nevertheless.

Throughout his career, Alex has always been the first person to the office, generally arriving between six and six thirty in the morning. When he began at the firm, the other young lawyers with whom he was presumably in competition secretly nicknamed him Eager Alex and Alexander Daybreak, but now he is a partner and he continues to arrive before the other partners, the other lawyers, the paralegals, the secretaries, the receptionist, and the mail-room workers. The only people he sees when he enters the Bailey, Twisden, Kaufman, and Chang offices on Fifty-Ninth and Madison are the security guards in the lobby—a recent addition to the building, since the attack on Lower Manhattan two years before—and the cleaners, who on most days are leaving with their buckets and mops and brooms and plastic bags filled with wastepaper just as Alex is walking in, dressed in his bespoke suit, his Turnbull and Asser shirt, and his Crockett and Jones shoes, which he polishes himself.

As usual, Alex uses the early-morning hours at his desk to clear away any lingering paperwork, to make little notes to himself about whatever cases or contracts he is working on, and to simply collect his thoughts, without the distraction of ringing phones, pinging e-mails, and other people. By nine o'clock, Alex feels well on top of his work. He is standing at the office's espresso machine—a gift from a well-known pop singer, thanking the firm for its pro bono work on behalf of the singer's chauffeur—when the first arrivals step out of the elevator: Alex's longtime secretary; his paralegal; his intern (the daughter of an old friend), all of whom know enough to ar-rive at work promptly; two other secretaries holding their breakfasts in white paper bags; an IT kid with a backpack and earbuds; Lew Chang's paralegal, who looks as if she has been crying, which more or less confirms Alex's suspicion that Lew and she are having a fling, a lawsuit waiting to happen; and Jim Johnson, the last one off the elevator. His face has been nicked and scraped by this morning's hasty shave, and his flowing hair has been sensibly barbered. A classic case of too little, too late.

"Hello, Jim," Alex says, indicating with a wave that Johnson follow through the outer office and into his corner lair, where Alex settles in behind his desk, a cherrywood Sheraton that used to be in Alex's house. With a second wave he directs Johnson to an old leather club chair, which looks comfortable enough but is so deep that anyone consigned to it must sit with his knees practically parallel with his chin.

After a minute of small talk, Alex, with the efficiency of a man who bills at $1,750 per hour, arrives at the point of this meeting.

"So, Jim. Pregnancy. We don't understand your reluctance to give us the name of your doctor. That seems odd to me, to both of us."

"Well, Alex," Johnson says, with a weirdly sarcastic edge to his voice, "it doesn't seem odd to me. Not in the slightest. I noted the look on your face when you saw Jill. And I think you'll understand this, *Alex:* I thought there just might be something more I could be doing to provide for my family."

"What look on my face, my friend?" Alex is aware that calling someone *my friend* is usually a way of saying you are not friends, and he notes with equal measures of amazement and amusement how quickly the gloves have come off between him and Johnson.

"Envy. A need to know. Desire. Sorrow. You name it."

"It seems as if you're doing all the naming, Jim."

"Yes, I am. And I am also naming the price."

"For giving us a simple piece of information?"

"Didn't you know, Alex? We're living in an information economy. Information is gold, it's oil, it's land, it's power."

"Okay, then tell me this, Counselor. And you don't have to divulge *where* you had this done—but what did you do? Is this some state-of-the-art in vitro clinic? In which case, I'd have to say: I'd be very surprised if there is anybody reputable or anyplace that's had any kind of track record that we've overlooked. Is this something that involves surgery? Because Leslie's been through enough of that. Is this some mumbo-jumbo faith-healing situation? Because if that's your great trump card, then, my friend, I might have to throw you out the window."

"Is there a box I can check that says 'None of the above'?" Johnson says, palpably enjoying his position in this back-and-forth.

"You know, when we sat together, week after week, in that dank little room at Herald Church," Alex says, leaning back in his chair, te-peeing his fingers, "there was a consensus, a kind of unwritten law, if you will, that we were all of us there for each other and there would be a sharing of information. I find your behavior, Jim, very strange, if not reprehensible."

"I can say two words, a man's name, and you and Leslie will be on your way to the nursery. But meanwhile, I have to do what's best for my family. Kids change everything, don't you understand that? This isn't about me and Jill anymore. This is about our son."

"Your son..."

"Yes, we peeked. Fact is, Jill's had a few complications and we've spent our fair share of time on the old ob-gyn trail."

"Okay. So it's none of the above. Tell me what procedure you used."

"It's called fertility enhancement," Johnson says. He leans forward in his chair and quickly stands up, begins to pace, rolling his shoulders, craning his neck, rubbing his long hands together, like an athlete alone in the locker room.

"So what is that?" Alex asks. "Vitamins? Diet?"

"It's all done in one appointment," Johnson says. "You're in, you're out, you're pregnant."

"Each and every time?"

"So he says. I won't lie to you, Alex. I don't really know his success rate. The people who told us about him were certainly successful. And he charges enough—not that that would be an issue for you." Again that quick zipper smile.

"And he's a doctor."

"Indeed he is." There's a bit of irony in Johnson's tone. "All very cutting edge, etcetera."

"I still don't know what it is he does."

"Fertility enhancement."

"I know. You said that. But that's what they all do. Fertility enhancement—you either interfere with fertility, and that's called birth control, or you enhance it, and that's called the last three years of my life and, oh, something close to three-quarters of a million dollars for everything from laser surgery to Chinese tea."

"This doctor treats both the woman and the man. He has a formula that radically increases the motility of your sperm and the viability of her eggs. God only knows what's in the stuff he gives you, but it fucking works, I'll tell you that. And I'll tell you his name, and how to get in touch with him, and everything else you need—but I need something too, Alex. I need to work here. My firm—well, you know all about it. It's a nothing place with flea-bitten clients and I'm not making any money, not the kind of money I need, not the kind of money I see around here. I'm an okay lawyer. Not great, I'm nobody's hero, nobody's salvation. But I know how to grind it out. Am I going to be one of the bright lights here? No, probably not. But I can do the work and I'm not going to embarrass myself or you."

"I'll say this for you, Jim. For you to come here and dangle this possibility in front of me and then to make it a precondition that I give you a job here—you've got to have some big brass balls to try something like this. Big. Fucking. Brass. Balls."

"Then, judging by your words and your tone," Johnson says, "I assume we have a deal. I'm asking for a three-year contract—and if you try to get rid of me for some personal reason or for some Mickey

Mouse screwup or for anything short of gross incompetence, I will sue you for breach. And retire."

After his negotiation with Jim Johnson, Alex called Leslie at her office and said he would be bringing dinner home tonight and there was something he wanted to tell her. He'd thought it was obvious what this conversation was going to be about—after all, she had been standing right there the night before in Central Park when he made his appointment with Johnson—but Leslie had seemed distracted on the phone and didn't ask for any further elucidation. She simply said, "Oh, all right," and left it at that.

And now, hours later, Alex is laying out the carry-in sushi and ice-cold dai ginjo sake in their dining room while Leslie watches him, sitting in a tufted leather Queen Anne sofa that Twisdens and their spouses had been sitting in since 1808, her legs drawn up, her arms wrapped around her knees, a distracted look on her face.

"I've been looking forward to this conversation all day," Alex announces as he pours the sake into two small pale green earthenware cups.

"There's something I need to talk about too," Leslie says. She brushes her bangs away from her eyes, takes a deep, steadying breath.

"Well, you first," Alex says.

From the next room, the telephone sounds—their answering machine is programmed to pick up on the first ring, and they hear Alex's deep voice instructing the caller to wait for the tone. (Alex believes that those who call it "the beep" ought to be thrashed to within an inch of their lives!)

"Remember meeting Mary Gallo?"

"From your office." Alex doesn't remember this person at all but he knows how to lead the witness.

"Yes. She's an editor, cookbooks mainly. I can see by your face you don't remember her—but you've met her."

"Of course I have," Alex says. Most of the people with whom Leslie works are interchangeable to him, but nice, awfully nice.

"Well, she and her partner just adopted. A little girl from Russia."

"Attachment disorder," Alex says quickly.

"What?"

"A lot of the Russian kids have attachment disorder. They don't bond." He takes a sip of sake.

"Alex. I want us to adopt. I'm sick of living this way. I'm tired of doctors, and diets, and I am most of all worried." She senses Alex is about to say something but she stops him with a gesture. "I am worried about what this is doing to *us*. Our marriage. Our *souls*."

"There's nothing wrong with our marriage or our souls," Alex manages to put in.

But Leslie is being carried by the force of all that she has kept pent up for months and she barely hears him. "I am sick of feeling like this, like a failure. I never want to hold my legs up like a beetle on its back after we have sex—it's ridiculous." She holds the sides of her head, as if to prevent an explosion. "I want our sex life to be about us. I want you to touch me because you love me and because you are attracted to me, not because I am ovulating, or am supposed to be ovulating according to the goddamned calendar and that horrible thermometer. I never want to see a calendar or a thermometer again. Ever. No, no." She puts up her hands as if Alex is about to interrupt, though by now he has decided to sit silently, let her vent, let the steam blow off. "I want a calendar, but full of dinner dates, and theater tickets, and meeting friends for drinks at the Sherry—remember? Remember our life together? What it used to be like? When was the last time we had dinner with people? When was the last time I had an orgasm?" She sees Alex's eyes widen. "I'm sorry, Alex. I don't even fake them anymore. At this point I'm like a clump of dirt waiting for the farmer to shove a seed in me." She reaches for his hand. "I used to be so sexy, Alex. With you. I was just blazing. You turned me on so much. And I want that back. We're not getting any younger, we're not going to live forever, and I don't want to waste any more of our time."

"May I speak now?" Alex says.

"I want you to," she says softly.

"Well, first of all, I take it that the remark about our not getting any younger primarily concerns me. Now that my fiftieth birthday is in sight. Though I must say, it feels more as if the fiftieth birthday has me in *its* sights, like in the crosshairs."

"No one gets younger, Alex. Life is a one-way street."

"Well…yes. That's true. But you're still a very young woman, and in a few years you're still going to be young, and you're still going to be beautiful—and young enough to be a mother. You get to my age, the pace quickens. I think you begin to age four years for every actual year, at a certain point. My time is running out."

"Your time is never going to run out with me."

"I repeat: my time is running out."

"Alex…"

"Jim Johnson came to my office today, Leslie."

Leslie falls silent. She drinks her sake and holds out her cup for Alex to refill.

"And?" she asks in a small voice.

"And now he is an attorney at Bailey, Twisden, Kaufman, and Chang."

"So he told you the name of their miracle doctor, I gather," Leslie says.

"Yes, he did. Dr. Kis, and he's in Ljubljana."

"Where?"

"Lub. Yan. Na. Ljubljana."

"Thanks for the lesson, Alex. Now you want to tell me where the hell that is?" Things seem to be moving along without her; she doesn't care to be a passenger on the SS *Alex* as it steams across the ocean of life.

"Slovenia, beautiful Slovenia." He cannot escape noticing the dejection showing in Leslie's face, and he covers his own nervousness by thoughtfully chewing an oily, briny slab of yellowtail. "Every girl's dream destination," he adds.

"Next week is sales conference," Leslie says. "I'm presenting my entire list."

"I'm sorry. I'm sorry for everything. I'm sorry I didn't consult you, I'm sorry about your sales conference, I'm sorry this new doctor is not in Paris, but most of all I'm sorry we don't have children in our life. We have to do this, Leslie. One last attempt, okay? We just have to."

"Alex, I'm done, I'm just…done."

"No, please. We can't quit now. I just gave this guy a job."

"You shouldn't have."

"*Leslie,* this child—"

"There *is* no child, Alex."

"I know, I know. But there could be. And I have never wanted anything so much in all my life."

"You haven't had a chance to long for things, Alex." She gestures around her, at the house, the furniture, the artwork, and all it implied: Alex is an heir and has never wanted for anything in his life.

Except this: another heir.

"That's not fair, Leslie. I want to have a child with *you*."

"Oh God, Alex. Do you think I don't want to have a child too? I want us to have that. But there are so many children in the world waiting for someone to take care of them. Wouldn't we do just as well to adopt?"

"I don't rule it out, really, I don't. But let's just try this. Can't we? All your kindness and intelligence and beauty—it would be a waste not to pass it along, not to keep it in the world. The gene pool cries out for it!" He smiles and lifts his brows, awaiting his smile's reciprocation.

"I'm going to assume you've already made arrangements."

Alex shrugs.

"When is the appointment?"

"Next Monday."

"But Alex, next week? It's not only sales conference but my sister is going to be in town and I offered her the third floor."

"So now she can stay anywhere in the house."

"How much is this going to cost?" Leslie asks.

"A ridiculous amount. And I've already paid half, since he insists on a wire transfer before the appointment. Which I know is highly irregular, but irregular might be just what we need right now, since nothing regular has done us the slightest bit of good."

"I can't stand seeing you so upset," Leslie's older sister, Cynthia, says to her. Cynthia, who co-owns an antique store called Gilty Pleasures in San Francisco with her boyfriend, has come to New York to visit Leslie and to attend a few auctions — she especially hopes to procure a set of twelve Chinese export plates made in 1775 for an English earl, each with his beaver and coronet crest in the center, flanked by a pair of mermaids.

"We're coming to the end," Leslie says. They are in the parlor and even though it is still light outside, the room is somber, filled with dark blue shadows and the sad perfume of hothouse roses that were supposed to be cheery. "If this doesn't work, I think we'll throw in the towel."

"The towel of the marriage?" Cynthia asks.

"Never. The towel of parenting."

"And he still won't consider adoption?" Cynthia asks. She does her best to keep her gaze fixed on her younger sister, but the parlor — indeed, the entire house! — is so filled with antiques, most of them in Alex's family for generations, that it's difficult for Cynthia not to take them all in with her appraising, admiring eyes. Just above the Queen Anne chair with its multicolored floral needlework in which

Leslie slouches is a two-hundred-fifty-year-old gilt-wood mirror surmounted by a swan's-neck crest, which in turn centers a feather-carved finial with a female mask nestled in palm fronds. It would probably sell for twenty thousand dollars, maybe more, in San Francisco. Also distracting Cynthia is the fact that Leslie has placed her teacup directly onto the George III mahogany tripod table next to her chair, a caramel-colored beauty with an exquisite piecrust top and leaf-carved feet.

"Look around you," Leslie says, indicating with a wave the walls covered in portraits of Alex's numerous relations, ranging from a British army officer with his scrubbed pink face and bloodred jacket; to a shrewd-looking older woman in an amber dress with Pomeranians on her lap and steel in her eyes; to a fatuous dandy in a royal blue tricorn and shimmering silk waistcoat, holding his cane delicately between two fingers; to some more recently minted Twisdens wearing the uniforms of their hobbies (riding breeches, yachting caps, painter's smocks) or their professions (Brooks Brothers suits, judge's robes, Episcopal minister's purple shirt and turned collar). "Alex wants to continue his family's line."

"And what are you?" Cynthia says. "Breed stock?" Childless herself, and living with a man who nearly everyone assumes is gay, Cynthia has never been a cheerleader for the conventional family.

"How about I love him and want to make him happy," Leslie says.

"And what about your happiness?" Cynthia asks. "All these procedures, your intimate life completely invaded. It's nuts. And your career!"

"Well, as I said, we're coming to the end of it."

"And what the hell is this new treatment that you have to leave the country to get? I mean, come on, Les. I'd be highly dubious. In fact, I'd be scared to death."

"Who said I'm not?" Leslie says.

Cynthia's attention is captured momentarily by a pair of Chinese reverse paintings on glass hanging above the fireplace. In one, a maiden kneels on a raft holding an oar and navigating rough waters, and in the other, a seated mother and a standing child are beneath a cypress tree, a pagoda on a hill in the distance. "Are those new?" Cynthia asks.

"Nothing in this house is new," Leslie says.

The primary home improvement Alex and Leslie have made is to triple-glaze the windows as a way of reducing the hum, honk, roar, shout, and screech of New York. Nevertheless, a piercing scream from the sidewalk one story below comes into the room with all the speed, force, and shock of a flaming arrow. Leslie and Cynthia hurry to the window and part the heavy velvet drapes.

Directly beneath them, a nanny in a white uniform and a blue top-coat holds the side of her face and continues to scream. She is obviously in excruciating pain, and a couple of passersby, frozen by the horror of the moment and the terror and torment of the woman, stand gawking at her as she walks in tight little circles holding her cheek and howling in agony. When she moves her hand away, the pink of her flesh shows through the dark brown of her skin. She looks at her palm, which is red with blood, while still more blood courses down her face, some of it pooling in her ear, most of it cascading onto the collar of her woolen coat, turning the bright blue wool brownish black.

Yet as terrible a sight as that is, what has riveted the attention of the people below on the street and Leslie and Cynthia as well is the nanny's little charge, a sinewy, long-legged, dark-haired, pale child of two or three, a boy, to judge from his clothes—red sneakers, blue jeans, and a little satin New York Giants jacket. He is sitting calmly in his stroller with his hands folded in his lap, his eyes expressionless, and blood drooling out of his mouth.

"Did that fucking baby just bite his nanny?" Cynthia exclaims.

According to Alex, the most irritating aspect of their appointment with Dr. Kis is that there is no way to fly directly to Slovenia unless they fly private. So he books Lufthansa first class to Munich, with a connecting flight on something called Adria, where first class will probably get you nothing more than a larger bag of pretzels. And so, on the afternoon of November 18, they set off on what Leslie hopes is the very last stop on their quest for a biological heir. The first leg of their flight is reasonably relaxed; they reach the meticulously maintained Munich airport around 7:00 a.m. and find a café in which to kill an hour before their scheduled flight to Ljubljana. They stow their Vuitton carry-ons under a black Formica table; inside of Alex's suitcase is an envelope with $20,000 in hundred-dollar bills, the second half of the payment to Dr. Kis, who insists on cash—he is gracious enough to accept American dollars, though he prefers euros. As luck would have it, someone has left behind a copy of the *Financial Times;* as they drink their *kaffeemilch*, Alex reads an article about attempts being made to restructure British Petroleum, and Leslie reads about the resurgence of international gangs who target rich families via kidnapping, identity theft, and blackmail.

"Look at this," Leslie says, showing Alex the newspaper's photo of two stubby-looking men with three-day beards, handcuffed, their balding heads down as they are led away by Russian policemen. "They tried to kidnap an American banker's child."

"Idiots," says Alex.

"You know..." They both say it at the same time.

"Go ahead," Alex says.

"I was just going to say I sometimes wish we weren't rich."

"Really?"

"Yes. Really. I wonder what our lives would be like. I mean, money is its own kind of ghetto, isn't it? Everything we do, everyone we know. And it makes us a target too. It's scary. So what were you going to say?"

"Me? I was going to say I wish we hadn't flown commercial."

*   *   *

The flight from Munich to Ljubljana is about forty-five minutes. The airport there, in terms of its size and sense of importance, is what you would expect if you flew into Poughkeepsie. Alex and Leslie disembark, along with a couple of elderly nuns, an Austrian businessman, and a stewardess in a peacock-blue blazer. They are brought to the main building in a minivan, the back door of which remains open to the cold, while not far away a jet begins its takeoff. Inside the shabby white building, there seems to be no passport control, no customs; in a few minutes, the Twisdens are out of the airport and in the back of a taxi reeking of air freshener. The driver, a woman in her thirties whose gelled, spiky hair reminds Leslie of those metal guards some people put on their windowsills to keep pigeons away, drives quickly past the frosted hillocks and icy evergreens lining the road into the city.

A sudden rain; it seems to come out of nowhere and all at once. The driver is reluctant to use the windshield wipers, turning them on for only a moment or two and then turning them off, waiting to turn them on again until the windshield has been pelted so thoroughly with rain that it looks as if it is covered with silver paint.

Alex feels the tension in Leslie's body, and he takes her hand, pats it reassuringly. "How you doing, baby?"

"Don't even say that word," Leslie says.

Soon, they are in the city. The outlying area exudes a kind of post-socialist anonymity, as if every building—every brick—feared being accused of putting on airs. But as they get closer to the city center, the architecture becomes less utilitarian, more decorative, and, after a series of switchbacks caused by various one-way streets and other streets recently closed to automobile traffic, they arrive at their hotel, which, from the outside, presents nothing more inviting than a wooden door such as you would use to enter a small church. Above it is a stone carving of an old man with his forefinger pressed to his lips, presumably asking passersby to keep their voices down.

Leslie has fallen asleep. Alex pats her knee as he pays the driver, and, commandeering both of their suitcases, he leads her into the hotel. Her eyes are half closed; he suspects that mainly she doesn't want to see *anything*. Check-in is at a charming little desk set to one side of a stone internal courtyard, where they are served by a sallow man in his thirties with thinning black hair and sad brown eyes beneath which hang the crepe of dark circles. *Kidney failure,* Alex thinks, handing over their passports.

There are potted plants everywhere—hundreds of them—and gloomy, age-encrusted paintings on the walls that remind Alex of the portraits of his ancestors back home except that these are of a jowly Madonna; a glowering bishop; a naked Holy Infant with sausage legs and a potbelly, wielding a sword.

Ljubljana is divided by a river. On one side is the Old Town, stony and Gothic, with twisting streets leading to Dr. Kis's office, and on the other is the newer section, with office buildings and modern apartments and the hotel where Alex and Leslie are staying.

Alex and Leslie will waste no time; they are booked to fly home the very next day. Their suite is spacious, with a large bedroom, a sitting room, and two baths. For efficiency's sake, they shower together, though Alex is out of his shower, dressed—he wears a blue suit, a white shirt, and a dark tie, as if he is on his way to court—and sitting in an armchair by the time Leslie, wrapped in a towel, pulls a modest dress out of her suitcase; he looks on with pleasure.

"You are such a beautiful woman," Alex says, shaking his head.

"I feel nervous and sad and I wish we weren't here," Leslie says, putting on the dress.

"Well, that's just the kind of positive energy we look for in a time like this," Alex says.

"I'm sorry, that's just how it is." She looks at herself in the mirror on the wardrobe door, straightens her collar, pats her hair, shrugs. "Can you at least promise…"

"You don't even have to ask," Alex says, rising. "This is it. The last crusade."

He takes her in his arms, overcome for a moment by his deep love for her and his regret that he has put them both through so many procedures as he pursues the holy grail of an heir. "If we come up empty here, no more."

"We can adopt, Alex."

"Mmm," he says, burying his face for a moment in her hair.

The man at the front desk calls a taxi for them, and, their bones aching with jet lag and fatigue, they wait, sipping coffee in the courtyard, but no taxi arrives.

"We're going to be late," Alex says. He excuses himself for a moment and consults with the desk clerk.

"Castle Trg is just a short walk," Alex says when he returns, holding an extra-large umbrella the clerk has given him.

"What's a *trg*?" Leslie asks.

"It means 'street.' And it's just over the Dragon Bridge," he adds, as if he were somehow familiar with this cold, rainy town.

"I don't think I want to be in a place where streets are called *trg* and bridges are named after dragons," Leslie says.

The real stone dragon of Ljubljana sits atop a castle in the hills overlooking the city, but replicas of it are every twenty feet or so on the Dragon Bridge. By the time they get that far, the rain is beating against their umbrella like a drumroll. Suddenly, the wind picks up, tearing their only shelter from Alex's hands. They watch helplessly as the black umbrella with its upside-down question mark of a handle spins its way down the river with the new city on one side, and the old city on the other.

They run. The storm is so fierce and their chances of staying dry are nonexistent, and somehow the whole thing is so absurdly awful they find themselves holding hands and laughing. Soon they are on Castle Street and facing the gloomy old building in which the doctor works.

A flashing red traffic light beats like a heart in the rain. Alex and Leslie cross the street and are nearly run over by a motorcyclist who, covered against the rain in a long black poncho, looks like Death itself.

The building is from the 1920s, designed in a vaguely Art Deco style. The doorway is curved; the windows are bowed. Two statues of women in robes holding swords guard the second story. Dr. Kis's office is on the top floor. Alex and Leslie, rain dripping from their clothes, ride one of those birdcage elevators up to the sixth floor and then must walk up two more flights of moist stone steps to the eighth floor.

"Does anyone back home even know we're here?" Leslie asks nervously as they approach the doctor's door.

"Your sister knows where you are, doesn't she?"

Leslie shakes her head. "I told her the doctor was in Switzerland."

"Why did you say that?"

"She was so worried and disapproving. I thought I should at least say it was in some country she'd heard of."

The top floor of Dr. Kis's could use a sweeping. It could also—and more urgently—use a good hosing-down. In front of a mahogany and milk-glass door, there is a scatter of magazines on the floor, as if no one has been here in weeks.

Alex makes a face meant to amuse Leslie, a face that says *Uh-oh, this might be the craziest thing we have ever done.* And with that he opens the door and they find themselves in a waiting room of sorts. There are a couple of flimsy chairs, a vinyl love seat. No other patients, no receptionist.

Silence, except for the sound of the rain spattering on the roof.

"Hello?" Leslie calls out.

"We might be a little early," Alex says.

"Alex?" Leslie says, her voice shaking. She lifts her arm to point at something, but fear has seized her nervous system so suddenly and so violently, it is all she can do to raise her arm a few inches.

Alex follows the path Leslie's eyes burn into the air and sees, standing in the corner...*something*. At first he thinks it is a bear. And then he sees it as a wolf. What it actually is is an immense dog, a black and brown rottweiler with vile yellow eyes. Its head juts forward, and a low growl rumbles in its chest.

Compelled by an ancient code of protectiveness, Alex stands in front of Leslie and feels her fingers digging into him. The beast steps closer and closer to them, and still closer. Saliva thick as sour cream hangs from the serrated pink edges of its mouth. Its eyes are imbecilic with avidity, and a smell of meat rises from its flanks and loins.

"Zeus! What are you doing out here?"

Both startled and relieved, they turn and see a dapper fellow in his twenties with a narrow face, a large, reddish mouth. He wears stovepipe trousers and a snug little sport jacket. His inky hair is gelled, and his thick glasses have heavy black frames. Obediently, the dog walks slowly to his side.

"Awfully sorry about that, folks," the man says in a British accent and in a tone that seems cringing and sarcastic at the same time. He hooks one of his bony fingers through the dog's collar and leads him into a room off to one side of the waiting area.

Alex and Leslie exchange glances. They are thinking the same thing. *What fresh hell?* But they have come too far and gone to too much trouble to turn back now.

A few moments later, the young Englishman returns. "Put a bit of a fright in you. He's actually pretty well behaved, old Zeus, but I know how it is; the first time I saw him I just about muddied my knickers. Reggie Woodward at your service. I am Dr. Kis's assistant, a position I would fill free of charge but for which, thank God, I am well paid." He smiles, exposing the jagged archaeology of his teeth, some brown, others, presumably new to his mouth, bright white. "Now, if you would be so kind as to follow me, we'll get the paperwork out of the way. And sorry for the state of this place—chalk it up to the disorganization of genius."

Dr. Kis's clinic is a warren of small examining rooms. Alex and Leslie follow Reggie into one of them that he has turned into an office, with a desk, three chairs, and a very serious-looking file cabinet with a lock on it. There is a dog-food bowl and a water bowl in the corner, and the remains of an immense bone, a giraffe femur, by the looks of it. On the wall is a poster showing some epic soccer match played in the snow, a line of stiff German flags in the background.

"Let us dispense with the monetary side," Reggie says. "I trust you have brought payment with you."

Alex hands him the envelope and they wait while Reggie counts it, all of it, right in front of them.

"That's more cash than we were legally allowed to bring into the country," Alex reminds him.

"Silly law, don't you think? I thought we had agreed upon euros," Reggie says. Noticing Leslie's alarm, he quickly adds, "Not to worry. Dollars will do."

"I notice we're the only patients here," Alex says to Reggie.

"Did you come here to meet people and make new friends?" he asks, putting the money back into the envelope. Seeing the look on Alex's face, he changes tack and says Dr. Kis makes only two appointments per week, spending the rest of his time on research, and telling him how fertility specialists the world over come to Slovenia to sit at the feet of Dr. Kis, and how he has the highest success rate of anyone in the field. Reggie speaks rapidly, in the kind of rote singsong that puts them in mind of a tour guide who has long since lost interest in the scenery.

"And now, one minute of science," Reggie says. "You'll be glad to know that the doctor's injections are all one hundred percent organic."

"I don't really see how you can use the words *glad* and *injection* in the same sentence," Leslie says. And though her little jest fills Alex's heart with love, he does wish she would be quiet and let matters proceed.

"Obviously I would lose my job if I were to tell you what materials the doctor uses, but he does want you to know that he has had great success—great, great success—using tissue from some of the most vigorous and fertile beings on earth."

"Beings?" Alex asks.

"Yes," says Reggie. "Living things."

"What kind of *being* are we talking about?"

"It's the results that matter," Reggie says. "Lions, tigers, bears—do you really care?"

"Yes, of course we do," Leslie says. "Alex?" Whatever exhaustion she was feeling has been dispelled, and her blood surges through her, and her eyes open wider with alarm.

"I should tell you," Reggie says, clearing his throat, "that often he uses just a small amount—a trace amount, really, undetectable, I should think—of…" The last word is uttered so softly that neither Alex nor Leslie can make it out.

"Of what?" Alex asks.

"Goby," Reggie says, with studied nonchalance.

"What's a goby?" Alex asks.

"A fish," Leslie says. She sees the look of wonder on Alex's face. "When you work in publishing, you learn all sorts of weird stuff."

"A fish?" Alex exclaims. "A fucking fish?"

"Oh, and by the way," Reggie interjects quickly, "here's a plus to our service that we've recently added. We connect you with a first-rate obstetrics practice right in Los Angeles."

"We live in New York," Alex says.

"Oh, yes. Sorry. No problem. We work with a terrific bunch of obstetricians there as well. We strongly advise you to stay within network. These doctors are very sensitive to the whole process. And, by the way, there's no charge for this service."

"The doctors see us free of charge?" Alex asks, rather skeptically.

"Oh, I wouldn't know about that," Reggie says. "But the referral is on us, that's what I meant to say."

In the middle of all this, the door opens and in walks Dr. Kis himself. He is about forty, tall and chaotic-looking, with bristling iron-gray hair, wrinkled clothes. He looks like one of those concert pianists in the movies, the kind who are struck with amnesia or who hear voices, who triumph briefly in the concert hall and then descend into a final madness.

He seems surprised to find Reggie speaking to patients. Reggie greets him in Slovene, and the doctor impatiently asks him a question, pointing to the dog bowls and the bone on the floor, and Reggie quickly picks them up.

"The doctor doesn't speak English, I'm afraid," Reggie says to Alex and Leslie.

"Really?" says Alex. "I was under the impression that most people in Slovenia spoke English."

"What can I tell you?" Reggie says. "Even geniuses have their limitations."

"Denar," the doctor says, extending his hand and slapping two fingers onto his palm repeatedly until Reggie hands him the envelope stuffed with hundred-dollar bills.

"This is going well," Leslie says.

The doctor says something else—everything the doctor says seems angry and impatient—and Reggie answers rather plaintively. Kis cuts him off with a furious wave, and Reggie tells Alex and Leslie, "The doctor will see you now," but it's almost drowned out by a violent clap of thunder. The electricity suddenly is cut and they all stand there breathing in the damp darkness for several moments before power is restored.

There are some doctors who inspire confidence, and others who don't. And then there are doctors like Kis, who inspire dread. We expect doctors to be clean, and he is not clean. Though his hands are scrubbed and he smells of antibacterial soap, his uncleanliness comes from something far below the skin. His eyes are distant; his expression one of exasperation and superiority; his touch is impersonal and slightly harsh.

After a very routine exam—stethoscope, blood pressure cuff—the doctor asks Alex and Leslie, in Slovene, when they last had sex, which Reggie translates with a kind of creepy relish.

"We had sexual relations nine days ago," Alex says with as much dignity as he can muster.

"And how was it?" Reggie asks, but quickly adds, "Kidding, I'm just kidding. We actually prefer a longer abstinence period, but nine nights will have to do."

Kis goes on to explain what the procedure involves. His voice contains no enthusiasm, or warmth, or even simple humanity. With Reggie translating, he speaks rapidly, like the voice at the end of a pharmaceutical commercial on TV listing in eight seconds the hundred possible catastrophic side effects of the new medicine. Kis looks off into the middle distance as he rattles along, and Reggie picks at his fingernails as he does his best to keep up with the doctor's rapid-fire delivery.

"We are going to increase the motility of your sperm and the receptivity of your eggs. We are turning a quiet glade in the forest into a teeming spot in the jungle. Life, life, everywhere life, wanting, taking, growing. We are going to turn you on. Up high. Like teenager and creature of the wild. Nothing will hold you back. Life! Life!"

Alex looks at Leslie, and the two of them start to laugh. The doctor is clearly insane, and the futility of their mission, plus the expense, and the jet lag, and the accumulation of three years of painful disappointments, leaves them with nothing but giddiness.

But the next thing Alex knows he is shirtless with the others looking on, and, without a word of warning or a moment's hesitation, Dr. Kis pierces the back of his right arm with a very large old-fashioned needle, and the silliness is gone, barely remembered. It is amazingly painful; the sensation goes to the marrow of Alex's bones, and while he is absorbing the pain, Kis takes out another syringe, equally large, and injects Alex in the neck, frighteningly near the jugular. Alex's heart races; he hears his own cry like the yowl of a fox in a trap. It crosses his mind that he is being murdered.

When the pain subsides, he says, "This is not very much fun," trying to be brave.

"Just be happy it isn't two years ago, when we used to give the injection directly into the willy," Reggie says.

Before Alex can react to that, Dr. Kis claps his hand over Alex's left ear, pushing his head down to administer the final and most excruciating injection—behind the ear. As he pulls the needle out, Kis steps back, looking as if he has just vanquished Alex in a fencing match.

"Now you are good to go," the doctor says in English. His words, heavily accented, buzz like flies.

Next it is Leslie's turn, and the ordeal that awaits her is now no mystery, since she has just witnessed Alex's agony. As he buttons his shirt, she shakes her head and says, "I'm sorry, but there's no way I'm putting myself through that. I just can't."

"Then it's not going to work," Alex says. He feels a rush of heat moving through his body, disconcerting, almost violent, but he doesn't react, not wanting to give Leslie anything more about which to be apprehensive.

"I'm sorry, sweetie, I really am. But." Leslie gestures helplessly.

Dr. Kis, again in English—there are phrases he knows for situations that often reoccur—"No refunds possible."

"Screw you with your refunds," Alex says, whirling on Kis, pointing his finger in the doctor's face. Turning to Leslie, he says, after taking a deep breath to calm himself, "It hurts for maybe two seconds."

"Alex, you were screaming."

"But am I screaming now? That's what counts."

"Really? Is that what counts? Nobody screams forever."

"Les…"

"I can't go through that kind of pain." Leslie makes a move toward the door, and Reggie steps directly in front of her, blocking her path.

"Go into the next room if you want this to work," Reggie says to Alex.

"Go! Go!" Kis says, waving his left hand while his right, hanging by his side, holds a fresh syringe.

"Get out of my way!" Leslie shouts at Reggie.

"Leslie, please," Alex says. "We've come so far. You're making a scene."

"Just go," Reggie says. "Quickly. Having you here is further upsetting her."

"Shut the fuck up, you idiot bastard," Leslie says. She attempts to push him aside, but despite his scrawniness and the utter lack of seriousness in his demeanor, he is unbudgable.

"All right, Leslie," Alex says, moving toward her, "can we just get this done?"

"I want to leave," she says, turning toward him, her eyes full of injury. "You're supposed to help me, you're supposed to be on my side, not theirs."

He places his hands on her shoulders and carefully draws her close to him. "It's going to be okay," he whispers into her hair.

She shakes her head no, at first sadly, and then with increasing emphasis, and finally with a vigor that is close to hysteria.

"Next room," Kis says.

Reggie leads Leslie back to the examination table and indicates with a movement of his chin by which door Alex ought to exit. He does as he is asked and finds himself in another examination room, this one, by the looks of it, not often used.

The examination table is bare, and the several tears in the upholstery ooze yellowish stuffing. The shelves are empty and the one poster on the wall seems to have been taken from an acupuncturist's office; it shows a human torso pierced on all sides by needles, and the sight of it makes Alex think of Saint Sebastian pierced by—what?—fifty arrows, but unkilled.

He hears Leslie's weak protests, and he goes to the door, driven by instinct. Yet before his hand can touch the doorknob he hears a strange ticking noise and when he turns toward it he sees Zeus walking slowly across the linoleum floor, a shower curtain of saliva hanging from his half-open mouth.

"No," Alex says in his most commanding voice. He hears scuffling sounds in the next room. "Zeus," he says, remembering. "Sit down."

Instead, the dog shoves his snout into Alex's groin. Alex presses himself against the wall, desperate to find even an inch of space away from the dog and his hot meaty breath.

"No," Leslie cries from the next room, wailing without hope.

And at the same moment, the dog rises on his back legs and wraps his front paws around Alex's right leg, about thigh high, and begins to thrust. Zeus humps away, thrusting, thrusting, stench rolling from his mouth and nostrils in scalding waves, his lurid red, glistening penis brushing against Alex's trousers, thoroughly wetting them.

When they finally get back to their hotel, the rain has stopped, though in its place are powerful wet winds that blow punishingly through the old city. Even if Leslie and Alex wanted to speak, the noise of the wind would drown them out, and it is just as well because they are unable to even look at each other just now.

Alex carries a white paper bag in which are two vials of bright pink liquid. Kis had given his final instructions in Slovene, and Reggie smirkingly translated. "Drink these when you get home and let nature takes its course."

The hotel has a cozy little business center where guests have the use of a brand-new computer, and while she is still able to Leslie ducks in to check her e-mail, primarily to see if there is anything from her assistant. There is nothing, and, after a moment's dismay, Leslie realizes it is too early back home for anything to have happened. There is one e-mail from Cynthia. *Your house is soooo lovely.* While she is at the computer and still thinking about it, Leslie tries to find out exactly what kind of fish the goby is.

Moments later she is back in their suite. Exhausted from the ordeal of the overnight flight followed by the far greater ordeal of their visit with Kis, they fall into their faux-king-size bed—really two standard mattresses with a large sheet pulled tautly over them—and are asleep almost immediately.

They awaken in each other's arms in a room that would have been dark as coal had not one of them forgotten to turn off the bathroom light.

"Where are we?" Leslie whispers.

"Don't ask," Alex says.

"Okay," she says. "Don't tell." She looks at her Cartier tank watch (third-anniversary dinner, Le Bernardin); they have been asleep less than two hours.

He leans over to kiss her but she recoils. He looks at her questioningly and she says, "Your breath."

"I wasn't going to say it," Alex answers, "but…yours too."

Despite everything, they are feeling urgently romantic. They have been given instructions by Kis to resume their sex life as soon as possible. Well, alone in a hotel bed in a strange city: it doesn't get more possible than that.

They roll out of bed and scamper into the bathroom to brush their teeth, rinse, gargle. Alex feels insanely young. Leslie's loins are scalding. They remember the vials Kis has given them, and Alex runs into the bedroom and retrieves the white paper sack, brings them in. They clink their vials together as if toasting each other with champagne and drink it down.

The taste is so strange that it cannot even be called repulsive—it reminds them of nothing they have ever tasted and so it is attached to no taboo taste. It's not salty; it's not bitter, or rotten. There are no words to describe it—except to say they both hope never to have anything similar pass their lips again. They drop the empty glass vials into the tin wastepaper basket beneath the sink, and the sounds they make ring out like gunshots.

"My breath still tastes weird," Alex says. He exhales forcefully and Leslie sniffs the air.

"Ick, ick, ick," she says. "Yet? I don't mind it. I am in a state of not-mindingness." She breathes into her own palm, sniffs. And then she squats and urinates onto the bathroom floor.

In the morning, the desk clerk rings their room at eight o'clock. They survey the wreckage of the place and the wreckage of their bodies—torn sheets, overturned chairs and tables, bent curtain rods, scratches, bruises, bite marks.

Alex says, "Whatever happens next, or really whatever happens for the rest of my life, last night…"

"I know," says Leslie. "Me too. Me three. Me…ten billion…"

"My cock is numb."

"You're lucky. Every place you went in is throbbing."

"Every place?"

"Every place."

They shower, dress, pack, make an attempt to put the room in order, but it's hopeless. They leave the housekeepers a very handsome tip and call down to the front desk, asking for a taxi to the airport. Ljubljana is deserted and looks desolate and somehow temporary in the cardboard-colored rain. The Art Deco core of the city gives way to socialist-realist outskirts, which in turn give way to open fields alternating with thick clumps of woodland where the pine and spruce are so dark green they look nearly black. The airport is bereft of automobile traffic. It seems astonishing and almost unreal that the airport in a capital city—even the capital of a country most people have never heard of—could be so quiet.

Takeoff from Ljubljana to Munich is delayed because of strong winds, and as their plane sits on the runway, Leslie watches as one of the little open-sided buses loops around the field, delivering passengers to an Aeroflot jet. Suddenly, a woman in her twenties, in a tight skirt and towering high heels, leaps off the bus and, after stumbling and falling to her knees, gets up and begins to run. Soon after, a man leaps off the bus and runs after her.

What is going on? Leslie cranes her neck to see—she has a vision of the woman lifted up off the runway by the force of one of the jet engines, sucked into the whirling turbine and devoured—but now the flight to Munich is set to begin and their plane turns sharply onto the runway.

The stewardess in her not-quite-turquoise blazer is nursing a cold. Across the aisle from them sit two elderly nuns; the thin sister comforts the large one, who is openly in tears, staring straight ahead and making no attempt to shield her face.

"What's wrong with them?" Leslie whispers.

"I don't know. Nuns have problems too. But you know what puzzles me even more? Since when do nuns fly first class?"

"By the way," Leslie says. "The goby eats its young."

They've been cleared for takeoff. The engines roar and the scenery races past. This is always the difficult moment on a plane for Leslie, and Alex takes her hand, pats it reassuringly. As they rise it looks like the thick forest is plummeting.

"I think I'm pregnant," Leslie whispers.

Pregnancy is as natural as anything on earth, but it also has a certain science fiction aspect to it: a seed is placed inside an almost invisible egg and then a near replica of the man or the woman begins to grow inside the woman's body. Breasts swell, hips enlarge, cheeks become rosy, moods swing. Pregnancy is not for the faint of heart.

Being pregnant may be one of the most feminine things a woman can do, but it sometimes creates characteristics that you'd otherwise find only in men, such as an increase in body hair. A pregnant woman can suddenly grow a line of hair on her swollen stomach, a kind of furry line of longitude dividing the globe of her belly. Sometimes the down on her upper lip will darken and thicken. Sometimes the peach fuzz on her chin will turn black and wiry. Sideburns emerge out of nowhere. Sometimes the breasts sprout dark hairs; sometimes the hairs spring up on the back, usually forming a little nest of dark fur more or less on the tailbone. Androgens, one of the hormones that accompany pregnancy, are the cause of this sudden furriness, and there is nothing to be done about it, and nothing to worry about either.

Except in Leslie's case, the hair growth is extreme, and particularly shocking since she was always so smooth and girlish. She was the kind of woman who needed to shave her legs and underarms only once a month; the hair on her head grew so slowly she had it cut once, maybe twice a year.

It is in the second month of the pregnancy when she realizes the changes taking place in her. One day, Alex wakes up around seven in the morning, just as Leslie is slipping back into bed. Her back is to him and he moves next to her to warm her up. He presses himself to her back and puts his arm around her. Her body shakes, and Alex realizes she is crying.

"What's going on?" he asks her.

She shakes her head, unable to speak.

He moves closer to her, as close as two bodies can be. "Hey," he says, "I'm here."

She hikes up her nightgown and takes his hand and moves it down and places it between her legs.

Alex tries not to show any reaction—no pulling back, no shudder, no matter how slight, nothing by which she might surmise how strange and unsettling this familiar private patch suddenly feels to him. But the difference is unmistakable; it feels as if her pubic hair has tripled and maybe even quadrupled in density, and what had once been a soft, wispy inverted pyramid is now a thick, coarse square. She holds on to his hand, as if to prevent him from drawing it back in revulsion, though revulsion is far from what he is experiencing. What he feels is perplexity and curiosity. How could this have happened? What does it mean?

Maintaining her control over his hand, Leslie slowly moves it up and down her private middle.

"Wow," Alex says, trying to sound impressed and not dismayed, "when did this happen?"

Leslie shakes her head, unable to speak.

"I think it's hot," Alex says.

But Leslie is having none of it. "I think it's disgusting," she says, scrambling out of bed. Alex wonders what time it is and lifts himself up on his elbows to get a look at the old GE digital alarm clock, a piece of junk from his college days in Williamstown, Massachusetts, he has not been able to part with. But the clock has somehow gotten itself turned around and he can't make out the numbers. He raises his wrist and holds it in front of him to read his Rolex and what he sees so startles and unnerves him he makes a strangled *aacchh* sound, repelled by the sight of his arm.

When he went to sleep some seven hours earlier, the hair on his arm was sparse and pale brown. Now it has darkened by several shades, and indeed seems more like canine fur than human hair. He shakes his head, as if to dislodge the fog of fantasy and hallucination from his mind, and a wet ribbon of drool flies from his mouth.

Alex goes into the bathroom, where Leslie is sitting on the edge of the tub, crying into her hands. She looks up at him, her eyes barely visible in the predawn gloom.

Alex turns on the lights and thrusts his arm out. "It's happening to me too."

Just as she had guided his hand so he might feel what had happened to her, Alex takes Leslie's hand and rubs it up and down the sudden fur of his forearm. In her distraught state, she isn't as protective of his feelings as he was of hers. "Oh my God, what the hell is that?" she says, snatching back her hand as if from a fire.

"What is going on here?" Alex feels light-headed, nauseated; he thinks for a moment he might actually pass out.

"He did this to us," Leslie says, her voice wobbling.

Alex wants to reassure her, but he can find nothing true to say that would soothe her soul. He merely shakes his head.

"He ruined us," Leslie says as she begins to cry. "He killed us, he turned us into…oh God, Alex. Don't even look at me. It's not just my pussy, it's everywhere. I'm just grotesque."

"We're going to be okay, I promise you. And we're going to have a family."

"This is what *you* wanted." Leslie hears what she has just said, and she suddenly snaps out of the whirl of grief that momentarily possessed her. "Okay, I can't go to work like this," she says, taking Alex's elbow and leading him to the door.

"What are you doing?" he says, pulling away from her.

"I'm going to get rid of this," she says.

"But how?"

"I'm going to shave what can be shaved. And I need you to go to the Duane Reade and get some bleach, it's called Jolen, I think, and it's made for lightening hair on your face, and I want you to get me some Nair."

"But…"

She shoves his chest with startling vigor. "Go!" she says. "And hurry. I've got a meeting with some European agents this morning and I can't be late."

* * *

For Alex, some of this vigorous hair growth is a welcome reprieve from the gradual balding he was experiencing in middle age. He realizes that his suddenly having such a healthy head of hair, thick and luxuriant, cannot possibly be *only* good news, but still he is quite pleased to have regained (as opposed to Rogained) his hair.

In fact, the physical changes do not bother or frighten Alex nearly so much as the psychological changes he is going through—and these he keeps to himself. His moods range from rage to utter tranquillity, and on both ends of this continuum he experiences an intensity of feeling as never before. Before the visit to Dr. Kis, most, if not all, of his emotions were mixed. Even the blackest sorrow had somewhere within it dark blue shimmers of hope; even the greatest joys held within them consciousness of joy's inevitable ebbing. His emotions were like hot-air balloons, and each of them carried the ballast of memory and knowledge. But now the ballast is gone and everything he feels is total, and practically overwhelming. He is not ever merely hungry—he is ravenous. He is not annoyed—he is in a seething rage. He is not feeling romantic—he is overcome with lust.

Soon, Alex is shaving morning and evening and clipping his fingernails every day. If he neglects his toenails, the nail on the big toe will saw through his sock—even when he clips them, in a month he goes through fifteen pairs of socks, until he no longer bothers to buy them from Brooks Brothers, although it had always given him a sense of continuity to purchase men's hosiery from the same store, the same counter, and perhaps even from the same stooped salesman as his father and his father before him had purchased theirs. Now Alex is buying socks in bulk from a discount clothing shop on Third Avenue specializing in seconds and discontinued styles, where he shops to the accompaniment of unspeakably loud hip-hop pouring down from the store's gigantic speakers, music that seems to him neither hip nor conducive to hopping, and that, with its throbbing rhythm tracks and furious-sounding vocals, is murder on his sensitive ears.

But he keeps his problems to himself, keeps them not only from the world at large but, as much as he can, from Leslie as well. He has always been the steady one. He has always been the one who kept track of their finances and their social engagements. In every way, Alex is the marriage's designated driver.

There is not a strand of new hair that appears on Leslie's body that does not horrify her. Women look forward to the rich glow that pregnancy gives their hair, but *not* if it is growing up their bellies or on the backs of their hands. As the weeks pass, Leslie comes to look upon her body as a country at war, a nation that was losing province after province to the invading hordes of unwanted hair. Leslie's morning toilette had always been a crisp, efficient fifteen minutes—a burst of shower, a dash of eyeliner, a little swirl of blush, and a quick anointment of her pulse points with perfume. Now she needs an hour or two to ready herself to face the world, and when she finally emerges from the bathroom, swathed in concealing scarves, her eyes show the colors of the flag.

Alex decides he will broach the subject of hair with Jim Johnson, who, despite having entered the firm in such a dishonorable way, has been doing a good job at Bailey, Twisden, Kaufman, and Chang. It is two weeks after the issue of Leslie's sudden furriness was raised—it has taken this long for Alex to put aside his desire for social distance from the unbecoming and irritating Jim Johnson—and when Alex makes the long walk through his firm's glass-and-mahogany corridors to Johnson's glorified cubicle, in a wing of the firm's offices that Alex has barely visited before, he is informed by a woman named Betty Varrick, a legal assistant (and secretary) shared by five of the firm's junior attorneys, that Mrs. Johnson had a baby and Mr. Johnson has not been in the office since.

"And when was this?" Alex asks.

"Oh, it's been three weeks, Mr. Twisden."

"Three weeks? That's a bit excessive, isn't it? Do me a favor, please, and get him on the phone and transfer the call to my office."

Back in his office, with its sweeping views of Midtown and Central Park, its antique Persian carpet, seventeenth-century globes, and fourteen-by-eighteen Samuel Fulton oils of bulldogs—not great art, perhaps, but somehow comforting presences to Alex—he goes over some routine papers while beneath his Sheraton desk, his well-shod foot taps nervously as he waits to speak to Jim Johnson.

Suddenly, startlingly, his phone rings. One of his assistants tells him that Betty is on the line and he instructs him to put her through.

"There's no answer," Varrick says. "I left a message."

"And you tried his mobile?"

"Yes. I did."

"And?"

There's a brief, uncomfortable pause. "The number is no longer in use."

"No longer in use?"

"I'm sorry."

Alex cancels his morning appointments and takes a taxi to the Johnsons' apartment, on Broadway and Ninety-Second Street. It is a large, drab building, five or ten years old, soaring up thirty floors between a

Verizon store and a Blockbuster Video. The lobby, presided over by a mournful-looking older doorman who seems to be wearing the uniform of a much larger man, still shows the evidence of the recently passed holidays—a large menorah with electric candles, each with a chunky flame-shaped bulb; a desiccated Christmas tree as frail and bent as an old woman; and a photograph of an African American Santa Claus, extremely buff, wearing a fur vest and red shorts.

"Mr. Johnson, please," Alex says to the doorman, brushing the snowflakes off the collar of his black cashmere topcoat.

"Which one? There are four Mr. Johnsons in this building."

"James. Or Jim."

"Make that three," the doorman says. "Those Johnsons are no longer in residence here."

"What?" Alex's voice is sharp, as if he is going to make the doorman revise his statement.

"Moved. In fact, there's a crew up there right now trying to get that place fixed up. You a friend?"

"Yes. Sort of. Employer, actually."

The doorman shakes his head. "Maybe you can tell me what the hell happened to that man. He was one of the nicest people in this building. Both of them, her too. Just as considerate and friendly and generous as you please. Very generous. The most generous people."

To doormen and waiters and all those people who serve us, we are *our tips,* Alex thinks. *An envelope full of cash, a hand to proffer it, and the rest a blur…*

"And then they just disappear," the doorman says. He cranes his neck, peers out through the glass doors at something he sees on the street, and then returns his attention to Alex. "Three months behind in the rent, is what I heard." He cocks his head and looks at Alex as if, as Johnson's employer, he might bear some responsibility for Jim's financial difficulties.

"I don't suppose they left a forwarding address," Alex says.

"They usually don't when they take off in the middle of the night. They didn't take anything with them. Just a couple of suitcases—the night doorman figured they were on their way to the airport or something. Plates and pictures and furniture and all the stuff they'd gotten for the baby, they just walked away from it—what was left of it."

"You say there's people working up there now?"

"If you saw the place you'd understand why."

"Would it be all right with you if I went up and had a look around?" Alex asks, and at the same time he places two fifty-dollar bills on the faux marble of the doorman's desk.

The doorman smooths the bills out, as if ironing them with his palm, and says, as he folds and pockets the money, "Nineteen C."

Alex goes up to 19C, and it is full of workmen talking and joking in Spanish as they drag furniture to the front of the four-room apartment. There is beige wall-to-wall carpeting throughout, and the carpeting is torn, stained, and—there is no other way to describe this—*chewed,* as if the Johnsons had been keeping wild animals here. Likewise, the walls are scored with deep gouges, and here and there holes have been punched in the plaster. The furniture the workers are disposing of is in a state of complete wreckage. Armchairs are without arms; wicker-bottomed dining chairs are without wicker; small sleeping pillows have been placed on the sofa as substitutes for missing cushions, and these pillows are covered in their own feathers. But all this mayhem is nothing compared to the foulness of this place. What is that smell? Rotted meat? Human waste? Cooking gas? Fear, of the most extreme, quaking, cowering kind? Or is it a combination of all these things, a hideous bouillabaisse of everything repulsive, hell's soup du jour?

The workmen have by now gotten used to the horrible odor, and their protective masks dangle on their cloth ties. They glance at Alex as they work, perhaps thinking he has some official connection to the building. With his hand covering his nose and mouth, Alex wanders from room to room, hoping to find something that will give him an insight into what has become of the Johnsons. He goes into the small utilitarian New York kitchen; shards of broken plates and glasses crunch beneath the leather soles of his Crockett and Jones oxfords. With some trepidation, he opens the refrigerator and, like a monstrous wave from an unsettled sea, the stench crashes down upon him, sending him reeling. His instinct is to slam the door shut, but he forces himself to peer into the refrigerator and what he sees is even more disturbing and disgusting than the smell: Ziploc bags containing rodents—mice, rats, squirrels, and a few plump, butterscotch-colored hamsters—are piled one on top of the other, all of them, despite the plastic wrap and refrigeration, in various states of decay.

Alex throws the door shut and staggers back, almost losing his footing on the shifting surface of all that broken glass. Three of the workmen have begun taking the furniture out, while the fourth is on his knees and starting in on the task of tearing up the remains of the carpeting. He glances at Alex but quickly looks away when Alex returns his gaze.

Alex walks into what had once been the Johnsons' bedroom. Stalactite-shaped stains render the bare mattress grotesque. A bedside lamp is on the floor, its long neck snapped in two. An oddly dainty and unmolested little bedside table stands next to the abandoned bed, some fake French Provincial probably picked up at Pottery Barn. Alex opens the table's single drawer. The blade of a straight razor greets him with a sinister wink of reflected light. Alex pulls the drawer all the way out. Besides the razor it holds a tube of Caswell-Massey shaving cream, and handcuffs.

Behind the bed, curtains cover a large window. Alex parts the curtains and sees the window has been completely covered in plywood. A little yellow Post-it is pressed to the wood, but the breeze of the moved curtain dislodges it, and it floats to the floor. Alex retrieves it, reads: *Help us.*

He hears voices—the workmen are coming back for more furniture. The one who stayed behind is saying something to them—Alex can understand just a smattering of it, but he surmises that his presence in the apartment is finally being questioned. He takes a quick look around. Is there anything here that can possibly tell him anything he needs to know? The Johnsons are gone. That is the overriding, salient fact of the matter. They descended into some horrible, disgusting squalor—and they fled.

On his way out of the apartment, Alex walks through the reeking kitchen again. He opens the refrigerator, takes one of the Ziploc bags, puts it in his pocket.

In the elevator going down, he shares the car with a woman and her two small children, but they get off on the sixth floor, where the building has a play area for children. Once he is alone, he takes his prize out of his pocket and devours the plump hamster in four quick bites. It is easily and without question the most delicious thing he has ever tasted.

It's called *shame* for a reason. Despite having many friends, as well as her sister, Cynthia, back in San Francisco, her mother, dear cousins, and colleagues, there is no one to whom Leslie dares confide the anguish she is experiencing over her increasing and inexorable furriness.

Her obstetrician, Dr. William Yost, examining her routinely, seems stubbornly unwilling to admit that anything is out of the ordinary. Yost is a fleshy, nervous man who wears a toupee that looks as if he bought it at a yard sale. His breath is bright and minty with mouthwash, though beneath that smell is the smoky trace of the cigarette he sneaked right before limping into the examination room.

"Oh, these things happen," Yost says as Leslie, in her paper gown, points out the swaths of fur inexorably growing everywhere on her body. "The important thing is…" He pats her stomach. "And everything is A-OK. We're all about the babies here."

Leslie squints at Yost. He is the second doctor she has seen at Turtle Bay Obstetrics and Wellness. The first, a woman named Dr. Eva Kosloff, an unusually tiny woman with mad blue eyes, was clear from the beginning that the eight doctors who shared this practice also shared the patients and that Dr. Kosloff herself might not be present at the delivery. Glancing down at her clipboard, she'd added, "So you come to us from the great Dr. Kis." And after saying his name, she seemed to have difficulty making eye contact with Leslie. "Did Dr. K. mention to you that some of the women he works with deliver a bit ahead of schedule?"

"He mentioned nothing of the sort," Leslie said. "But the sooner the better. Look. I need to do something about this." She lifted her arm, showed her. "Can you take care of this for me?"

"Not really my field," Kosloff said, quickly turning to take her leave.

Leslie, usually so good at coming up with solutions to life's difficulties, is simply paralyzed with self-revulsion, and even finding a dermatologist who might help her is made difficult by her doing it in secret. She trolled the Internet and found a doctor down in Greenwich Village whose office she now sits in, taking her place in the waiting room with two wealthy-looking Indian women in gorgeous saris, both of them chatting amiably while their unibrows expressively rise and fall. Also there is a glum teenager, slim and tall, who could have been a model were it not for a noticeable mustache, and a demure woman in a pantsuit who sits with her knees pressed together and her purse in her lap and who has the sideburns of an Elvis impersonator.

Her cell phone chimes in her purse and she reads the message from her assistant Robert. Are you in the bldg? Jacket proofs are up and they look horrible!!

No, I am not in the building, Leslie thinks. *My disgusting self is in the office of a hair-removal specialist, thank you very much.*

At last, it is Leslie's turn to see the doctor, Carole Ann Ryan, a lantern-jawed young woman with a pageboy haircut and oversize glasses with red frames that match her hair. She glances at her clipboard and asks, "So what seems to be the trouble?" though even with most of Leslie's body covered it is obvious she is struggling with extreme hirsutism.

Leslie's eyes blaze as she fixes the doctor with a long stare until finally she pulls the tails of her blouse out of her skirt and exposes a torso that is darker and thicker with hair than it was even the day before. Dr. Ryan, despite her extensive acquaintance with scars, boils, eczema, psoriasis, rashes, oozing acne, and cancerous growths, has never seen anything that comes this close to turning her professionally strong stomach. Leslie notes the quiver of the doctor's throat as she swallows her shock, and her light brown eyes widen behind her thick tinted lenses. She reaches for a chair and drags it toward her and sits, heavily, releasing a sigh.

"Are you being treated for endometriosis?"

"No. Why do you ask?"

"Oh, sometimes the treatment can lead to a certain amount of unwanted hair. How about weight loss? Have you lost a great deal of weight lately?"

"Are you even looking at me? I'm pregnant. I'm gaining weight."

"Okay. I'm just ruling out the normal causes."

"Normal? Does any of this look normal?"

"So…you're pregnant," Dr. Ryan says, glancing down at Leslie's new-patient questionnaire on her clipboard. "That's very exciting. You do know that a certain amount of hair growth often accompanies pregnancies."

"This is not a *certain amount,*" Leslie says. She tells herself to calm down, but rage boils within her.

"The important thing is to try and enjoy your pregnancy," the doctor says. "It's a very special time in a woman's life."

"I can't live like this. I have a job, I'm in public. This is not doable."

"If your insurance covers laser hair removal, we can do that for you right here. And if not, we can direct you to a couple of reliable places where it can be done nonmedically."

Something catches Dr. Ryan's attention—the light has touched the hair above Leslie's upper lip in such a way that it makes it seem thicker than before. Curious in some horrible, childish manner, Ryan steps closer to Leslie and then, her brow furrowed, her lips pursed, looking like a kid about to turn over a rock to see what vile squiggly things might be beneath it, she pokes at Leslie's mustache with one finger.

And with lightning speed, like a beast in the wild and with no more premeditation than an apple falling from a tree, Leslie sinks her teeth into the doctor's finger. The doctor screams in pain and terror, grabs her right pointer with her left hand.

Leslie is standing now, unperturbed by the doctor's howls of pain. She feints a move toward Ryan, causing the doctor to cower in fear. She places her hands on Ryan's shoulders and shoves the doctor so hard against the wall that the glass cabinet attached to it comes loose and crashes to the floor.

Dr. Ryan is temporarily out of commission, but Leslie hears the sound of rushing footsteps, and she bolts down the gray-carpeted corridor, into the waiting room, and bursts through the doors leading to the common hallway on the fifth floor. No time to wait for the elevator; she takes the stairway. She hasn't had any real exercise in years but she finds it surprisingly easy and even pleasant to be running. There's a spring in her step, but what is stranger than that, and more disturbing, is there is a quietly humming joy in her heart. It's the first moment of real happiness she has had since taking Alex's hand on the plane back from Slovenia. Her thought back then was *I'm pregnant;* now what fills her heart with wild music is another thought: *Get out of my way!*

*   *   *

Shortly after Leslie returns home, the police arrive to place her under arrest. On the ride to the station, she contacts Alex and calls their lawyer, Arthur Glassman, and because of Glassman's efficiency and Leslie's lack of prior arrests, he is able to quickly post a minimal bail and get her out of there.

They get back home about seven. Glassman is full of bluster and pride about having gotten Leslie released so quickly. Leslie pours drinks for the men and sparkling water for herself and they sit in the front parlor listening to the rattling-beads sound of rain against the window and the whoosh of traffic below.

After finishing half her drink, Leslie excuses herself and says she must take a hot shower to get the stinky putrid smell of the lockup off.

"Oh God, yes, by all means," Arthur says, rising from his seat. He is a well-turned-out man in his early sixties, in an English suit and expensive shoes, with a full head of kinky white hair and merry blue eyes. He takes Leslie's hand and gazes at her in his fatherly manner, though he is also inspecting her, wondering if he might discern some visible sign of madness that would cause Leslie to take a serious nip out of a doctor's hand.

When Leslie is out of the room, Arthur sinks back into his seat. "This is not going to be easy, you know," he says. "I mean, she actually did bite that woman."

"Is that a question?" Alex asks.

"No, it's not a question. The woman was bitten, and she has Leslie's teeth marks on her. Teeth marks are more identifiable than fingerprints."

"I'm sure they are."

"Alex. What is going on?"

"I don't know. Pregnancy? It changes women, everybody knows that."

"Yes, that's true. But Leslie is the first pregnant woman I've known to bite a dermatologist. Look, the pregnancy thing is a card we can play, and I'm sure I can get this settled with probation and community service. There's no way they are going to lock up a woman of Leslie's stature, pregnant or not. But we're going to have to cop a plea. You understand? We're going to have to hammer out some sort of agreement, and I promise you this doctor is already using her good hand to dial some bottom-feeding personal injury lawyer and she is going to hit us up in a civil suit."

"You just do what needs to be done, Arthur," Alex says.

"You still haven't answered my question, Alex."

"There are things that happen, Arthur. In people's lives, their bodies, their marriages; private things. But whatever it is, I'm sure it will pass."

"What does her doctor say? And who is your obstetrician, by the way?"

"Oh, this Dr. Blah-Blah, who the fuck knows? It's a practice with eight doctors and we see someone different each time. It's strictly a moneymaking outfit, but we're fine where we are. The last thing we want is some helicopter obstetrician hovering over us. Listen, Arthur, we've waited a long time for this and now the only thing that's important is to keep her safe and comfortable and for us to have this child."

"I realize that. But this Dr. Blah-Blah or any of his colleagues, they haven't noticed anything…untoward in Leslie? Nothing out of the usual?"

"What are you implying?"

"I'm not implying anything, old buddy. I'm just asking."

"Do you see something out of the ordinary in Leslie?"

"Other than her practically eviscerating her dermatologist?"

"Not funny, Arthur."

"Not meant to be. But something's going on. If you don't want to get into it, we can just drop the subject. But if there's anything you want to let me know, this is the time to do it. Right now. You're on the clock anyhow."

"Actually," Alex says, clearing his throat, "it looks as if it might be more than one. We might be looking at twins. And there's an outside chance of triplets."

"Oh my God."

"Why do you say that?"

"I don't know. It just came out."

"You don't think we'll be good parents?"

"I didn't say that."

"But you said 'Oh my God,' as if some catastrophe were on the way."

"It popped out of my mouth, Alex. No offense intended." He finishes his vodka, places it on the end table with some finality, and stands up to leave.

Alex thinks how amusing it might be to pounce on Arthur, to shove him on the chest and bring him to the floor—not to hurt him, just to remind him who is boss, who is on top and who is on the bottom. Who is paying the bills. Who is paying the cost to be boss. Yeah!

And here Arthur comes, his arms open for a comradely embrace, his stout belly pushing at the middle button of his suit jacket, his cuff links winking in the overhead light. He puts his arms around Alex, pats him manfully on the back, and says, "Be well, old friend. We'll talk in the morning. And please make my apologies to Leslie—but I have to get home. Rhonda and I have tickets to *Phantom of the Opera* tonight. I have zero interest, but Rhonda is young and she wants to see it. She actually thinks it's an opera."

"Okay then," Alex says, suddenly ravenous. He has a vivid vision of steak tartare as he walks his old friend to the door.

Between the arrest, the pending civil suit, and the tone of Leslie's e-mails and telephone calls, Cynthia feels compelled to leave her life in San Francisco and come to New York to look in on her younger sister. Cynthia is not the worrying kind, but there is no ignoring the tone of her communication with Leslie. After being installed in her own suite of rooms and putting her clothes away in the George III mahogany serpentine front chest, Cynthia wants to take care of Leslie's increasingly vexing grooming issues.

There is reason to believe that word about Leslie has circulated throughout the dermatologist community in New York, but Cynthia is quite certain that within the vast network of skin-care specialists in the city—Hungarians, Russians, Koreans, licensed and unlicensed—someone will be able to give Leslie at least temporary relief through electrolysis. Leslie's experience in Slovenia has made her reluctant to see an Eastern European, and as luck would have it, Leslie finds on the Internet a woman named Lu Park who has a skin-care business in a walk-up building four blocks east of Leslie's house. This time, hoping to avoid a repeat of Leslie's experience at Dr. Ryan's—Leslie blamed it on her own embarrassment about her condition, a somewhat flimsy excuse that Cynthia decides not to prod—Cynthia gives Leslie a double dose of Xanax, rendering her rubbery and practically speechless. The hair removal, which takes a full five hours and which Leslie basically sleeps through, proceeds without incident.

It is left to Cynthia to pay Lu Park, a woman in her forties with girlish barrettes in her dark hair and hands that feel as hard as wood. Lu Park asks Cynthia, "She your sister, right?" And when Cynthia says yes, she is, Lu Park shakes her head and says, "Two other women, big pregnant, same problem. Both come here." She counts the money angrily as she speaks, as if there is not quite enough there to compensate her for her troubles.

The next day, Leslie is still exceptionally groggy from the sedative. Her skin looks red and feels burned and it is an easy decision to give work a miss and stay home with her sister. Over a late breakfast of French coffee and croissants, Leslie, her voice low, her words slurred, finally confides to Cynthia about her visit to Dr. Kis.

"I've never been so scared in my whole life," Leslie says.

"How could you go to such a quack?" Cynthia says while at the same time admiring the pattern on the Spode coffee cup.

"Not such a quack, was he?" Leslie says, patting her distended middle. "We tried everything and everyone, and Dr. Kis is the one who succeeded."

"Dr. Kis? Honestly his name?"

"We really didn't even know that much about him, to tell you the truth. But I thank God for him now." She pats the great hump of her stomach again.

"I remember when we were kids," Cynthia says. "I was the one who wanted babies and you were always the one who said you would never let that happen. Now look—I've got two cocker spaniels and an apartment full of antiques, and the way it looks now, I am never ever going to be a mother. And you! You're bursting at the seams."

"When you're married to someone, you want to please them."

"He's married to someone, he's married to *you,* and I don't see him pleasing *you.*"

"Go fuck yourself," Leslie says. The words ring out like gunfire, and in the miserable silence that follows, Cynthia's face colors and Leslie feels waves of shame and astonishment. "I'm sorry," she says. "I don't know where that came from. That was nuts." But even as she says this, the sisters both have a pretty good idea where it came from—the same place Leslie's sideburns came from, and the same place that launched the attack on ruddy Dr. Ryan. Leslie is in catastrophic hormonal imbalance.

"God, Leslie, I'm the one having her period and you're the one acting crazy. And by the way, I don't suppose you have any supplies on hand. I didn't come fully equipped."

As if to silence herself and prevent any new outbursts, Leslie fills her mouth with what remains of her croissant. It feels very unfoodlike in her mouth, as if she has taken a bite out of a pillow. To moisten the wad of unsweetened pastry, Leslie takes a large swallow of coffee, and the introduction of the hot liquid causes her to choke. Holding on to the edge of the table, she coughs without restraint, as if she were alone, or not entirely human. She sticks her tongue out and expels food from her mouth—Cynthia is shrinking back now, shielding herself with her pale rose damask napkin—but even ridding herself of the croissant and coffee cannot quell Leslie's coughing, and before long she has made herself sick, and she vomits up the early bites of her breakfast as well as remains of last night's dinner, little chunks of chicken floating in a broth of bright yellow bile.

"Leslie!" Cynthia says, as much in admonishment as concern.

Leslie's eyes are glassy. Her mouth hangs open. She brushes her fingertips across the little mound of sick that quivers on her lovely Spode breakfast plate. And then she places her fingers in her mouth, sucks them dry.

"Leslie, stop! What are you doing?"

Leslie looks as if she is about to answer. Her mouth opens, but no words come out. Just a low moan, an *ahhhh* that rattles in her throat like a pebbles in an empty can. She pushes back from the table, starts to get up, and tumbles hard from her chair onto the floor, where she writhes, moaning, drooling, her eyes wide, frightened, and unseeing.

"Leslie!" Cynthia cries. She kneels beside her sister and tries to soothe her by patting her shoulder, stroking her hair.

Blanca, the housekeeper who works there three mornings a week, comes into the room with a large bowl of fruit and, seeing Leslie on the floor, her legs thrashing, her shoulders hunched, lets out a cry of sympathy and distress. After placing the bowl on the table, Blanca hurries into the kitchen and calls Alex's office, and after a few delays and misunderstandings, she is at last connected to him.

"Mrs. Leslie is sick," Blanca says to Alex.

"I'll be home in minutes," he says to her. The offices are not far away; most often Alex doesn't bother with the firm's car service, and this time he runs the ten blocks between his office and his house. Normally the little jaunt takes ten minutes; today he makes it in three—he cannot recall ever moving so quickly, so effortlessly, not even in the full flush of vibrant youth. He feels as if he is propelled forward by a turbine engine. Other pedestrians step out of his way and turn to watch in astonishment as he speeds past them.

"Where is she?" Alex asks Cynthia as soon as he walks in.

"She's in bed," Cynthia says. As Alex goes past her on his way to the bedroom, Cynthia tries to stop him by placing her hand on his arm. "She's sleeping."

Alex pauses, looks at Cynthia's hand on his arm. His nostrils dilate as he detects the faint aroma of her menstruation. The smell; the unexpected, alluring delicacy of her fingers and her painted fingernails; the sound of her breathing; the scent of her scalp; the out-of-balance nervousness of her posture; her eyes—all of it come together to create a sudden and overpowering rush of desire. Never, even as a teenager drunk to the point of lunacy on his own hormones, has Alex felt so helplessly swept into the vortex of lust.

"You're really a very beautiful woman," he manages to say.

"Alex, that's actually sort of creepy."

He smiles. He agrees with her. Yet he reaches for Cynthia, catches her wrist. He has a vision of entering her, of licking her flesh, of pulling her limb from limb, and the vision is so real and so unsettling that his legs tremble. Yet he maintains his grip on her.

"I'm going to kiss you now," he announces.

"I don't think that's a good idea, and you better not," says Cynthia, and in the years to come she will have ample opportunity to wonder if she ought to have said something stronger and put up a more spirited defense when he drew her roughly to him and pressed his lips against her mouth. Yet in the moment, she is severely weakened by not being quite able to believe Alex is serious about all of this—there is something so *clobbered* in his expression—as well as by her desire not to create a scene, and he is able to achieve his kiss, a rank, moist, and un-welcome thing.

"Hey!" Leslie shouts, standing in the archway dividing the morning parlor from the library. She is wrapped in a blanket. Her eyes blaze. "Leave him alone!" she cries, and with that the blanket falls from her, revealing her heavy pregnant middle and expanses of raw reddened skin where the fur has been removed—yet even here little bits of stubble have begun to reappear. Leslie pulls Alex away from her sister and savagely slaps Cynthia in the face with such force that Cynthia ends up on her back.

"Not me!" Cynthia manages to scream. It looks as if Leslie is going to strike again, and in a panic Cynthia rolls away from her. She hits the legs of an end table, and an old China trade vase shakes, totters, and finally topples over, striking Cynthia on one side of her face, cutting her deeply.

"He's mine!" Leslie says, her voice a metallic growl. She lifts her hand in preparation to bring it down hard, but her gesture is frozen in midair, and she looks to one side, as if she has heard something troublesome. "Oh!" she says, grabbing at her naked crotch.

Five months and three weeks into her pregnancy, Leslie's water has broken. Clutching her stomach, she climbs off of her sister, and looks beseechingly at Alex, who is now wrapping her in the blanket and leading her out of the room.

"Blanca!" Alex shouts, "*una ambulancia, por favor. ¡Rápido! ¡Ahorita!* The baby is coming!"

He meant to say *babies.* They are expecting two, but in fact there are three, two perfectly formed, a boy and a girl, and the third twisted, de-formed, a hideous mixture of bone and gel, a muddle of matter, with something of a mouth in it, something that looks like an eye, a hand. Eastview Hospital has the experience and the technology to deal with premature babies, but some babies are not meant to be, and the doctors and most of the nurses there know how to whisk away the occasional monster that will not live, or should not live, and, above all, should not be seen by the mother. Or the father. Or anyone else. They are horrible genetic mistakes, and the world must be free of them. The lives of those so hideously unfortunate can be snuffed out like a match—it is so simple, and the life it would otherwise have to endure would be so painful and hopeless: the tiny little murder is really an act of charity.

The doctor tending to Leslie is neither Kosloff nor Yost nor any other doctor she has seen at Turtle Bay Obstetrics and Wellness. He is a young, good-looking man—something of the ski instructor in his build, his floppy blond hair—who whistles while he works. For the two of Leslie's babies who might survive, there are incubators on hand, but once the boy and girl have been cleaned off and their airways cleared of Leslie's viscosity, it becomes apparent to the obstetrician and the nurse that there has been a miscalculation. The twins, a boy and a girl, are very much alive, with beautiful, shiny heads of hair; they don't need incubators or any other kind of medical intervention. They need their mother, and the doctor and his nurse swaddle them and hand them over to Leslie, who, despite her exhaustion, is smiling happily, and reaches for them in a gesture of pride and possession as old as life itself.

Each of them has the same birthmark, a little red squiggle on the right hand. Adorable!

The second nurse comes back to the delivery room. Her name is Amelie Gauthier, a French Canadian, about forty years old, scrawny, fiercely religious. She tucks her twinkling gold crucifix under the top buttons of her uniform, and when the doctor gives her a questioning look, she purses her lips and briefly nods, indicating that the inconvenient matter of the third child has been dealt with and that nothing further on the subject needs to be said. The doctor looks at her questioningly again, to make sure that all is understood, and Nurse Gauthier looks away.

PART 2

TEN YEARS LATER

Lead us not into temptation...
—Matthew 6:13

For a long time, for as long as he can remember, this child has feared the night. What worries him is not that there might be a ghost lurking in the darkness, or a skeleton or a one-eyed icky thing or a zombie or Freddy or Jason or any other kind of Halloween monster. And yet, when the last of the light has disappeared from the sky and he is in his room, his thoughts become increasingly fearful. He thinks of being chased; he thinks of being caught. He hears footsteps coming up the stairs to the third floor, where his room is next to his sister's, his twin, his best friend, his only friend. He thinks of harm coming to her. He hears voices, he hears barks, he hears squeals. But worst of all is when things go quiet and the silence of that house makes him wonder if all the world outside his door has vanished.

No; that isn't the worst part. The worst part is when he falls asleep and he dreams of saber-toothed tigers and other flesh-eating animals. Sometimes in his dreams he sees them from a distance. Sometimes they are close by. Sometimes they chase him and he escapes, sometimes they catch him, and sometimes the creatures are right over his bed and in the dream he opens his eyes and looks right in their faces.

No; that isn't the worst part either. The worst part is that there is no one whom he can tell these things to, and no one to protect him. The worst part is the faces of those creatures are the faces of his parents.

The worst part is he knows that in some way he cannot put words to, some way that has yet to fully reveal itself, the dream is true.

"Do you know where that old baby monitor is?" Alex asks Leslie as they share a midnight snack. Naked, they sit in the kitchen, the table lit by a single bulb.

"Why do you need it?" Leslie asks, her voice deep and sensual, fully relaxed from their lovely time in their bed.

"I was thinking of putting it in the cellar," Alex says.

"Oh no. I don't think that's a very good idea. I don't want to hear what goes on down there." Her plate is empty now; she wets her finger, dabs it in the juice and the salt.

"No idea?"

"Of?"

"Where that old baby monitor is. I thought it was in one of the closets in the master bedroom."

"Why would we keep it?" Leslie asks.

"It seems like someone had been poking around in there."

"I'm sure we threw it away," Leslie says, reaching across the table and helping herself to a piece of gristle Alex has left on his plate.

Their voices are tinny, scratchy, as they come through the beige plastic grillwork of the old plug-in baby monitor. And he can hear what they say only when they are relatively close to the box he has sneaked into his bedroom. His mother is first to speak.

I'm tired. What about you?

I'm all right.

Are you feeling sexual?

I wasn't until you asked.

Adam's hand reaches quickly down and turns off the speaker, which he has set up next to his bed. He knows what is coming next. He has heard it before. Once. And once was enough.

In the morning, Adam slides the baby monitor far under the bed and waits for his door to open.

"Good morning, sweetheart," his mother says. She is dressed in jeans, a turtleneck sweater; her thick luxuriant hair is pulled back. She looks so happy today. Her lips are dark red; her teeth icy white.

"Good morning."

"Hi," Alice, his twin, says. She is already in the hall with their mother, dressed for school.

"Hi, Alice," Adam says. He pulls the covers back, climbs out of bed. He is a delicate boy, with a bit of prettiness in him. His limbs are long and thin, his hands look as if they might be suitble for coaxing Chopin out of a baby grand. He is a pensive boy. Friendless except for his sister, he takes no pleasure in sports or in any other pastime that calls for more than one person. He likes chess, but his only opponent has been a computer program. Alice won't play. She is artistic, dreamy, and has no interest in games in which pieces are captured and thrown into a box. He says he wants to be a doctor, and Leslie sometimes thinks that the first person Adam will ever touch will be laid out on an examination table.

Leslie loathes doctors, and her antipathy is shared by her husband, but far be it from either of them to discourage their son. "Whatever you do, we'll always be proud of you and always love you," they say to him.

Adam gathers his clothes and sets out for his little private bathroom. He is meticulous in his grooming habits, maybe even a little compulsive. It has crossed Leslie's mind that Adam might be a little OCD, or be suffering from some underlying condition that makes him unnaturally concerned with cleanliness. But sending him to a shrink, or to anyone else to whom he might open up and reveal his home life, is out of the question, unfortunately.

Just one of the many avenues toward normal life that has a gigantic DO NOT ENTER sign strung across the entrance.

Look what I found!
  What is it?
  Taste it.
  I'm not tasting it. Not without you telling.
  Oh, big strong man.
  Laughter. Much, much laughter.
  Come on, you big furry cocky crazy guy, taste it.
  If this is cat I'm going to kill you.
  It's not cat.
  It looks like cat. Sniffing noises. *What is this?*
  I told you it wasn't cat.
  It's actually quite good.
  Duh.
  And then—oh, not, not this again—the sound of eating, chewing, tearing, gulping, coughing, hacking, snarling, ravenous, unhinged, mad, mad eating.

Volume down. No, Adam can still hear them. Power off. Monitor under the bed. It occurred to him today that if his father or mother came in and found the baby monitor while he was asleep they might kill him. For real.

"Are we going to get a new dog?" Alice asks her mother the next morning while they wait for Adam to come down for his breakfast.

"I think so, sweetheart," Leslie says.

"It's too sad," Alice says. "I don't want any more pets." She has her notebook open in front of her and she draws in it with a number 2 pencil.

The waffles rise from the toaster and Leslie puts them on a plate and brings them to Alice.

"I know, baby, it's hard to lose a pet. But most of these poor things come from the pound. They were going to put them to sleep anyhow."

"Ginger didn't."

"Ginger came from one of those awful pet shops that I think should be against the law."

"Then just maybe no more pets for a while," Alice says. She is long and lean like her brother, but without the alarming delicacy. She is hardier, more emotional but also more confident. She, too, is friendless, but she gives no outward signs of loneliness or even shyness. She is a world unto herself. She wears her thick hair in braids and she loves to run, jump, and climb. When her parents take her to the park to let her burn off some energy, it makes them proud to see her fleetness, her grace and dexterity, though there is always a moment when she dashes out of their sight and they wonder for a few terrible moments if she is ever going to return, if she has perhaps figured things out and decided to make a run for it.

"What are you drawing there, sweetie," Leslie asks.

She steps behind Alice and looks over her shoulder at the notebook. Alice has made an amazingly lifelike drawing of Gray Guy, a cat that was in their possession a few weeks ago. Gray Guy sits with his square head cocked, his skinny tail wrapped around his ankles. He has a multitude of long whiskers and his eyes are at once mysterious and vacant.

Alice feels that her artwork is private but she cannot resist the desire for her mother's approval and she looks up at Leslie hopefully.

"That is fucking amazing," Leslie says, despite her many promises to herself to watch her language around the kids. "May I have it?"

"Sure," Alice says with a shrug. She tears it out of the spiral notebook, and Leslie puts it on the refrigerator, secured by a magnet shaped like a hamburger.

At that moment, Adam walks in, scowling.

"When can we stop being locked in our rooms at night?" he asks, an unfamiliar edge in his voice. He is usually such a good boy....

*   *   *

If walls could talk. The old Twisden house had been slipping into delinquency and disrepair for quite some time, but now the slippage has become more of a headlong plunge. Leaks, cracks, drafts, and all kinds of mechanical malfunctions go unrepaired. Furniture is torn, stained, broken—and much of what has survived has been brought to auction. Likewise the once prized paintings of the various Twisden ancestors—the ministers and sea captains and industrialists and surgeons and puffed-up arbiters of New York social life that had been for years peering down at the twins from their gold-leaf frames— have disappeared now, one by one, and are presumably hanging in the corridors and drawing rooms of arrivistes, people with the means to bid on the artifacts of someone else's family history, their own backgrounds being either unsightly or nonexistent. The helpers that once kept the house running so smoothly have similarly disappeared, one by one, until, recently, the last of the domestic employees, a housekeeper, had her employment cut from two days a month to no days a month, and the house immediately fell several quick levels on its way to complete chaos, like an elevator car hanging at a severe tilt from one fraying cord.

Despite the house slowly slipping into a state of ruin, Alex and Leslie keep careful tabs on Adam and Alice. Now that Alex barely shows up at his office and Leslie has not worked in publishing in several years, they both have time, a great deal of time to devote to parenting. One of them normally walks the twins to school each morning and whoever does not have the morning shift is there in the midafternoon, waiting for the kids across the street from Berryman Prep, twelve blocks north of their house. Both Alex and Leslie prefer to wait as far from the school as it's possible to be while still remaining visible to the twins when they emerge from the castlelike doors of the prestigious and pricey school. They don't want to socialize with the other parents and the nannies who are also there to collect their charges, don't want to engage in any idle chitchat, don't want to swap gossip about the school or the neighborhood or the mayor or global warming or some great new restaurant or the Cy Twombly retrospective at the Met or the latest shake-up at Lincoln Center, and with even greater vehemence they do not want to enter into a stream of sociability that might suddenly bring them to the shores of what to them is the Land of the Worst-Case Scenario—an invitation to a playdate, a birthday, or a dinner party. In fact, they dread invitations the way a criminal might dread a subpoena or a search warrant.

It goes like this: The twins emerge from school at 3:00 p.m., cleaved to each other almost as tightly as they were in the womb. Their eyes are cast down, their gait is labored, as if shyness and a desire not to be noticed are strapped to their backs like rucksacks. Simultaneously, they gaze up, just to make sure that their mother or father awaits them, half hidden by the bulk of a parked car or the shade of a London plane tree. They cross the street and move quickly toward home, stopping for nothing but red lights and traffic. Though the twins are athletic, they must struggle to keep up with their mother, whose stride is long and graceful and who always seems to be two or three steps away from them and whose gaze is constantly shifting, her glance as sudden and sharp as the snap of a finger as dogs walk by on their leashes and squirrels leap from branch to branch. But when Adam and Alice walk with their father, their efforts to keep up with him are futile and they must remind him that they are half his size and hope that he will slow down and allow them to keep up. He looks startled, and for a moment it appears as if he is going to be angry, and then that moment passes and he swoops them up in his arms, both of them, and carries them as if they weighed nothing, nothing at all. His strength is amazing....

Once they are home, their schedules are as unvarying as the wind-up tune of a music box. They are each given a glass of low-fat milk and a protein bar. They are allowed one hour of television. They are allowed one half hour of video games. They clear places for themselves on the dining table and dedicate themselves to their homework for at least two hours. They play with their father, who likes to roughhouse, which is almost always a great deal of fun but now and then it gets out of control, and one of the twins ends up hit or scratched and must bite back tears. At six thirty, the family watches the news on TV, and at seven, dinner is served. Lately, these evening meals have settled into a pattern of utter sameness—pasta wheels in a sauce of butter and salt for the children, roast beef for the parents.

When they are called to dinner, the twins do not want to be rude or risk hurting their parents' feelings, but the truth is that the prospect of sitting at the table and watching the adults consume beef so rare that it is more blue than red and swims in a pool of what Alex and Leslie call gravy but that Adam and Alice see as blood is really more disturbing than the prospect of being sent to bed with no dinner at all. But every time, the meal is gotten through. They are served dessert. Homework is checked. A silence settles over the house; the ticking of the grandfather clock is as loud as nails being pounded into the lid of a coffin.

It is November and the darkness comes quickly, as if night is a garrulous old man who cannot wait to tell his terrible story, and with the darkness comes Adam's and Alice's bedtime or, at least, their exile.

Adam lies in the darkness of his room with the receiver of the baby monitor resting on his stomach. It rises and falls as he breathes.

Nothing is being transmitted. All he can hear is the whoosh of electricity, like wind blowing through his parents' bedroom.

Then he hears their footsteps. At first he is startled, thinking they are coming to his room. He pushes the monitor under his covers. But he realizes that what he has heard is their footsteps approaching their own bedroom, and he disentangles the twisted wires of the monitor and places the speaker once more on his stomach.

I feel something happening in me, Alex.

I'd like to give you something to feel in you too.

Stop it, me serious.

You smell so good.

The sounds of scuffling.

All right, all right, what is it?

I'm having thoughts, Alex.

Thoughts are okay. Thoughts are good. Thoughts are what make us human, right?

Bad thoughts, Alex.

What happened here?

Cut myself shaving. Alex?

What?

Don't you want to know what my bad thinks are?

Thoughts.

Right. Don't you want to know what my bad thoughts are?

I think I know, Leslie. We don't have to talk about it.

It's about the children.

Shhh.

Our children, Alex. Our children.

Crying sounds.

I know, baby. I know. Shhh. It's okay.

Crying. Then: *Do you have these kind of thinks too?*

A long silence. At last, the father speaks, softly. *Yes.*

I can't sleep.

Leslie. Please. I'm exhausted.

I smell smoke.

It's not from here.

Her smelling it!

Who's smelling it, Leslie. Who?

Me!

Then say, "I smell smoke."

I smell smoke. You pedantic motherfucker.

I just happen to think it would be nice if we sounded as if we were . . . you know. Whatever. Something decent.

I smell smoke, Alex.

It's from next door. Their fireplace. The smoke from their chimney wafts near our window.

Wafts?

Blows.

What if there is a fire, Alex? In our . . .

House?

Yes, what if there is a fire in our house.

Don't scratch me like that.

Sorry. I thought you liked it. But what if?

There's not going to be a fire. But if there is, Leslie, we call the fire department and we leave the house. Just like anybody else.

But what about our children?

What about them?

They're locked away.

Yes. I know. We must.

But they'll be trapped.

There are fire escapes right at their windows.

With gates, Alex. We put gates over those windows and the gates are locked.

And I have the key. We go up; we unlock the gates.

I don't have the key.

You shouldn't have the key, Les.

Because why?

Because I have more control over myself. I'm sorry, but that's just a fact.

Well, I know where the key is. It's in the candy dish right over there. So there. Asshole.

Nice.

Oh, I forgot. Mr. Sensitive. Mr. Well-Born.

What is wrong with you?

I think I'm going into heat.

Adam quickly turns off the monitor. His heart scrambles around his chest as if it were looking for a way out. *I've got to get out of here,* he thinks.

The next morning, the twins are released from their rooms by their mother, who seems to be starting another cheerful day. She is wearing brand-new blue jeans, which might mean she actually went to a store. Though she is smiling, Adam notices she has a new bruise on the side of her face. He and Alice know that sometimes their father hits her. But they also know that sometimes their father is hit *by* her. And sometimes they just play sort of rough with each other and things happen....

Family secret.

The children walk behind their mother, down the third-floor hallway, past empty spots on the walls, where once gloomy oil paintings hung, forbidding portraits of their supposedly important ancestors. An antique Persian runner once covered the floor here, and royal blue carpeting once covered the stairs, but all is bare now.

"I hope you two are hungry," their mother says. "I made a really nice breakfast."

"Not so much," Alice says.

"What did you make?" Adam asks.

"Eggs!" Leslie says. "Beautiful fresh eggs."

"I had a good dream last night," Alice says to Adam.

He shrugs. Dreams don't do it for him.

"I dreamed someone shouted—I was out walking and someone shouted 'I love you' out of a window," Alice says. "He said, 'Hey, I love you' and...I don't know. Other stuff. 'I'll wait for you' and like that."

"Nice," says Adam, only because he is polite.

On their way downstairs, they pass their parents' bedroom. Normally, the door to this room is shut, but today it is wide open, and the children glance in, curious about the mysteries of the parental chamber. Alex, in maroon-and-white-striped pajamas, his long, lustrous hair hanging in a dark curtain, is on the floor, effortlessly doing push-ups—in fact, the push-ups come so easily to him that he increases the degree of difficulty by clapping his hands together after each one as if he were not a middle-aged lawyer enduring a professional rough patch but an eager young Marine in basic training.

"Hi, kids," Alex says, showing off a bit by clapping his hands *twice* after this push-up. The bedroom is a mess: furniture overturned, clothes everywhere, plates and saucers, bowls, cups, knives, and dirty napkins.

"Hi, Daddy," Alice says.

Adam mumbles something indistinct. He is noticing the coarse tufts of body hair surging out from between the buttons of his father's pajama top, as well as the hair at the bottom of his father's legs, exposed where the pajamas have ridden up during exercise.

Adam is also noticing something else—the little candy dish on the night table on his father's side of the bed, a dish that Adam now knows contains the key to the accordion-style burglar gates that secure their windows.

"Come on, you're going to be late for school," Leslie says, noticing that Adam is lingering behind.

In the kitchen—where scented candles burn to somehow camouflage the smells of fresh meat—the twins sit at the plain wooden table, and their mother presents them with a skillet filled with scrambled eggs, enough to feed ten people. The mound of eggs is so massive that the sight of it robs both children of whatever small appetite they had, but neither wishes to court controversy and they do their best to eat enough to satisfy their mother that her efforts have been appreciated.

Soon Alex comes into the kitchen. He is not dressed for work but is in his pajamas and robe—it's been months since he has gone into the office. Money is an issue, and even though they are basically supporting themselves by selling off their huge cache of valuable belongings, the disposal of all these pricey antiques is not without effort. In fact, it is practically a full-time job.

With everyone absorbed with breakfast, Adam quietly excuses himself from the table, mumbling something about needing to go to the bathroom. He walks as quickly as he dares up the staircase to the second floor, though there is no good reason why he would not use one of the bathrooms on the first floor. Certain things in the lives of the twins are predictable—they will be locked into their bedrooms shortly after dark; pets will appear and disappear, though by now they have learned to remain detatched from the animals who come through the household, just as they have learned not to go anywhere near the cellar door at the far distant end of the house; they will hear strange sounds through the night and they are never to ask about them. They are never allowed to invite children over to their house, nor are they allowed to make anything but the briefest visits to the homes of their classmates—not that invitations are any longer forthcoming. And family secrets must be kept. Divulging any detail to outsiders about the life of that house would be like blasting a hole in the hull of a submarine.

Adam is halfway up the stairs and he stops, listens. All he can hear is his own nervous breathing. He takes another step up. Stops. Waits. Listens. And then another. He hears his father coughing, and the *hack hack hack* of it seems to be coming from right behind him. Adam dares a peek over his shoulder—there is no one there. The coughing ends with a little whoop that turns into laughter. Adam exhales and takes the rest of the stairs two at a time.

He tiptoes into his parents' bedroom. A number of vanilla-scented candles burn on the mantelpiece and on the windowsill, but even with the camouflage of perfume, there is a heavy scent of bodies in the air. Adam glances at the king-size bed, which has been carefully, almost primly made, with the corners tucked in and the pillows just so. But there is nothing prim about the deep gouges in the wall behind the brass headboard, and though Adam has seen them before, he cannot help but stare at them.

He reminds himself he must hurry. At any moment one of his parents might become suddenly aware of his absence and come bounding up the steps in that uncannily speedy way both have of getting from one spot to another—sometimes they move so quickly, it is like watching a movie where there has been a break in the film: a character can be on the porch one moment and in the next frame unnervingly be standing in the living room. Adam uses his finger to stir the coins that fill the spare-change dish on his father's night table. All he finds are quarters pennies dimes and nickels.

"Adam?"

Adam hears his father's distant call and looks up, his heart pounding. He stirs the change more vigorously, this time managing to spill some of it onto the table and the floor. But it's there! The key! He shoves it into his back pocket and starts to pick up the change, though his fingers are rendered practically useless by his fear, and each coin defies his grip.

He hears footsteps coming up the stairs. He has no choice. He must leave a few of the coins on the floor—and get out of there.

But when he looks up he is no longer alone.

Alice stands in the doorway of their parents' bedroom, her eyes blazing, her face icy and pale.

"What are you doing?" she whispers.

"Is he up there?" their father hollers from downstairs.

"I've got him," Alice calls back, her voice shrill. She squats next to Adam and the two of them pick up the rest of the coins and then hurry toward the steps, at the bottom of which Leslie, already in her coat, stands at the mirror in the foyer, adjusting her hat and looking thoughtfully at her reflection.

"We're getting out of here," Adam whispers to Alice.

"To where?"

"Not sure."

"Adam…"

He grips her arm and practically hisses, "They're going to kill us."

"Come on, kids!" Leslie calls from the bottom of the stairs. "Late for school!"

Gone are the days when the children would be taken to Berryman Prep by private car, and gone, too, are the trips to and from school in a taxi. Now, no matter what the weather, they walk, accompanied by either Leslie or Alex. Today, Leslie escorts them to Berryman Prep. She holds their hands as she speed-walks up Fifth Avenue. She never walks them on the western side of the street, the sidewalk next to Central Park, though as they race along she seems always to be glancing toward the park, at the pigeons rising up in pink and gray clouds, at the mad squirrels scurrying up and down trees as if at every moment their lives hung in the balance. Today, as Leslie hurries the twins toward school, the squirrels seem to vex her so much that at one point she stops right in the middle of the street and stares across Fifth into the park, her eyes blazing, her neck craned forward, her black-stockinged legs slightly trembling, and with what sounds to the twins something like a whimper trapped deep in her throat.

"What's wrong, Mom?" Alice asks.

The question seems to snap Leslie to attention, and she blinks as if coming out of a hypnotic trance. Her smile is wide, radiant. "Nothing's wrong my precious. Just…" She taps herself on the head. "Still sort of in dreamland, that's all."

Because Berryman requires uniforms, both Adam and Alice are dressed in blue blazers. Adam wears gray trousers; Alice wears a gray pleated skirt that falls to one inch below the knee. They walk in silence for a few moments, and Leslie's face brightens. "Hey, did I ever tell you two what the happiest day of my life was?" They are stopped at a light on Seventy-Ninth Street. She holds on to the twins' jackets, as if they had no sense and might at the slightest provocation race into traffic. Cabs, all of them carrying passengers, stream by; and then a flatbed truck carrying hot-dog carts that will eventually be distributed to street corners all over the city; followed by a school bus for children with special needs; and finally a crosstown city bus with two advertising posters on its side, one for a local bank offering low ATM fees and showing a man dancing with a dollar sign, and the other one advertising a new horror movie called *Blood Sausage* and showing a nearly naked female corpse hanging from a slaughterhouse meat hook.

"The happiest day of my life was when you two were born," Leslie is saying. "What a dream come true. And twins! Oh me, oh my, it was like winning the cosmic lottery."

The twins steel themselves. They have heard this song before— and sometimes there's a verse in it about the baby who did not make it out alive, and this verse is tearfully delivered, and it makes them feel awful, sick to their stomachs with pity for their mother's unhappiness, and even sicker with helplessness.

But today there is no dead baby, no tears, just happiness, sheer glowing happiness.

"We wanted you guys so much, and believe me, there is not a day that goes by when I don't feel grateful to have such beautiful, terrific kids. And don't forget, I was once a kid too. And I know how hard it can be. Sometimes the other kids aren't that nice. Is that sometimes how you feel? Alice?"

Alice shrugs. She feels so distant from the other children in her school that the question of their niceness doesn't often occur to her— in fact, it *never* occurs to her.

Leslie puts her hand on Alice's shoulder. "I think the way some of the kids nowadays are being raised—it's just crazy and irresponsible. And I know—we both know, your father and I—that you might wish you had a little more freedom, but one day, I promise you, one day you'll look back on what we have done to keep you safe and healthy and you'll thank us, you really will."

They are close to the school now. The architecture of the place used to terrify Adam—immense terra-cotta bricks, carved Doric columns, a gargoyle here and there, Gothic windows. Berryman Prep looks as if it were built in New Haven, Connecticut, and somehow drifted down from the Yale campus and found a spot on the Upper East Side. It speaks of tradition, privilege, learning, and a great seriousness— in other words, it proposes childhood without childishness. Directly across the street from venerable Berryman is a public school made of pale bricks with greenish pseudo tiles on the ground floor that frame windows that, because of askew venetian blinds, all look cockeyed. Next to the public school is a large blacktopped playground where hundreds of middle-school children dressed in every imaginable color and in every kind of clothing from Levi's to djellabas call out happily to one another as they stream toward the entrance before the morning bell rings.

"Can I ask you a question?" Adam says.

"Of course, my precious," Leslie says. She gathers him close, kisses the top of his head.

He can hear her breathing in the scent of his scalp. It makes him shiver, though he knows it is just her way of loving him.

"Why do we have to get locked in at night?"

"This again?" his mother asks.

"We don't want to be locked up anymore," Adam says.

"It won't be forever," Leslie says.

"I don't get it," Adam says.

"Neither do I," says Alice.

"So we don't eat you up," Leslie says, her right hand tousling Adam's hair. She says it as if it were a joke, but it has the sound of the most truthful thing she has ever said to them.

* * *

When Alex and Leslie enrolled the twins at Berryman Prep, the staff went to some lengths to make sure that the twins were not in the same classes. The feeling was that, for all of its wonders and beauties, being a twin was something children also had to overcome, or compensate for, and the more time the Twisden children spent separately, the better they would do in their studies, the more friends they would make, and the more chance they would have to develop into autonomous, well-adjusted adults. Apart, the twins seem to long for each other, and neither of them has met with much social success. They are not outcasts, nor are they the victims of teasing or exclusion. They simply do not click with the other students. They are withdrawn, sleepy, mumbly—they seem like sad children.

Today, Alice is with her fourth-grade science class traipsing through Central Park. Their teacher, Edie Delaney, insists that there is more nature to be observed in an acre of Central Park than in an acre of the Serengeti Plain, though it is also the case that she likes to sneak a few quick puffs of her Marlboro Lights while leading these supposedly educational expeditions.

"All right," Edie Delaney announces, jiggling her Bic lighter in the pocket of her trench coat, "here's what we're going to do. Remember that hundred-year-old London plane tree we saw in the beginning of the year?" She points to the tree, which stands a hundred or so feet away, its bark mottled green, yellow, and black, like camouflage wear, floating in a sea of its own dropped leaves. "Did everyone bring their notebooks? Hands?" The fourteen children in her class raise their hands. "Great. Gather around the tree and make the best drawing you know how. Okay?"

They look at her with some skepticism until Jeremy, whose father is a matrimonial attorney known as the Piranha of Park Avenue, steps forward and says, "This isn't art class, right?"

"No, it's not, Jeremy, and that's an excellent point. It's a science class, and a very important part of science is observation." Edie takes a deep breath; her lungs are poised for a cloud of nicotine-rich smoke and seem horribly disappointed to receive only air. "So what I am going to need you to do now is *observe and record*."

In short order, Edie repairs to a nearby bench, seating herself so she can suck down a few long drags of her cig while at least being able to imagine she cannot be seen by her students, and the class makes its way toward the London plane, with Alice, as usual, straggling behind—she has developed a strategy in which her exclusion from the group appears to be a function of her slow pace and not a rejection of her company.

Just as Alice makes the first lines of her drawing, her attention is drawn to the sound of crunching leaves and twigs, and she turns toward the sound and sees that beneath a hawthorn bush, a large one, about the size of a refrigerator, there is a pair of flashing eyes. Someone—a child—is crouched there, hiding. And she can tell from the way the child breathes—and oh, she can hear; how she can hear!—that his heart is wild with fear. So much fear that it makes Alice afraid too.

Her hand begins to shake. She forces herself to draw the London plane, but the lines she makes jump up and down like the record of an electroencephalogram. She closes her eyes, breathes. *Who are you?* she thinks. And a voice within her answers: *Don't look at me!*

A moment later, a man on a silly-looking bright red gas-powered scooter comes putt-putting by. The man has lank brown hair down to his shoulders, a thick beard the shape of the blade of a shovel, and he wears a long woolen coat. The scooter may look silly, but the man looks fierce, frightening, and very, very angry. He moves his head to the left and the right, scanning the walkways and the open spaces. He is looking for something, and Alice is sure that that something is crouched beneath the bushes, hiding and in terror.

"Caleb!" the man calls. "Come on, man. Everything's cool. Caleb?"

He stops, kills the motor on his scooter, and looks around with increased intensity and concentration. He senses something...

"Caleb?" he says, more softly this time. He makes a kissing noise such as you would use to reassure a dog or some other animal. He waits. Waits. Finally, he reaches into his pocket and takes out a small silver cylinder, places the end of it in his mouth, and blows—his cheeks puff out. None of the other children seem to notice the high shrill piping sound of the whistle, but it is just short of unendurable to Alice. The suddenness of the pain it causes her is as frightening as being grabbed in the dark, and she claps her hands over her ears, her heart racing, her legs cold and wiggly as snakes.

After a couple more blasts on his excruciating whistle, the bearded man is satisfied that Caleb is nowhere near, and he starts the engine of his scooter again—the deep, gassy sputters of the little machine are a relief to Alice after the audio-dagger of the whistle.

When the scooter is out of sight—though she can still hear it putt-putting, even over the river of noise that flows southward on Fifth Avenue—Alice makes sure Ms. Delaney is not looking and then scurries over to the bush where she saw the flashing eyes. She parts the stiff, bare branches. There is the smell of dirt and decaying vegetation, and mixed in somewhere the juniper tang of feline urine. The branches are stiff and resist Alice as she struggles to part them, and for a moment she thinks the boy is no longer huddled there.

"Hello?" she quietly calls.

"*Go away*," a scratchy, frantic voice answers. "Go away or I'll kill you."

She falls back, landing on her seat, so frightened that the world seems to snap and shiver before her eyes like a flag in a high wind. With her hands behind her and her heels dug into the ground, she crawls backward, away from the bush, away from the voice, in a panicked crabwalk.

Partly because of his advanced reading skills, and partly to minimize the number of classes he shares with his sister, Adam is put in a combined fourth-through-sixth-grade English class, where the students this semester are studying the Bible as literature with one of the school's more popular teachers, Michael Medoff. Mr. Medoff is a tall, well-built man in his early thirties, with wavy hair, a scimitar nose, olive-green eyes, and a kindly but distant manner that draws children to him. Today, he is trying not to stand too close to any of the kids because he senses that his skin reeks of rum. He has trouble metabolizing alcohol, and last night he and his boyfriend, Xavier, were out late at a club frequented by Cuban exiles whose ideas of merriment and personal freedom seem to have no boundaries. (Michael's idea of personal freedom is to be able to choose whatever he cares to read, with no papers to grade or classes to prepare.)

The fourteen students here today sit at a large oval table while Medoff paces near the front of his classroom reading aloud from the King James version of the Old Testament.

"Okay, here's God in a particularly vengeful frame of mind," he says. "This is from..." He glances at the Bible in his hands. "Jeremiah."

"Jeremiah was a bullfrog," more or less sings Ry Finnegan, whose father produced about 10 percent of *Rolling Stone* magazine's Greatest Rock Albums of All Time.

"The Jeremiah of the Old Testament is *so* not a bullfrog, Ry," Medoff says. And, not able to resist reminding the boy that the teacher not only gets the reference but knows the lyrics, he adds, "He was *so* not into joy for all the fishies and making life terrific for you and me. Listen." He looks at the Bible again and reads, " 'And I will make this city desolate.' And if that doesn't make you wonder about God's anger-management issues, maybe this will. 'And I will cause them to eat the flesh of their sons and the flesh of their daughters, and they shall eat every one the flesh of his friend.' "

Medoff looks up, smiling. He loves these kids, their brightness, their newness to the world, and he can hardly wait to start kicking ideas around. Yet as his eyes lift from the book, the first thing he happens to see is Adam Twisden-Kramer, whose face has suddenly drained of all color. If Adam were an old man, or even middle-aged, Medoff's first thought would be that he was having a heart attack or a stroke. His breathing is shallow, and beads of perspiration are on his forehead now, and the wings of his nose.

"Adam?" the teacher manages to say as the boy slides from his chair and onto the floor in a dead faint.

All day long the key has burned like a coal in Adam's pocket. Now it is night, nearly ten o'clock, and he and Alice have been locked in their bedrooms since six thirty. He connects with her phone and texts her: We get out of here.

2 early, she taps back.

Cant wait.

He climbs out of his pajamas and back into today's school clothes. He takes the key out of his pocket, and at first it does not fit into the lock that keeps the burglar gates shut, In fact, it seems to have nothing whatsoever to do with the lock. But even as his spirits spiral downward, Adam continues to twist and turn the key, and before too long he can push it into the invisible canal within the lock. He twists the key, and though it does not really turn, there is enough of a jiggle to lead him to believe that with a little patience he can make it work.

The baby monitor is on the bed, the volume turned up so he can hear if his parents leave their room and come to check on the twins. The speaker emits a steady whoosh of static; it sounds like a cat that can't stop hissing.

From far below, and not broadcast through the monitor, comes the howl of a dog—Adam cannot tell whether the sound comes from out-side or from a neighbor's house or from the cellar of his own house, that dank, terrible place he will never, no matter what, step foot in—he'd rather die.

He hears their voices, his mother's and father's coming through the monitor.

So sleepy, his mother says. *That tasted amazing.*

Gives new meaning to the phrase 'good dog.'

Don't. I just like to think of it as meat.

Have you given it more thought?

I hate thinking. I really do. I completely hate it.

It's something we need to think about, Leslie.

I don't even understand.

We just go there. We get on a plane and go there. If he could lead us in, he can fucking well lead us out.

Lead us out where?

Look at us, Leslie!

Suddenly, the lock surrenders to the key and unclenches itself from the gate, allowing Adam to push it to one side. He stands there for a few moments, closer to freedom than he has ever been.

He hoists the dark maroon JanSport backpack from its resting spot on a chair. He unzips it to make certain he has remembered to stuff in the things he imagines he might need: three changes of underwear, three pairs of socks, a cord to recharge his phone, three Rice Krispies bars in their shiny foil wrappers. He looks around his room—what else should he be taking?

But he must hurry. This much he knows. He unplugs the baby monitor, stows it hastily beneath his bed. He takes a last look around the room, wondering—fearing—that he will never return to it. Where will he go? He has no idea. He looks at the walls, the floors, the hooked rug, the poster of the giraffe with the funny look on his face, his pillow, his books, his toys, his computer. He turns off all the lights in his room but turns the small television on. "Good-bye, room," he whispers.

He stops. Is someone coming? He leans toward the door, listens as hard as he can with his eyes closed, his breath held. All he can hear is the working of his own heart. *I'm going to be a heart doctor one day, I'm going to fix hearts.* The thought calms him for a moment—the future is like a guardian angel. But the creaks and twitters of the old house chase the angel away.

He listens to the silence. He cannot shake the feeling that his parents are standing just outside his door. They are preternaturally capable of sensing his every move, and even capable, it often seems, of reading his mind. Of course they know he has opened the safety gates. How could they not?

He wonders what they will do to him. The thought of it is too immense, too wild and overwhelming; it is like trying to see a polar bear in the midst of a blizzard. All you can do is squint and wait to be devoured…

He thinks of the baby monitor tossed carelessly under the bed. Maybe he can retrieve it, plug it back in…

But it's far too late for that.

He walks across the unlit room, which he could navigate blindfolded. He presses his ear to the door. Waits. Listens.

"Mom?" he whispers. And hears in reply only silence. With a little more fear in his voice: "Dad?" Again, the silence. Is it the benign silence of emptiness or the silence of a beast waiting to strike? No matter how hard Adam presses his ear to his bedroom's door, the silence persists.

With the gate out of the way, his next task is to open the window— a window that has not been open for as long as he can remember. His small hands clasp and yank the brass lifts on either side of the lower sash, but the window does not budge. His face is fiery; his slender fingers feel as if they are about the break. Adam steps back, his heart racing. He sees that the thick wooden frame encasing the window has been painted so that there is not even a crack of space between the window and the molding that holds it in place. Once he saw his father struggling to open a window that had been painted shut. His dad had hammered the heel of his hand up and down the window frame, breaking the paint's seal, and then opened the window with no further trouble. But Adam does not dare bang away—such noise will surely bring his parents upstairs, if they are not already there, waiting.

Adam takes a series of deep breaths, telling himself, *You do this, you do this, you can.* He grabs the brass lifts, expels his breath with a strongman's mighty huff, and to his great surprise the window opens with a long crackle.

There is no time to be proud or happy. Adam climbs out of the window and steadies himself on the windswept landing of the fire escape, reminding himself that if he looks down into the frozen, barren patch of backyard three stories below, he will surely fall. He takes a moment, waiting for his heart to slow down and for his breaths to come more easily. *I'm going to make it,* he tells himself.

A kind of iron gangplank connects the part of the fire escape he's standing on to the landing beneath Alice's window. He looks toward it and sees her peering nervously through the steel diamonds of the burglar gate. He's pretty sure that the key that opened his gate will work on hers as well. It has to. It must....

And if her window has been painted shut? He will open it. He has found a strength beyond what he knew, or even imagined. He has tapped into his will to survive.

The fire escape is slippery. It vibrates in the wind. It seems to sway when he moves; it wants to pull away from the bricks of the building. The rusted bolts attaching it to the side of the house chirp and squeak.

Slowly, Adam takes a step toward his sister, and another step. The metal groans beneath his feet, but as frightened as he is, there's no turning back.

He looks out into the night, which is as unfamiliar to him as the terrain of some distant planet. He has seen it only in pictures and through his window, but now it strikes him as somehow more alive than he had ever imagined it. There is the sound of traffic. He can hear two people laughing on the street, invisible, but vivid too, like they are right there beside him. A plane pushes its lights across the inky sky. The sound of distant music, the thrum of the bass. The world!

He hears knocking. Knuckles on glass. Terrified, he turns toward his room, expecting to see his father's furious face and the angry come-here gestures beckoning him back. But all he sees is the darkness of his old room. The knocking comes again. It's Alice. She's scared. She wants him to hurry. It's her turn to be set free.

In the building just west of the Twisden house, a similarly built town house that has long since been divided up into steeply priced "cozy" apartments, a very large, tired, and discouraged middle-aged woman named Dorothy Willis lives on the dwindling inheritance left to her by her parents. She has been writing a book about an animal actor of the 1950s named Francis the Talking Mule, a book that she had thought would be easy and amusing to write, but, like everything else in her life, it became sadder and more difficult as it proceeded until she was practically unable to eke out a page, a paragraph, or even a sentence. But she remained at her desk deep into the night, playing computer solitaire, eating, trying not to eat, and surveying the backyards and lit windows of her neighbors.

For the most part, the windows of the houses within her view are curtained, and Dorothy must piece together narratives from shadows and silhouettes. It's a bit like trying to figure out what people are saying in a language you don't know. Is that figure of a man going up and down someone chinning himself on a bar, or is some repulsively energetic sex act being performed? Is that woman draping her arms around the silhouette of a man comforting him or seducing him, or, given the fact that neither of them has budged in twenty minutes, are they not people at all? Dorothy knows it's rude and just a bit creepy to spy on your neighbors, but the people in the adjoining buildings are not really neighbors. She doesn't know their names or anything else about them, which coats them all with a veneer of unreality.

As to the comings and goings in the expensive little yards below, there are often diverting things to look down upon during the warm months, but since the beginning of November the gardens have been empty save for the ever-diligent pigeons and squirrels, and a few fat rats. A couple of times, once near dawn, once around midnight, she saw Mr. Twisden digging a hole in his backyard and then burying something in a blue plastic sack, but he was so unhurried and confident that it never occurred to Dorothy that anything untoward might be happening.

But tonight she sees something that amazes her right out of her seat, though she has been sitting for so long that her legs cannot hold her bulk steadily and she immediately falls back down into the expensive orthopedically designed desk chair she treated herself to when the Talking Mule project began. But even huffing and puffing from a sitting position she sees it: a little boy is crawling through the window and scrambling onto the fire escape. Dorothy's first thought is that the house next door is on fire, in which case the whole block might soon be engulfed in flames, most particularly the house she lives in, in which case she is in mortal danger. So once again she forces herself out of her seat and this time she goes to her window. There he is, the child, looking up at the sky—he does not look like a kid escaping from a house on fire. Yet he looks too young to be sneaking out at night to meet some little sweetheart. Dorothy presses her bulk against the window to get a better angle, and she peers out: There is no sign of flame, or smoke. And no one else but this solitary child is moving.

Oh my God! The boy almost slips off the fire escape, but he rights himself. And now he is walking toward a lit window about fifteen feet away. Dorothy is breathing with such force that her inner humidity is clouding the window. She wipes the vapor clear and by now the boy has been joined by another child, exactly his height and weight. A girl, maybe, through Dorothy cannot be certain. She herself had once been coltish and thin and had to be urged to eat. She once climbed, too, the live oak that ruled the little kingdom of their Baton Rouge backyard....

Suddenly she sees the two children clambering down the metal staircase, the end of which sways back and forth, like the point of a blind person's cane. They are in the yard, through the gate, gone.

Kids, Dorothy says to herself. Well, show's over. She gathers herself and is about to return to her desk, her book, her bag of Bugles, when all of a sudden a head pops out of the boy's window. It must be the father. Dorothy has seen him many times, this well-built, unfriendly man, often with a hat pulled down over his brow, warmly dressed even when the weather called for short sleeves.... He looks left, right, up, and then down, and wastes no more time holding on to the illusion that those children are somehow nearby. The window slams shut and by the time Dorothy makes her way from her back window to the front of her apartment, both the father and the mother are on the street. They stand in the gauzy swirling cone of light dropped by a streetlamp, touching each other nervously as they look up and down the street. They lift their faces. They seem to be.... what? Sniffing the air? How strange. They are. They are definitely sniffing the air.

After a moment of consultation, the mother takes off in one direction and the father lopes off in another. Dorothy keeps her eyes on him. He stops, cranes his neck to see farther down the block, and then does something that almost causes her to topple over: in a seemingly effortless single move, he jumps from the sidewalk to the roof of a parked car. He seems not to be subject to the laws of gravity. From his new perch on top of the silver Mercedes, he looks up and down the block for any sign of either of his children.

Michael Medoff sits at the kitchen table, which was built into the wall in order to save space in his five-hundred-square-foot apartment on the ninth floor of an old apartment building on Twenty-First Street, near Second Avenue. The apartment would be small even if he lived there on his own, but he shares these two and a half rooms with Xavier Sardina, and the two of them, broad-shouldered and not particularly graceful, are continually trying to navigate around each other, like dancers unsure of the choreography.

Tonight, Xavier is clearing the remains of their dinner while Michael spreads out his homework on the table.

"That's disgusting," Xavier says over his shoulder as he slots tonight's china into the dishwasher rack.

"What?"

"You wet your fingertip and pick up bread crumbs from the table and eat them."

"I'm still hungry."

"You didn't even finish your dinner."

"No time. I've got to grade sixteen essays about *Oliver Twist* and I have only…" Michael looks at his watch, an ocher-faced Elgin, a legacy from his grandfather. "Two hours before you force me to go out dancing."

Xavier lowers his chin, arches his brows, but does not allow himself to be drawn into what he is sure is a conversational trap. Xavier and Michael go to a dance club called the Third Degree just off the West Side Highway between Bank and Bethune every Tuesday night, and every Tuesday night Xavier feels Michael's reluctance to attend. Michael's idea of a great night is for the two of them to sit on the sofa watching the Tennis Channel on their immense high-def screen with a bowl of low-cal popcorn between them, whereas Xavier revels in New

York's gay nightlife, the later, the louder, the more amped-up and tee-tering on the brink of chaos, the better.

Though Xavier left Havana and its homophobic inanities more than ten years ago and has been living in New York ever since, he continues to celebrate his freedoms with an almost desperate vigor, as if the right to dance with a man in public, to live with a man, to hold his hand on the street, to share a candlelit dinner with him in a public place, all these things and a thousand other sexual liberties might be revoked at any moment. Michael generally chooses to accommodate Xavier's restless appetites. Though they have been together for nearly five years, Michael retains some sense of being Xavier's host in America, as if Xavier has cabbed in from Kennedy with his heart set on taking as large a bite as humanly possible from the Big Apple. If Xavier is bored or lonely even for a day or two, Michael considers it his fault and feels as if he is not only letting down his foreign visitor but somehow putting the United States itself in an unfavorable light. Xavier exhausts him—their evenings together are rarely spent at home; they careen from discos to gallery openings to wine tastings to dinner parties to poetry readings to bookstore events to theater lofts and jazz clubs—but Michael recognizes that without Xavier he might settle into his own personality's default position: a dour shut-in, content to leave the house for work and little else.

"You work so hard for your students, Michael," Xavier says, letting the water in the kitchen sink heat up before using the sprayer to rinse the dishes—the torrents of hot water available strike a chord of delirium in Xavier almost as resonant as the pleasures of sexual freedom.

"Well, Zavy, it's called doing your job," Michael says.

"For rich kids, no? Why not go across the street to the public school and teach children who are poor and need you?"

"Every kid is poor, really," Michael says. "Every kid is powerless. And every kid is at the mercy of his family. If they're not loved and cared for, they're screwed. Anyhow, I like my job, and I never forget that I am under something of a microscope simply because…"

"There must be a million gay teachers in New York, Michael," Xavier says. He turns off the hot water, dries his hands on a dish towel. "So why you think you so nervous in your school?"

"For very good reasons, Zavy, and you know it. Starting with a homophobic headmaster." Michael catches the towel Xavier has thrown at him, uses it to dab off some imaginary crumbs on the side of his mouth, and tosses it back.

While the towel is in midflight, the buzzer near the front door goes off, a rasping, piercing noise that the two men have dubbed the Penetrator.

"Who is that?" Xavier says, with some irritation.

The buzzer sounds its gray, grinding noise again, and Michael pushes his chair back and rises to answer the call. He presses the Talk button in the beige intercom next to the door, and the doorman, a thick-voiced elderly Irishman named James, announces that Adam Twisden-Kramer is in the lobby and wishes to be allowed up.

Adam Twisden-Kramer? The visit is so unexpected that for a moment Michael can't connect the name to anyone he knows. But then: of course. Adam. Adam is neither the best nor the worst of Michael's students, yet Michael holds a special fondness for the boy, recognizing in Adam's downcast eyes and soft voice a version of himself at ten years of age, when his body and mind embarrassed him beyond endurance. Of course, there is the fainting incident…. The way the boy hit the floor with the whomp of a stack of magazines, right in the middle of class. Michael had rushed to him, held him, picked him up. As Adam regained consciousness, he opened his eyes and saw that he was borne aloft in his teacher's arms, and for a moment there was a wide flickering stare of fear, followed almost immediately by a kind of all-encompassing peacefulness. The boy was like a young sailor swept from the deck of his vessel who learns in an instant that the sea will not swallow him but will keep him afloat. He had closed his eyes and breathed a deep sigh of relief.

There had always been a diffidence in the boy, a melancholy that made him compelling to Michael, and though Adam has yet to ask for anything special, nor has he engaged Michael in anything more than the most passing conversation, Michael has sensed for months that the boy wants to connect with him and seek some guidance, perhaps even solace. He is almost always the first of the students to come into class and he is always the last to leave, and even though his test scores are just slightly better than average and his papers are full of misspellings and grammatical errors, and the ideas they contain rarely go beyond a simple parroting of the remarks Michael has made in class, the effort Adam makes is not only palpable but endearing. If A for effort has any meaning, Adam is an A student.

And yet his suddenly showing up here is confounding. Even though Michael's address is far from a state secret, Adam would have had to make some effort to find it. And though there is nothing in the by-laws of Berryman Prep that explicitly prohibits a student from calling on a teacher after school, it is simply *not* the done thing, and frankly, it feels as divergent from the culture of the Berryman community as whistling in the corridors, picking your nose, or, for that matter, being openly gay.

"Send him up," Michael says through the intercom, though as soon as he says it, it seems like a mistake. Perhaps he ought to have gone down to the lobby and dealt with whatever Adam wants—having him come up is a dangerous precedent, and, worse, it is going to turn the rumor of Michael's homosexuality into an established fact: no one seeing Xavier and him sharing this small apartment would have the slightest doubt about the nature of their relationship, no one—not a child, not a grandmother, not a visitor from outer space, no one.

* * *

Faster, faster, faster faster faster—dodge, cut, hide, run again, faster still.

Alice, clutching her backpack, pounds down Lexington Avenue, not sure if her mother is still chasing after her, afraid to look and see.

It has all gone horribly wrong—she and Adam were not halfway down the fire escape before suddenly the lights of their house came on, square by square, like a model of a brain coming into consciousness. And then: shouts, threats. And Adam going south and her going north, yelling to each other: *Call me!*

She is amazed by how good it feels to run, and how easy it is. She has muscles she didn't know she had. She is in possession of a grace that was hers all along. Through the morass of fear and uncertainty, there comes a sudden blaze of sheer animal joy. Before this night, she had no idea what her body could do....

Michael waits for Adam by the elevator, and when the doors slide open the boy emerges, wearing just a light jacket even though it is a cold wet November evening. The jacket is streaked with rain and dirt; it looks as if he has taken a fall in it. But what makes the jacket particularly strange-looking—and makes Adam himself look mentally unbalanced—is that it has been tucked into the boy's jeans. His sneakers are soaked; leaves cling to their soles. He has scratches on his pale cheeks, and tiny twigs in his hair.

"Hello, Mr. Medoff," he says. "Thank you very much for allowing me up."

The elevator doors sigh shut behind him and the boy stands in the hallway, the path to nine other apartments on this floor, all but one with their doors firmly shut.

"Adam? What are you doing here?"

The boy opens his mouth to speak, but all that is released is a deeper silence. His eyes brighten as they fill with tears.

"Adam?" Michael says. His misgivings about this unexpected visit are suddenly cast into shadow by larger concerns. The boy seems to be tottering, and Michael reaches a steadying hand toward him, and at the touch of his teacher's hand, Adam feels his knees buckle, and only quick reflexes allow Michael to catch him before he hits the floor.

He half pulls and half carries Adam into the apartment. "Oh my God," Xavier says, dropping the dish towel and hurrying over to help. He closes the door behind Michael and the boy. He lifts Adam's legs and helps to carry him to the sofa. "What happened?" Xavier says.

"I have no idea," Michael answers, his voice unsteady. He crouches next to the sofa and gently shakes Adam's shoulder. The boy's eyes slowly open. They are an unusual shade of brown—closer to tan, really, and the whites of them are dark cream. They fix Michael with a stare stunning in its neutrality, neither friendly nor unfriendly, neither frightened nor trusting: all they do is *see*.

The boy tries to lift himself up on his elbows, but he is too exhausted, and after making it halfway, he gives up and falls flat again. He reaches behind himself and unhooks the backpack's straps and lets the thing fall onto the floor. "I didn't know where else to go," Adam says, staring at the ceiling now.

"You've got to tell me what's going on." Michael glances up and sees that Xavier has retreated to the kitchen, the cloak of their privacy already unraveling, thread by thread.

"I don't know," Adam says. "I'm not sure." He tries again to lift himself up on his elbows. This time he has more success and manages to swing his legs off the sofa and sit up straight. He rubs his hands over his face as if he were washing it with soap.

"Where did you get those scratches? Do you want to go to a hospital? And I need to call your parents right now."

"You can't," Adam says.

"Adam, this is my home. It's not a hideaway for guys who've had some kind of blowup with their parents. You understand?"

Adam nods. The chaotic smells of the night—wind, rain, soot, the burned-transistor tang of urban darkness—still cling to the boy's hair. There is something in his proximity that strikes a sudden terror in Michael.

"But I can't go home," Adam says. He lowers his head and clenches his fists.

"I need you to tell me why. If something is going on there—I mean, if something is happening that makes you feel so afraid—I need to know. You understand?"

"No, no," Adam says, very quickly. He waves his hand as if to dispel the notion of child abuse. "It's not that."

"Then what is it?"

"They're away."

"Away?"

Adam hesitates before shaking his head. "They're in Canada," he says.

"Canada?"

"Yeah, Montreal."

"And they left you alone?"

"Yes. With my sister."

"Who's looking after you, Adam?"

"No one."

Michael narrows his eyes, tilts his head. Somewhere along the way, he has settled on this gesture as a way of extracting the truth from his students, though he has no idea if it works or not.

"Our mother has family in Montreal," Adam adds.

"Family."

"Yeah. A brother. He's the mayor or something."

"Your uncle is the mayor of Montreal."

"Maybe not anymore."

"Adam. I'm going to need to contact your parents. And right away. You can't be here if no one knows where you are."

Adam shrugs. "But they're not home."

"You can give me their cell number."

"They don't have cell phones. And anyhow, you need a special chip to make them work in Canada. Like for Europe or anywhere."

Xavier comes out of the kitchen—he wasn't making himself scarce after all—carrying a tray upon which is a mug of warm apple cider with cinnamon and a peanut butter sandwich cut into quarters.

"Here you taken this now so you no get seek," he says to Adam in the most atrocious accent Michael has heard from him in years.

If seeing another man in his teacher's apartment has any meaning to Adam, if it confuses him or confirms a theory, there is nothing in his demeanor to betray it. He reaches for the mug and looks up gratefully at Xavier.

"Oh, thanks," he says. He holds the cup of hot cider and glances at the coffee table. "Is it okay to put it on your furniture?" he asks his teacher.

"Of course," Michael says. He sees that the boy's hands are trembling.

Adam leans forward a little as he brings the cup to his lips. At the moment he is about to drink, the phone rings, and the noise startles him so profoundly that he makes a sad little yelp, and his hands move as if to cover his face, which spills nearly the entire contents of the cup of cider onto his shirt and his lap.

Michael and Xavier have put Adam into the bedroom, where he removes the first of his clean pairs of socks from his backpack and changes into them. In Adam's absence, Xavier and Michael sit on the sofa, not daring to speak for fear of being overheard but communicating their distress and confusion with shrugs and shakes of the head. Michael mouths the words *I'm sorry,* to which Xavier curtly frowns and waves his hand. Michael takes Xavier's hand, links their fingers together, and squeezes.

Michael finds his class list and looks up Adam's contact information. There are work numbers for both parents and a home number. One category is left blank—In Case of Emergency. Michael dials the home number; not only is there no answer, but there is no answering machine, no voicemail, just the unfamiliar experience of a phone ringing on and on and on.

"Mr. Medoff?" Adam's voice comes floating out from the bedroom.

"I'm here, Adam."

"Could you come here for a quick second?"

He enters the bedroom. The bed is made, the pillows stacked one on top of the other, a pair of slippers on either side, half hidden by the bedspread. Everything looks tidy, almost antiseptic, like a Holiday Inn. The room is gloomily lit, with only one of the bedside lamps on. Adam stands in the center of the room holding his T-shirt. The boy is skinny; his nipples are brown buttons; his belly button is raised and hard—it looks like a beehive; and most oddly of all, his chest is starting to get hair on it.

"My back feels weird," Adam says.

Adam turns, and Michael sees his back has been clawed as if his skin were wrapping paper and someone was overly eager to see the gift within.

"Oh my God, Adam, what happened to you?"

"Is it bad?"

"Yeah. Doesn't it hurt? It looks very bad."

Adam's small round shoulders bob up and down. Though silent, he is crying. He covers his face with the T-shirt.

"All right, this is completely insane. We need to get you to an emergency room. What the hell happened to you, Adam? Were you attacked?"

The scratches are deep red and the skin alongside of them is livid. Michael forces himself not to turn away and tries to compose his expression—he can feel his own grimace pulling at the muscles in his face, his neck.

"It's okay, I just want to know if it's bleeding," Adam says. "It feels wet."

"No, it's not bleeding. Put the shirt on."

"I'll mess up the shirt."

"It doesn't matter. We've got to get that looked after."

Adam puts the T-shirt on, pulls it down over his torso, faces his teacher. "I'll be okay."

"What are you doing here, Adam? What happened to you? What's going on? Who's supposed to be looking after you? I find it hard to believe your parents just took off for Montreal and left you and your sister alone."

At the mention of his sister, Adam's face takes on a look of utter anguish.

"I need a place to stay."

"I want you to tell me what happened to you."

"I fell. In Central Park. On some rocks I was climbing."

"They seem like gouges."

Adam doesn't answer immediately, but then he shakes his head. "No. I fell."

"Where's your sister anyhow? Where's Alice?"

Adam tentatively reaches toward the bed and touches it, first with just his fingertips, and then with his entire hand. Before Michael can ask him what he's doing, the boy collapses facedown onto the bed, draws his knees up to his chest, and tucks one hand under his head.

"Adam?" Michael stands over the boy, who seems to have fallen into a deep sleep. A stroke, a poison dart, death itself could not have extinguished consciousness so quickly and so totally. Gently, Michael shakes the boy's shoulder. "Adam? Come on, son, you can't..." He shakes his shoulder again, this time a little more forcefully. A low, vibrating sound comes out of the boy, something between a moan and a growl, and the sound of it touches a primal nerve in Michael, chilling his blood, raising the hairs on his arm, and causing him to hold his breath as he steps backward.

*   *   *

With the bed occupied and only one sofa in the apartment, that night Xavier heads uptown to Inwood to sleep at his sister's apartment. Shortly after moving from Havana to New York, she and her husband separated—he has moved to New Haven to work as a security guard at Yale, and though he is there with the good excuse of taking a much-needed job, it is an unspoken truth between them that Raul has fallen in love with a woman in Bridgeport with whom he spends every spare moment—and now the long New York nights are particularly lonely for Rosalie.

"Bring me a pack of Winston cigarettes," Rosalie says. "And the sugar and I have coffee for morning." Her English is still something of an adventure, but she refuses to speak Spanish with her brother, or with anyone else. It might have been part of what drove Raul away, thinks Xavier. Plus her bossy manner. However, he feels bad for having anything but gratitude for her generosity; who else in this city could he call with the announcement that he was on his way over for the rest of the night? New York is a place of great friendliness, but limited hospitality.

He is half a block from his apartment house now. The night is cold and wet. Tires from the passing cars, taxis for the most part, whisper and hiss over the wet pavement; the streetlamps reflect on the windshields, which are dotted with rain. In Havana, drivers use their windshield wipers as little as possible, but here they wave frantically back and forth even in a drizzle.

His plan is to walk to Twenty-Third and Park Avenue South and catch the East Side train to Grand Central Station, where he will connect with the shuttle that will bring him to Times Square, where he can board the A train to his sister's neighborhood. As Xavier walks west on Twenty-First Street, he notices that each step he takes is mirrored by the step being taken by someone across the street. When Xavier speeds up, the man across the street quickens his pace too, and when Xavier deliberately slows down, the man across the street slows down as well. He seems to dodge the circles of light dropped by the streetlamps, and the night is too thick to see anything but his shape. Xavier has a vague idea that this same fellow was posted across the street from the apartment and had begun shadowing Xavier from there, but Xavier was engrossed in his phone call and wasn't paying close attention.

Usually there are plenty of people out on the street, even on this basically residential block, but the bad weather has limited the population to just the two of them. Xavier is in terrific shape and he knows how to handle himself in a fight, but he feels a rush of dread. Should he stop in his tracks, at which point the man across the street can either continue on his way or state his business? But no: here in New York it is not always a matter of strength and courage or even martial art; here, the shitty people carry weapons, often guns.

Is it someone who wants to rob him? All he has in his wallet is about thirty dollars. He would hate to lose even that small amount of money. Rosalie wants her Winstons and her sugar...

Xavier stops, and sure enough the man stops too. Xavier turns to look at him directly, but the man pivots away, glances up, as if there is something in a lit window up high that has captured his attention. Xavier could cross the street, though he is not sure what he will do once he is there. As he prepares to step off the curb, a taxi approaches, its plastic tiara lit, signaling that it's ready to accept the next fare. He raises one finger. Like most cabbies in New York, the driver has perfected braking so that the handle of the rear door is directly in front of the passenger.

The cabbie is a Sikh. The earpiece of his cell phone snakes under his turban. "Yes? Where can we go?" he asks. Xavier is about to say he wants to be taken to Twenty-Third and Eighth, where he can board the A train, but before he can get the words out he sees the man who has been tracking him suddenly dart into the street.

"Go!" Xavier shouts to the driver, who is fiddling with his earpiece with one hand and tripping the meter with the other. Yet the urgency in Xavier's voice is not lost on the driver, and he puts the cab into gear just as the man rushes toward the door and attempts to open it. Instinctively, Xavier lifts his arm to shield himself, as if this man were a landslide of rocks and mud about to come crashing down on him. The man slams his gloved hand against the window, almost popping it loose from its casing, and roars with anger, frustration. He has a large head, coarse features, bushy hair.

The taxi heads west and Xavier looks out the rear window, his heart twisting and clawing within its box of bones. The man is running after them. His feet seem barely to touch the ground.

"Oh, this is a crazy city in a crazy country," the driver says. He places his hand on top of his turban as if it might blast off his head.

"Just go," Xavier says. "Make the light."

"The light is mine for making."

As the taxi picks up speed, the man stands in its wake, in the middle of the street. Headlights are coming up behind him, and for a moment Xavier thinks he is going to witness this man being plowed beneath the wheels of oncoming traffic. But at the last moment he steps out of the way, and disappears into the darkness.

Xavier allows himself to relax. He leans back, closes his eyes for a moment, but as he does, he feels the taxi slowing. They have not made the light after all. It shines deeply red, a bullet hole in the darkness. Xavier again turns in his seat to look out the rear window of the taxi, just as the door to the cab's backseat is yanked open.

It all happens so quickly, the driver barely has time to react. Xavier feels the man's powerful hands grabbing at his jacket, smells the man's tangy, meaty breath as he pulls him close. As if Xavier is trapped in a horrible dream, he is lifted from the seat and pulled from the taxi. Through the cardio chaos of blood pounding in his ears and the sound of his own terrified shouts, he can barely hear the cabbie's cries of alarm. He feels his attacker's hand on his chin. One finger, sharply nailed, is shoved in his nostril, another pokes at the edge of his eyes. Suddenly, consciousness disappears, as if his brain were an electrical appliance and someone just kicked the plug out of its socket.

For years, Adam has wondered what the night was like outside the confines of his locked room. He has heard so many times from his father about the things that can befall a child at night, and reason has been heaped upon reason to justify Adam's and Alice's imprisonment. He has heard about muggers and slashers and kidnappers. He has been taught to fear those in the city who are less well-off than he and his family, those huddled masses who have had enough of huddling and might at any moment come sweeping through the unguarded gates of Manhattan's loveliest quarters with vengeance in their hearts and murder in their eyes. But as much as he has been taught to dread the night and all of its countless dangers, what Adam has truly come to dread is the sullen click of the lock after his door is closed, that final metallic clunk that says: You must stay here.

As he grew older, Adam came to long for freedom from that locked room—the bed, the desk, the carpet, the steel-gated window—with a kind of blind, consuming passion. And when he began to realize that, rather than keeping them safe, his parents were keeping him and his sister in the place where they were perhaps less safe than anywhere else on earth, the desire to escape became a kind of mania. Yet now that he is finally out in the night, out in the great wide world, finally free, he is puzzled and saddened to realize that his heart is anything but filled with joy. Is he more afraid here in this strange apartment, this strange, chilly room, than he was locked in his own bedroom? Perhaps not. But here the fear is less familiar, and so it is somehow more painful and destabilizing to feel it.

Awake again, he spreads his arms to see if he can reach from one side of Mr. Medoff's bed to the other. He stares up at the ceiling. He looks at the dull, somehow saddening little lightbulb in the ceiling, hiding behind a milky glass fixture. The fixture itself holds a dozen desiccated flies in its concavity. He hears Michael's footsteps in the next room. How strange it must be to live in such a small place, where people are never really apart. He hears Michael clear his throat. It's almost as if the teacher is right here in this room, standing next to him. Next, Adam hears the electronic chirp of the keypad on a telephone being pressed.

I want to live, Adam thinks. A simple enough thought, but words he has never formed in his mind before, and they seem to have a magical power, a kind of abracadabra spell-casting power that opens the floodgates and releases an inner sea of emotion. A moment later Adam's face is scalding as he is overcome with his own instinctive drive to survive.

As he has done countless nights before, he calms himself by closing his eyes and counting his breaths. As he quiets his mind, his body has a chance to assert itself and clamor for its own need for sleep. He falls into a sudden slumber as if walking off the edge of a cliff.

He dreams of his father. Eating meat that swims in a pool of its own…Well, Alex calls it gravy, but Adam would have to say it's blood.

How much time passes? A minute? Five? Adam awakens to the sound of his cell phone chiming in his jeans, which are draped over the footboard of his teacher's bed. *Oh please, be Alice.* He looks at the screen. *Yes!*

She has sent him a text message: Ware r u? In the darkness—the older he gets, the keener his eyes—he texts back @ m medoff 400 e 21 r u ok?? He clutches the phone and stares at the little screen as it slowly goes dark. Finally, Alice answers back: go 2 parc. Alex's response is instant. What park?? He shakes his phone as if to hurry his sister's response, but again the screen goes dark, and this time it stays that way.

Alex Twisden forces himself to walk casually, Xavier's unconscious body slung over his back. Alex wants to look to the world like a man carrying his drunken pal home after a night of killer martinis, and maintaining a steady pace and a calm expression are both key to the masquerade. He walks north on Madison Avenue, along a route with few restaurants and clubs and practically nobody on the street. When he does pass someone—say, a short, spiky-haired woman walking a rather delicious-looking dachshund, or a couple of Korean businessmen in animated conversation—he purses his lips and nods brusquely, which has become the universal sign for *I see you and I see that you belong here and I do too.*

Alex is counting on the likelihood that the cabdriver will not want to sacrifice the rest of his shift by reporting the assault to the cops and will instead continue to cruise the streets of New York, trying to make a living.

When another taxi comes into view, Alex lifts his hand to hail it.

At that same moment, Xavier starts to regain consciousness. It is like slowly rising from the deepest part of the sea, a sea filled not with water but with soaked cloths, mud, faces.... He opens his eyes, sees the dim upside-down world. This much he knows: someone is holding him. He squirms, hoping to get away, as his wallet falls from the inside pocket of his leather jacket to the curb a hundred thousand miles below.

And Alex, standing between the curb and a streetlight and feeling the shift in his human cargo, says in the most comforting tone he can summon, "Don't worry, pal, I'm taking you home." The cab stops in front of them.

"I was attacked. Who are you?"

"A friend. Just tell me your address."

Xavier tells Alex his address, and when asked for it he also supplies the apartment number. Reaching for the taxi door, Alex turns nimbly so that Xavier's head knocks with considerable force against the streetlight's thick metal stem, plunging him back into unconsciousness— perhaps even killing him, for all Alex can tell.

"Whoa," the driver says, seeing the state of Alex's companion. The cabbie is young, with dragons and Chinese characters tattooed on his arms and neck. "You going to a hospital?"

"No, we're fine," Alex says good-naturedly. "Some people shouldn't drink."

"Tell me about it," the driver says, starting the meter. "Where to?"

Alice has never been out on her own after dark. In fact, she has barely been anywhere by herself in the daylight hours. But tonight she has run through the streets of the Upper East Side, past curious doormen who follow her with their eyes, past restaurants with limousines black as hearses idling in front of them, past jewelry stores and nail salons closed, locked, and gated for the night. Every step of the way she senses someone is close behind her, either gaining on her or, momentarily, falling back, but she does not dare turn around. She feels someone pounding down the pavement, hands outstretched, trying to grab her and take her back to the house, which would be more than she could bear. It would be the end of her.

She is in jeans; Nikes; a black ski parka; a Peruvian wool cap, red, orange, and blue. Her backpack, too full to properly close, has been hastily stuffed with clothes, schoolwork, a package of lunch meat, and the phone she uses to text her brother. When she comes to a sudden stop, her phone seems to fly out of her backpack. It hits the sidewalk with a clattering noise and spins crazily onto the street, where it is promptly crushed beneath the wheels of a FreshDirect truck, delivering groceries even at this late hour. Next comes a taxi, then a Con Ed van, then another taxi, then yet another taxi, and all of them inflict their damage on the phone, though surely it was dead at the initial blow.

Now without her phone, she feels as if Adam has vanished. She has only one clear thought: *The park!* She is not even sure why Central Park seems to her the only safe place in the city right now, but she yearns for the fragrant darkness of those dormant acres, the trees, the shadows, the tunnels and stones, the countless secret places.

She *knows* she is not alone. She can feel herself being watched. She looks behind her. Smoke pours out of a Con Ed construction site in the center of the street, lit by a large yellow light that pulsates like a frightened heart. Alice's skin feels horribly alive. Her mind races. Her thoughts are no more distinguishable to her than snowflakes in a blizzard. She sees a figure emerging from the smoke. *Run!* she tells herself, but her legs are heavy and when she can finally get them to move she immediately stumbles.

But it's not her mother. It's a homeless man pushing a shopping cart that overflows with cans and bottles. His cargo's rattle echoes in the night.

She enters the park at Sixty-Fifth Street, hopping over the little stone wall and traipsing through the frosted foliage. She feels a powerful urge to relieve herself, but there is no way she can do it, no way, no way, no way.

There is a playground nearby for little kids. No way she is going to pee in a playground. Alice remembers coming here with Adam when they were small, always with either their mother or their father, and with a nanny in tow. She remembers them all, the parade of appearing and disappearing nannies, but remembers them dimly, like songs heard just once or twice, a long time ago. There was Pilar, Sonia, Mercedes, Erin. There was Mrs. Calhoun, Susana, Susan, Sue, and Sue Ellen, and then there was Cher, with her deep tan and cobalt-blue eyes the color of airport landing lights, who was full of hilarity one moment and dumbstruck with private unhappiness the next, and who turned out to be a man—Adam saw him taking a leak at Ray's Famous Pizza.

With each nanny there was a sudden infusion of fun, of brightness, gaiety, but each one's term was fleeting. Some of them managed quick, apologetic good-byes to the twins, others simply vanished, and now, standing at the wrought-iron gate to the playground and watching the empty swings moving in the night wind, Alice has a distinct, piercing memory of sunlight through the latticework of her eyelashes as one of the nannies—Mercedes?—pushed her between her shoulder blades to make Alice swing in the bucket seat next to Adam—"We're flying, we're flying," he said—while she whispered anxiously to her friend, another nanny, who was standing next to her, her own charge asleep in a stroller. "I'm so scared," Mercedes had said. "I see what they eat."

A silent squad car, its emergency lights flashing, races from east to west through the park, and Alice, too, moves west, zigging and zagging, feeling the cold and the damp seeping through her sneakers. Soon she is on a long, broad paved walkway with benches on either side. The spires of the immense apartment houses of Central Park West momentarily come into view, their windows dim and gauzy.

The next thing she knows, she is crouched behind a large bush, her pants down, squatting, breathing a long sigh of relief as the pee spatters onto the frozen leaves, and a thick soupy smell of her own urine rises in a cloud of steam. She can't believe she is doing this. And yet she cannot stop. The relief of it is greater than the weirdness and greater, too, than the looming fear of being discovered. She stares straight ahead, emptying her mind along with her bladder, closing her eyes, allowing herself to relax in the familiar internal darkness that is her self, her essential, private self.

Yet this piece of internal real estate, which has forever been her refuge, is suddenly invaded by the leering, snarling figure of…her mother. Her mother! Her bright green eyes, too intense. The fresh spray of flowery perfume. The face of her wristwatch floating on a wave of amber hairs…The woman who all of biology and all of culture has urged Alice to trust. *I see what they eat,* the nanny hissed.

Alice opens her eyes, banishing the memory. But the relief of the cold darkness is immediately overturned by the sound of *something* breathing rapidly behind her. Gasping, she pulls her pants back up, but in her haste she trips herself and falls to her knees. *"Oh oh oh,"* she whimpers. Where her pant leg has risen, there is an inch of bare flesh between her cuff and the top of her sock, and she feels something cold and alive touch her skin. With a cry, she turns to see what has touched her.

Oh. A little shaggy white dog with rabbity red eyes and askew ears, panting eagerly, the way dogs will when they think they have found a friend, and with an odd urgent air about him, as if he has someplace important to be and he's running late. Alice reaches for the dog, who cautiously moves a little closer to her. Instinctively, Alice pounces on him and closes her fist on his scruff. *Eat.* It is not really like thinking; it's more like hearing a command uttered by a creature who lives inside of her, not a girl or a boy, not a human or an animal, just a creature, something alive, the essence of life, really, life before it was divided up into *kinds* of life. She stares at the squirming little dog. His pink belly is scored with scratches; his fur is dingy, dusty, with so many twigs and leaves stuck to him that it's a wonder birds don't lay eggs on him. His penis, aroused by fear, emerges moist, glistening red from its sheath of flesh. Alice brings him closer and closer to her mouth; she can practically taste him. "No, no, no," a girl's voice says, and it takes her a moment to realize that the voice is her own. With a cry of anguish she drops the dog. He lands on his side, scrambles upright again, and, rather than running for his life, reapproaches Alice, rubbing the side of his face against her arm, making little high-pitched imploring whimpers.

He runs a few feet away, stops, turns toward her. She understands: he wants her to follow him. She crawls out from behind the bush and by then the dog is twenty feet away from her. She thinks of all the dogs, large and small, that have passed through their house. She imagines her immunity to that grief to be like a scab over a cut, a cast-iron crust that would never again allow that part of the body to bleed.

The white dog, sensing that she has slowed down, stops, looks over his shoulder at her, and proceeds to run again, with Alice close behind, winding this way and that, deeper and deeper into the darkness of the park.

Xavier hears the sound of his mother's stiff broom sweeping and sweeping the floor of their apartment on Máximo Gómez. *Stop, stop, it will never be clean,* he wants to shout at her, but he is somewhere—where?—and his eyes are shut, screwed closed so tightly that, try as he might, he cannot open them. Her sweeping, her infernal, mad sweeping seems to surround him.

Por favor, he whispers to her, but she must not hear because the sweeping only becomes faster, louder. Now it seems she has taken another broom in hand and is somehow sweeping double—no! In triplicate! How many brooms can this woman manage? And what kind of broom—what kind of mother—would blow such foul wind in his face? Blindly, he tries to push her back and feels the wet of her demonic open mouth. Has she come to devour him? In the mad logic of this feverish state, it is not inconceivable, though it was always his father who most disapproved of Xavier, his mother who loved and protected him.

He smells shit. Has he disgraced himself? Is that why she is sweeping him away, out of her life, into the hard street?

His eyes finally open, but it is like trading one darkness for another. But gradually this second darkness becomes the lesser darkness. Not so solidly black, just a deep, sad gray. And through that gloom comes the quizzical glare of red eyes staring at him. The sweeping turns out to be the sound of panting. An animal.

A flash of memory: the upside-down world streaming by as he is carried down the street…

He scrambles to a sitting position, backs up, and feels the cold crisscross of the cage into which he has been locked. With him are eight dogs, some large, some small, his companions in captivity. Frightened, he tries to back up even farther, pressing himself against the chain-link fencing. His feels something soft flattening out under one of his palms, and something pebbly and hard beneath the other: shit and kibble. The dogs move closer, panting, wagging, whimpering. Xavier has never owned a dog, never wanted to, doesn't really like or understand them, but one thing is clear: these poor trapped things are looking for help.

"Hey, what the fuck! Help. Someone. Down here." Xavier shouts with what little strength he can muster—the effort of it sends pain shooting through his body in every possible direction. And it's all for nothing, really. He can feel the deadness of his cry. This place, wherever he is, has been soundproofed to the max—studio foam, sound-absorbing curtains, acoustic tiles. Calling out down here is like crying yourself to sleep with your face pressed into a pillow.

With the white dog gone, it is as if her world is empty—she has nothing to follow, nowhere to go, and a sudden crushing aloneness comes over her, as heavy and real as rain. She stops, hears something....She makes herself stop panting so she can hear better—a kind of rolling, growling, grinding noise. A couple of hundred feet away, skateboarders are using the stone steps of the staircase leading to the Bethesda Fountain to practice their moves. Likewise, they use the sides of the benches and the rounded concrete borders of the walkway to mount their wheels upon and to conduct their ceaseless arguments with gravity and good sense. There are ten of them, tall and short, skinny and broad. Though she knows none of them and is naturally shy, Alice moves toward them—anything seems better than solitude right now. She stands at the top of the staircase near a clump of dead honeysuckle, a few white flowers frozen in place. There is a smell of horse manure in the air and the distant clop of a horse-drawn carriage, the driver in a top hat, the passengers huddled beneath heavy blankets, trying to make the best of it. When the carriage rolls closer, the dappled gray horse lifts its head, its enormous nostrils open wider, and it whinnies, high-pitched and crazy.

The skateboard kids are like no other teenagers she has seen. Their jumps are wild, reckless, and almost every one ends in a fall, a real tumble, a skin-tearing skid along the cement, a bone-shattering thud—though none of them seem to get hurt. Or is it that they all refuse to show any sign of having been hurt? A few of them seem almost to fly, holding on to the edges of their boards as they crouch down, howling with excitement as they rise and fall.

Her heart pounds with anxiety as she is compelled toward the skaters. Her need to be with others is almost a mania; she struggles for contact as if solitude were a sea that could swallow her forever.

Adam! Where are you?

A long line of benches flanks either side of the walkway, with a space of four or five feet between each bench. Between two of the benches is what first looks like a chaotic clump of blankets but on further inspection proves to be a wheelchair. Child-size. And sitting in it is a boy or a girl covered in a hodgepodge of blankets with mud streaks and dead leaves stuck to them. A ghostly white light glows from the middle of it.

"Come here," a voice from the wheelchair says.

Alice is too frightened to go to it and too frightened to turn away.

"I won't hurt you," the voice says. "Like how can I? You know?"

"Who are you?"

The child in the wheelchair is silent. The blankets shift and stir and then comes the grinding whir of the wheelchair's power being activated, and whoever it is in that chair is slowly rolling toward her.

Every fiber in her being urges Alice to run, but she wills herself to be still—as frightened as she is, she cannot bear the idea of hurting the feelings of someone unfortunate.

As far as she can tell, it's a boy in the chair, though he is covered from head to lap, only a small portion of his face visible. The light shining from his lap is a computer, the shell of which is covered in green-gray-and-black-camouflage-patterned fabric. One small hand clasps the filthy satin edge of the blanket he wears like a monk's cowl, moving it a little to the side so he can speak. The fingers of that hand are stiff. In fact, they are plastic. The entire hand is plastic.

"My name's Bernard," he says, his words slurred, blurry, hard to understand.

"Oh," Alice says. Her heart is beating so furiously, the world looks unstable, like something reflected in a pool of water.

"What's your name?" Bernard asks.

"Alice."

A silence. The sound of breathing as the boy gathers himself. "*Bon soir,* Alice."

"You speak French."

"Mother from Canada taught me some."

Alice stops herself from asking him to repeat what he has just said; replaying it in her mind, she deciphers the words. If a cement mixer could speak, it would sound like this boy....

"Are you cold?" she asks him, looking at the many blankets he has draped himself in.

"Come close," he says.

"Why?"

"Close."

She realizes that explaining the why of anything might be more than he can do, yet, still, she is proudly reluctant to come even a step closer to him. Right now, about ten feet separate them.

The boy's other hand crawls out like a shy animal from the shelter of blankets. The hand is bony and is attached to a wrist that pokes out from a loose-fitting sweater. He pushes a button on his motorized chair and rolls closer and closer to Alice. *Run, run!* she tells herself, but she cannot bring herself to do so—it's one thing to run from danger, quite another to run from the fear of seeing something ugly.

Bernard stops his chair just as the skinny, deeply grooved tires touch the tips of Alice's shoes.

"Lap," he says. And when Alice fails to respond he says it again, more forcefully.

She looks down and in Bernard's lap, half hidden in the folds of blanket, is a gleaming silver tube—a flashlight. "Yeah?" she says.

"Take."

She does as he commands, picking it up gingerly so as to avoid touching him or even the blankets. The metal is freezing cold. The flashlight itself, though small, is surprisingly heavy. She turns it on, pointing the light toward the ground—her shoes, the broad sidewalk, the scatter of fallen leaves plastered to the cement.

Bernard uses his living hand to move the plastic hand a few inches to the left, exposing more of his face, and Alice, knowing what he wants her to do, slowly lifts the beam of the flashlight until it is shining directly on him.

He has one eye, and his nose is just two slits, no protrusion. His chin is long and comes to a point, and his mouth is hideously small. His skin looks as if it had been burned, had healed, and then been burned again. One of his ears is exposed and it seems no larger than a half-dollar, and it is covered in hair…or is that fur?

"Oh," Alice says, her voice full of pity. She hadn't meant to say anything, but it slipped out, and now she says it again.

"Bad luck, right?" Bernard says. "Poor me." He glances down at his computer screen, frowns, pokes at a couple of keys. His movements are swift, decisive.

Alice notices something else about his living hand. A birthmark. A red squiggle, just like she has, and Adam has too.

"Look," she says, thrusting her hand toward him.

One of the skaters breaks off from the pack. He seems to have noticed Alice's presence and he rolls noisily half the distance between the two of them. He stops, dismounts, and steps hard on the back of the board, flipping it up, catching it, and continuing on with it resting on his shoulder like a rifle. He is tall, rangy, and he looks about fifteen and uncared-for. His clothes are dirty and would not serve for a cool day in September, much less this cold November night. His hair is long, matted, and he carries an aroma of wind and rain and smoke and bad food. Instinctively, Alice steps back, and she feels her shoulders hunching up and her hands tightening and bending, as if to claw at him if he makes a threatening move.

"Hey, Bernard," the boy says.

"Hi," Bernard says, his voice somehow communicating friendliness and respect. "You guys were doing no-heads."

"More to skating than hotdogging, old friend. So?" He cocks his head toward Alice.

"You're the best."

"Nice of you to say so, Bernard. Hey, does your mother know where you are?"

"Maybe."

"Well," the boy says, shifting his skateboard from one shoulder to the other, "she probably does. The thing about your moms is she knows everything." Turning toward Alice, the boy asks: "How old are you?"

"Almost eleven," Alice says, "and you better not bother me."

"Eleven?" He sniffs noisily. "No wonder."

"What?"

"I think you're one of us, and if you're only eleven…." He laughs. "Then you don't even know it. First you gotta bleed."

"Shut up, that's disgusting."

"You're still a child," he says. "Your time will come, and it's going to be great. Are you close yet?"

"What are you talking about?" Alice nervously looks around, wondering which way she will run if this boy makes her any more afraid.

"Downtown," he says, tapping the fly of his jeans. "Or uptown," he adds, slapping his chest. He sees the look on her face. "Don't be afraid," the boy says. "I'm just asking. But when it happens, you'll see, you will definitely understand." With a complicated set of movements, like a West Point cadet on a parade ground, he moves his skateboard from his shoulder onto the pavement, mounts it, and skates to Alice's side.

"She's okay, brother," Bernard says.

"What are you doing here?" the boy asks, his voice less harsh now. "You running?"

"My dad's going to come and get me in a minute," Alice says.

"I'll bet."

"Well, he is."

The boy looks deeply into Alice's eyes, squinting and frowning, like a lawyer reading a contract's fine print. "You're mad afraid of your father."

"No, I'm not."

"And your mother too, right?"

"You don't even know them."

"So maybe I don't and maybe I do. But I will tell you one thing about them—they are hairy bastards, right?"

Alice doesn't have the will to further insist. She lowers her gaze, shakes her head.

"Eli, Nell, Oliver, Djuna." The boy counts the names off on his fingers. "Chelsea, Kim." He ends in a shrug. "I'm pretty young to have so many dead friends."

"I guess."

"You know what happened to them?"

"How should I know?"

"You could actually guess, if you thought about it."

But Alice does not want to think about it. She shakes her head.

"Think."

"I don't even know you," Alice manages to say.

"Their fucking parents killed them."

"Yeah, right."

"It's true. Ask Eli, Nell, Oliver, or Djuna. Ask Chelsea. She was six. Ask Kim. We lost him two weeks ago." The boy reaches into his back pocket and pulls out a wrinkled photograph of a golden-skinned boy with long floppy hair, wearing jeans and a blue-and-white sweatshirt that says I ♥ SLOVENIA.

"Is that him?" Alice says, her voice shaking.

The boy puts the picture back in his pocket and pulls out a cell phone, which he flicks open like a switchblade. He steps back and takes a picture of Alice. "In case you disappear," he says.

"Can I use your phone?"

"Do you have any food?" he asks.

"I don't walk around with food."

"My name's Richard, but everyone calls me Rodolfo."

"I'm Alice."

"Do you have any money, Alice?"

"No."

"Honest?"

"Honest. Can I use your phone?"

Rodolfo is silent for a few moments. Finally, he pats Alice's shoulder. "Hungry? Come on, we'll show you how to get food. You like to hunt?"

He turns toward Bernard. "Go home, Bernard. Your mom's a nice lady and if she wakes up and sees you're not there she's gonna freak out."

"What about your phone?" Alice says.

"My parents cut off my service a year ago," Rodolfo says.

Michael gropes for his wristwatch, which he had placed on the coffee table, thinks for a moment that it is somehow ten past six until he turns the watch the correct way and sees it is twenty minutes before one, which makes more sense. But still: Who could be ringing the buzzer at this hour?

He decides to do nothing, at least not right away. It could be one of his neighbors making a mistake, or it could be some dopey kids screwing around in the lobby. He sits up, leans against the arm of the sofa, waits. A few moments go by and he is about to make another attempt at sleep when the phone rings. Startled, Michael grabs it immediately.

"I know it is late," says Rosalie, Xavier's sister. "But I wait for Xavier and he no here."

"He's not there?"

"No. I wait."

"What the fuck?"

"Yes. Me too, What the fuck?"

The buzzer sounds again, this time in a series of short bursts that seem to convey furiousness on the part of whoever is downstairs.

"This might be him, Rosalie. I'll talk to you later."

"I'm calling police," Rosalie says as he hangs up the phone.

Michael decides to meet fury with fury and when he speaks into the intercom, his voice is ragged with irritation. "What in the hell do you want?" he says through clenched teeth. "Is that you, Xavier? Where's your key?"

"This is Alexander Twisden, Mr. Medoff. My son is in your apartment, and I have come to take him home."

Michael cannot immediately rid himself of the idea Adam planted in his mind—that the Twisdens are in Canada, and Adam and Alice have been left alone. "Who is this?" Michael says into the intercom, gruffly, though not quite so aggressively as a moment ago.

"Would you like me to come back with the police?" the voice says.

Rather than answer, Michael buzzes the lobby door open. He quickly climbs into his trousers, pulls a cotton sweater over his undershirt, and jams his feet into his shoes, dispensing with socks. The thought of being seen even remotely undressed in this small apartment with one of his students—one of his *boy* students, no less—asleep in the next room fills Michael with waves of panic, as if he is descending a staircase in the dark and suddenly finds a step missing.

Alexander Twisden emerges from the small elevator and looks up and down the hallway, his nostrils flared in disdain. He sees Michael standing in front of the door to his apartment and walks toward him with the long, princely strides of a man who knows that everything he says, wears, and does is important, a man who knows how to project his personal power so well that only a complete fool would fail to note it.

"What are you doing, Mr. Medoff?" Twisden says as he brushes past Michael and enters the apartment. "I have to tell you, I am stunned by your lack of judgment."

"Adam told me you were out of the country."

"Oh, Adam told you." He expels air, as if no words could adequately describe the idiocy of Michael's remark. He surveys the apartment, and Michael feels a slow, cold twist of dread, wondering what this place looks like through those icy eyes. "So?" Twisden says. "Where is he?"

Michael clears his throat. A strong coppery scent emanates from Twisden, and as Michael backs away from the odor, he notices that there is something red caked beneath a few of Twisden's fingernails.

"He's asleep," Michael says. Somewhere in the back of his mind, banging distantly like a shutter in a window too far away to be seen, is the thought that somehow Twisden has gotten this information from Xavier...

"Adam!" Twisden says loudly. "Please come out here."

"Okay, okay, hold on," Michael says, pushing back a little as a way of regaining his confidence and his self-respect. "You can't come in here and start shouting. I've got neighbors on all sides."

"And I'm sure they'd be thrilled to know you are keeping one of your little boy students tucked away in this shit box of an apartment."

Alex Twisden's bluster may often have had a disarming and even disabling effect on his adversaries, but when the bluster is used on Michael, it has a nearly directly opposite effect. He feels himself tremble at the volume of Twisden's voice and the rancor of his words, but the effrontery of it, and the implied assumption that Michael is some poor weakling who will quake and tremble when faced with the bluster of a Real Man, brings out the innate stubbornness at the core of Michael's personality. Gay men from intolerant small towns are among the toughest people in America.

"Hey, back off, all right?" Michael says. He sees Twisden's eyes widen. "He showed up here in the middle of the night. He said you were out of the country. I mean, come on, what is going on?"

"What's going on? You would presume to question the way my wife and I are raising our children. There is no one who cares more about their children than we do. No one. But I think the question here, Mr. Medoff, is what kind of teacher turns his little apartment into a clubhouse for ten-year-old boys."

The two men are silent for a moment, and in the silence Michael hears a soft *click*. Adam has locked the door to the bedroom.

"I find your tone offensive," Michael says. "And I find—"

But he doesn't have a chance to list the things he objects to because Twisden has grabbed him by the shirt and now runs him into the wall, where he hits with a bone-bruising thud.

"Adam?" Twisden calls, in a surprisingly tranquil voice, considering that he is pinning Michael to the wall at the same time.

Both men's eyes turn toward the bedroom door, but Adam is silent.

"I'm going to have you fired," Twisden whispers to Michael.

"I'm going to have *you* arrested," Michael says.

Twisden gives Michael a last shove and goes to the bedroom door. He tries the handle, but it barely turns. "Adam, please, come out. Now. I need you to come out now." He waits, listening, tries the handle again, and finally steps back and runs his shoulder into the edge of the door. The effort of it barely shows on Twisden's face, but the result is a splintering of the door's frame. Casually, as if this were a perfectly acceptable and normal way of entering a room, he reaches through the jagged opening and undoes the lock on the inside. He brushes the splinters and dust from the shoulder and sleeve of his jacket and walks into the bedroom.

The bedroom is filled with shadows going this way and that at mad angles. A bedside lamp has fallen to the floor, turning shoes into hills and chairs into watchtowers. The white cotton curtains dart and dance away from the open window. In the midst of the commotion, Adam has fled.

"I am dialing nine-one-one right now," Michael says as Alex goes to the window. He flings it open to its widest and looks up and down. The rusted, pigeon-spattered fire escape is flush with the outside of the window.

"Oh God," Alex says, running his hand through his thick head of hair. "Oh please. My little boy! My son!"

With amazing agility he slips out of the window and stands on the fire escape, looking up, down, and side to side, but Adam is nowhere to be seen. He dips back into the bedroom, shaking his head.

"It's ringing," Michael says. He holds the phone toward Twisden.

"Why would I be afraid of you?" Twisden says. "With all that I've got going on in my life, how would I ever be able to find the time or the energy to be afraid of you?" And with that, he brushes past Michael, making sure to jostle him, almost, in fact, knocking him over.

"Asshole," Michael says, somewhat quietly, secure in the knowledge that Twisden is already halfway out of the apartment building. He hurries to double-lock the door behind Twisden and then turns to survey the damage done to the bedroom door.

When he goes back into the bedroom itself, Adam is sitting on the edge of the bed, shaking with fear.

"Why did you lie to me, Adam?"

The boy looks up at him, helpless and afraid. He shakes his head.

"I think I just made a huge mistake, Adam. I should have—"

"No," Adam says. "You can't."

"I can and I must. He's your father. I'm going to call him, and I'm going to take you home. This is nuts." He reaches for Adam to get him off the bed.

But the boy takes Michael's hand in both of his and presses it to the side of his face, his eyes squeezed shut, his mouth twisted.

"Adam?"

"They're going to kill us."

This is what children say when they are worried about being sent to their rooms, or being grounded, or having their iPods taken away for a week. But Michael knows that in some cases—not so few as we would like to imagine—this is what children say when they are genuinely and legitimately afraid of suffering harm at the hands of the people pledged by nature and the law to protect them.

"What do you mean, Adam?" Michael says in a soft, calm voice.

Adam shakes his head.

"Does your father hit you?" Michael asks.

"No."

"Do either of them?"

"No."

"Spank you really hard? Shake you? Twist your arm?"

"Nothing like that."

"Then what? Threaten you?"

The boy shakes his head and shrugs, looks away.

"Then what are we talking about here, Adam?"

"What I know."

"And what's that? What do you know?"

"That late at night something happens to them. They get different."

"Adults have their own time, they have adult time. And they are different then than they are when they're with their children."

"It's not that."

"Are you sure?"

"Yes."

Michael sighs. "I don't know, Adam. It sounds like things are basically okay at your house."

"They're going to kill us," Adam says, his face reddening, his voice rising. "I don't think they can help it. But at night something happens. I'm not lying. This is true, I swear to God. They want to…"

His voice breaks, and he looks down, his body trembling.

"They want to eat us," he says, in barely a whisper.

Bernard's mother comes home after her shift plus overtime at the hospital to find the boy in his bed, fully clothed and sobbing. The sight of this is more wearying to her than upsetting—she has seen him like this countless times. In fact, lately, as he grows up, more often than not she finds him in various states of despair, from loneliness because of his isolation; frustration because his physical limitations are so severe; or shame and revulsion, if he has disobeyed her stern warning to keep away from the mirror, all mirrors, any mirrors, and anything else with a reflecting surface, be it a toaster or a spoon.

The mother, Amelie Gauthier, sits on the edge of his bed and pats his back. She is tired, so tired, more tired than a human is meant to be. She is feeling the exhaustion driving through her like a steady rain. She glances at the boy's motorized chair; the seat is thick with crumbs, the detritus of the cakes and cookies he munches day in and day out. His ever-present laptop is open; his screen saver is the face of Jesus. Faith in Jesus is the one thing she has been able to give him….Her open hand travels up and down his curved, bumpy spine, feeling the practically prehistoric rise and fall of it. She knows this boy's body as well as her own.

"Bernard?" she whispers.

"Oh, Mama, Mama," the boy whimpers. "Sick, I'm sick."

"Shhh. Mama knows. Mama's here."

Their tiny apartment on West One Hundredth Street is dark; its few small windows look out onto the darkness of the building's air shaft, at the bottom of which, fourteen stories down, is a mysterious pile of broken bottles, soup cans, discarded lamps. The thick gloomy shadows of the apartment itself, depressing on the face of it, is actually a kind of blessing to Amelie and Bernard, muting the visual impact of Bernard's countless deformities and hiding, as well, the chaos of their quarters.

There is no proof of Bernard having been born. The closest thing to any record of him is the hospital's report of him emerging dead from his mother's womb. Amelie has raised him in complete secrecy, allowing him contact with only the wild children who inhabit the city's parks and the virtual world he inhabits on his computer. Because of this, all of his numerous and often pressing medical needs have been taken care of by her, and if their apartment were ever to be fully lit, it would look like a medical-supply locker, full of gauze, syringes, ointments, bath chairs, transfer benches, intermittent catheters, every conceivable type of pillow, and pills of all kinds: antibiotics, mineral supplements, vitamins, sedatives, painkillers, antispasmodics, laxatives, various antipsychotics, and sleeping aids, all of them pocketed by Amelie and brought home in her never-ending quest to make Bernard *1 percent* more comfortable and functional.

"What did you do today, Bernard? Park?"

"Yes."

He rolls over, showing himself to her, as if he has already thought this through and wants her to experience the full impact of what he will say.

"They run so fast."

"I know, I know."

"And I sit."

"You're here."

He shakes his head, at first slowly, sadly, and then with increasing vehemence, until it looks as if he is having a seizure.

It's unbearable to Amelie. Her heart is breaking and her eyes are closing—how can she feel simultaneously this sad and this sleepy? A million times over she has relived the moment she took the gnarled, doomed newborn that this child once was, swaddled him in a sheet, and made him her own. They were going to kill him! They were going to throw him away as if he had never happened! As if he did not have a heart, a brain, feelings, a soul.

Bernard holds up his hand for his mother to see. "Saw another," he says.

There was a time when she could easily decode his communication, but it takes more energy than she has now, and as her own powers steadily decrease, buried beneath a weight of accumulated years and exhaustion and isolation and discouragement, she finds that she and the boy, rather than growing increasingly close to each other, are actually drifting apart. *Saw another? Saw another what? Another hand?*

He sees the combination of confusion and indifference in her face, and he holds his birthmarked hand up higher by way of explanation.

"Girl, my age. Nice too."

"Really?" Amelie's attentiveness rises. "Last night?"

"Yes." The poor scrambled and twisted child's good eye fills with tears, which he brushes away with his hand—the red squiggle is moist for a moment.

"Was she with the others?"

"They took."

"Took?"

"Her."

"I see." She hears the gurgle of the boy's bladder emptying. As usual, he seems completely unaware. He has that look of his—a kind of frightened stare, as if he has seen something dangerous that he is powerless to prevent. Without warning, he coughs deeply, and a bubble of saliva emerges trembling from his tiny mouth. If he were a comic-strip character, this would be the dialogue balloon, and it would say: *Why was I ever born?*

This question, unthinkable once to Amelie and never ever spoken, has come to haunt her. In that way, the child has eroded her once-impregnable faith. When she spirited him out of that hospital while those two rich fools were cooing and sighing over their twins, seemingly unaware that triplets had been born, there was no question in her mind whether she was doing the right thing. She was saving a life just as surely as a fireman who carries someone out of a burning building or a cop who takes the gun out of a lunatic's hand. He was not going to be handsome or fleet, that infant she was saving, but Amelie did not care about beauty or the usual paths to success—in fact, they filled her with a kind of contempt, their very easefulness suggesting something sneaky, morally lax, unfair, and vile. But what she had not taken into account was that by rescuing this child from the oblivion to which the doctor was all too eager to consign him, she was condemning him to something that might be worse. With the sudden horror that is the emotional equivalent of an avalanche of ice, she thinks: *I have done more harm than good.*

Bernard tries to sit up, fails, and mewls with frustration, his hand clawing at the air as if the very invisibility of oxygen was part of the prison that held him fast.

"I know it's sad for you, my darling," Amelie says.

"Yes."

"So hard."

"Alone," he says. "Alone."

"The girl," Amelie says.

"Mmm. Nice to me."

"With the birthmark."

"Nice."

"Did she tell you her name?" She knows the answer; she has often thought of the two with whom this poor thing was born. She even knows where they live—several times she has succumbed to temptation and walked past their house, and once she has even seen them, being walked to school by their mother.

"So did you talk to your new friend?"

"Have no friends. Just you, Mommy."

"I know, baby, Mommy knows."

"Mommy."

"It's so hard, isn't it?"

"So hard."

"Every day," Amelie says.

"Hard."

"And getting harder too, isn't it, baby?"

"Scared."

"So hard, life is so hard."

"Scared, Mommy."

"Shhh." Amelie puts her hand into the pocket of her nurse's smock, touches the little bottle she has been carrying around for days: Dilaudid. Slowly, her fingers close around the cool glass. She has been thinking about this all day, all week. Her original plan was to shake thirty drops onto Bernard's tongue and drink the rest of it herself. Now, however, her mind is going in a different direction.

"I have something for you," she says. "It tastes a little icky, but it will make you feel better."

He looks at her hopefully. "Nommy."

"Stick out your tongue." She takes out the bottle of synthetic morphine, shows it to him.

Trustingly, Bernard sticks his tongue out of his abbreviated dash of a mouth. His tongue is short, almost square.

"Mommy loves you."

"Mmm," he says.

"You know that, don't you?"

It would be easier to die, for both of them. But she must not; she will not. Life must be protected above all else.

"This is going to make you feel a lot better. Okay? No pain. Just beautiful sleep."

" 'kay."

Patting his perspiration-soaked forehead with one hand, she deftly unscrews the cap of the little bottle with her thumb and forefinger. The cap hits the floor, rolls beneath Bernard's bed.

"Can you open wider for me?"

"Mmm."

She shakes the bottle over his tongue.

"Icky icky," he whines.

Alex has done what he can to chase Adam down, but he has failed to locate him, and now, dejected, he returns home, where he sees Leslie, who has had no more luck finding Alice than he had finding Adam.

She is on the sofa in their sitting room. A valuable—very valuable!—cherrywood-and-horsehair settee used to be in the spot where she now lounges; it has been replaced by a very, very informal piece they recently picked up at the Housing Works thrift shop, a butterscotch-and-vanilla-colored sofa still smelling faintly of the patchouli incense its former owners burned. The upholstery is already beginning to unravel. Indeed, this has been the case in a lot of their furniture, and inasmuch as they are aware of how rough they are with their belongings, it is always a battle between selling the things off quickly for the money needed and holding on to the old things and maintaining the connection they give them to their former life. Not so very long ago, it fell to Alex to be the cold, realistic one when it came to their once-beautiful possessions, and it was Leslie who balked and often bargained like a child, promising to be more careful and weepily saying the antiques were precious to her, even though she had in the past often complained that the furniture was uncomfortable, the paintings were oppressive, and the various decorative items made her think of a stage set for *The Mousetrap*.

"I'm frightened," Leslie says, supine. She is covered in a crocheted blanket; her eyes stare up at the ceiling, at a blotchy water stain.

"They'll be back," Alex says.

"They don't know what they're doing out there. Someone could hurt them."

"No one's going to hurt them," Alex says. He sits heavily in an armchair that has been covered by a bedsheet to hide some stains left by a hasty meal.

"I still don't understand how they got out," Leslie says.

Alex bristles for a moment, thinking she might be trying to lay the blame for their escape at his feet. In the past, placing blame was the only really glaring weakness in Leslie's character. Somehow, phrases like *Did it not occur to you* and *What exactly did you expect to happen?* fell trippingly from her sharp tongue. Now, however, that desire to fix blame has disappeared, or perhaps the *ability* to do so is no longer hers.

"I don't understand how they opened the…the whatchamacallit," Leslie says.

"The gate," Alex says, supplying the word, though he has told himself a thousand times over that he ought not to do that. "I think one of them pocketed my key. Probably Adam. Though I wouldn't put it past Alice. She's quiet, but she has her ways."

Leslie, still lying on the sofa, covers her eyes with her forearm, breathes deeply. "I love them so much. It feels like…crazy weather."

"I know."

"I love them."

"I know, baby. I know."

"I love them."

Alex gets up from his chair, goes to the sofa, sits on its edge, and strokes Leslie's forehead. There are a few patches of microscopic stubble where she has pushed back on the boundaries of her hairline, restoring with a razor and tweezers its original shape, but other than that, her skin is soft, and it makes him feel good and useful to sense her breathing begin to calm as he touches her. He covers her brow with his open hand, as if he were checking her temperature. He imagines he can feel her *mind,* which he pictures as a thing in pieces, glittering but broken, like a crystal goblet that someone has smashed.

"How did they get out?" Leslie asks, unaware that Alex has just tried to answer that question. Her memory! Once it was an orderly place, filled with names, dates, ideas....Now those things are still there, but they share the space with smells and sounds, and soon, Alex fears, those wordless memories will take over more and more of the other memory's domain. It was a wonder she was able to keep her job at Gardenia Press at all, even after voluntarily reducing her workload and her days in the office in the hope that increased time would give her at least a shot at completing her tasks. And it is a wonder that Alex's own thought processes have not deteriorated as much as hers; at least not yet. At least, not as far as he can tell....

Leslie kicks the blanket off and scrambles to her feet. She vigorously rubs her hands over her face as a way of waking herself, making herself ready for what must come next.

"We go," she says, and then hears what she has said, which is not always the case, and quickly corrects it. "We should go. We can't stay here if they are out."

"They're going to come back. Adam was at his teacher's apartment, but he got away from me. You should see that place. Oh my God, whatever happens to us, however much money we lose and whatever life puts in front of us, we could never live in such a horrible apartment. We still have this." He gestures toward the ceiling stain, the walls with the paper coming off in long curls and the pale squares where paintings used to hang.

"We have nothing, Alex. Nothing. And you know it. I don't even know if I trust you with our children. And I don't know if you trust me. And I don't even know if I reserve that trust."

"*Deserve,* honey." He doesn't mean to correct her, not now—too much going on. "They'll be back, Leslie," he says. "We just have to have faith. And we should be waiting for them."

"Should should should fucking should," Leslie blurts. She sits back down on the sofa, half on the cushion and half on the balled-up blanket. "I want to kill myself," she says. "I do not want to be alive."

Alex nods. "I know." He moves closer next to her, takes her hand. "But we can't," he says, his voice soft and mournful.

"I know," Leslie says. "More's the pity."

"Are you at all hungry?"

She shrugs. "I could eat. What do we have?"

"Cuban."

"A human? I thought that's what we…Oh God, I'm glad Adam and Alice aren't here. It's all happening too fast."

"We resisted for as long as we could."

"Have you resisted? Or have you been helping yourself without me knowing about it?" Leslie narrows her eyes.

"I have not, and I resent your asking."

"Where is he?"

"In the cellar, with the others."

"With the dogs?"

"In a cage. I think it's time. Everything inside of me is telling me it's time."

"I'm not ready," Leslie says, but she can feel her mouth watering.

"I feel like a teenager," Alex says. "Just before having sex for the very first time. No force on earth could have stopped me."

"Once we do that, there's no turning back."

"Not necessarily," Alex says.

"You have done it before, haven't you. I can tell just by how you're talking about it."

"He looks delicious, Leslie. It's so horrible and so exciting. I mean, really, think about it. When was the last time we enjoyed ourselves? I mean, really and truly enjoyed ourselves?"

Leslie cocks her head, listens. And listens some more. Finally, she smiles. "I can't hear a thing from down there. You did such a good job. I'm proud of you."

"We Twisdens don't do things halfway, my dear. Come. Let's go downstairs. I want you just to take a look at him. Just a peek, a sniff. Nothing more."

He offers his hand and she takes it, allowing him to pull her to her feet. They go down to the first floor of the house and approach the heavy wooden door beneath the staircase.

"We're really so terrible," Leslie says, though she is feeling such intense love for Alex at this moment that she can't help but smile.

"We can't help it, my dear."

"What's with all the *my dears*? So fancy."

"Just trying to hold back the night," Alex says.

Leslie shakes her head as Alex takes out the old jailer's key, large and rusted, and fits it into the top lock.

"We should be ashamed," Leslie says.

"We are. A little."

"We should kill ourselves."

"You don't believe that."

"I do."

"Well, we can't. It's simply not in our nature, not anymore. No animal except humans can commit suicide."

"What about lemons?" Leslie says, brightening.

"*Lemmings,* my dear. And they are not committing suicide. They have no idea what the hell is going to happen when they go off the side of the cliff."

"What a bunch of dummies, right?"

"Right. Total idiots." Alex turns the key and the lock responds with a deep metal thump. Leslie places her hand on Alex's arm, hoping to slow things down.

"Then maybe we can hire someone to kill us," she says. "You can have it done for a thousand dollars."

"We're not killing ourselves and we're not hiring someone to kill us. Leslie! What is wrong with you? All this negativity. It just saps the life out of everything."

"There is a human being locked in our cellar."

"I understand that."

"Our children have run away from home."

"I once ran away from home too. You probably did as well, at one time or another."

"No, no. I did not."

"Well, it happens. Kids…run away."

"They ran away because they're afraid of us."

"You don't know that. They could have taken off for any one of a thousand reasons."

"No, I know. And you know too. They are…" She waves her hand in front of her face the way she does when she cannot think of a word and needs her husband to supply it for her.

"Afraid," he says.

"Afraid of us," Leslie says. "And they should be." She gestures toward the cellar door. "And now we're both scared to death that they're going to find someone out there and tell the world what goes on in this house and the next thing we know the police are knocking at our door. Right? Isn't that what you're really most afraid of? Not that some harm will…" Again, she waves her hand, looking for help.

"I don't know what you're going for here," Alex says. "Befall?"

"Yes. Befall. You're not worried that something will befall them. You're worried they're going to tell." Tears fill her eyes.

*   *   *

"Are you sure you're not hungry?" Rodolfo says to Alice. The two of them, along with Rodolfo's skater crew, are crouched behind a few large boulders, where they have lit a small, smokeless fire. A cowboy hat filled with squirrels sits on the ground; a bit of blood has seeped through the tawny felt. A couple of the boys wait eagerly while squirrels roast in the flame, others have not bothered to wait and are enjoying the raw bounty of their late-night hunt.

When Alice first realized what these boys and girls were going to do—as they climbed the trees, shook the branches, and pounced on the awakened, frantic creatures when they hit the ground and scurried hopelessly to escape—she was horrified, but she has quickly gotten used to this new reality, though not so much that she will allow herself even a bite of squirrel meat, no matter how hungry she is.

Rodolfo is crouched next to her, and to be polite he covers his mouth with his hand while he chews. Alice is relieved to see he has at least chosen the meat that's been cooked.

"You'll see," he says to her. "You'll get used to it. One day you'll like it way more than a fucking Big Mac. Oops. Sorry for the swear."

"I don't care about swears," Alice says.

"You want me to take you somewhere so you can get some indoor food?"

"I just want to find my brother."

Rodolfo nods. "Yeah. I know."

"Adam."

"How old is Adam?"

"We're twins."

"Yeah?" Rodolfo smiles. He has a beautiful smile. Light from the fire brightens his eyes. "A lot of us are twins. We've got triplets, and Jeff, Louise, Marcel, and Adrienne are...what's it called? Foursies."

"Quadruplets," Alice says.

"Yeah. That's right. Quadra. Quadrapal..."

"Quadruplets," Alice says.

Rodolfo slaps his forehead and sticks out his tongue and rolls his eyes, laughing at his own impression of a mentally challenged person. Suddenly serious, he asks, "So, you go to school?"

"Yes!"

Rodolfo shrugs and says, "I tried. Sort of. I guess." He makes the cartoon-stupid face again and stands up quickly, offering his hand to Alice. "Come on, I'll get you the kind of food you're used to."

"I need to find my brother."

"I won't let anyone hurt you. Come on." And then, in the voice of the guy who announces the baseball games on TV, he adds, "Let's do it!"

Rodolfo summons the others with a whistle, loud and piercing. They obey him without question or hesitation. After stamping out their little fire, they dispose of the squirrel bones, heads, and tails. Afterward they march in a kind of rough formation, following Rodolfo and, by extension, Alice through a thickly grown part of the park until they emerge near the running track circumnavigating the reservoir. In the warm months, this oval of blue water, as bright and blue as a child's eye, is home to ducks and geese, a geyser of water shooting up from its middle at all hours to keep the water clear. Now, however, the reservoir is covered in a thin sheet of ice, the eye of an old man, gray and clouded.

"We're going in!" Rodolfo announces, lacing his fingers through the fence that has been put up to prevent just such a thing from taking place. A cheer of unanimous agreement rises up from his troops—except for Alice, who at first thinks he is just joking around. But when she sees the mass of them kicking off their shoes and resting their skateboards against the fence, she realizes that Rodolfo is not kidding.

He sees the look of incredulity on her face. "Come on!" he says, as if only a fool or a very strange person indeed would think twice about plunging into the reservoir's icy water on a cold November night.

"No way. It's freezing."

"Only at first." He puts his hand on her shoulder. She shrinks back until she realizes his touch is friendly, gentle.

"I'm not doing that."

"Just come in with us, Alice. I promise."

"What?"

"You'll like it."

"I'll catch cold and die."

"You're more safer here than you have ever been."

She's not sure what he means by that, but there is something about it that feels true.

Some of the boys and two of the girls have taken off their jackets and their shirts, and one boy—Alice gasps when she sees this—has stripped all his clothes off, and now they all scramble up and over the fence with no more effort than a group of kids mounting the steps of a front porch. In ones and twos they break through the thin sheet of ice—little more than sludge, really, with the consistency of cake batter—until, except for Rodolfo and Alice, all of them are in the water, as seemingly carefree as seals, plunging in here and reappearing there, splashing one another, grabbing, laughing, dunking, their voices a din of unfettered youthful energy rising up from the reservoir with so much force that Alice could imagine it carrying all the way up to the distant, hazy moon.

"They're going to get in trouble," Alice says. She cannot tear her eyes away from them. She is filled with admiration and horror, envy and scorn.

"We don't care."

"You better care, mister," Alice says, hearing her mother's voice within her own.

"We've already faced the worstest," Rodolfo says. He sounds sincere, and he also sounds as if he is boasting. "What can anyone do to us that would be worser? Sure you don't want to go in? It's really fun."

"No way," Alice says.

"No probs," says Rodolfo. He pats her reassuringly on the shoulder and reaches into the pocket of his Levi's jacket and plucks out something to eat, which he quickly pops into his mouth.

What's that? Alice wonders. It is red and kind of moist-looking. He can't offer her one because it is a freshly harvested heart, plucked like a little red egg from the nest of fragile bones in the chest cavity of a squirrel.

"Before we go downstairs, I want to show you something," Alex says to Leslie, leading her by the hand to the wreck of a room that he has been calling his study—the hope had been that the nomenclature would impose a kind of order on the room, make it a place where work was actually done, tasks completed, dollars earned, and dignity preserved. But slowly and inexorably, this room has fallen into horrid disrepair, as have all the other rooms. He cannot even remember when he last did a lick of legal work at home. The best he can manage is to keep track of the sale of family heirlooms, but even this sad bookkeeping has descended into chaos, with sales and money still to be collected jotted down on stray scraps of paper that have been absorbed into great heaps of similar scraps of paper, many of them rendered illegible by the various spills and smears engendered by the frequent snacks he brings into this room, snacks that in his former life would have been unimaginable: hunks of raw meat, giant cans of chicken broth, rawhide chews manufactured for rottweilers and that both Alex and Leslie have found ideal for easing the extreme jaw tension they so often feel—if every love affair must share at least one joke that no one but the couple would find funny, theirs is the rawhide chews.

In the middle of Alex's desk is his laptop computer, which he has struggled mightily to keep clean and thereby distinct from the room's general grunginess and dishevelment. He keeps the case closed, and to further protect the computer he drapes an old shirt over it—the sight of that beautiful broadcloth sometimes gives Alex a pang of sadness, a wash of nostalgia for his former life, when he argued cogently and ate at impeccable tables, when even time itself seemed rich, as it inevitably does when you are billing clients more than a thousand dollars for every hour that ticks by. This computer has been a kind of pit into which he has frequently fallen; time he means to spend here getting his life in order has often been completely wasted playing inane computer games or chasing down the flimsiest notions in a kind of pretend research. Between eBay, pornography, and watching animal videos on YouTube, hours go by in which Alex exists in a kind of fugue state from which only the sudden onset of hunger can arouse him, and now, though he still attempts to keep his computer separate from the mess that surrounds it, he has come to view his Toshiba as yet one more dysfunctional thing in his life, and there are even times when he considers picking the thing up and smashing it to pieces.

"What are we here for?" Leslie asks as he guides her toward his desk.

"Sit down and watch this," Alex says. The machine's welcoming chord plays as the computer powers up, the screen fills with blue light, and then his wallpaper picture—an adorable fawn with its head tilted to one side—comes into view. The keyboard is smudged and there are more than a few hairs on it, but neither Alex nor Leslie notices. With a few vigorous keystrokes he enters the YouTube site and starts a video.

It's Dr. Kis, looking as if not ten but thirty years have passed since they were in his office. The YouTube heading over the video reads FLESH AND BLOOD! Kis is staring at the camera as if he were being photographed following an arrest, unable to look away or disguise himself and hoping that by over-opening his eyes, pressing his lips together, and slightly dilating his nostrils, he can somehow alter his appearance, transform himself.

"Oh my God, Alex, it's him." She grabs Alex's arm.

"I know, I know."

Leslie is open-mouthed with wonder. She shakes her head. "I thought we tried everything. How did you find him?"

"I just found it. What difference does it make?" He pauses the playback. "Do you want to see it or not?"

Leslie stares at Kis's ravaged face. She reads the video's heading—FLESH AND BLOOD—and suddenly has an inkling of how Alex stumbled across it, the keywords he must have been typing into his computer's search engine, the gruesome and shameful nature of his curiosity. Flesh, blood, who knows what else? She has no desire to humiliate him or cause him any further discomfort.

"Play it," she says. She touches his shoulder.

He looks at her with love and gratitude. There is a closeness between them that surpasses anything he has ever imagined. He clicks Play.

"Bonjour," Kis says in a very quiet voice.

"In English, Doctor." The voice comes from behind the camera.

Is it Reggie? Leslie wonders. *That dreadful little pimp...* But no, the voice is without that snide, complicitous quality Leslie remembers from Ljubljana. This voice belongs to someone heavier, sorrowful, someone who might even be kind.

"Where is he?" Leslie asks.

"Ach," Kis says, throwing up his hands. He takes a breath, smooths his shirt front.

"You know what?" Alex says, suddenly pausing the video. "He looks like he's on his way to The Hague." He sees the blankness in Leslie's expression. "World Court?"

"Oh," says Leslie. But she shakes her head, still a bit lost.

"You know, a lot of military men in what used to be Yugoslavia behaved rather badly during their civil wars. There was a lot of slaughter."

"Back in olden times?"

"Well, not really. Mid-nineties, around then."

"I wasn't even born yet."

"Of course you were, Leslie. What are you talking about?"

"Stop testing me! I'm not in the University of Alexander. And anyhow, he's a doctor, right? He's not a millinery."

"Military."

"What is he saying? Let's hear it. Maybe. I don't know...you never know. Maybe there's something here." She knocks Alex's hand away and clicks on the Play icon to continue the YouTube video.

"Hello," Kis says. "My name is Slobodan Kis, and I have been practicing medicine in Slovenia, primarily in my home city of Ljubljana, since 1987."

"Oh my God," says Leslie. "This is too much. This is just really fucking too much."

"For many years I was fascinated by the mysteries of human reproduction," Kis says. He pauses, swallows, dries the corners of his mouth with the back of his spotted, trembling hand. "I treated infertile couples in my home city, and eventually all over Europe, and finally from everywhere—China, U.S.A., United Kingdom. I had some successes, some failures. And one day in the summer of 1999, I devised a fertility treatment that indicated we were at a new threshold in the science of human reproduction. Blending endocrinal materials from human and nonhuman sources, I began to administer injections that had a stimulating effect on the human reproductive system that was nothing short of miraculous."

A wave of static goes through the image, flashes of light like the branches of a bare tree, and for a moment the image of the haunted old physician is a jumbled, disjointed negative of itself. But quickly it comes together again, and now Kis is holding an immense photo album covered in a plush, quilted material that looks like it's from the sofa in a fortune-teller's waiting room. With some difficulty, Kis opens the book, and in it, eight to a page, are snapshots of children, from infants to young people in military uniforms. "These human beings are alive today because of me, my work, my science." He turns the pages, first slowly, and then quickly, as if the whole enterprise is trying his patience, and the pictures flash by.

"Whoa," a voice says, a teenage boy. "I think I saw us in that book."

"Who is that?" Leslie asks. "What's going on?"

"Two kids. We're watching them watching him," Alex says. "They're the ones who posted the video."

"Oh Jesus," Leslie says. "This is making me sick."

The video camera with which the two young boys have been recording Kis's video swings off to the side, revealing a disheveled bedroom, a window with tattered green curtains, and a flat-screen TV showing Kis's video.

"Rewind it," one of the boys says.

"What the fuck, Mario," the other boy says. "I'm not fucking rewinding it." Still, he does as he was asked, and they freeze the image of Kis's book of accomplishments.

"That's us!" Mario says, and he runs to the TV and jabs his finger against the screen. "We're in there!" He is a slight kid with shoulder-length hair, sloping eyes.

"Look at what's happened to this guy," Alex says. "Look at his eyes, his face. Look at what he's become."

The boys start the video from where they'd paused it.

"A doctor is not measured by his successes alone," Kis says. "The failures often eclipse much of the good."

"Yeah," one of the boys says tauntingly, "like you messed up, dude."

"Big-time," the other boy says. And they both dissolve into laughter.

As if hearing the taunts of the boys, the doctor falls silent, looks down at his hands, which rest on the table before him.

"He looks a hundred years older," Leslie says. Her hand is on her chest as she tries to slow her breathing, but the sight of this man, no matter how time-worn and melancholy, no matter how desperate and fugitive his manner, brings her back to that time in his offices when he seemed to tower over her, an overpowering presence who seemed almost to rape her with his needles.

"Do you want to talk about the canine component of the serums you were using?" the kindly voice prods.

"No, I am not talking about that."

"Well, the whole purpose—"

"Don't speak to me of purposes," Kis says, suddenly regaining the imperial manner both Alex and Leslie so vividly recall from their own meeting with him.

"Nothing of the canine component?" the voice says rather sadly. The doctor shakes his head. "And nothing of the ursine?" Again the doctor shakes his head. "And nothing of the vulpine?"

"There is nothing vulpine in my serum. Fox are not good breeders. You must be mad."

"And nothing lupine?"

A long pause. Then: "It doesn't matter."

"It doesn't matter?" one of the boys screams, his voice rising on the wings of incredulity.

"It matters to us, Doc," the other boy cries.

"If we live, we're coming to kick your ass," the first boy says. One of them zooms the lens of his video recorder so that Kis's face is closer, grainier.

"Stop it for a minute," Leslie says.

Alex does what she asks.

"Can he fix us?" Leslie asks.

"Do we even want that?" Alex says.

"Are you insane?"

He opens his mouth to say something but remains silent.

"Can he fix us, Alex? Does he say anything about that?"

"You can hear for yourself," Alex says, restarting the video.

"In my serum," Kis says, clearing his throat, straightening his shoulders, "I use many different strains of genetic material. What is my crime? Trying to bring happiness and relief to people? Vigor. That is the watchword." He closes his fists, shakes them, bares his teeth. "Strength. So many of these infertile couples, they wait too long, they live too soft, they worry, they obsess about nonsense. They fatten. They tire. I give them back the vigor. And health. Good blood, wildness. You understand? I put the wild in them."

"Jesus," one of the boys mutters, no longer finding it funny.

The boy with the camera turns it away from the video of Kis and toward his brother, who has hair down to his shoulders, shaggy sideburns, and the beginnings of his first mustache. He looks hollow-eyed, frightened, but needs to put himself forward for the camera's sake. He holds up his pointer finger and his pinkie and sticks his tongue out as far as he can, as if he were some heavy-metal hair god acknowledging his headbanger audience at a concert.

"Oh, that boy. That poor kid," Leslie says.

"Wait," Alex says. "This is what I most wanted you to hear."

"In pursuit of vigor," Kis is saying, "I introduced certain kinds of fish oils. Yes. You understand?"

"We're not stupid, you fucking wack," one of the boys fairly screams.

"I believe in fish oil, quite apart from my fertility research. For joint health, lowering triglycerides, depression. Even skin tone." He glances unhappily at his own hands and puts them onto his lap and out of sight. "I perhaps made an error...."

"An error?" the kindly voice asks.

"Yes."

"Can you say more about that?"

"Is that what is required?" Kis asks.

"It would be helpful," the voice says.

"We're going to find you!" one of the boys bellows, his youthful energies returned.

"And tear you up, man," his brother adds.

"And scatter you to the wind!" they both shout in unison, their voices now a virtual howl.

Leslie reaches for Alex's hand, looks up at him with very, very frightened eyes.

"I used oil harvested from a most common fish," Dr. Kis says softly. "I was concerned with availability. Eventually, I settled on *gobiodes*."

"English, please, Doctor."

"The goby fish. An everywhere fish. Cold water, warm seas, aquariums."

"And there was a problem with this?" the voice asked.

"Here we go!" one of the boys calls out in an amusement-park sort of voice, the kind people use when the roller coaster is creakily inching up its initial ascent.

"Yes, a problem. This particular fish has a particular nature."

"And this nature was?" the interlocutor prods.

"The goby is a cannibal fish. It feeds on its own kind." Kis's voice is clipped, factual; whatever it costs him to say these words will remain his own secret.

"Specifically?" the cameraman asks.

"I am working all the time," Kis says, now with emotion. "Don't you understand? All the time. Perfecting, taking out the bugs. And learning perhaps how some of the unfortunate side effects can be reversed."

"You see? He can reverse this," Leslie says.

"Not yet," Alex whispers, indicating with a gesture that Leslie should listen to what Kis says next.

"But you were saying about the fish," Kis's gentle interrogator asks. "This cannibal fish."

"What do you want me to say?"

"What we discussed before."

Kis heaves a huge sigh and looks off into the distance. "It's a cannibal fish. The goby."

"And specifically?"

"Specifically? This is what you want? Okay. Specifically, the goby fish likes to eat its own young. It seems to be its preferred form of nourishment. These are legal matters now. You understand? My lawyers advise me that there is very little I can say until these issues are resolved."

With a popping noise and a hiss, the video goes dark. In the sudden silence, Alex and Leslie can hear the faint screams of the man caged in their cellar.

"We shouldn't be hearing that," Alex says. "I must have left the door open." He starts to stand up, but Leslie stops him with a hand on his forearm.

"What has he done to us?"

"I don't know."

"Alex."

"Worst-case scenario? Exactly what we think."

"We are a danger to our own children." Leslie's voice is plaintive, as if all she desires is for Alex to disagree with her.

"Sometimes," he says. "We have our good days, and we have our bad days."

Again, the faint cries rise from the cellar. Leslie turns toward the sound with a startled expression, and Alex wipes the saliva from the corner of his mouth with the back of his hand.

The howls make him hungry.

The sun trembles red over the small slice of the East River Michael can see from his windows. It is a little before 6:00 a.m., and pale thin stalks of light rise on the streets below. Michael is exhausted. He has barely slept and he is overwhelmed by worries—what to do about Adam, what Adam's insane, bellicose father might do next, and as if that were not enough, he is also consumed with worry about Xavier. Since Michael learned that Xavier never made it to Rosalie's, his mind has felt like a fish hooked by two different fishermen, being yanked and reeled toward two different shores. He is at once deeply worried that Xavier has been hurt or is in some other kind of trouble and is also furiously certain that Xavier has decided to punish him for basically turning him out of the apartment and has retaliated with some tawdry hookup. Or maybe Xavier's finding another bed for last night was part of some larger retaliation, based on his boredom with Michael's slow social metabolism, Michael's stay-at-home mentality. Hadn't Xavier regularly complained they didn't go out often enough and were not a part of the throbbing nightlife?

When Michael gets out of the shower and comes back to the front room, half expecting to see Xavier tearfully repentant or, perhaps—best-case scenario!—slightly injured, he finds Adam sitting on the sofa, which is still covered with bedsheets and blankets. Adam cradles a bowl of cereal and eats ravenously. He glances up at Michael with an expression both nervous and fierce.

"I was just about to wake you up," Michael says, trying to sound parental, even though he is wearing only a towel.

"I get up early."

"Well, it's time to go to school."

Adam concentrates on his cereal.

"Adam?"

"Can I have some more cereal?"

"Of course. You want me to get it for you?"

Instead of answering, Adam springs off the sofa, scampers into the kitchen, and pours so many Cheerios into his bowl there is scarcely room for milk.

"Since you're coming with me, you're going to be a little early. We get there before the students." He watches Adam shoveling the Cheerios into his mouth.

"Please don't make me" Adam is finally able to say.

"You have to. It's school."

Adam shakes his head no.

"Come on, Adam…"

"That's where he'll look for me."

"But that's exactly what's going to have to happen. Whatever is going on between you and your folks, you're not going to solve it by running away or hiding out here."

Adam shakes his head, more and more insistently.

"Well, you can't stay here. I'm going to school and you're going to have to come with me."

"He is going to kill me. Or maybe Mom is. Or both."

"Adam! Come on."

"They are. They do things. They're different from everyone. They can't even help it."

"Are you sure, Adam? Are you sure you're not just super-angry right now and this is what you're feeling?"

"You saw him. He was right here. You saw him."

"I know. And all I saw was a dad looking for his kid. I should have given you to him right then and there. I wasn't thinking clearly."

"Yes, you were. You could tell."

"Maybe I should call him right now." Michael glances at his wrist to see the time, but he's not wearing his watch. He's not wearing anything—just the towel. A creepy, guilty feeling comes over him, the kind that comes not from doing anything wrong but from doing something that leaves you wide open to misinterpretation and accusation. He realizes there are still plenty of people who think gay men can't be trusted around male children, though to Michael being with anyone younger or smaller or lighter or smoother has zero appeal— he likes the weight and smell of someone substantial on him, a commanding air, a firmness of touch. He even likes a certain degree of sheer bossiness, something for which Cubans in general seem particularly disposed. *Xavier! Where are you?*

"I don't want you to call him," Adam says, very softly.

"Then you better get ready for school, and we'll get this all squared away once we are there."

"I don't want to."

"Adam, I think you're old enough to understand this. I am a teacher. It's my job. And I could get fired for coming between one of my students and his parents, or even for just the perception that I am."

"Even if the parents are going to kill the kid?"

"No one's killing anyone, Adam."

"Yeah?"

"Yeah. Come on, be reasonable."

"I am."

"Okay, as your teacher I am legally required to call Child Protective Services. I have to tell CPS that your parents are trying…" Michael stops himself, though it's already too late. He has ventured into territory he should have never gotten near. The parents at Berryman Prep are for the most part wealthy, demanding, entitled alpha-dog types, and the school's administration has always followed a policy of accommodation and catering to the wishes and whims of the parents upon whose large tuition checks and occasional endowments Berryman depends, a policy that was not a whit less stringent for being unspoken. Though carved over the Gothic-style front entrance were the words *knowledge is freedom,* a more truthful motto would have been "The customer is always right," and at Berryman Prep, the customer wrote with a pricey Montblanc pen.

"How come you don't believe me?" Adam says, his lower lip beginning to tremble.

"Adam, I'm not here to debate with you. We're going to school and we're leaving in ten minutes. Once we are there, if you don't tell me to do otherwise, I'm going to make that call."

Ten minutes later, Adam emerges from the bathroom, washed, his hair wet-combed, his face frozen with unhappiness. Wordlessly, he follows Michael into the elevator and through the lobby. It is a cold, steely morning, with a stiff wind that carries the scent of burned coffee.

Adam has not even bothered to zip his skimpy jacket. Michael stops himself from telling the boy to bundle up against the cold. None of them seem to close their jackets anymore; none want to seem like vulnerable boys.

As they descend the steps to the subway, surrounded by others on their early-morning commutes, Michael, suddenly sensing that the boy might do something foolish, takes hold of Adam's arm—not tightly, but with just enough force to remind the boy that someone is in charge. Yet the touch of the teacher's hand seems to electrify Adam, who twists away from Michael.

"Settle down," Michael says, but as he gives Adam an admonishing look, the boy's eyes narrow and his lips part, revealing two rows of bright white teeth. Too bright. Too sharp. The sight of them unnerves Michael momentarily, and he stumbles on the subway steps. He regains his balance by gripping the railing, and the next thing he knows Adam has yanked himself free, turned around, and leaped away. It almost seems as if he is flying.

"Adam!" Michael cries out. Maybe half the thirty or so people on the staircase show some interest in the commotion Michael is creating, while the others either don't hear or are absorbed in difficulties of their own, or perhaps they both hear and care but have been trained by city life to always reveal as little as possible.

Michael chases after the boy. He has no choice. And, also, no chance. He sees Adam knife into the crowd on Twenty-Third Street, dart this way and that way, at absolutely awesome speed—and then, to Michael's horror, the boy dashes into traffic to cross to the gloomy greenery of a small park. A beat-up-looking truck hauling large sheets of plate glass brakes quickly to keep from hitting Adam, and Adam rises as if there were wings on his heels and steps onto the truck's hood, using it as a platform from which to vault across the street. And disappear.

"Did you see that?" a middle-aged man in a cashmere topcoat and a brand-new baseball cap says to Michael. "I'll bet you a sock full of nickels that kid is on one of those energy drinks."

There is a cold, steady drizzle soaking the streets and the tops of the parked cars when Michael arrives at Berryman. It's still a few minutes before classes begin; most of the younger students are already there, deposited by caretakers who have other duties to attend to or by their parents, faces stark and worried in the weird light of their smartphones, who must be prompt because they have early-morning meetings to chair. "They hold their phones out like Hamlet addressing Yorick's skull," Michael once said to Xavier—and the thought of Xavier brings Michael's hand reflexively into his pocket, where he finds his own phone and calls his great dear friend's cell for the tenth time that morning.

"You're here!" announces Davis Fleming, Berryman's headmaster. Fleming is large and fleshy, but with his broad smile, well-scrubbed skin, and silvery hair, he looks like a large boy cast as the father in a school play. Fleming's grandfather and both his parents attended Berryman Prep, as did Fleming himself. He lives in a Berryman-owned apartment next to the school, and, except for college and a honeymoon to an island off the coast of South Carolina where he and his wife (Berryman, class of 1983) had their honeymoon, he has never been farther than ten miles from these corridors. But despite the animation in his face and the unvarying, unyielding smile, there is annoyance in Fleming's voice and a bit of steel in his hand as he grips Michael's biceps through the slick chill of his leather jacket.

"What can I do for you?" Michael says, falling into step as Fleming marches through the hall, past the glassed-in case with fading old pictures of by-now-aged Berryman athletes taking flatfooted set shots in basketball games a half century ago, where the time eternally shows six minutes to go; and wrestling boys in black sneakers and unitards, their expressions hovering between nobility and teenage hormonal haze, lawyers now, surgeons, bankers, grandfathers, dead and buried, some of them. Michael and Fleming are in the old wing of the school, with its Gothic touches and scuffed maroon floors, where the light is dim and somehow humid, like the watery gloom of a submarine. Fleming doesn't keep his grip on Michael's arm, but he continually touches it nonetheless, as if Michael might need reminding that flight is not an alternative.

"Can you tell me what this is about?" Michael finally asks.

"About?" Fleming says, as if the word itself were peculiar.

"Why am I basically being abducted here?"

"I think you know the answer to that, Mr. Medoff."

There's nothing Michael can say to that. He *does,* more or less, know why he is following Fleming to his office.

But what he is not prepared for is that both the Twisdens are already in Fleming's office, Leslie, the mother, in flared trousers, a turtleneck, and a long raincoat, and the horrible father pacing back and forth like a beast in its cage, snarling into his cell phone. When Fleming leads Michael into the office, the furious parents turn toward him with devouring eyes.

"Where is our son?" Alex says, snapping his phone shut.

"And our daughter," adds Leslie. Her voice shakes; her eyes are red, presumably from crying.

"Yes," Michael says, and clears his throat. "Yes."

"Yes what?" Twisden says.

Michael tries to quickly consider his options, and in the confusion and uncertainty he decides it is best to stay as close to the truth as possible, though he is loath to state that Adam spent the night in his house, and that upon rediscovering him after Twisden's late-night visit, Michael did nothing to inform Alex, thus, by implication, entering into a state of collusion with the little boy. "I haven't seen Alice, and I have no idea where she is," he says to Leslie.

"And what about Adam?" Twisden says. He is wringing his hands with suppressed rage; there is something reddish beneath two of his fingernails. He sees Michael glancing at them and he quickly puts his hands in the pockets of his expensive-looking suit jacket and steps closer to Michael—years of tough negotiating have schooled him well in the body language of intimidation, and even though his career is sputtering now (at best!), he knows how to impose his will.

"What about him?" Michael says.

"Did he go back to your little love nest?"

"My love nest? What is that supposed to mean?"

"You know damn well what that means," Twisden says.

"I resent that," Michael says.

"If you would just answer Mr. Twisden's question, we could get this matter squared away," Fleming interjects. "Please, Michael, let's stop all this...posturing. A child is missing."

"Two children," Leslie says. She wraps her raincoat tightly around herself, though it is as warm as an armpit in Fleming's office.

"Mrs. Twisden," Michael begins, but Leslie cuts him off.

"Ms. Kramer," she says.

"I don't know where your daughter is. I'm sorry."

"And our son?" Twisden says.

"I don't know where he is either." He knows what question will come next and chooses to offer more of the truth rather than endure the viselike grip of Twisden's inevitable interrogation. "Your son came back to my apartment last night after you left," Michael says. "He was cold, he was wet, and he seemed very, very frightened."

"You see?" Twisden says to Fleming. "It's exactly as I told you."

"And why didn't you call Mr. Twisden and Ms. Kramer the moment he first arrived?" Fleming asks.

"Adam told me they were out of town."

"And he believed him," Twisden says, as if nothing could be more unlikely or absurd.

"Yes, I did."

Alex and Leslie exchange quick glances.

"And what other tales did our son tell you?" Alex says, this time with a shade less bluster in his voice

"Mr. Medoff," Fleming says to Michael. "This is highly irregular."

"If you so much as touched him," Twisden says, shaking his head and grimacing, as if sickened by the punishment he would be forced to mete out.

Michael has never seen eyes quite like Twisden's—so intense, yet with no more emotion than halogen lamps.

"And now where is he?" Leslie Kramer says. "What have you done with him? And why in the *hell* did you not call us when he returned to your apartment?" The atomizer of whatever perfume she is wearing seems to have been given several extra pumps this morning; her lipstick appears to have been applied with a trembling hand.

"It was…it was a strange situation," Michael says. "I thought Adam had taken off again, and when I realized he hadn't—well, he begged me. This morning, I tried to bring him to school. But he ran away. He's very frightened—of both of you. And because of certain things he said to me, I am obliged to make a formal report to Child Protective Services." Michael's heart is beating so furiously that he is certain everyone in the room can hear it.

"He ran away from you?" Twisden says, as if this in itself were an admission of Michael's malfeasance.

"Yes," Michael says. "Just as he ran away from you. Just as he *hid* when he knew you were drawing near. Just as he spent hours hiding in the park before that. We're talking about a boy who came to me cold and wet and frightened out of his wits, and let me tell you—let me tell you and you and you, too, *Mr.* Fleming, I wasn't the one who was frightening him. I was the one he came to for protection. And I believe he ran away from me on our way to school because he knew his parents would be here looking—"

But that is all Michael is able to say because Twisden has pounced upon him. The furious lawyer's hands are on Michael's chest, and Michael staggers and falls backward, and the objects in Fleming's office recede like the cars of a speeding train on its way to the darkness of a long tunnel. And now he is inside the tunnel and instead of the deep confident howl of a train whistle, he hears his own voice, hoarse and anguished, scared and unstable, and when the darkness relents he has awakened to a view of the recessed track lighting in Berryman Prep's nurse's office. Looming over him is the soft, moon-shaped, somehow nun-like face of Jeanette Cavanaugh, the school nurse, and the worried, guilty face of Davis Fleming, who is not only frowning but wringing his hands.

"Hello there, Michael," Fleming says as Michael's eyes open. "Wow! You had yourself a good old-fashioned knock on the noggin." He seems to have settled on the strategy of treating Michael's being attacked by a crazed parent as some sort of delicious, madcap adventure the two of them can now share.

"Don't move, not yet, and not too quickly," Jeanette Cavanaugh says.

"How did I get here?"

"I carried you," she says.

"I tried to help, but she wouldn't allow it," Fleming hastens to add. "This is one strong lady."

"Where are they?" Michael says, lifting his head, propping himself up on his elbows. The pain seems located primarily in the back of his neck and the top third of his spine, a twisting, cold pain, the sort that makes you wonder what will come first, the moaning or the throwing up.

Jeanette hands him a bright blue ice pack, the outside of which is white with freezer burn. "I'm going to give you something for pain," she says.

"What's on the menu?" Michael asks.

"The strongest we keep is extra-strength Tylenol."

"Give him extra," Fleming says, as if money for the extra pills were coming out of his own pocket, and costs be damned!

Michael struggles to his feet. The room flaps and flutters like a flag; he holds on to the edge of Nurse Cavanaugh's medical-supply cabinet for balance. "I'm all right, I'm fine," he says, as much to himself as to them. He pats his pockets, looking for his phone, and asks Jeanette if he might use hers.

"Who are you calling?"

"The police. Of course. I mean—come on."

"Michael," Fleming says. "First CPS, now the police. That's not necessarily the way to handle this."

"Are you kidding me? Are you insane?"

Fleming looks at Jeanette, clears his throat. "Jeanette, may I use your office for a private moment or two with Mr. Medoff?"

Jeanette has been looking at Fleming with some degree of disbelief, and now, when she hears his request to vacate her own office, her eyes widen and she shakes her head. "If you insist," she finally manages to say.

"Terrific," Fleming says. He waits for her to leave and as soon as the door is closed he turns to Michael and with great urgency says, "I want you to allow me to handle this situation, Michael. I have friends at CPS and I will make sure a report is filed. As for the police, I think we had better let cooler heads prevail. Make no mistake about it— what Mr. Twisden did to you is unacceptable. What I don't want to happen is for you to be dragged into some pissing match with his guy. You understand? They are going to accuse you of molesting their son, Michael. And I think you know me well enough to understand that there is no greater champion of gay rights in the world than me, but I don't care how liberal and up-to-date New Yorkers are supposed to be, gay teachers are vulnerable. When it comes to children, everybody is just a teeny-tiny bit reactionary. I wish it were not the case. I wish we lived in a better world."

"Did I ever tell you I was gay?" Michael asks.

Fleming seems taken aback by the question.

"Then why do you refer to me as a gay teacher?" Michael persists. "Do I look gay? Do I talk or walk gay? Did I one day come to school with a rainbow scarf?"

If the personal side of Fleming is rattled by Michael's questions, the administrative side is unflappable. "Your personal life is of no interest or importance to me. But it is to the Twisden-Kramers, and I don't want them making accusations, I don't even want innuendos. The Twisden family is prominent in this city. Both Adam and Alice are full-paying students who receive not one penny of school aid, which helps us to continue our outreach program for the sons and daughters of doctors and dentists and other less fortunate New York families. If you want to rattle the parents' cage you will (a) not get anywhere, (b) risk a valuable resource for the Berryman community, and (c) and this is the most important part, Mike, and I say this not only as your supervisor but as someone whom I would like you to consider a friend, you will find yourself in some disgusting sex scandal. And the thing about sex scandals is everybody loses—especially the accused."

As Michael prepares himself to rebut what Fleming has said, he is interrupted by a sharp knock at the door. Both men turn toward the sound and before either can say *Come in* or *Please Wait,* the door opens and they are confronted by the sight of Mrs. Fillmore, a squat, fierce woman who has worked as a secretary at the school for the past thirty-eight years. She has white hair cut in an oddly girlish way, and large black-framed glasses.

"We got a call from the police," she says, looking at Michael. "Someone found a wallet belonging to Xavier…Rivera, or something? They can't find him, but there's a card says in case of emergency, contact you."

"Where did they find it?" Michael asks.

"Someone brought it into the precinct. Don't worry, I'm sure the Good Samaritan kept all the money—if there was any. They found it in a gutter somewhere on Twenty-Third Street."

It feels to Michael as if his heart is being punched to death.

Rodolfo has been as good as his word and has taken Alice to a place where she can eat, get warm, and sleep. It's a large apartment on West End Avenue, in a building that once was fancy but has gone down in the world, and now there is no doorman, and the elevator is self-service. The apartment itself is on the tenth floor, unlocked and unkempt. Rodolfo warms a can of soup for her, plunks down a carton of milk, and makes some toast—though he butters it with a heavy hand, crumbling it to bits. As soon as she has eaten, she is overcome with fatigue, and suddenly nine hours have passed like a shooting star glimpsed from the corner of your eye, and Alice awakens on a soft green sofa the pillows of which have a sharp but comforting animal smell. This must have been the favorite sleeping spot of the family dog.

"Hello?" she calls out softly, tentatively, sitting up, rubbing her eyes with the heels of her hands. When her feet touch the ground, they land directly on Rodolfo's shoulder—he has curled up next to the sofa and slept on the floor.

He reacts quickly to her touch; in less than a second, he is on his feet, in a slight crouch, his eyes sharp and wary. Seeing Alice, he relaxes, smiles. "Are you hungry?" he asks.

Alice shakes her head. "I can't remember where we are," she says.

"We're at Peter Burns's crib."

"Who's that?" Alice hears voices in the next room, laughter, the scuffle of feet.

"A friend. A kid. Don't worry, he's cool."

"This is a *kid's* apartment?"

Rodolfo shrugs. "Sort of."

A boy about seven years old races into the room looking agitated and afraid. "Hey, Rodolfo, you better come. Luke and Dave are starting to fight."

"Let them," Rodolfo says with a wave.

"But last time…"

"It's okay. Just let it happen."

The boy shakes his head, submissive but dissatisfied. And a moment later, a hideous yowl comes from the next room, followed by a long rumbling growl that feels to Alice as if it were coming from right below her feet. She covers her ears the way she does when the subway comes roaring into her station.

"Come on," Rodolfo says, taking her hand. "I'll show you the place. You can come here whenever you want. It's ours."

As Alice allows Rodolfo to lead her across the largely bare living room, with its windows covered by bedsheets and its walls without pictures, she notices a couple of other sofas shoved into far corners. On one of them someone is sleeping, but so tightly curled that Alice cannot say if it is a boy or a girl, and on the other a teenage boy sits with his back to a teenage girl, who is vigorously brushing his long russet-colored hair. Rodolfo opens a door and just before he leads her into a long corridor, dimly lit by wall sconces with faltering flame-shaped bulbs, the young boy comes racing in again, this time even more agitated than before.

"Rodolfo! Please. You've got to help. He's going to kill him!"

Rodolfo heaves a sigh and lifts a wait-a-second finger. "The kitchen's at the way end of the hall," he says to Alice. "When food…" He shakes his head. "I mean, *there's* food in it."

He saunters casually into the depths of the apartment with the boy, and Alice makes her way down the dim hall, past a series of closed doors, some with the paint peeling, others with deep gouges in the wood. She figures that behind one of these doors is a bathroom, but she is afraid to open one and see something unforgettable.

This is the first morning in years in which she has awakened and has not had to wait for her father or mother to unlock her bedroom door.

She knocks lightly on a door chosen at random. "Hello?" she says, and waits. "Hello?"

She hears what sounds like someone clearing his throat, followed by words rapidly whispered back.

"Come in!" It's a woman's voice, cheerful and inviting, like a lady in a bakery or a nice teacher.

"Sorry," Alice says. "I'm looking for the bathroom?"

"There's one in here, sweetheart," the woman says. "You can use it."

"Come on in," a man's voice joins in. The voice is not so friendly—it sounds tired, unhappy.

Now she has no choice but to open the door. The room is dark. Blankets have been hung over the windows. The only illumination comes from a single Little Mermaid night-light, but even in the heavy shadows of this room—bereft of furniture, freezing cold, and with the overwhelming, disorienting stench of burned hair, rotted food, feces, and urine—Alice can make out two figures, grown-ups, sitting on the floor side by side with their knees drawn up and their eyes blazing.

"Hello there, little girl," the woman says. And now Alice can tell that the lady's voice is not really sweet but meant to sound that way.

"Hello," Alice says. Her eyes are becoming used to the sludgy gray gloom of this room and she is starting to make out more clearly the two adults on the floor. They both have long graying hair and neither of them wears anything on top; on the bottom they both wear satin running pants—the man has hiked up one of the legs on his and he is scratching and scratching at something that seems to be bothering him on his shin. There is a bowl next to them and another one that has been tipped over.

"I don't recognize you," the woman says. "I'm Peter's mother. Are you a friend of our son?"

"I guess.

"How old are you, sweetheart?" the mother asks.

"Ten and a half."

"Oh! What a nice age!"

The father picks up the metal bowl that's been tipped over and skitters it across the floor toward Alice's feet, where it rattles and echoes. "You're looking for a bathroom, right? It's right over there." He points to a door behind him. "And while you're in there, I wonder if you could fill this up with water. Cold water. Let it run for a while before you fill the bowl. There's sediment in the pipes in this old building."

The urgency to reach the bathroom is irresistible. She picks up the bowl and walks into the small bathroom at the back of the parents' room, wondering why they can't get their own water, why they are crouched on the floor, why they are wearing practically no clothes in this chilly room, why the room is so dark, why it smells so horrible. But the behavior of adults is often inexplicable, upsetting, and bizarre, and she is so accustomed to cutting slack for those who are honor bound to cherish and protect her that she is now in the habit of judging no one.

The bathroom is small and cold and smells of ammonia. The floor is covered in layer upon layer of newspaper, some of it damp, some of it torn. There is only a small sink for washing; the turner for the hot water has been removed, exposing a long rusted bolt. The toilet is a catastrophe, and Alice hovers above it as she relieves herself. At least there's toilet paper, but with stupid jokes printed on every square, and some of them show drawings of girls with big boobs, their elbows resting on the rims of gigantic martini glasses.

The medicine cabinet that must have once been above the sink is gone, and Alice looks at the blank, torn-up wall as the cold water thunders into the bowl. She carries it to the huddled parents. "Where should I put it?" she asks.

"Oh, thanks so much," the mother says. "So nice of you."

"Put it right over here," the father says, patting the space between him and the mother.

Moving slowly, carefully, lest she spill a drop of the water, Alice approaches them. She can feel her heart squirming like one of those squirrels the nasty boys captured in the park.

"Right here," the man says, patting the floor again, his voice sort of slurry this time.

"Graceful you," the woman says in a cooing voice. Her nostrils open wide and then close tightly and open wide again.

Alice puts the bowl between them and in an instant the man lunges at her and grabs her wrist. His mouth is open wide, and a sharp, foul smell pours out of him. Alice is almost blind with fear. She twists her arm, trying to get free, but now she has more to contend with: the woman has grabbed her ankle.

"Please don't hurt me," Alice says, but the feel of her, her delectable young flesh, and the sound of her pleading only make them more avid to—to what? Hurt her? Mangle her? Eat her? She doesn't know. Suddenly summoning more strength than she knew she possessed, she yanks herself away from both of them, freeing first her leg and then her arm.

She staggers back and they lunge for her, their fingers bent, the nails like claws, their eyes ablaze with appetite. Yet just when it seems as if they are going to pounce on her, she sees something that, even as it saves her life, strikes her as the most terrible sight of all: they are both brought up short, yanked back in midair. Both of them are manacled, bound to the radiator and the heat pipes with heavy lengths of chain that are attached to them at their waists and their calves in a kind of pitiless bondage straight out of the Middle Ages, when the mentally ill were brutally restrained and forgotten in asylums with nothing to warm them but their own madness.

But are they mad? They seem so to Alice as they continue to hurl themselves at her, as if one more thrust might break the heavy iron links that confine them. Alice has lost her footing and she is sprawled on the cold floor, half shielding her eyes from the piteous sight of these two people growling and howling and doing everything in their power to get their hands on her, and half transfixed, fascinated, mesmerized by what she sees, and then she scuttles away from them on her backside, propelled by her heels and her hands.

The door to the room flies open. It is Rodolfo, in the company of a boy wearing tight black jeans and a hoodie.

"Mom! Dad!" the boy in black jeans shouts. "What the fuck?"

Alice scrambles to her feet and runs to Rodolfo's side. He puts his arm protectively over her shoulders. He is slightly smiling.

"Peter," the woman says. "Unlock us." She is on her hands and knees.

"Cover yourself, Mom," Peter says. "In front of my friends? What's wrong with you?"

"Be a good boy, Peter," the father says. "Do what I ask."

"Stop asking."

"Be a good boy," the father says. His voice drips honey. "Come on."

"I want to go out," Peter's mother wails. "I want to breathe fresh air. I want to see the sky."

"Do what's right, Peter," the father says.

"Why would I ever do anything for either of you?"

"We gave you life, Peter," his father says.

"Yeah. And then what?"

"We better bounce," Rodolfo says to Alice.

"No," Alice says, shaking herself free of the arm he has draped over her. Her eyes are wide, and her heart is pounding; her mouth feels full of the sweet and bitter taste of knowledge.

"Please, son."

"We always loved you," the mother says. "Always. No matter what. No matter how it sleeve."

"Sleeve?" Peter says, his voice curdled with contempt. "You can't even talk anymore."

"Do what I ask," the father says.

"I meant *seemed*," the mother says. "No matter how it seemed, we always loved you."

"You can't keep us like this," the father says.

"What am I supposed to do?" Peter asks. He has gotten closer and closer to them, but if they were to make a run at him, the chains would stop them in their tracks a few inches from the spot where Peter stands. Even as he extends his hands pleadingly toward them, he keeps his elbows tucked to his sides so his fingers aren't in any danger.

"I must pee," the mother suddenly cries out. "Go away!"

The father nods sagely and, with a magisterial wave of the hand, gestures for Peter to leave.

Alice sees that Peter's shoulders are shaking. She realizes he is crying. Alice doesn't know why, but the sight of Peter's heaving shoulders makes her think of Adam. Peter turns away from his parents and walks toward Alice and Rodolfo, making no attempt to hide his tears, which stream down his face.

"I'm not like them," he mutters to himself. "I'm nothing like them."

When he closes the door, Alice asks him, "May I use your phone? I have to call my brother."

Michael sits in his apartment, watching the light move across the floor as the morning sun slowly makes its stiff journey across the city. He has been waiting and waiting and waiting for the phone to ring, waiting for some news of Xavier. He has dozed off a couple of times; he has made himself tea; he has gone quickly to the bathroom, taking the wireless phone with him.

The only person to ring the apartment has been Xavier's sister. Where Michael is sad and feels defeated and alone, Rosalie is defiant, furious, angry at the police for not finding her brother and for barely looking for him, angry at Xavier for going missing and, Michael senses, angry at Michael too—for unspecified reasons, but probably revolving around her essential disapproval of two men living together as lovers, especially when one of them is her little brother.

Michael takes a deep breath, covers his eyes, massages his temples. How is life going to proceed?

The phone rings, startling him. He is sure it's the police. "Yes?" he says, barely audible, even to himself.

"Michael? It's Davis Fleming."

"Hello," Michael manages to say. He looks at his watch. School began an hour ago. Well, fuck them, fuck everybody, everything. Even fuck should get fucked. "I'm calling to thank you for not coming in today," Fleming says. "I thank you, and Berryman Prep thanks you too."

"What?"

"It was very sensitive of you and I want you to know it's very much appreciated. Best to keep a low profile while we figure out how to deal with all this stuff."

It has taken Michael a moment to understand the purpose of Fleming's call, and now that it's clear that Fleming doesn't know that Michael is dealing with something far graver than Fleming's petty institutional concerns and homophobic bullshit, he grips the phone with savage fury. He wants to scream at Fleming—but words fail him. A sound, however, comes up from his depths and pours out of his open mouth and he just lets it come, louder and louder, as his face fills with fiery blood and the tendons at the side of his neck turn to steel.

"I didn't know."

"I didn't either."

"I was so scared."

"Like me."

"Yeah."

"Phone."

"Yeah, fucking phone."

"Really bad."

"Really."

"Those guys."

"I know. They're weird."

"But they helped."

"I guess."

"They did."

"Whatever. I just think from now on we better not split up."

"Definitely."

"I mean, let's really twin out."

"What?"

"Just stay together. Okay?"

"I'm hungry."

"Ick. I can't even think about food. Feel my hands."

"Why?"

"Just feel them"

"They're cold."

"Freezing cold."

"What does it mean?"

"I don't know."

"Am I human?"

"Ha-ha."

"I mean it."

"Of course you are. And so am I."

"Will we always be?"

Silence.

"Will we?"

"I don't know."

It is an unexpectedly beautiful day in Slovenia, and Dr. Kis sits at his desk with sunlight streaming in through the window behind him. He is dressed in a fine new blue suit. He is freshly shaved and barbered. He looks relaxed, almost happy.

Standing before him is his friend with the movie camera. "Okay," the friend says. "Why don't you tell us what you have come up with."

"English?"

"Yes. Then we will do a couple of other languages. But let's start with the English."

Kis clears his throat. "Now?"

"Anytime you're ready, Doctor."

"Hello, this is Dr. Slobodan Kis speaking to you from the free and independent country of Slovenia." Kis clears his throat again, this time more forcefully.

"As some of you know, I have been offering fertility treatments for nearly fifteen years. People, many hundreds of them, have come to me, so many without hope. I have not been able to give each and every client a child, but my success rate is unprecedented in modern fertility medicine. There have been articles in *Paris Match* in France, *Der Spiegel* in Germany, *OK!* in Russia, *Town & Country* in the United States, and of course numerous medical journals. There is no question, no question whatsoever, so make no mistake, my friends, I am, in all due modestment, the leading fertility physician in Europe, and the world.

"Have there been errors? Of course there have. Have some been…unfortunate? Yes, without question. But two things we must put first.

"One. Do my clients complain that my treatment is ineffective and does not work? Well, the answer to this is a resounding no."

Suddenly, Kis falls silent. He takes a deep breath and pinches the bridge of his nose.

"You okay?" the man with the camera asks.

"I just need to rest."

"It's going very well, Dr. Kis. It truly is. Just pick up from where you left off."

"The second question," Kis continues, "is of course all-important and that is what about the health, short-term and long-term health, of my clients? Well, I can state with complete certainty that here the record is perfect and spotless. Especially if you compare the Kis method with artificial insemination, in vitro fertilization, fertility drugs—well, then the picture is rosy indeed. My clients suffer no infections, no urinary difficulties, no loss of energy, nothing but vigor and the joys of parenthood."

Kis juts his chin forward, and his eyes are suddenly fiercely cold, an eagle guarding its nest. His lips turn stubbornly downward and he folds his arms over his chest, the very portrait of a man who answers to no one.

"Um...Dr. Kis? I think the reason we're making this?"

"Foolishness," Kis says.

"Is that there have been...problems? Problems that must be addressed? People who should be reassured? Given hope?"

"Ach," Kis says, with a wave. "Okay. Is this what you need to hear? In some very rare cases—perhaps, at the most, two out of every ten—the mixture given to our clients has been more powerful than...Well, no, that's not what I am going to say. What I will say is this. You leave that other part out, okay?"

"Just continue, Dr. Kis."

"For the very few clients who may wish to have some of the side effects of the treatment taken away, completely erased, poof, gone, then I want to tell you that I have studied this problem and now there is a simple solution, and so if you wish to see me, you are of course welcome, with nominal costs. I am not here to get rich. I am already very rich—too rich! And if you worry that when your children make the hormonal change, perhaps they will begin showing excesses of energy, sexuality, whatever the problem...Most of these fears are baseless, by the way. These children are fine, and so are you. Much ado about nothing, as the Bard of Avon put it. But if you want to deal with whatever side effects there are, then you are most welcome to it. It's all very simple."

"Do you want to give a little bit of detail about what some of the side effects have been, Dr. Kis?"

Kis smiles. "I'll leave that to others," he says.

"Don't do that, please don't do that," Leslie says to Alex as he walks past her to check the temperature of the water in the bath they plan to share.

"Don't do what?" Alex asks.

"I don't like to be sniffed. Especially no from behind. Not."

"I wasn't."

"You were, and please don't."

"Sorry."

Leslie wraps a towel around her lower half, which makes Alex feel twice as naked.

As Alex leans over the tub and tests the water with his fingertips, Leslie has an impulse to push him down and hold his head under. Yet following in the wake of that murderous urge is a feeling of love for him so powerful and so incoherent in its devotion that her legs go weak.

"Do you remember our life before we became parents?" she asks him.

"Of course I do. How could I not?"

"I mean, really member it." She shakes her head, as if to erase her little mistake. "I mean, remember."

"We were so rich," Alex says.

"I never cared about that," says Leslie. "I loved you so much. And I still do."

"Everything top of the line. Now…now I'm glad we have hot water."

"People said I was your…" Again, the word eludes Leslie, and since this comes so close on the heels of her saying *member* instead of *remember,* her spirits plummet, and she feels a cold wave of discouragement break over her.

"It doesn't matter what they said."

"But what was it? What did they say?"

"They said you were my trophy wife."

"Yes, that was it," Leslie says. She laughs, holds her arms out wide, looks at herself—her drooping breasts; the rippling muscles of her abdomen; the roughness of her skin, the result of so many waxings and peelings and laser treatments—and then she looks at Alex. "No trophy now, right?"

Rather than comfort her with words, Alex puts his arms around his beloved wife, holding her close. Kneading her shoulders, he slowly turns Leslie around and embraces her from behind, slowly entering her, moving back and forth, side to side, and breathing into her ear, which, even in the consuming, lovely mindlessness of this sudden lust, he manages to remember is something she likes. "It's like sweet wind in my ears," she has said. "Like we're flying."

A little later, they soak together in the bathtub, which, though luxuriously large, is not really large enough to hold them both, and so Alex soaks on the bottom and Leslie is half on top of him, half to his side. They feel so close to each other. They both look deep within themselves and find no words to describe their feelings.

"Do you want me to wash you?" Alex asks.

"No soap, just water," Leslie answers.

"Where do you think they are?" Alex wonders. "Do you think they're together?"

"I don't know. Maybe." Leslie cups some water and brings it to her face. "I hope so. It's not good."

"What's not good?" He tries to keep any hint of impatience out of his voice. But he has not failed to note that Leslie's conversation is becoming more and more dominated by missing words and wrong words and general verbal confusion. Now and again it happens to him too, but his difficulties are nowhere on the scale of hers. And if it is language that makes us human, then Leslie is becoming slowly less and less human, and the grief he feels at this prospect is not based on judgment—the distinction between *human* and *animal* has long since ceased to make much difference to him—but is, rather, based on the fear of losing her. And he is losing her. He can feel it. She is fading just as surely as loved ones can begin to disappear when they become gravely ill or start to succumb to Alzheimer's disease—there is less and less of them, until one day they are gone.

"You're a scrubber," Leslie says, followed by a low laugh.

A scrubber? Alex supposes she means he has scrubbed her back with a washcloth.

"We were talking about the kids," he says.

"I know."

"I was wondering if they are together and you said, 'It's not good.' "

"Alex. Please. I won't be condescended to."

There's a welcome edge to her voice. Lately her main emotions have been rage and confusion, but this last remark drips with sarcasm, and Alex's spirits lift.

"But what did you mean?" he asks.

"I was a highly respectful editor at a terrific New York publishing house, so don't talk to me as if I were some kind of idiot."

"I'm sorry, I didn't mean to," Alex says, but all he can think is: *You said* respectful.

"They need to be together, Adam and Alice," Leslie says, as much to herself as to Alex.

"I worry."

"I love them so much. No matter what, they're my...they're my babies."

"What if they go to the police?" Alex says.

"To say what? What could they say?"

"Whatever children say. They are clearly frightened—why else would they be running."

"They know nothing," Leslie says.

"Hey, my parents thought I knew nothing about their private lives—but I knew my father was having an affair and that he had a collection of photographs that could have filled a porn museum, and I knew my mother drank to excess, and I knew all kinds of other things too that they assumed I was in the dark about."

"Those are silly secrets," Leslie says.

"Silly maybe, but not so secret."

"Our secrets are different."

"Worse, you could say."

"And we guard them with everything we have. All we do is keep our secrets; it's the main thing."

"But we can make mistakes," Alex says. He realizes he has been scrubbing Leslie's back for over a minute, and the skin is bright red—which seems to highlight the wisps and curls of hair on her shoulder blades. "Letting them get out of their rooms was a bit of a fuckup, wouldn't you say?"

"They tricked us," Leslie says, nodding.

"And they show no interest in coming home."

"Maybe they want to and they are not able."

"They're running, Leslie. We need to get them back in the fold before they start telling tales."

Leslie doesn't say anything. She is engrossed suddenly with trying to touch the tip of her tongue to a bead of water that hangs from the tip of her nose.

"Leslie?"

"Hmm?"

"What are you thinking about?"

"I'm remembering."

"What are you remembering?"

"I have a mother too. Or maybe no more? Maybe she died?"

"No, she's alive. She's old, she's sick."

"In San Francisco, right?"

"That's right."

"San Francisco, California."

"Right."

Leslie is silent for a moment. She lifts her hips out of the water, soaps her middle, and then relaxes and watches the soap bubbles zizz off of her.

"With my sister."

"Yes."

"Cynthia."

"Your memory's getting better again."

"Oh, yeah, it's super-duper." Her voice curdles with sarcasm. "I actually remember my sister's name. I think I will be working as an editor again before too long."

"You ought to be a little more forgiving of yourself, Leslie."

She reaches behind herself and lovingly pats Alex's cheek.

"How much longer?" she asks.

"How much longer?"

"This," she says. "This life." Before he can answer—or before his *not answering* becomes too sad—Leslie begins to kick her legs in the bathwater. The water starts to foam, and as she kicks with more and more vigor, waves of soapy water slosh around the tub.

"Take it easy," Alex says.

But Leslie's fluttering legs only work harder and faster and soon the water is flying every which way.

"Stop!" he cries. But she does not stop. And the chaos she is creating is somehow infectious. It triggers something in Alex, some love of fun, some curiosity about what will happen next. And first with his hands and then with his legs he too begins to beat wildly at the water inside their tub. No doubt about it—it's fun. The walls are soaked, thick sudsy gray puddles form on the floor, but who cares? It's fun! It's really fun. Alex's and Leslie's barks of excitement and shrieks of laughter echo against the room's black-and-white tiles.

Across the country, in San Francisco, Cynthia Kramer is showing a mahogany tripod table from the era of King George III to yet another young married couple with bewildering amounts of dough to spend on fragile antiques. Unlike many of her customers, these two actually seem to have a great deal of knowledge about the objects they crave, and after they ask Cynthia a question about a painting or a pair of candlesticks, they listen keenly to whatever she says, all the while trading little conspiratorial glances, as if trying telepathically to decide whether or not to offer on a piece. Gilty Pleasures on Castro is still *the* place to shop in northern California for people interested in old English and early American furnishings. The problem with the business now is the same problem it has had for the past ten years, and that is half the time it is closed. Cynthia used to be open all day long six days a week, but after a disastrous trip to New York and the heartbreaking alienation from her beloved sister, and the crushing depression that the loss of Leslie caused in Cynthia, she can manage only two or three hours a day. Her energies simply will not return, despite the cavalcade of cheerful little pills that march through her system. Now the sign on the door says BY APPOINTMENT ONLY above the telephone number of a cell that lives in the glove compartment of her car, a phone whose ring she often as not can't hear and whose backlog of messages she rarely checks.

Right now, her shop is filled with English and early American pieces, many of them coming straight out of Leslie and Alex's house, arriving in crates, unasked-for and unacknowledged. She cannot look at one of them without feeling in the pit of her stomach the terror of that afternoon ten years ago when her sister out of nowhere began accusing her of making a move on Alexander Twisden. The injustice of this cannot be forgotten, the betrayal, the ugliness. Cynthia's boyfriend once tried to convince her to forgive and forget, and even went so far as to suggest she was being rigid, unreasonable, that she was holding on to the insult long past its expiration date. But what was the worth of his advice? Of course he believed in forgiving and forgetting—he was already having an affair and making preparations to leave her.

Yet what can she do with the pieces that arrive? Throw them off the Golden Gate Bridge? Leave them in front of the Salvation Army over on Mission Street? And so she has been selling the vases and the dinnerware and the silver and the mahogany, and the needlepoint and the carpets and the oppressive-but-pricey paintings as they come in.

And why? she often asked herself. Why were Leslie and Alex divesting themselves of their fine furniture, some of which, she has noticed, has had the varnish gnawed off the legs and arms? What was going on in that terrible, crazy house? And what about her niece and nephew, neither of whom she has ever met?

"I'm not really entirely certain this isn't a reproduction," the male half of the newlywed couple says, hoisting a bronze Regency inkwell, the lid of which resembles a book, a Bible perhaps, presided over by an unclothed cherub, all of it set upon nine inches of black marble.

"I can assure you that it's original," Cynthia says. "It's been with one family for over two hundred years."

In actuality, it is one of the items Leslie had sent to her shortly after Cynthia left New York and fled back to San Francisco.

"It's very beautiful," the wife says, tapping her finger on the cherub's naked bottom. She smiles apologetically at Cynthia, and, in a flash, Cynthia sees the whole tedious landscape of their marriage, how this poor girl will be forever smoothing over all the feathers that her husband rudely ruffles. She will be picking up the dirty socks of his bad behavior until she drops dead—or gets the hell out.

Just then the phone in the shop begins to ring. Cynthia squints at the caller-ID box on the phone, but the plastic is smudged and her eyes are not really very good, and so, as usual, despite the technological prompt, she has no idea who is calling. Normally she doesn't bother to pick up, but this time she does, primarily as a way of keeping herself from saying something rude to the young man.

"Gilty Pleasures," she says instead of hello.

The sound of breathing, heavy and troubled. She ought to hang up—listening to some pathetic creep pleasure himself is not her idea of a good start to a day. But she gives it one more try and repeats the store's name.

"Cindy," the voice says, and there are only two people alive who still call her that, and one of them, her mother, is in a coma.

"Hello, Leslie." Cynthia glances at the arch clock somberly ticking next to the telephone; it's eleven in California, two in the afternoon in New York. Assuming Leslie is in New York. She may be in France, or on the moon. Cynthia waits for Leslie to give the reason for the call, but all there is is more breathing. It's both alarming and annoying, and Cynthia is about to hang up.

"Cindy?"

"What do you want, Leslie? I'm surprised you would even—"

"I'm sorry. I'm so sorry."

Cynthia presses her lips together, but she feels the strong pressure of tears filling her eyes.

"Are you okay, Les?" She cannot help herself.

"No."

"No?"

"No, I'm not, I'm not…" Leslie is crying—or is she? Horrible, strangulated howls of what seems to be grief pour out of her, but they do not sound like anything Cynthia has ever heard before. She wonders— Alex? Has something happened to Alex? Or has Alex—whose disgusting, insane behavior was, finally, at the root of the fight between the two sisters—left her, hit her, done something unforgivable?

"What's going on, Les? Why are you calling?"

"My babies…"

Oh my God, Cynthia thinks. *What could be worse?*

"What's happened to them?"

"I don't know."

"You don't know?" Cynthia hears the chime of sleigh bells followed by the vigorous closing of the door—the newlyweds have moved on, looking for another antique store in which hubby can demonstrate his expertise.

"They ran away!"

"Both of them?"

"Yes."

"How long ago?"

"I don't know."

"You don't know. How can you not know?" Cynthia feels herself being drawn into the old and beautiful familiarity of her relationship with her younger sister, and she tries to stop the process—it's like having ten years sober and suddenly being tempted by a bottle of Boone's Farm.

"Two days, maybe?" At this point, Leslie tends to mark time in meals, but she knows if she says *four eatings ago* it will push Cynthia away. She feels a twist of impatience. How is it that Alex can still use his wristwatch, pay bills, talk to people on the outside?

"Have you notified the police?" Cynthia asks.

Leslie is silent. Finally, she says, "Yes."

"And what do they say?"

"Nothing. They won't help."

"They won't help?"

"You have to!"

"I have to what?"

"Help us. We're flap…"

"Flap?"

"Not flap. Um…frantic. We are frantic.…"

* * *

Cynthia lives in a six-room apartment in Telegraph Hill, and after closing Gilty Pleasures earlier than planned she sits at her breakfast counter drinking green tea and eating shortbread cookies. She hears music from her neighbor's apartment, bright, happy, up-tempo music, folk-rocky good-girl music, music that sounds like a mockery of Cynthia's inner life.

She dunks her shortbread cookie into her tea—the nice thing about living alone is you don't have to be too fussy about your eating habits, or anything else pertaining to manners. She swirls the cookie around, wanting it to absorb the maximum amount of moisture before she eats it.

The crumbs from the cookie disperse in the tea, floating this way and that. There is something about it that trips a memory, and Cynthia is instantly transported to her childhood home in St. Louis, to the playroom in her family's drafty Tudor near Washington University. The two sisters are playing tea party, but with their own personal pop bent to it—they are two married women making tea for their husbands, Daryl Hall and John Oates.

A tornado of longing for her sister whirls through Cynthia. She covers her face and weeps into her hands. It feels all right to weep, to shed the tears she failed to shed when her connection to her sister was severed. Once she has composed herself, she opens up her laptop and books her flight to New York. She chooses the first flight out the next day, but then she cancels that reservation and finds another flight for today, 4:00 p.m., which will get her to JFK a little before two in the morning, and then she changes that to the red-eye, which will get her in around six.

Adam and Alice have, for the time being, fallen in with Rodolfo and his wild friends. Peter has gone into some sort of rage and no one can hang out at his apartment where the manacled parents are kept, but none of the gang seems to care about this one way or the other. They are all used to getting bounced out of places. Camps, schools, restaurants, movie theaters, playgrounds, amusement parks, beaches, their own homes. Some disperse to Central Park; a couple of them mention something about Carl Schurz Park way on the Upper East Side; and the rest, including Alice and Adam, simply walk as a pack two blocks south and one block west to an apartment on Riverside Drive.

Here the ruination of the place is so extreme that in comparison, Peter's place seems cozy. The new hanging-out spot is the home of a fleshy, sneering girl whom everyone calls Chiquita. She wears a brown-and-white Peruvian wool cap and has several tattoos that run like angry tears from the corners of her eyes down her cheeks. Her voice is low and foggy; she sounds as if she has a bad cold, or has just awakened. The apartment is on the top floor of an older building on Riverside and when Chiquita brings her friends in, the doorman pretends to find something interesting in the tips of his shoes, making not the slightest gesture as the rank file of boys and girls streams past him, with their smell of smoke and wind and squirrel and hormonal chaos trailing after them like exhaust out the back of a bus.

The wooden floors of Chiquita's apartment are bare and so scratched and warped that it looks as if a hockey team has been over them with their skates on. Except for a high-backed sofa, there is not a stick of furniture in the apartment, and the sofa itself is piled with everything from broken ice trays to lamb bones.

The windows are covered with sheets and blankets. The wind makes its frigid way into the apartment; the window glass has long been shattered, and all there is are empty mullions. The walls, where holes have not been banged through them, are thoroughly defaced with incomprehensible graffiti, everything from anarchist As to ravings that are apparently obscenities in an unknown language, judging from the furious energy that seems to emanate from the letters.

Teenagers of indeterminate gender chase and grope each other, and there is shit on the floor. Literally, shit on the floor.

Alice instinctively takes Adam's hand.

"What's with your sister?" Rodolfo asks, sneering. Ever since Alice called Adam and he found his way over to the West Side, Rodolfo has been weird toward him. When they walked on the sidewalk, Rodolfo continually "accidentally" bumped into Adam, sometimes so hard that he forced him off the sidewalk. When he speaks to Adam he stands too close to him, and he also likes to throw playful punches, usually stopping an inch short of Adam's stomach, but when the target of the punch is Adam's arm Rodolfo is not always so careful to stop before contact is made.

"She's fine," Adam says.

"It's disgusting in here," Alice says softly, though there is no way Chiquita can possibly hear her—Chiquita has taken a scrawny kid by the back of his neck and pushed his face down onto the crunchy sofa, with its freight of bones and other kinds of garbage.

"Really?" Rodolfo says. "You want to go somewhere else?"

"It stinks in here," Alice says, defiantly.

"Why not let's go to your house then," Rodolfo says.

"We can't," Adam says.

"Shut up," Rodolfo says, rather placidly.

Adam feels a slow cold flutter of fear that begins in the pit of his stomach and radiates like ripples in a pond up and down his body.

"You shut up," Alice says, glaring at Rodolfo and gripping her brother's hand even more tightly.

Rodolfo smiles. "You've got good spirit," he says. He thumps his hand against his chest. "All right, both of you. Come with me, and just shut the fuck up and listen to what I say."

Rodolfo leads them to an empty room at the back of the apart-ment. The walls have just been painted dark gray, and the windows are open to air the place out, though it is still so full of fumes that Adam and Alice cover their mouths and noses as soon as they walk in.

"First you got to give me a kiss," Rodolfo says to Alice.

"Sorry, I don't kiss," Alice says through her splayed fingers.

"Come on. Please."

"No way."

"Please?"

"Just let her alone," Adam says.

Rodolfo dismisses him with a wave "Okay," he says. "Here's the deal. There is a guy over in Europe and a lot of people went to him because they couldn't have kids. My parents went to him fifteen years ago; they were one of the first. He's a doctor, the Europe guy. But a fucked-up one. Really fucked up. And I think your parents went there too. A lot of people did. Hundreds. Sometimes it worked out fine. And sometimes it didn't work out."

"There's nothing wrong with us," Adam says. He hears mayhem coming from the front of the apartment—a girl's screams, the kind where you don't know if she's having fun or really upset—but he makes himself keep his eyes right on Rodolfo.

"Maybe there is and maybe not," Rodolfo says. "How old are you again?"

"Ten," Adam says with a shrug, as if he might be older but has lost track.

"If anything's weird, it usually shows up later. But how about your parents? How fucking weird are they?" He sees the looks in their eyes, feels some small measure of pity for them. "It's not their fault. And it wasn't my parents' fault neither."

"Either," says Alice.

"You're pissing me off," Rodolfo says. "You two are running because you're scared, and Rodolfo is here to tell you, you're scared for a reason. These people get fucking weird. You know what I'm saying?

They get hungry, they get thinking all crazy and shit. No matter how much they love us."

From the front of the apartment comes the sound of a scuffle, shouts, and breaking glass. Rodolfo's eyes light up, and with a skater's grace he pivots and runs toward the noise, leaving Adam and Alice alone in the cold, redolent room.

"We should get out of here," Adam says.

"To where?" Alice asks. "It's cold out."

"It's cold here, and it's dangerous."

"So where? Home?"

"Would you do that?" he asks.

"Would you?"

He shakes his head no. "Why do they want to hurt us?" Adam asks.

"I don't think Dad wants to hurt anyone," Alice says, uncertainly.

"He's worser than her."

"Worse," Alice corrects.

A sudden loud bang. A leaded-glass door leading to a balcony has blown open. Cold air rushes in like water through a breach in a ship's hull, and the two children rush across the room to shut the door, their heads bent against the stiff icy wind.

Yet at the moment they are closing the door, they hear a voice, merry, welcoming, and adult.

"Hello there, you!" the voice says. If a voice could have an actual weight, this would be a very fat voice, a voice with a full belly.

The twins wordlessly consult each other and venture a look out onto the balcony to see who has called to them.

What they see is so horrible and bizarre that they both stand transfixed despite the cold and the wind that threatens to lift them up, twirl them around, and send them hurtling to the street below. There is not one adult, but two. And both of them are immensely fat, stuffed into chairs so tightly that it seems doubtful that either of them could ever get out. Checked blankets are draped over their knees, and they sit there looking out over the railing of the balcony as if on the deck of a ship sailing around the South Pole. One of them seems to be a man and the other a woman, though, really, there is not much difference in appearance between them. Both have long hair, matted and knotted. Both wear filthy overcoats, split at the seams—silky white satin lining oozes from beneath their arms. They wear rubber boots; the floor of the balcony is slick with something wet. A giant fried-chicken bucket is between them.

"Don't worry about us," the bloated parent closest to the door says to Adam and Alice. "We're armless."

"Harmless," the other one corrects. Now that he has spoken, it seems he is the male of the couple. "Time was we could ramble and rumble with the best of them."

"Y-y-yow," his wife says, lazily pawing at the cold gray air with her left hand while groping uselessly around the empty Popeyes chicken bucket with her right.

The husband squints at Adam and Alice, cocks his head to one side. "Twins. Am I right?"

Alice and Adam nod. They have an impulse to run—but to where?

"I'm surprised more of us didn't twin," the husband goes on. "But as far as I can tell, most of you little ragamuffins came out one at a time. And I guess it's a good thing too. It's hard enough keeping you guys in check."

"You can say that again," the wife concurs.

"You know," the husband says, sighing and rubbing his swollen belly, "I love my daughter, we both do. What parent doesn't? But would I repeat all we went through?"

"Don't do that," the wife says. "Don't do that Donald Rumsfeld thing of asking yourself questions. That I can't stand."

"Well, we'll just agree to disagree on that, okay?" the husband says with a quick knifelike flash of his icy smile. "But if we're making suggestions, then I suggest you just let your mind wander off somewhere while I talk to these twins, who, I believe, have never been here before. Am I right about that?" He points to Adam.

"I never been here," Adam says.

"Me neither," says Alice.

"Well then, welcome." He beckons them closer with eager waves.

Automatically, Alice moves toward him, but Adam stops her with a hard squeeze of her hand, a gesture that does not escape the man's notice; he frowns and knits his brow.

"So I'm assuming," the man says, "that your parents were clients of the great and wonderful and miraculous and trailblazing Dr. Kis, who probably by now is the richest shithead in all Slovenia."

Adam and Alice, having no idea what he's talking about, remain silent.

"Am I right?" the man persists. "Are you two products of Dr. Kis?" He points at Alice, who he has already decided is the more vulnerable of the two and so more likely to succumb to his pressures.

"I don't know," Alice says, shrugging.

"Really? You never heard your parents speak of the great and all-powerful Dr. Kis? No mention of Ljubljana? No private little jokes about the drug fiend who works as his assistant?"

The children are silent.

"Why don't you answer?" the woman says, at last withdrawing her hand from the bucket and energetically licking her fingers.

"We don't go to doctors at our house," Adam finally says.

Chiquita comes onto the balcony pushing a supermarket cart. The cart, as seems to be the case with so many of them, has one errant wheel in front, and it is filled with chicken—roasted, fried, and raw.

The two bloated adults fall silent, their eyes widening with anticipation as their daughter wheels the thirty pounds of poultry toward them.

"I do like my chicken," the father says, his voice rich with desire and self-mockery.

"Always did and always will," says the mother.

"Not like some," the father says, as if in his own defense. "With their taste for live meat—or human beings."

"Was never our thing," the mother agrees.

"No accounting for taste," the father says.

"I wouldn't mind taking me a nibble of one of these little morsels," the mother says, laughing, gesturing toward the twins.

Chiquita gives Adam and Alice a hard, questioning glance before turning to the business at hand, which is to put today's haul near her parents without getting too close to them.

"Do you guys need to be hosed down or anything?" she asks as she slides the buckets, flats, and packages of chicken over to her parents.

"No hurry, sweetie," her father says.

"Come over here and give me a kiss," says her mother.

"Yeah, right, I'll be doing a lot of that," Chiquita says.

"Come on," her mother insists. "Give me some sugar."

"Don't," her husband advises. "You're only going to make things worse."

"You're lucky I don't kill you both," Chiquita says without much passion, as if she is simply pointing something out.

"What do you call this?" her mother says, indicating her gargantuan girth and her husband's.

"No one forced you to eat," Chiquita says. As she backs up, she steps on Alice's foot, then turns around and glares at her.

"You know we can't help it," the mother says, taking one of the raw cutlets in hand, sniffing it for a moment, and then tearing into it.

"You were always fat," Chiquita says, turning back and jabbing her finger toward her mother.

"That is completely untrue, and totally rude," her father says. He has chosen one of the roasted chickens, which he has dropped onto his enormous lap.

"You would have eaten me, if you could."

"But we didn't," her father reminds her. "Ask your little friends here, ask them if they feel safe around their parents. The temptation. The terrible temptation."

"Lead us not into temptation," her mother intones, attempting to lift her hand.

"At night," the father continues, "especially at night, when the will is weakest. To have a delectable thing right there in your house, sleeping, half naked. We resisted that temptation. Most cannot. It overwhelms, it cripples, it humiliates. Yet we resisted. You don't know how lucky you had it. Oh, how sharper than a serpent's tooth it is to have a thankless child!"

When the father mentions teeth, the mother, in a sort of involuntary reflex, curls her lips, revealing to Adam and Alice her own teeth, which are deeply discolored, of normal size in the center but enormous and dagger-sharp on either side.

Early the next morning, Cynthia, who took a taxi from JFK, stands in front of her sister's town house looking up at its dark windows, each one filled with reflections of bare trees, the empty branches looking like desolation itself. She is furious with herself for failing to dress for the cold New York weather; every gust of wind feels like punishment for her haste. She places her small suitcase on the sidewalk and blows on her hands to warm them. A postman walks past in a hat with fur flaps, looking like a Russian soldier. He glances at Cynthia, stops, and shifts his bag from one shoulder to the other.

"You visiting there?" he asks Cynthia.

"Why do you ask?"

"You can tell them I stopped delivering. Mail just piles up—it's a hazard. So if they want their mail they can go over to the branch and pick it up. You tell them that, all right?"

"I didn't say I was going to be visiting anyone," Cynthia says, but the mailman has already passed her by and she is not sure he heard her.

She tries Leslie's phone for the sixth time this morning and is bounced over to voicemail yet again. *I didn't come all this way to stand on the street,* she thinks, and, after picking up her suitcase, she mounts the five-step staircase to the front door. An air of dereliction is over everything. Unswept leaves have been frozen onto the porch landing. The glass that borders the front door has been papered over from the inside, so no one can peek in, not even for a glimpse of the foyer. A whiff of something dank and possibly even rotten wafts from the house. When Cynthia rings the doorbell, the button wobbles in its casing, and when she pushes it again and again and presses her ear against the door, she hears nothing but the thump of her own heartbeat. The bell is surely not working, and so she knocks, casually at first, with a light rap of her knuckles, and then vigorously—yet still there is no answer.

Oh! Cynthia remembers something, and it's too bad for her, because it would have been better forgotten—more than ten years ago, when Cynthia often traveled to New York to buy stock for Gilty Pleasures and used her sister's beautiful home as her headquarters, Leslie and Alex had graciously given her a set of keys so she could come and go at will and feel that the place was truly her own. Had she ever gotten around to throwing those keys away?

Cynthia opens her handbag and finds her key ring, a tarnished silver circle three inches in diameter holding at least twenty keys: for her car, her bicycle lock, her health-club locker, her summer rental at Stinson Beach, her mother's apartment, her mother's and her safe-deposit box, and four keys for her own apartment. She can't really tell one from the other, but the third one she tries in Leslie's door slips right in. Cynthia's breath catches in her throat, and the lock is satisfied with a deep, resonant click.

She pushes the door open, though something within her tells her not to—something frightened and wise and insistent. She steps in, calling out for her sister as she walks with utmost trepidation into the foyer.

"Leslie?" she says, stepping into the first room to her left, what was once a sitting room graced with lovely old pieces and presided over by the stern gazes of various extinct Twisdens: admirals and bankers, with their ruffles, their flushed cheeks, their bright, avaricious eyes. Now the room is used only for the storage of things that there seems to be no earthly reason for storing—boxes of oversize plastic bags, piles of sheets and towels, broken cutlery.

Cynthia senses that someone has crept close behind her, and she whirls around, but there is no one there, just the faint trace of her own breath in the cold watery air.

As so often happens, fear lops over into anger and she is suddenly furious with her sister for breaking the long silence between them. And where in the hell is she? Cynthia stops, breathes, reminds herself that she is being unreasonable. Leslie called in the first place because she was frantic that the twins had gone missing. And Leslie is not here probably because she is out somewhere in the city searching for them. It doesn't matter how many people are on the hunt—no mother is going to sit home and wait for a call when she could be out looking herself.

"Leslie!" Cynthia calls. Her voice echoes through the house, up and down the empty stairways. She gropes for the light switch, turns it on. Weak, anemic light drifts from the overhead lamps.

"Alex?" Again she waits, and again all she hears is her own voice, bouncing around the house like the lonely cry of a ghost.

Cynthia crosses the foyer, this time going right rather than left, and enters what had once been a library, a temperature-controlled home for first editions, most of them bound in leather, many of them hundreds of years old. The dark cherry shelves are still there, but they are empty now, and the old leather chair placed near the shelves, where once you could curl up and read, has sprouted a spring from its seat cushion, and the arms are ragged, as if cat-clawed. It smells like cats. It smells like cats, best-case scenario....

Her heart is pounding harder and harder. She can feel it in her throat, even behind her eyes. Something is wrong.

"Leslie!" she calls out, and she can detect the fear in her own voice. She puts down her suitcase, clears her throat, calls again, but the fear is still there. It will not go away. It grows like spores, like cancer, choking her. She lowers her head, tries to clear her throat more forcefully, and wonders: *Am I going to puke?*

No, she's not going to get sick, not just yet: She's going to scream. She's going to scream because something has touched her from behind, something cold and a little bit slimy, and it has touched her on the bare skin on the back of her leg, just above the line of her boot. She whirls to see a rat, dashing from one side of the room to the other, glancing at Cynthia over its shoulder as it makes its way to its escape route in the tile-lined fireplace. As it disappears into a crevice, she hears a chorus of twitters and cheeps, the colony of kith and kin awaiting it in the dankness of the inner walls, where the vermin conduct their parallel lives.

Cynthia's legs wobble, as if fear exerted a weight upon her that is more than she can bear. She staggers forward and is about to steady herself by grabbing hold of the mantel, but the commotion of the rats freezes her. She backs up without remembering she placed her suitcase on the floor, and she trips on it and must wave her hands frantically to stop herself from falling flat on her back.

"Leslie!" she cries, as much out of fury as fear.

Yet the fury has a cauterizing effect. It scorches the terror and kills it at its root. The next thing Cynthia knows, she is heading up the narrow staircase leading to the second floor, where, back in the time when she was a regular visitor here, most of the socializing took place. How happy everyone was! How comfortable and beautiful and full of style and ideas! The tinkle of cocktail glasses, the sexy whisper of silk, always the smell of fresh roses, their dark red petals beaded with mist...Why oh why oh why did they not remain satisfied with what they had? Why the mania to have a child, the very thing (of this Cynthia is convinced) that ruined everyone's life? Why did Leslie go along with Alex's mania for an heir? For surely it was Alex's doing, surely his vanity and stubborn old-school values were behind the project. Why was someone who would never think of having a reproduction on his wall so mad to reproduce?

The stair creaks beneath her weight. Cynthia stops, waits, listens. This time she does not call out her sister's name but proceeds again toward the house's second story, one stealthy footstep at a time. But when she is halfway up, something stops her. A sound. From below. What is it? Barking? A human cry? She turns. Waits.

Adam and Alice make their way through Central Park, heading toward the Upper East Side for no better reason than they are marginally more familiar with that part of the city. It is not even noon, but it looks as if evening has already rolled over the city. Dark, heavy clouds hover threateningly over the defiant spires of the great apartment houses on either edge of Central Park. Rain? Snow?

Alice shivers, and Adam puts his arm over her shoulders as they bow their heads and walk quickly into the wind. A woman in high-heeled boots has just had her umbrella flip inside out and she turns in a circle trying to get it under her control, as if the broken black thing were going wild with the pain of its own brokenness.

"Are you okay?" Adam asks his sister.

"I'm okay. Are you?"

"I wonder where we're going."

Alice smiles; this somehow strikes her as funny. "I wonder too," she says.

After a few moments of silence, Alice says, "Mom and Dad aren't like those two up on the balcony."

"I guess not."

"I still think they're nice," Alice says.

"Me too," says Adam. "Most of the time. But you know what?"

"What?"

"We can never go back."

Suddenly, they stop in their tracks. They both see it—the dark, windblown, somehow familiar silhouette of a man at the crest of a hill not more than fifty feet away from them.

"Fucking fuck," Adam whispers.

Alice squints. Her nostrils dilate as she cranes her neck forward.

"It's not him," she says.

As the man jogs past, it becomes obvious it's not him, and they hold hands and run, laughing, their hair streaming behind them in the cold wind as they move like beautiful wild creatures across the park. *Not him! Not him!*

They don't speak of it, but they veer in a northerly direction as they continue their dash toward the Upper East Side, heading toward Berryman Prep, though they could not say why. Neither of them believes that this will be a safe place for them. If their parents are not sitting there at this very moment waiting for them, then they will surely come by at some point. Or someone from the school will call them. Do they think that Michael Medoff can somehow help them? Not really. They are not thinking of anything in particular. They are cold, they are tired, they feel frightened and alone, and they are heading toward their school because it is a weekday and that is where they belong. What they would really like to do is go home. They would even like to be locked into their rooms. They want to see their parents—even as they run from them. But all of that is wrecked, all of it is impossible. So they are running toward school because right now they simply don't know where else to go.

In all the many times Cynthia has been in this house, she has never been in the cellar—why would she? Yet now here she stands. A door beneath the staircase. She puts her ear to it—silence. But she waits until she hears it. A low, rumbling growl. She turns the engraved copper doorknob—but it won't budge. She twists it back and forth—but it is locked tightly.

She knocks against the old, heavy wood. "Hello?"

And sure enough: barks rise up, exhausted and hopeless, the calls of animals who have barked and barked and now assume no one will ever hear or care but who must bark nevertheless.

But wait…There is something else. Another sound. Another *kind* of sound. A sound within those sounds. A human voice.

With ever more urgency, she tries to open the door. Key…key…Where would the logical hiding place be? She reaches as high as her arm can stretch and feels along the crown molding over the door frame, the invisible dust like seal skin. She feels the cool metal teeth of a large, old-fashioned key.

Without meaning to, she brushes it off its perch, and it rattles to the floor, skitters along the bare wood, and comes to rest somewhere beneath an old, vaguely Victorian table upon which Leslie and Alex have piled hundreds of pieces of mail, everything from catalogs and magazines to Con Ed bills.

The dogs below begin barking with renewed vigor. But where has the key gone? It's shadowy beneath the stairs, and even in the bright part of the day it's nearly dark here. Cynthia gets on her hands and knees and reaches beneath the table, blindly groping for the key. She sweeps her hand back and forth. Dust has accumulated here, as thick as the web of seeds inside a cantaloupe. "Acchh," she says.

Her back is to the front door, so she does not see the wedge of light that has fallen over her, as long and narrow as a sword. She did not hear the opening of the front door, and she does not hear the footsteps drawing closer and closer to her. She has no idea that she is no longer alone.

Leslie is looming above her, her eyes yellow with rage.

* * *

Michael can no longer tolerate the lonely tension of sitting in his apartment waiting for *someone* to tell him *something*. He has called every hospital in the city. He has called a few of their friends, not one of whom seemed to grasp the severity of the situation—"You haven't heard anything from Xavier, have you?" has been taken by all of them as pertaining to some huge domestic squabble rather than as the emergency Michael knows it is. He can also no longer tolerate the bored, bureaucratic tone of the cop who answers his calls at the precinct and who tells him to "Sit tight," as if Michael's nervousness was slightly annoying and possibly even getting in the way of the search for Xavier— a search that Michael is certain is not taking place. And, finally, he cannot tolerate the hourly phone calls from Rosalie, whose suspicions of disaster are, as time passes, even stronger than his own.

And so he walks the streets of his city. Where to look? There is no logical place. He stops in the Greek coffee shop they both like, and he hits a couple of similar establishments, the one they go to when the one they like is crowded, and the one they haven't gone to since Xavier found an eyelash in the yolk of his poached egg. Nothing. Michael weaves in and out of shops—shoe stores, magazine stores—and he scours the faces of passersby, as if one of them might betray in a glance some knowledge of Xavier's whereabouts.

He walks north, following the route of the Lexington Avenue subway line, which rumbles beneath him as he goes. He walks quickly, then slowly, then quickly again; a half hour passes, an hour. He pulls his cell phone out of his jacket and sees it is actually Xavier's phone. He flips it open to see if anyone has called. Nothing, nada, bupkes…He calls the landline in the apartment. Nothing…He calls his own cell phone and listens to the ring, but, no, that's intolerable. The thought of that phone ringing in Xavier's pocket as Xavier lies— what? Dead? In someone else's bed? Cuckoo in some clobbered amnesiac state? Intolerable…Michael stops, tries to catch his breath.

He forces himself to calm down. Nothing could be less productive than losing hope. When he finally takes a deep, normal breath he realizes he has walked all the way to Berryman Prep, its schizophrenic architecture—half of it was built in 1894 and half of it in 2007—carved against the steely sky.

Alex walks the streets of New York looking for any sign of his children. His eyes sweep the crowded sidewalks left to right. He sees everything and everyone. His jacket is unbuttoned. He takes deep sweet breaths and when he exhales, long plumes of exhaust stream from his nostrils.

He thinks of Xavier, whom he has already tasted, marinating in his own juice in the holding pen. The thought sends a shiver of delight through Alex, a ruffle of pleasure in the pit of his stomach. It reminds him of how he felt as a young, young man when he thought about having sex, and just the dream of it could send a fandango of sweet pleasure all the way through him, as true as a tuning fork; just the thought of it, the fantasy, the possibility…He stops. A memory! When was the last time he had a real memory? When had his mind sifted through the debris of the past and found something to seize upon? Memories are what make us human…and he is having one.

But as quickly and unexpectedly as memory comes, it departs, leaving him blank, confused. He finds himself standing on the corner of Fifty-Seventh and Fifth, with the businesspeople and the shoppers and the blind pencil seller with his delicious-looking dog. *Where am I?* he thinks. He wipes his nose with his sleeve. Looks around. *Oh, yes.* It comes back. He must find his offspring.

Seeing her sister after all these years has jolted Leslie back to a state of near humanity, and she sits with her now in the kitchen, weeping openly, so overcome with sorrow, and worry, and a swirl of other, unnameable emotions that it is nearly impossible to speak.

Cynthia watches her sister weep into her own hands. She surveys the kitchen with ever-increasing revulsion and alarm. The sink is full of dirty dishes—no: filthy dishes. Dishes that might be impossible to scrape and get clean and would be better thrown away. The floor is not so much dirty as oily, greasy. It is a trial even to walk from one part of the kitchen to another. How do these people live like this? It's no wonder the children have disappeared—they are hoping to escape the gross microbial infestation of this place! It's a wonder they weren't removed! The dopey calendar on the wall is a year out of date. The only nod toward an existence beyond sheer animal survival is a vase full of cut flowers, but even here the gesture has turned rancid: the flowers are dead and blackened, and the water in the vase is dark green and has a putrid smell.

How can Leslie—who as a girl refused to drink soda from a pop-top can because the tab went down into the can, possibly bringing with it an avalanche of germs—how can she live this way? How?

"I've tried so hard to be a good mother," Leslie says.

"I know, I know," Cynthia says, though the only knowledge she has of the quality of Leslie's maternal efforts is the state of this house, which suggests the profoundest sort of neglect.

Leslie uncovers her face, slaps her hands once, rather briskly, against her cheeks. "You know, I never really wanted children."

"I know. I didn't either. We're not the breeding kind, it seems."

"But you stuck to your guns," Leslie says.

"I didn't have an Alex pressuring me."

"We can't blame Alex. People are when they are."

Cynthia furrows her brow. *People are when they are?*

"What do you mean?" she asks.

"I mean *where*," Leslie says. "No. *Who.*" She lowers her eyes. "I'm very tired."

"What are the police saying?" Cynthia asks.

Leslie's eyes widen, and she looks as if she is going to say something but stops herself. "Nothing," she finally manages. She tries to look directly at her sister, but it is more than she can do. Her eyes, instead, take in the disorder of the room. "Sorry the place is such a mess," she murmurs.

"Do you mind telling me what's going on?" Cynthia says. "Where is all your stuff, for God's sake?"

"Oh, Alex sold it. Most of it. Some of it…you know, just sort of wore out."

"And do you mind telling me why Alex is suddenly selling antiques that have been in his family for generations?"

"Because we need money. Things aren't going so well at work. For either of us, really. The economy and all. And this place…it's expensive keeping it up."

"Yes, I can imagine. You have a whole house in the middle of Manhattan. Why don't you move to something smaller? An apartment."

"Privacy, I guess. You can't put a price on privacy."

Suddenly, as if to prove her point, howls rise up through the floorboards, muffled, distant, but unmistakable.

"Leslie!" Cynthia says. "What the fuck?"

"What?" Leslie says, as if she cannot imagine what the matter might be.

"What do you have down there?"

"Oh, that…Yeah. Our dog. Some of the soundproofing came down. It's so difficult getting people to do anything, and Alex and I have to do everything ourselves."

"Why do you need soundproofing for a dog?"

"Well, yeah, dogs. More than one."

"How many?"

"Two?"

"Are you asking me or telling me?"

"Three," Leslie says. She shifts in her chair. She swallows.

"What is going on here, Leslie? I am exhausted. I've come clear across the country. And I did it for you. I did it because you are my sister and I love you. I love you in spite of…" She gestures toward Leslie's face, her body, to indicate the damage done. "But now I want some real answers."

"Don't pressure me, Cyn."

"What am I hearing down there? That's not two dogs, or three…"

"I feel cornered, Cyn." A note of hysteria has entered Leslie's voice. She flexes her hands, stretching her fingers to their full length, relaxing them, stretching them again.

"I'm asking you what's going on."

"You're asking and asking and asking!" Leslie screams. She leaps up from her chair, and her eyes dart this way and that, as if she fears something is about to come after her, or perhaps she is looking for a way to escape.

"Leslie! Sit down. You're acting—"

"Don't tell me what to do! My children are missing." Leslie picks up the vase filled with dead reeking flowers and throws it against the wall, smashing it to pieces. Her face is contorted, her eyes two red wounds. She lunges for the sink and begins to empty it, smashing cups glasses plate and platters. "My babies! My babies! I have to have my babies!"

Cynthia cringes in her chair and her heart begins to race. She covers her ears against the nerve-racking sounds of all that shattering glass combined with the wails of her distraught sister. And—what's this? Howls from the cellar. Louder than before. Louder than ever, as if the beasts caged below are rising on a ladder made of their own yowling agony and will be in this very room in no time.

Suddenly, Leslie is still. Drool pours from her mouth. Her eyes are cast down, and she breathes heavily, trying to calm herself. Gradually, inch by inch, she lifts her eyes and turns to Cynthia. She is breathing through her mouth.

"Something's happening," she says.

"Leslie," Cynthia says.

"Something's happening."

"Shhh…shhh…sit down."

"I'm changing," Leslie says. "Oh dear God, please help me." She sits down and covers her face with trembling hands.

"Leslie!" Cynthia cries. "I'm calling an ambulance."

But as suddenly as Leslie ceded control of herself to the hunger and the rage within, she regains her composure.

"I need you to do me a favor, Cynthia. And I know—believe me, I know—you do not owe me anything. I have been a horrible sister. I have been a monster."

Cynthia's eyes fill with tears. Despite everything, it's unbearable to hear her sister talk like this.

"What do you want me to do, Leslie?"

Leslie wipes the corner of her mouth with the back of her hand. Slowly, she rises from her chair and makes her way across the kitchen. She pulls one of the cupboard drawers out—but with so much vigor that the entire thing jumps out of its track and she is left holding it as various carving tools clatter onto the floor, making their terrible racket. Leslie reaches for the largest of the several knives and carries it back to the table.

It is deeply frightening to Cynthia to have her sister approaching her with a weapon, and she is only marginally less frightened when Leslie slaps the knife down onto the table.

"Pick it up," Leslie says, sitting down.

"All right," Cynthia says, grabbing the knife. She feels safer with the knife in her hands. The blade is two feet long, eight inches wide. It looks as if it was made to carve an elephant.

"Now what?" Cynthia asks.

"Use it."

"What do you mean?"

"I mean use it. On me. Get me out of this. Please."

"Leslie. You're not in your right mind."

"Do you think I don't know that? I lock my children in their rooms at night. And you want to know why? Because I'm terrified of what I will do if I see them."

"What do you think you'll do?"

"Devour them. Rip the flesh from their bones." Leslie lifts her chin, pulls her shoulders back; there is a note of defiance in her voice. "And now they know it too. Kids, they know everything. You really should have had children, Cyn. It's an amazing experience. There's nothing like it."

"This is crazy talk, Leslie. I'm going to get you some help."

"There is no help for me, Cynthia. I can't even kill myself. I need you to do it. I'm begging you. Please."

"Leslie…"

"Just do it. You've got the knife. Now use it. Use it! Use it, you fucking stupid cow."

By now, Leslie has risen from her chair. She seems almost to be levitating, riding the current of her own fury. Her eyes show no white whatsoever. The veins, stiff and straight as chopsticks, bulge from her neck, and her face is crimson. Afraid for her life, Cynthia clutches the knife tighter and holds the point toward her sister to stop her from getting any closer while Leslie lets loose with an unending and almost indecipherable torrent of obscene insults, calling into question everything about Cynthia—her looks, her fertility, her truthfulness, her smell.

But after emptying this sewer of invective and seeing that no matter what she says she cannot incite Cynthia to use that knife, Leslie sinks back into her chair, closes her eyes. In the sudden silence, both women hear the distant muffled howls from the cellar below.

"Come on," Leslie says, "follow me. I'll show you how bad it's gotten."

Davis Fleming paces his office, silently mouthing the words of the address he will give next week at the Berryman alumni dinner, which, in what strikes him as a kind of kick-up-your-heels, devil-may-care snubbing of Berryman tradition, will be held *downtown* at a newly opened Italian restaurant called Trattoria Gigi. Normally, this dinner is held at a venerable Upper East Side venue called Wittenborg's, but even the most dyed-in-the-wool Berryman traditionalists have begun to notice and discreetly complain that Wittenborg's food has become somewhat tired, and some would say inedible. This downtown Italian restaurant has garnered enthusiastic reviews and it serves the kind of trendy delicacies the younger alumni seem to crave. The tuna carpaccio has garnered a great deal of praise, and one food writer has remarked that no one in town can foam a Jerusalem artichoke quite like the chef at Trattoria Gigi. Fleming could not care less. His only concern is making up some of the school's battered endowment, which is still depleted in the aftermath of hideous stock-market fluctuations. So if the younger alumni crave Jerusalem artichoke foam, then Jerusalem artichoke foam it shall be. These fresh young zillionaires have weird tastes—in parenting, in clothing, and in food. And my God, do they fret over food. It is so odd to Fleming how much emphasis some people put on what they eat....He himself goes for the basics, just like his father and his father before him. Give him a piece of meat, a half a potato, a green salad, and a glass of ice water, and he will be fine. Maybe a scoop of strawberry ice cream, a cup of coffee— and never mind if it has been organically shade grown!

Thinking of ice cream and coffee somehow eases Davis into a kind of reverie, and he stands now in his office, holding a triple-spaced copy of his remarks, gazing out his window, seeing without actually *seeing* the familiar view of the wrought-iron fence surrounding the school and the sidewalk and pedestrians and street and cars beyond. Then something *does* jolt him out of his dreamy, slightly sleepy state: he sees Michael Medoff walking slowly toward the school, his face stern and unshaved, his gloved hand holding a coffee in a to-go cup.

"Oh no," Fleming says. How can this be happening? He thought he and this idiot had an agreement.

He drops his prepared remarks onto his desk and charges out of his office, putting his coat on in the quiet corridor as he races for the front entrance.

"Mr. Medoff!" he calls as soon as he is outside. Fleming's voice is rich with bonhomie, but his smile has all the warmth of a hacksaw. Medoff is lurking near the entrance, though he shows no sign of intending to actually enter the building, which somehow makes his presence near the school even worse, and more irritating.

"What are you doing here, buddy?" Fleming says, slowing his pace as he approaches the young teacher.

"Doing?" Michael says. He looks around, as if just now realizing where he is. His hair is tousled; the whites of his eyes show little lightning bolts of red. "I'm…just walking."

Fleming glances up at the dank gray sky that looms above them like a chilly platter of raw fish. "Really? Out for a walk?"

Michael nods.

"I thought we had an understanding," Fleming says. He gives Michael's shoulder a couple of vigorous pats. "I thought you understood what's at stake here."

"I have done nothing wrong, Davis, and you know it. The Twisdens are making me the issue when the issue is clearly them. Have you called CPS yet?"

"The point is, Mike—"

"Don't call me Mike. Okay?"

"The point is that in a school atmosphere—especially an elite institution—where there is smoke there is fire."

"Did you just come up with that?"

"You know what I'm talking about. The Twisdens are going to make this about you."

"Yes, you're talking about me being a h-o-m-o."

"I'm talking about allegations of misconduct."

"I repeat: h-o-m-o."

"I'm not going to play little PC games with you, Michael. We're both professionals. We both understand what's involved in protecting this place as a learning environment."

"That boy is terrified. Have you even asked why?"

"What occurs in families is often difficult for outsiders to understand. But here's something everyone understands—he was in your apartment. Do you have any idea what kind of trouble that could cause—not only for you, but for the whole of Berryman Prep? We are days away from a major fund-raising event. We don't need this shit, okay? You understand? We do not need this shit. Am I talking your language?"

"Are you talking my language? Because you said *shit*? What the fuck is the matter with you, Davis?"

"There's not a mark on these children. They do well in school. There's no sign of distress. Believe me, I've been in the kid business for a long, long time. What did the boy say to you that's made you so determined to make everyone's life miserable? Did he say that he was being beaten?"

"No, he did not."

"Sexually abused?"

"No."

"Anything?"

"Yes."

"What, Mr. Medoff? What?"

"He said that their parents were…" Michael breathes a long sigh. "He thinks, they both think, that their parents are going to eat them."

"Really."

"Yes."

"And you believed him. You are willing to put the reputation and possibly even the financial health of this institution on the line because a ten-year-old boy came to your apartment in the middle of the night and told you his parents were going to eat him up, yum yum yum."

Before Michael can say another word, little Adam Twisden-Kramer rushes to him and throws his arms around his teacher's waist.

Michael, exhausted and brittle with tension, almost loses his footing from the force of the collision, but when he looks down and sees the boy, his dark hair damp, his face pressed into the wool of Michael's coat, his eyes squeezed shut, there is nothing to do but pat the kid lovingly, hoping to impart some small comfort with a touch.

"Hey, hey, what's going on?" Michael says. He sees Alice standing a few feet away, looking on, her face pale and fearful. He looks at her questioningly as Adam continues to hold on to him.

"Do you see this?" Fleming says, his eyes wide, his head shaking back and forth, as if he has just discovered incontrovertible proof of a crime. "This is not a teacher-student relationship here."

Adam appears oblivious to what Fleming is saying and implying and, in fact, doesn't even seem to hear his voice. His grip on Michael only tightens.

Michael pats the top of the boy's head. His hair feels half frozen, thick and a bit oily. At his teacher's touch, Adam looks up, his eyes wild and frightened.

"Hi," the boy says, his voice shredded by uncertainty.

"Are you coming to school?" Michael asks.

Adam shakes his head. Alice tentatively steps a little closer.

"People are looking for you, Adam," Fleming says. "Your parents are worried sick. All of us are. Where have you been?" As he asks this, Fleming reaches for Adam, takes him by the arm. But Adam yanks himself free of Fleming's grip.

"Leave him alone," Alice says. It's almost impossible to believe that voice—grave and harsh and full of threat—could come out of the willowy little girl shivering on the sidewalk.

Fleming is unnerved by it for a moment but he regains control of himself and raises a finger and slowly points it at Alice, a gesture that in the course of his career as an educator may have frightened many a ten-year-old into submission but that on this cold morning has absolutely no effect on Alice.

"I wish I was grown up," Adam says to Michael in little more than a whisper.

"It's not all that it's cracked up to be," Michael tells the boy, stroking his hair. Suddenly, Michael brings himself up short: How will it look to people who see him petting this beautiful ten-year-old boy? What will people make of it? What will they assume? What frightened, hateful thoughts will form in their minds? How is it that heteros, with their long history of savagery toward children (Abraham's willingness to run God's bloody errand was only the beginning!), with their centuries of raping, exploiting, slaughtering, and starving children, have managed to project the propensity to harm onto gay people? Fuck it all. He puts his arm around the boy.

But the boy resists. He sees something. And Alice sees it too.

"I am going to need you two to come inside and we can call your…" Fleming is saying.

Michael has followed the trajectory of the twins' frightened stare and now he sees what they see—Alex Twisden, his shoulders hunched, his head down, his hands jammed into the pockets of his long leather coat. He is rapidly approaching Berryman Prep, and those he passes on the sidewalk step quickly to one side. It would be best not to be jostled by this glowering man, in whom anger and energy seem to sizzle like meat on a grill.

Fleming senses that the twins are about to bolt, and he has the presence of mind to grab Adam by the wrist and Alice by the lapel of her autumn jacket. It is like grabbing a trout under the water or somehow getting your hands on a rabbit in the wild—the smallness of the creature in no way prepares you for its strength and its will to escape your clutches, a will completely undiluted by manners or any hope that you might somehow be merciful.

Adam makes a sound—it's like a quick exhalation of breath, with a guttural dragging noise in it—and twists away from Fleming, while Alice tucks her chin in, takes a quick sniff of Fleming's hand, and then bites it—not so hard as to draw blood, but with enough force to make him relinquish his hold on her.

"Hey!" is all Fleming is able to say. As the twins take each other's hands and run in a westerly direction, he shouts at them, "Welcome to suspension, you two!" He turns, glaring, toward Michael, as if this turn of events were Medoff's fault too.

Michael tosses his to-go cup into the nearby trash can and sets out after the twins—he doesn't know why. Perhaps to bring them back, perhaps to learn why the very sight of their father—Twisden is just now crossing the street at a diagonal, seemingly blind to the traffic—would make Adam and Alice run for their lives.

"Bring them back!" Fleming calls out after Michael. "Bring them right back here."

Fleming watches for a moment as Michael races after the two children. And now they have stopped—they see him coming. Adam reaches out for his teacher with both hands, as if Adam is on a ship that has just left the pier, and Michael, a moment late, must now leap over the freezing waters to get on board.

Suddenly, Fleming feels a powerful thud against his shoulder, and he has to grab onto the fence to stop himself from losing his footing and falling onto the sidewalk.

"You idiot," Twisden says through clenched teeth. "You had them in your hands!" And without another word he speed-walks past Fleming, a hundred, perhaps a hundred and fifty feet behind the twins and Michael. "Kids!" Twisden calls. "Come back! Kids? Come on. Please. I'm not going to—" He stops himself from saying *hurt you,* and in the momentary silence of the suppression, his mouth fills with the imagined taste of blood. His hand goes to his throat and he takes a deep, shuddering breath. *Oh no, no no no,* he thinks. *Please don't let this be happening.*

Without realizing it, Alex has stepped into the street, and his moment of remorse is suddenly invaded by the flat, brutal sound of a car horn. A taxicab has come to a screeching halt a few inches from him, and the driver, a dark young man with little round glasses and a ponytail, is leaning on his horn.

Alex walks to the taxi and opens the door. The driver is reaching for the billy club he keeps wedged between his seat and the door precisely for moments like this. He raises the club to strike Alex, but Alex catches it in mid-arc, pulls it out of the driver's hand, and sends it skittering across the street, where it disappears beneath a parked van.

"That honking hurts my ears," Alex tells the driver before setting off down the street after his children, at first in a kind of easy lope, and then faster and faster. He pulls his phone out of his pocket and dials Leslie as he runs.

Leslie has gone—as soon as the call from Alex came in, telling her that he had found Alice and Adam, she grabbed her coat and raced out. Alone again in the house, Cynthia sits on a falling-apart sofa in front of the fireplace, the cracked tiles of which open into a hidden highway for the countless rats that live within these walls. She has been sitting there immobile for—who knows how long? She is in a state of shock, trying to understand what has happened to her sister while at the same time trying desperately to expel it from her mind. The conflict between these two contradictory impulses has filled Cynthia's head with a swarming, incoherent chaos that sounds like the buzzing of a hive. She claps her hands over her ears, and the drone of her confusion is louder, more insistent.

And now the miserable commotion from deep within the house rises up through the floors like the smell of rot. Cynthia gets up from the sofa, cocks her head, listens. She hears the high hopeless yipping of what she guesses is a small dog, and the whimper of puppies, and the deep, exhausted woof of what sounds like a large hound. The key!

She remembers it all of a sudden, jams her hand into her pocket—and there it is. She feels its sharp jagged notches, and the steely cold of it somehow accelerates her heart. She pulls the key out, tightens her hand around it, and wonders if she is going to faint.

But her fear is not as great as her will to survive, and she holds on to her perch of consciousness, sensing that if she succumbs to the inner darkness that beckons her, all will be lost. Slowly, deliberately, with every fiber of her self-control, Cynthia forces herself to the stairway and makes her way to the cellar's locked door, all the while clasping the key so tightly that when she opens her hand to look, it is as if the shape of it has been branded onto her palm.

The animals below sense her presence—at first they go silent, as if experience has taught them that the approach of human footsteps can sometimes bring food and attention and sometimes terror. But soon the sound of the key trembling and scraping its way into the lock excites them—their hunger triumphs over the flickering memories of the terrible things they have already seen, and they begin to vocalize, making beseeching sounds from whimpers to howls.

Cynthia turns the key. The lock is resistant, but then with a heavy clunk it turns. Her hand grips the handle, the cold, greasy brass of it. She pauses—mixed in with the cacophony below is...a human voice. Can it be true? Can there be a *person* down there? Yes, the sound is unmistakable. A man. But what is he saying? At first it sounds like a threat—like, *Don't come near. Stay where you are.* But that's not it. She listens more closely. She pulls the door open—just a crack. She raises her knee up against it, in case someone or something comes rushing forward.

Hi, Diane, that's what the voice is saying.

"Hello?" Cynthia calls down. "Hello?" She opens the door wide and peers into the damp darkness below. What could she do for a man locked in a cellar who is calling for Diane? Who could he be? Why would he be lurking down here? And who in the name of holy hell is Diane?

She feels along the wall near the door and finds the light switch, turns it on. One dim, bare lightbulb comes on, hanging from its fixture about halfway down the wooden steps. Light seems to leak from the bulb with the weakness and uncertainty of water dripping from a faucet. How can a light make everything seem darker? The plank right below the light shows dark gray, but all that seethes beyond it has been plunged into the blackness of a moonless, starless winter night.

"Hello?" Cynthia calls down again, and hearing the trembling fear in her own voice, she clears her throat and repeats it, forcing herself to sound more capable, less afraid. The dogs respond to her voice with wild, piteous barks and yowls, and she hears the crash and rattle of their cages as they throw their bodies against them. Suddenly, there is a moment's pause in the canine clamor, and in this brief silence she hears the human voice again. And he is not saying *Hi, Diane*. Would that he were! He is saying over and over and over again, with a kind of mindless insistence, like a prisoner beating a tin cup against a stone wall, "I'm dying, I'm dying," his voice dull and hopeless.

Cynthia takes hold of the light fixture and tries to aim the bulb down toward the bottom of the stairs. The bright chrome of a cage winks briefly in the glow and then recedes into the darkness again, to be replaced by the staring needful eyes of a dog. A line of knives hanging from something… The fixture is finally too hot to hold on to any longer and with a little yelp of pain—which sets the dogs off once again, louder than ever—she lets it go, and the light swings back and forth, casting dizzying, maddening shadows everywhere.

Cynthia's consciousness is now all but split in two. What is most reasoned in her mind counsels her to turn, go back upstairs, and close that heavy door behind her. But her *instinct* urges her forward, into the darkness and the noise of that cellar, and step by step she approaches the bottom of the staircase, to the ever-increasing passion of the caged dogs and the bleating, pathetic sound of the human being who also awaits her, who is only able to repeat over and over: *Dying dying dying*. And, finally, *Please help me*.

The floor of the cellar surprises the bottoms of her feet—she was expecting wood or cement, but it's dirt, packed and hard, and so cold that the chill of it goes right through the soles of her shoes and into her bones. Her legs tremble and nearly buckle; she reaches blindly at nothing to steady herself. And then, a surprise: she stumbles forward, hears a faint click, and suddenly the entire cellar is illuminated—the lights have been switched on by a motion detector, and now the cellar is as bright as an operating theater. Cynthia reels, blinks back the brightness.

That moment of blindness. How she wishes it could have lasted longer. Not just a moment—an hour. Not just an hour—an eternity. For what she sees now is by far the most gruesome sight she has ever beheld, or even imagined. What she sees now makes death preferable to having to live with the memory of what is right before her eyes.

Michael doesn't mean to be a part of it, but there is no escaping it. He doesn't want to believe them, but he does.

The children are holding his hands; the children are frightened and they are running, and Michael is frightened and running too.

Why not go to the police? But what can the police do? Two ten-year-olds on one side, and a respected lawyer dripping money and prestige on the other? At the very most, the police will "look into it." It could take days, weeks, months before the folder landed on the desk of someone who'd give it a second look. And meanwhile...

They are more than half a block in front of Alex, but Michael dares a glance over his shoulder, and just as he feared, Alex is gaining on them, running with his head down and his elbows close to his sides, his arms moving back and forth with the implacability of pistons. There is a mindless, tireless purity to his gait, and for a moment Michael is overcome by the certainty that he could run for all he is worth and run faster and farther than he has ever run before and it still would not be enough. His very humanity is laced through and through with discouragement and self-doubt and these things beat a path straight to the sad, defeated heart of surrender. A zebra on the veldt will run forever, the beating of its hooves unimpeded by pessimism, its breaths uninterrupted by terror—indeed, the closer the lion gets, the more the zebra becomes at one with the singular task of flight. Safety! Safety! Even with the lion's jaws around its hindquarters, the zebra will continue trying to escape. But a human being? Shortness of breath, a fiery stitch in the side, the sudden insanity of thinking that perhaps if you stop and try to reason with your pursuer, you will be better off—all these things conspire against you, and Michael wonders for a moment: *What chance do I have?* And, even more subversively: *This has nothing to do with me.* And, even more subversively than that: *This is hopeless....*

But at that moment, Adam tightens his grip on Michael's hand, and Alice likewise squeezes his other hand, and with the childish, trusting touch of these twins, his fate is sealed. He cannot and he will not betray them. He will not tell them to listen to their father. He will not try to convince them that things are not as bad as they imagine them to be. He will not beguile them with fantasies of the all-powerful police coming to their aid. With the touch of their hands they have said something that is beyond *I love you,* beyond desire, beyond any emotion and any commitment Michael has ever known. They have said *I trust you with my life,* and the immensity of this lifts him, and makes him duty bound.

"Turn right on Madison," he tells them. "And go—let's go, let's go."

Adam shoots him a look of acknowledgment too deep and too enveloping to be called gratitude. It speaks of a connectedness beyond the human ledger of what is asked for and what is granted, a sense of oneness that would render "Thank you" an expression of mere politeness, not much less insipid than "Have a nice day." Alice lifts Michael's hand so that his knuckles lightly touch her cheek, and it is like a contract signed in ink. No: in flesh. Actually: in blood.

In the time it has taken for Michael to have these thoughts, Alex has closed the gap between him and the children, from about two hundred feet to something close to one hundred. It's clear to Michael that if this is a contest of speed, he and the twins are going to lose.

"Our main hope is that he doesn't want to make a scene," Michael tells the twins. "He'll stay close but I bet he's afraid to make a grab."

Berryman Prep's narrow east–west street is jammed with traffic— a truck has stopped somewhere between Fifth and Madison, and the drivers in all the cars stuck behind it lean frantically on their horns, filling the street with miserable braying honks, as if a herd of elephants has been penned and fears a slaughter is on the way. On either side of this strip of prime real estate, jacquard curtains are discreetly tugged to one side and the windows of the twenty-million-dollar town houses fill with frowning faces.

As they near the corner of Madison, Michael risks pulling the children out into the street, between two yellow cabs that are stuck in traffic, and once the three of them are on the other side of the street, he races west with them, toward Fifth Avenue. His instinct tells him that they will have more of a chance to elude Twisden if they can somehow get to Central Park. But Twisden is not so easily thrown off the trail. He doesn't bother to cross the street then himself, but he keeps pace with them and is just about to cross to their side of the street when suddenly the traffic unclogs and Alex must stop for a few moments and wait for an opening.

Michael senses an opportunity for safety: a FreshDirect delivery truck, filled with groceries for the housebound and the wealthy, slows down and comes to a stop directly to the left of where he and the twins are on the sidewalk, momentarily blocking them from view.

At that same moment, they hear a rolling rumbling sound behind them, and in virtual unison, the three of them turn to see a pack of young teenagers riding skateboards along the sidewalk, crouched on the decks of their boards and seeming to give no thought to the pedestrians who scramble to get out of their way.

"It's Rodolfo," Alice says with a shiver of excitement.

"Rodolfo?" Michael asks.

"He's real name's Richard, but everyone calls him Rodolfo," Alice says. Her voice is bright with the pride a child feels when she has the answer. "I met him in the park."

"Hey, man," Rodolfo says as he rolls up next to Adam and puts his arm around him, almost knocking him over.

The driver of the FreshDirect truck lights a cigarette and rolls down the window to let the smoke out.

Rodolfo and his friends surround them—a couple are familiar to Alice, the others are not. It's not obvious who is a boy and who is a girl; it seems really not to matter very much. There is something similar about all of them—it is as if there is more energy going through them than their bodies can contain. Impulse, appetite, sex drive, willfulness all seem to wrestle and writhe within each of them, like monkeys in a laundry bag. One of the skaters continually shakes his head, like a swimmer trying to dislodge water from his ear canal, though maybe this is a girl. Another—stovepipe thin, ponytailed, reeking of smoke and burned coffee—stomps on the stern of his/her skateboard, causing the bow of the deck to pop up like a jack-in-the-box. Yet in the chaos there seems to be some kind of design. They form a ring around Michael and the twins, preventing them from moving, but also obscuring them from view.

"Follow me," Rodolfo says. He sniffs, snorts, clears his throat, and rolls his shoulders.

"Who the hell are you?" Michael asks.

"My house is right over here."

"Have you been following us?" Alice asks.

"We saw you," Rodolfo says. "Come on, no time to talk."

He leads them to a four-story town house made of rust-red brick with white wooden trim around the windows, a house that someone has recently bought and that is now being gutted. Two dark green metal dumpsters are curbside, filled with rubble. A plywood ramp has been placed over the front steps, allowing the work crew to wheel sand and bricks out as the inside of this stately old house is demolished.

"Where's your family?" Alice asks him.

"Who the fuck knows?" Rodolfo says. He puts his arm around Alice, pulls her close to him, sniffs the top of her head.

"Don't," she says, pushing him away.

"Maybe later," he says.

Rodolfo directs Michael and the twins to follow him up the ramp. Michael looks over his shoulder, fervently hoping that the FreshDirect truck is still blocking Twisden's view. But the truck is finally moving again—though now Twisden is surrounded by Rodolfo's friends, who are doing whatever they can to block his view.

The locks to the enormous carved wooden door to the entrance have been cored out and filled with pinkish putty, and now the door is secured by a single padlock. But the rivets that attach the plate to the door have been loosened, and when Rodolfo hits his shoulder against the door, it opens immediately.

"He'll find us!" Adam cries as Rodolfo pulls them into the house.

As dank and chilly as it is outside, it is even more bone-chilling inside this house. The deep, earthy smells of cement, sand, plaster, mud mingle with the sharper, somehow more alarming smell of sawed and splintered wood, of burned-out electric wires, and also of the frantic human smell of a desperate man who comes at night to plunder the copper wires and pipes and whatever little scraps he can find for resale. Even now, the twins' nostrils quiver and dilate at the sour-sweet aroma of sweat extruded through the soft mesh of skin already permeated by cheap brandy and Risperdal.

Broken bars of weak gray light come through the hastily nailed boards over the windows. The entrance foyer reminds the twins of their own house, some twenty blocks south. Though they are standing on cardboard that bears the muddy prints of many, many wafflesoled work boots, they imagine that beneath it are the honey-hued oak parquet floors of home, perhaps with the same starburst inlays. Despite everything, and against all logic and all instinct toward self-preservation, Adam and Alice long for home with the openhearted helplessness of children. Like all young mammals, they are genetically encoded to trust their parents and believe that the people who brought them to life are their havens in a heartless world. It is in their brains, it is in the wash of their spinal fluid, it is their most basic and necessary engineering to believe that their mother and father are here to protect them, and they hold on to this instinct no matter how compelling the evidence to the contrary—and even then, even after they let go of the illusion and begin to run for their own lives, doubt shadows their every move, as they are reacting to a reality that is in essence inconceivable, a truth that continually feels like a lie manufactured by their own failings or by the misfirings of their own feverish minds.

"Ever wish you were adopted?" Rodolfo asks Adam.

"No."

Rodolfo's grin is gummy, bordering on the equine. "My peeps had to sell this place. The new owners hired a bunch of guys to come do the reno, and they found a lot of shit that was really fucking weird. Now the new owners are in court trying to get their money back—but guess what? That money is gone, and so are Mr. and Mrs. Pomerantz." Rodolfo waves his fingers as if saying good-bye to the picture of his parents that floats in his mind.

"We'll hang here until it's safe," Michael whispers.

"Maybe," Adam says. At first Michael wonders if Adam is questioning his plan, but a moment later he realizes that *maybe* means that *safety* seems like a total long shot.

"I'll show you around my lovely home," Rodolfo says with a host's sweep of the arm. He guides them deeper into the house, into a room that was perhaps the parlor but has been so thoroughly taken apart that all that exists of the walls are unpainted wooden slats holding in fiberglass insulation. The ceiling has been completely removed, offering up the underside of the second floor, wide oak planks with the sullen silver tips of two-inch flooring nails poking through them.

"This was a very sad room," Rodolfo says.

"Why sad?" Alice asks.

"I found my dog Casper in this room, afterward." He says it in an exaggeratedly bright tone and rubs his hands together like a magician preparing to pull a coin out of someone's ear. "In fact, every room in this house has an awful memory. Upstairs was where I once walked in on my parents having sex, and my father threw me down the stairs, and then my mother came down and I thought she was going to help me, but she was just as bad. And in the bathroom is where I found our cat, Shirley MacLaine." Rodolfo notices an old mahogany telephone table missing one of its legs leaning against what is left of the wall. He picks it up as if it weighs almost nothing, lifts it over his head, and sends it flying toward the lath work, where it hits with a ferocious crack.

The children cringe. Michael looks around, trying quickly to see if there are other ways into this place and other ways out. Michael checks his watch. It's 11:30. Normally, he has a nearly unerring sense of time—as a teacher, he can tell without glancing up at the clock how close he is to the end of the period, and at home he knows without the use of a timer when to scoop out the eggs bobbing and clicking in the bubbling water so they will be perfectly soft-boiled. But now he is so far off course it's as if he has entered a new dimension, one where $E=mc$ quadrupled. How is he standing in a squat with a bunch of feral teenagers as they spin tales of their abuse? Why isn't he at work? Where is Xavier? His main thought is that he and the twins need to stay in this house at least fifteen minutes before venturing into the street again. That's all he can say for now. That's what a lifetime gathering wisdom and experience has added up to. Fifteen minutes parked right here.

From outside: the whoop of a fire truck's siren, its urgencies echoing back and forth off the facades of the houses. And then: the blare of the truck's horn, as powerful as the warning blast from an onrushing train. What clearer illustration of a world gone wrong than a fire truck stuck behind drivers hunting for parking spaces while somewhere a building is engulfed in flames?

The sound is unsettling to Michael but unbearable to the twins and Rodolfo, who cover their ears against the noise, screw their eyes shut, hunch their shoulders, grimace, as if in pain.

When the fire truck is finally able to get through, the noise subsides and the kids uncover their ears, breathe sighs of relief.

"Don't worry about your father," Rodolfo says.

"He's really strong," Adam says.

"And fast," says Alice.

"This is insane," says Michael.

"We didn't do anything wrong," Adam says.

"We didn't," Alice adds. "No way. Nothing big. It's not…"

"It's not fair," says Adam.

"It's not," says Alice. "He's crazy. They both are."

"No one's going to kill you," Michael says. "Or hurt you." But even to himself, his words and the voice with which he delivers them seem weak and unconvincing.

"There's something wrong with them," Adam says. "Really really wrong."

"They used to be nice," Alice says.

"Sometimes they still are," Adam says. He is suddenly worried that they have gone too far in their criticisms and that somehow, through some dark magic, their words are going to make themselves known to their parents.

"Some of the parents try not to hurt," Rodolfo says, nodding sagely. He speaks to the twins as if he were many years their senior.

"I think that's why they lock us up," says Alice.

"Wait," Michael asks. "Lock you up where?"

Adam and Alice fall silent. They have been taught all their lives to keep family secrets, and even now, when they are on the run, the fear of betraying their parents is immense and palpable.

"Guys," Michael says, hoping for many, many reasons that the situation he finds himself in is not as abnormal as it seems, "come on. Kids have issues with their parents. I had issues with mine—big ones."

"We don't have issues," Adam says.

"We don't even know what issues are," adds Alice.

Michael hears something, a throaty flutter, a sudden warning displacement of the air—and the twins hear it too. They all three of them look up toward the sound in the back of the house, in a room in which half the floor has been taken out, revealing the hundred-and-twenty-year-old joists onto which the planks had once been nailed. On the part of the floor that is still intact, there is a heap of tarps and drop cloths, paint and plaster splattered. For a moment, it seems as if something is stirring beneath the pile....

And there, above, is a family of pigeons, two large gray-and-pink adults with feathers puffed up against the cold, and two pigeon chicks, downy and pale gray, looking not unlike ducklings. One of the adult pigeons is hovering over one of the chicks and regurgitating what looks like spoiled cottage cheese into its wide-open beak.

"Yo," says Rodolfo, "I never fucking saw a baby pigeon." He licks his lips, moves forward a bit.

"The parents hide them until they are big," Adam says. "That stuff the big one is throwing up into the baby is called pigeon milk; it makes them grow real fast."

"Is that the mother feeding them?" Rodolfo asks.

"The mother and the father both do," Adam says.

"Amazing," Michael says. "It's like they're giving their babies their own bodies to help them grow."

"At our house it's sort of different," Alice says.

* * *

When Cynthia recovers (though not really: she will never recover) from the sight of Xavier—his left arm all but missing, only one bone and some rags of flesh still attached to him, like red streamers on a child's handlebar grips, and strips of the human meat of him peeled away from his left side—she tries to figure out a way of releasing him from the blood-and-waste spattered cage in which he is kept; failing that, she stumbles up the steps, dialing and redialing 911 on her smartphone, which has been struck dumb by the depth and soundproofing of the cellar, until she is standing in the front hall talking to a dispatcher, a woman with a Jamaican accent who instantly diagnoses the combination of hysteria and catatonia in Cynthia's voice and speaks to her in comforting but efficient tones, assuring her that an ambulance will be there within minutes, and when Cynthia, almost weeping now, says that perhaps the police need to come as well, the dispatcher assures her that will happen too. She askes Cynthia, "You going to hang in there for me, aren't you?," the simple humanity of which so touches Cynthia that she begins to sob.

The EMT workers and the police arrive at the same time. Cynthia directs them all to the cellar, and they find Xavier unconscious in his cage. Cynthia, who has not followed them down but who sits on a graceful, fragile little cherrywood chair pressed against the wall a few feet from the door to the cellar, her eyes shut, her head dangling, and her stomach churning a thick batter of bile, hears the cops and the EMT workers talking, hears them breaking open the cage, hears one of them say, "On three!," and then hears more talk, murmurs both urgent and indistinct.

The EMT workers emerge first, carrying Xavier strapped to the gurney, covered up to his chin by a sheet that is slowly turning red. Next to emerge are the two police, who place Cynthia under arrest, read her her rights, and lead her out of the house, each of them touching her on the back.

* * *

One of the baby pigeons ventures out from its nest and hops along the beam. It quickly loses its balance and falls straight to the floor. It does not even flap its wings or make any other attempt to stop or cushion its fall. Luckily, it lands on the mass of drop cloths directly below.

The older pigeons are in a state of extreme agitation, vocalizing and moving their heads quickly back and forth while ruffling their feathers. Despite their obvious concern, it takes a few moments for this worry to be transmitted through their nervous systems and converted to an actual action. First the horrible fact of the fallen chick must be absorbed, then the other chick must be secured in the nest, and, finally, the two adult birds must swoop down to the floor, landing a few feet away from their baby, who is lying motionless.

The adult pigeons hop this way and that, but they do not go directly to their inert young one. Thousands of years of roundabout, suspicious, circuitous movement cannot be undone by one fallen squab, but eventually the two adults arrive at the mound of tarps and drop cloths, and just as they do there are two separate signs of life, one reassuring and one completely unnerving.

The reassuring sign is that the downy little pigeon, sensing the proximity of its parents, shakes and shudders back into animation, rights itself, and starts to scramble off the tarps that broke its fall.

The unnerving development is that a bare arm emerges from the side of the heap. The arm is slender, dark, and alive with purpose. With suddenness and blind accuracy, it grabs the pigeon chick. The adult birds coo and flutter with the gravest concern, and now the leaden lump of old tarps begins to heave as a tremendous agitation ensues beneath it.

"Oh man," Rodolfo says, more in annoyance than amazement. "Don't tell me."

Emerging from the pile are two teenagers, a boy and a girl, both essentially undressed. The boy is broad-shouldered, muscular, with a Chinese character tattooed on the side of his neck. He is wearing a pair of dark gray briefs and holds the pigeon chick in one hand and a bottle of some kind of booze in the other. The girl is slight, pale olive in complexion, furtive. She has the manner of a trapped animal, though one that might cause more fear than it feels. Her hair is short and looks as if she has just cut it herself using a child's dull scissors. She lifts a corner of one of the tarps to cover her nakedness.

"WTF, Max," Rodolfo says to the boy. "I told you about coming here."

By way of an answer, Max grabs his crotch. He holds the baby pigeon in front of his face, moving his eyes as the chick's head turns this way and that and tightening his grip as the chick tries to twist free.

"Put it down," Rodolfo says. "Put the fucking thing down."

"Why?"

"Because you're freaking out my guests."

"Your guests?"

"What are you—stupid? Put it down, man, I'm not kidding." Rodolfo starts to walk toward Max, and Max, perhaps as a way of freezing Rodolfo, opens his mouth and prepares to ingest the frantic chick, whose pinkish feet fearfully throb like two frightened, scaly hearts.

"I'm hungry," Max says. There is a dull, clobbered quality to his voice, as if he has been huffing gasoline, or has suffered a blow to the head, or is simply not very bright.

"Give it to me, Max," Rodolfo says, his hand extended.

"Who the fuck are you?" Max says.

"You should go away," the girl says. "We were here first."

"First of all, Emily, you never tell me what to do. This is my house."

Emily looks around and makes a joke of looking very impressed. "Wow. Nice crib, man. Really, this place is the shit."

"You're embarrassing yourself."

"Yeah?"

"Yeah. Get some clothes on."

"Like this?" She drops the edge of the tarp that she had been holding and throws her shoulders back, puckering her lips in a jokey but painful imitation of an old-fashioned seductress. Her skin shows bruises everywhere—her thighs, her ribs, the insides of her arms, her neck, as if she has been frantically groped by someone with ink-stained fingers. The neglect and adventure of her life is all over her, like the signs of a fatal disease.

"Look at you," Rodolfo says, shaking his head.

"Mind your own business," Max says. "We're starting our family." He brings the pigeon chick close to his mouth—it's only an inch or two away from being devoured—then suddenly stops, frowns, turns it this way and that.

"If you eat that," Rodolfo says, "I'll rip your arm off and beat you to death with it."

"It's dead," Max says.

The twins, in the meantime, have gathered closer to Michael, instinctively gravitating toward him, the only point of safety in a world that has tipped into the grimmest sort of madness. Michael puts his hands over their eyes, but even as they cleave to him, they will have no part of the blindness with which he seeks to protect them—they have had enough of the darkness.

"You was squeezing it too strong," Emily says, nodding sagely while half covering herself again.

"Sorry," Max says to Rodolfo. "I was going to give it to you."

Rodolfo is standing just inches away from Max now. He slaps him hard on the head. In the empty house, the sound is particularly resonant, as if someone has furiously hit the arm of a leather chair with a razor strop. The blow sends Max reeling back. He gets entangled with the tarp and nearly falls, and as he scrambles to keep his balance he accidentally drops the dead pigeon. It lands on its back, its prehistoric little feet pointing toward the demolished ceiling.

"I'm sorry, I'm sorry," Max says, bowing his head, clearly afraid to make eye contact with Rodolfo.

"Is it dead?" Alice asks Michael, who nods his head.

"Why are they like this?" Adam asks, indicating the three teenagers with a gesture.

"I don't know," Michael whispers. "I'm sorry."

Rodolfo picks up the dead bird. He shows no squeamishness or any particular emotion about picking up something dead. He glances at it before tossing it to Max.

"It's yours," he says. "Don't waste it."

Max catches the thing and smiles cravenly. "Eat up while it's still fresh," he announces. And a moment later he has stuffed the entire chick into his mouth. It is more than he can comfortably chew. His cheeks balloon out, and his eyes widen and swell, and moments later he is wincing and shaking his head.

"You no like?" Emily asks, laughing.

He shakes his head emphatically no, and then opens his mouth and, using his finger as a kind of scoop, tries desperately to get everything of that little pigeon out, though it is a mass now of blood, down, feather, bone, beak, eye, tiny avian organs, and saliva.

Rodolfo says to Emily, "You would have his child?"

"So give me yours, bitch," she says.

Max is trying to retch up a bone lodged in the back of his throat; it feels to him as if he has swallowed a dart. He makes huge hacking sounds, but nothing comes up except a bit of pale yellow bile.

Suddenly, the front door flies open with a crash, which is followed by the sound of pounding feet rushing toward them with the fury of a river that has breached its dam. Alex Twisden has found his way in and is dragging one of Rodolfo's crew behind him—a fleshy kid with ice-white hair and bare hammy arms protruding from a cutoff blue-jeans jacket. The kid makes a last-ditch dive, tackling Twisden and bringing him down face-first. But Twisden, despite the sickening thud with which he hits the floor, seems undeterred. With a dexterity and grace that is half beautiful and half terrifying, he catapults to a standing position and whirls to face the boy who brought him down. With gestures so quick and efficient they seem devoid of anger or any other emotion, Twisden grabs him by his jacket and hoists him up, as if the boy—who is shouting now, and snarling, and flailing his arms—weighs no more than a kitten. Twisden shakes the kid a couple of times and throws him against the door frame just as the rest of Rodolfo's crew comes running in. Two of them are bleeding from whatever confrontation allowed Twisden to make it into the house in the first place, but all of them are shouting and ululating madly, boosting their own courage as they make a run at Adam and Alice's father. They are not afraid; they are doing what comes naturally to them.

"Daddy!" Alice cries, instinctively reaching out toward Twisden, until she sees the look in his eyes and shrinks back.

One by one, Rodolfo's gang of cast-off, fearless friends pile on Alex. He strikes out with his hands, his feet, his elbows, but despite his strength and his pitilessness—there is blood everywhere, there is crying too—he cannot get free of them.

"Come on," Rodolfo says, shoving Michael and the twins deeper into his old house. "Back away." He herds them past Max and Emily; past the adult pigeons, who continue to hop and flutter mournfully; and toward a sheet of plywood that has been covering French doors leading to the back garden. Rodolfo rips the wood down—nails and splinters fly—and then, stepping back, he rams his foot through the glass and mullions, creating an opening just large enough for them to barrel through. "Go on," he says, his voice trembling with urgency. "He's hard to hold."

Then: "Wait," Rodolfo says, with a hand on Alice's shoulder. With his forearm, he knocks away some of the jagged glass, and then, with a quick nod, he gestures for them to make their way through.

Adam is the first one, and then it is Alice's turn. She whispers *Thank you* before maneuvering through the shattered French door, closing her eyes and holding her arms straight up, trying to protect herself from the deadly-looking shards that make going through the window seem like entering a shark's open mouth.

"You're next, Teacher, let's go," he says to Michael, and Michael makes his way through the smashed windows, but because he is larger, he is not able to fully escape the tear and bite of the glass that remains, and as he lands in the spongy, half-frozen grass behind the house, he is picking out triangles of broken glass that have pierced deeply into the weave of his coat.

The back garden has, aside from its small lawn, a ruined outdoor fireplace, junked lawn furniture, a stone cupid missing its head, and broken bricks where a bit of patio used to be. What was once grass trod on by a family that might have at least imagined happiness is now a delinquent frozen patch of uncared-for lawn that's degenerated into a botanical feral state, a chaos of sticker bushes, knotted vines, and voluptuous weeds. And half covered by all the growth is a jumble of bones, most of them small and difficult to identify, but one at least clearly a pelvis, and another a small skull with large canines.

"Go!" Rodolfo shouts down at them. Behind him are the dim shapes of his friends doing their best to wrestle Alex to a standstill.

Stumbling over the bones, the twins and Michael rush toward the tall wooden gate in the corner of the garden, but it is bolted shut and they must scramble over it—no problem for either Adam and Alice, but a challenge for Michael, who must try it four times, with the twins, invisible now on the other side of the fence, urging him on in increasingly desperate tones.

But at last—with visions of Twisden hurtling across the yard and grabbing his legs—he hoists himself up. The toes of his shoes bang frantically against the gate's wooden planks as he pulls himself higher and higher, and, after balancing for a moment with his knee on top of the gate, Michael flips himself forward and lands between the twins, and the three of them just stand there, wondering what to do and where to go.

Rodolfo and his crew, accustomed to chaos, to sudden exits and constant danger, have scattered in all directions.

Michael catches his breath and looks at Adam and Alice; their eyes are trained trustfully on him, and this trust, which seemed such a benediction before, now sends a chill through him. How can he ever protect these two? How can he even know whether he is about to deliver them directly into the arms of their furious father? How can he know if he is in the process of forever ruining his own life?

The three of them go to the front of the town house, hoping there, at least, people will be present, witnesses, and that will make them marginally safer.

Is he still in the house? Have the wild boys and girls knocked him unconscious, tied him up—killed him? Michael scans the block up and down, back and forth, looking for Twisden. There is a mail carrier; here comes a dog walker with eight, nine, maybe ten dogs, little and brown, black and white, big, shaggy, and gray. There is a mother's helper pushing a stroller with a plastic rain guard covering her little passenger, who sits there like a tiny pope, his pudgy fingers splayed.

And there is Twisden, sitting on the fender of a battered old Volvo parked directly across the street. He can be wherever he wants to be. He can take these children whenever he thinks the time is right.

He slides off the front end of the car as softly as a shadow moving along a wall.

Fifth Avenue is less than two hundred feet away, and they speed toward it on the south side of the street while Twisden keeps pace with them on the north side.

"Daddy, Daddy!" Alice screams. "Leave us alone!"

Her cries arrest the attention of a few passersby. Some stare, but no one tries to interfere, or intercede.

"Just come here," Twisden shouts over the traffic noise. "Okay? Come on, honey. What are you doing? What are you afraid of?"

"You, Daddy," Alice yells back. Her face reddens, but despite the emotion she doesn't break stride. In fact, they are all of them running faster and faster—the race is on to get to the Fifth Avenue light before it turns red again.

"Yeah, Dad," hollers Adam, emboldened by his sister's outburst. "You can go fuck yourself!"

"Adam!" Twisden says, almost leaping in front of a rattletrap of a plumbing-supplies truck, "how dare you use that kind of language!" He stands now on the other side of the street, his fists on his hips, his head shaking censoriously.

It seems to Michael that something is preventing Twisden from making a full-out attempt to grab the kids. Some part of him is wary of what others will see, what they might think or even do. Twisden's plan is to wear them down, to keep pace with them, to make it impossible to get away from him until one of the kids, or both of them, or maybe even Michael himself is so exhausted and discouraged that surrender will seem the best option. Maybe that's what the death instinct is...not a drive toward death itself, but the brute, inexorable reality of death gnawing away at life until it just snaps.

"Come on, quick," Michael says, pulling the kids forward and dashing across Fifth Avenue just as the light goes to green and the herd of automobiles begins its charge, as if once they are past this one light they will never have to stop again. Car horns blare their owners' displeasure as a few of the drivers must wait an extra half second for Michael and the twins to make it to the west side of the street.

Here the sidewalk is somewhat narrow. A few feet away is the pale gray stone wall bordering the eastern edge of Central Park. Between the pavement and the wall are wooden benches, freshly painted bright green, and occupied, for the most part, by young women from the Caribbean, bundled against the cold, with hoods and scarves and earmuffs and gloves, talking to one another while they keep an eye on the swaddled infants in their care. A few of these young women, with their lonely eyes and weary smiles, watch as Michael and the twins run past them. Michael is the first to clamber over the wall, fighting off the chaotic tangle of the immense, empty forsythia bushes just on the other side of the wall. Scrambling to get his footing, he reaches over the wall, grips Alice under her arms, and lifts her.

Twisden is there, closer than ever, walking along the sidewalk next to the wall, his hands in his pockets and his lips pursed, as if he were whistling. How did he gain on them so suddenly? Can he really move this quickly? And if he can, what hope is there?

As if to answer the question as soon as it crosses Michael's mind, Twisden is now just a few feet away. Escape? There is no escape. Hope? There is no hope.

"Dad!" Adam screams, feeling the nearness of his father, hearing his breath, smelling him.

Michael quickly lifts Adam to bring him over the wall, but he hasn't acted quickly enough. And he is not strong enough. And today, it would seem, is not his day.

Nor does it seem to be Adam's. His father's hand closes around his ankle with the heartless stubborn strength of forever, and he is captured.

Alex turns Adam around and clasps him fiercely by the shoulders, holding him up so that the tips of their noses are practically touching. Heat ripples off Twisden, as if he were burning inside. "Is this the little boy who told his father to go fuck himself?" he says.

"No," Adam says, barely.

"Is this the little boy who tells family secrets?"

"Adam!" Alice screams.

Michael must restrain her to keep her from climbing over the low wall and getting caught herself. He pulls her toward him. They back up, stumbling, nearly falling over the twisted vines armored against the winter, cold and hard.

"Give me my daughter," Twisden says, his voice boiling, yet inside that rage there are ripples of doubt. How can he hold on to the boy and catch the girl? What are people seeing right now? What are they thinking?

"Dad, please," Adam says.

Alex turns toward Adam's voice, as if startled.

"They're getting away," Twisden cries.

"Put me down, Dad, please, put me down."

A young couple walking their Australian shepherd have stopped, and they stare openly at Alex and Adam while the dog sits, ears flat, hackles up, its docked tail twitching nervously.

"Wait until you have children," Alex says with what he dearly hopes looks like a good-natured grin. He hoists Adam up and holds him in the crook of his arm, as if his son were a three-year-old who has gotten tuckered out during his playtime and now must be carried. The very familiarity of the image seems to reassure the young couple, though if they had taken note of the apprehensiveness of their dog, they might not be quite so sanguine. And, of course, they can't be faulted for not noticing how fiercely the man is gripping his son's leg. But the privacy of family life, like the primacy of private property, is a given to most people, and the young man yanks his dog's leash author-itatively and the couple continue on their way.

"Dad?" Adam asks in his smallest, most timid voice.

Alex, who has been making certain the couple and their juicy-looking dog are indeed walking away, turns toward the sound of his son's voice.

Adam has exactly one second to implement his plan, and he does not waste it. As soon as his father is fully facing him, Adam runs his finger into Alex's eye, stabs hard and remorselessly into the cool jelly of it.

Alex howls with pain. He grabs for the pulsating flame of his eye and covers it with his hand, dropping Adam to the ground.

"I'm sorry," Adam whimpers as he scrambles over the wall and runs toward Alice and Michael, who have been waiting for him, thirty yards beyond.

On the other side of the curving roadway connecting the east side of Central Park to the west is the monumental Metropolitan Museum of Art, and Michael leads the twins quickly and crazily across the road, dodging taxis, trucks, and cars. They run as fast as they can, past the sellers of postcards and pastel portraits and giant pretzels, fewer here than usual because of the raw weather.

The massive white stone staircase leading to the museum's entrance looms before them, at the top of which hang banners announcing the World of Watteau, Treasures of the Topkapi, and Representations of Evil—this last one made of dark red silk and bearing the silhouette of Lucifer, his arms raised high, one hand holding a pitchfork, the other a human head. Not daring to glance behind them, the three push through the doors. Inside, they slow themselves so as to not court unwanted attention, but they still move quickly as Michael guides them to the ticket booth. He has only a couple of dollars in his pocket but, though the admission price is hefty, it is also voluntary. "Three, please," he says, pushing a single toward the woman in the booth, who impassively slides over three lapel pins, giving them access to the museum and its trillions of dollars' worth of treasure.

And here comes Alex, as arresting and incongruous in this great hall as a wild animal. He bursts into the great echoing main lobby, looking this way and that, his left eye deep red, his teeth bared. Whereas Michael and the twins even at the height of their fear are careful to remain somehow under the radar of the museum staff and the thousands of visitors, Alex feels no such need. After whirling around several times and failing to pick his children out from the waves of museumgoers that wash across the great room, he begins to shout: "Adam! Alice!"

"Oh God," Alice murmurs, hearing her name bellowed, hearing its second syllable echo, seeing the people stop in their tracks.

A teacher and a couple of parent volunteers are escorting a class of sixth-graders from a nearby Catholic school—the boys in maroon blazers and white shirts, the girls in maroon skirts, kneesocks. Michael and the twins use them as a moving screen as they make their way toward the main staircase.

The shouting has released Alex from his inhibitions and from his desire to appear as if he were a man like any other. His voice, powerful, strident, is nevertheless full of anguish. "Alice! Adam!" The names shouted out so vehemently—who knows what he is really saying? *Adam?* It could be a word in Arabic, which it truly does sound like after bouncing around the acoustic chaos of the Met's lobby. People are openly staring at him now. Since New York entered the Age of Terror, sudden noises are more disquieting than ever, and a man acting in a strange, possibly possessed manner puts people very much on alert.

Still, Alex's piteous cries awaken compassion in some, though the overriding fact remains that he is causing a terrifying, completely destabilizing disruption, and whatever good reason he may have for carrying on like this, he should not be standing at the foot of one of the greatest collections of art and antiquity in the world and creating a disturbance of this magnitude, and so everyone feels a sense of relief when from every corner of the main floor, security guards come rushing toward him.

Still using the parochial-school class as camouflage, the twins and Michael have gotten to the second floor, though they can well hear Alex bellowing below, a sound as gut-wrenching as the roar of a lion. Alice's hands are over her ears; Adam's jaw is set, and his eyes are flat, almost dead.

"Keep going, keep going," Michael says, tapping Adam's shoulder. Alice is lagging behind and he reaches back for her. She takes his hand. When Michael glances over his shoulder at her, he sees the tears streaming down her face.

"Sir? Sir? I'm going to have to ask you to be quiet."

This request is given by one of the twelve security officers who have come at Alex from all points, though it seems to be something a bit *more* than a request, since it is delivered as the guard—a tall, portly man with a shaved head and dark nostrils—pulls out a thirty-one-inch expandable steel baton.

When the mass of people on the grand staircase reach the Met's second floor, some go straight ahead, some turn right, and others head left. Everyone heads in a separate artistic and historical direction—to see swords and chalices, or Dutch masters, or black-and-white photographs from the early twentieth century, or crowns and scepters from kingdoms that history has disposed of, or the innumerable examples of the arts and crafts of various preindustrial peoples: baskets, hammocks, bowls, and knives that some explorer thought so highly of that he decided to pack them up and ship them to New York.

Still following the sixth-graders, the twins and Michael veer slightly to the right and enter the first room of the Lucifer exhibition. To anyone looking, Adam and Alice are in this class, and Michael hopes that he will pass for either a teacher or a parent volunteer.

Straight ahead is an enormous painting of a saber-toothed tiger walking through a pale green savanna, a deep blue sky above. The tiger's head is squared, equine; his mouth is open and his incisors are immense, stained, it seems, by bloody meat. Its eyes are dark, utterly alive and remorseless.

* * *

Alex has decided not to flee *or* fight, though the mental image of himself slashing and biting and pummeling those guards is so vivid and so real it feels like a memory. Yet as the guards draw closer and closer, he raises his hands and composes his face into a look of as much innocence as he can muster.

"Hey, guys, guys, guys, come on, I'm sorry," he says in a slightly abashed tone.

"We're going to ask you to come with us, sir," says the baton-wielding guard as he approaches Alex. He walks steadily forward, but he holds his metal wand in front of him as if it has magical powers. The guard takes note that he is approaching an individual whose left eye is as red as a cup of tomato soup.

Among the other guards, all of whom are silent at this point, closing in on Alex one small step after another, a kind of prewar escalation is taking place—one has a pair of handcuffs, another has drawn a Taser gun, and another has a small silver can of pepper spray.

"Look, guys," Alex says. "I realize I was making a commotion, and I'm sorry. I'm a lawyer." He starts to reach into his jacket but stops. "May I show you my identification?"

"Keep your hands where we can see them, sir," the lead officer says.

"Okay, no problem. I understand. But there's something you need to understand too." Alex feels one of the guards almost on him, and he whirls quickly, fixes the man with a stare that is so unexpectedly powerful that the guard stops for a moment.

"I am here for my children," Alex says. "My children are right here in this museum—where, by the way, I am a member, and where my father sat on the board of trustees. Not that it makes a difference."

By now, about two hundred people have gathered around to listen and watch this drama unfold.

"I am going to ask you to calm down, sir," the guard says. He takes a small tentative step toward Alex.

"I am calm. And I apologize for the…" For what? The word is gone. Alex realizes that his immunity to the aphasia that has increasingly vexed Leslie is running out. If the decay of her speech is any harbinger of what will happen to him, his days of being able to easily express himself are coming to an end.

"Listen to me," he says, though he has always believed it is a crass and hopeless announcement of your own impotence to demand to be heard, Mark Antony's speech to the rabble notwithstanding.

"No, sir, I need you to listen to me."

The guard is just about to grab Alex by the wrist when Alex utters the magic word. "My children have been kidnapped by a pedophile and he has them somewhere in this building. You want to toss me out of here—fine. You want to put me in jail? I'll spend my ten minutes in jail. But in the meantime, that pedophile has my kids and I want to know what you are going to do about it."

It turns out that the sixth-graders are more than a little revved up by the various Representations of Evil, and before long a few smart-ass remarks lead to a deluge of comments and jokes, which in turn leads to shoving, tugging, and the striking of poses—even in a world of Internet porn, the sight of a few painted bare breasts seems to have unhinged half the kids. And so, after quickly learning that their threats are either disbelieved or simply not heard, the adults in charge play what they believe to be their trump card. "If you guys can't calm down, we're leaving this museum and going right back to Our Lady Gate of Heaven," the teacher says, her voice rising, hardened.

Just then, however, one of the parent volunteers, a lovely young mother dressed as if for a date, comes clattering back into the room in her daring high heels. She has been downstairs to get a map of the museum and while she was there she heard Alex's heartfelt plea to the guards. "There's an old guy downstairs," she says, "and he says there's some pervert up here who's got his kids. A bunch of the guards are running around."

"All right, let's go," the teacher announces, and for the moment the class is docile, obedient, and they follow her out of the Lucifer show's first room. Michael, Alice, and Adam are suddenly bereft of human camouflage—at this point they are in front of an immense brown, gray, and yellow painting of Death astride a horse, the Devil and his strangely shy-looking steed trotting beside him in a landscape littered with human skulls. And in the relative quiet left in the wake of the sixth-grade class's departure, they hear what sounds like an army's worth of footsteps pounding up the grand staircase.

Alex Twisden has swayed the jury of guards, and they are on their way to apprehend the terrible man who has his children.

As soon as they hear the guards rushing up to the museum's second floor, the twins break into a full-out run, with Michael close behind, marveling at their grace, their speed. They have no idea where they are going—the only plan is to *go*. They race past a couple of elderly women, one of them in a wheelchair; past an art student who has set up her easel and is copying a Hieronymus Bosch triptych; through the next gallery and the next as the display of Lucifer in art continues, and half the patrons wear earphones as they listen to the mellifluous voice of an art historian explaining the symbolism and historical background of the work. Those who are listening to the lecture seem to have no idea that two children and a man are racing through the rooms, and those who do notice can make no sense of it, and through sheer confusion (plus a desire to remain safe and uninvolved) they are virtually motionless as Michael and the twins run for their lives.

Kings and queens, soldiers and frightened hares, rich merchants, peasants, and allegories of salvation, all of them in elaborate frames, go flashing by as one room turns into the next. Michael and the children who cleave to him as their only hope search for a way out of the museum. Now and then they see a sign signifying an exit, but when they race toward it they find themselves in yet another gallery. They are lost in a maze of priceless art.

"Over here," Michael says, so winded he can barely get the words out. He is pointing to a small sign that shows a stick figure making its way down a sketchily rendered staircase. They find themselves in what feels like a little-used corridor, rather dimly lit, housing glass cases jammed with Egyptian artifacts. But when they get to the staircase, there are multiple yellow ropes blocking it off and a sign that says DANGER.

"We need to separate," Michael says.

"No, no," Adam says, coming quickly to his teacher's side.

"Don't leave us," Alice says. Her eyes glitter like pulverized quartz. "Please."

Michael puts his arms around both children and gathers them close. He had not known how fierce and incoherent love could be, how it can turn within you like a wheel of fire. He will do anything to protect these two, even as he grapples and gropes his way toward a sense of what he is protecting them from.

"We're going to be okay," he says. He kisses the top of Adam's head; the boy's scalp is drenched with sweat. He pulls Alice even closer to him. "Okay?" he whispers to her. "Okay?"

"Thanks," she manages to say.

"They're looking for a grown-up and two kids," Michael says. "If we split up, we have a better chance. So here's what. Find your way out, one way or another. Go to the Eighty-Sixth Street entrance to the park and walk south. Okay? Walk south on the sidewalk as close to the museum as you can get. And count fifty benches. All right? How many benches?"

"Fifty," Adam says.

"Fifty," says Alice.

"And that's where we'll met."

"Then what?" Alice asks.

"We'll figure it out," Adam says.

"Yes," Michael says. "We will. I promise you that." To his surprise, his voice wobbles. It is unable to bear the full freight of his emotion right now. "We will figure it out."

They stow their jackets, figuring that anything that differs from Alex's description will be to their benefit. Adam heads right, Alice goes left, and Michael hopes to look like any single man strolling through the Met as he wanders past ancient and near ancient art, and the art of Korea, and Chinese art, even stopping now and again to admire an urn, a spoon, an intricately stitched orange-and-blue robe. His heart is drumming at an impossible, unsustainable speed, as if it knows its moment of extinction is near and wants to quickly use up the allotment of beats it has been granted by fate.

Look normal, look normal, he tells himself.

While he is involved in this impersonation of a man of leisure, gazing at the finery that once belonged to a dowager empress, he is suddenly touched rather brusquely on the shoulder—somewhere between a tap and a clasp—and when he turns around he sees a Latina museum guard and a NYPD beat cop with a reddened face and a handlebar mustache.

Michael manages to look at the two of them with a mixture of curiosity and annoyance. He raises his eyebrows, as if to say *Yes?*

"Identification," says the cop, allowing himself the shorthand of the all-powerful.

Michael speaks to them both in fluent and very, very rapid French, all the while pointing this way and that, hoping, first and foremost, that neither of them speaks French, and next that his gesturing will be complicated enough to further frustrate them and send them on their way.

Whatever quick description these two have been given, the partic-

ulars of Michael—a man alone speaking French!—convince guard
and cop that they are wasting their time with him, and in a moment
they continue their haphazard search for the pedophile and the two
little innocents.

Meanwhile, Adam is making his way past European sculpture, Is-
lamic art, and musical instruments, walking quickly, with his hands
in his pockets and his head down, as if he were looking for something
that he dropped on the floor. He finds a staircase leading to the first
floor, and he stops at the top of it and takes a deep breath. *Let me go,
let me go,* he whispers to himself. He holds on to the banister. It is
warm from the body heat of hundreds of hands. His legs tremble. He
forces himself to feel lucky and takes the first step. He can see there
are guards waiting at the bottom.

His only hope is that they are looking for a grown-up with two kids
and so one child all by himself, looking relaxed and happy, swinging
his arms back and forth, will be allowed to pass.

At the same time, Alice moves through the European paintings, past
the muddy, moody Rembrandts, past the rearing white horses, the
smoke-wreathed battlements, the choppy seas, the hopeful dawns, the
enigmatic women in capes and mantillas, the haughty men in beige
britches and shining boots. She is counting her breaths and is now up
to four hundred. Leaving the paintings behind, she finds herself in a
gallery filled with statues, some of them broken, some intact: Is that
Neptune? Is that Pan? Is that a wolf or a dog? There is a din of voices
in this room and once again she meets up with the sixth-grade class,
who have finally pushed the teacher and the parent volunteers over the
edge; the students all seem to know it as they abjectly march in single
file with their eyes cast down while the teacher, who seems to be in a
state approaching despair, mutters, "Remind me never to take you all
anyplace nice."

Alice falls in line with the class as they make their way down the main staircase. She is walking next to a girl a few inches taller than herself, a girl with thick braids and dark brows. The girl glances at Alice and seems to register the fact that Alice is not in her class, nor is she someone whom she has ever seen before, but this knowledge is eclipsed by her unhappiness about being removed from the museum. "Do you think this place used to be a castle?" the girl asks Alice.

"I guess," says Alice, though she knows better.

Despite the search for the so-called pedophile and the two so-called abducted children, it looks not that much different from any other day at the Metropolitan when the class and Alice reach the first floor. There are police standing at the exits, but their expressions are mildly curious, and their posture is relaxed. And meanwhile, people are streaming in and out, alone and in pairs and in groups, tourists, art lovers, lonely people, young and old.

The police at the door pay scarcely any attention as the sixth-graders and Alice stream past them and outside. She continues to count her breaths as she steps out into the cold gray afternoon.

Michael is counting too: benches. Walking backward so he can see Adam or Alice approach. But where are they?

He is at the limit of what he can endure. He has been in a constant state of anxiety since Adam appeared at his apartment. He has entered a world he has never imagined. The rug of reality has been yanked from under him by an unseen hand. He feels alone, abandoned, un-equal to the task. And Xavier: *Where in the fucking hell are you?*

At the fiftieth bench, he stops, sits, facing east. Before him is a statue of King Jagiello, the fifteenth-century unifier of Poland and Lithuania, the grand duke of Lithuania, vanquisher of the Teutonic aggressors at the Battle of Grunwald. The statue was brought to New York by the Poles for the 1939 World's Fair, and while it was here, Poland fell to the German army, after which monuments celebrating the defeat of the Teutonic hordes were not welcome in Poland, and so the bronze statue stayed put, and it has been here ever since. The king's armored horse looks rather demure, its head cocked to one side, its eyes startled and wide as it gazes down and off to one side, as if to avoid the sights of the slaughter sure to come. But Jagiello himself brims with military bluster, his crown firmly perched on a head of flowing hair, his expression stubborn and royally confident, his arms raised in a V, a long sword in each hand, the swords themselves crossed in an X, one tip pointing north and the other south.

"May I trouble you for a light?" a voice says.

Startled out of his reverie, Michael sits up straighter. Something tells him not to turn around. A thumping heartbeat later, Alex Twisden is sitting next to him. Twisden smells of earth and wind; his shoes are splattered with mud.

"Get the fuck away from me," Michael says in a quiet voice.

"Why are you in my life?" Alex asks. He folds his arms over his chest, stretches out his legs. "Why do I even fucking know you?"

A couple of nannies wheeling their well-swaddled charges walk by. It has gotten colder, and when the nannies open their mouths to talk, clouds of vapor come out and hang in the air like dialogue balloons in a comic strip. One of them glances at Alex and whispers something to her friend, who looks back over her shoulder at Twisden as the two women go on their way.

"I'm going to call the police," Michael says.

"Good! The police are looking for you. The crazy fag who took two children away from their home."

"The children are terrified of you, Twisden. Terrified."

Alex lays his hand on Michael's knee. Pats it. Squeezes it. Pats it again.

"You're a good person," Twisden says. "I know this."

Michael doesn't say anything. From a distance, he sees Adam, walking slowly, counting the benches.

"I would like to know what my children have said about their parents."

"What are you worried about? What is the thing that you don't want them to say?"

"Don't joust with me, Mr. Grade-School Teacher. You're way above your pay grade. I do this for a living. Rule number one: you don't ask a question unless you already know the answer."

"But I do," Michael says. "I do know the answer. I know exactly what you want to keep secret."

Twisden laughs. Michael wonders if he is merely trying to conceal his feelings by pretending he finds all this terribly amusing, or if he is laughing over what is about to happen, which only Twisden himself can know.

"You're gay, aren't you," Twisden says, suddenly very serious.

"Oh yes. Indeed. Extremely gay. Gay as the day is long. Über-gay, turbo-gay. Why? Are you having feelings?"

"Look here, teacher boy. Your sexuality is of no interest to me. But like any parent, I am not going to sit idly by while some gay teacher seduces my son away from his family. You find him attractive. And by now maybe you're finding the girl a little…shall we say: interesting."

"You're insane." Michael makes a move to stand. He knows Adam is getting closer and closer, and he not only wants to get away from Twisden but also is hoping, against all probability, that Twisden has not yet noticed his son slowly approaching.

But Twisden is fast and he is strong. He clasps Michael's shoulder and presses him down as if he is leaning on a plunger that will explode sticks of dynamite.

"What's your hurry? Do you think I don't see my son making his way toward us? He's my son. *My son!* There is nothing in the world I care about more. He's mine. Not yours. Mine. Do you understand me? It's just natural. You'll see. One day you and Xavier might adopt a nice little Chinese baby, and you'll be surprised how protective you'll come to feel."

"How do you even know Xavier?"

"Hmm," Twisden says, tapping his forefinger against his chin. "That's an excellent question. How do I know Xavier?"

"Where is he, Twisden?" Michael attempts to rise again and this time manages to twist away from Alex's grip. "You are going down, man." Michael glances over his shoulder. Adam sees him and he also sees his father; he has stopped right where he is, eight benches away. About twenty benches away from Michael, Alice walks, her head down, pointing at each bench as she counts it off.

From the opposite direction, he hears a shout. "Alex? Sweetheart?" It's Leslie, walking quickly, her trench coat open and filled with the wind, puffed out like a sail, her hair blowing. She starts to run.

Michael turns toward Alex and pulls his phone out of his back pocket, flips it open. "It's over. You understand? Over."

Twisden slowly get up. He is three or four inches taller than Michael and he makes every inch of his advantage count — posture, proximity, a palpable willingness to do harm. He tries to snatch Michael's phone away before he can dial 911 and hit the Send button, but Michael turns quickly so his back is to Twisden, which is a successful maneuver inasmuch as it protects his phone and the integrity of the call, but in every other way it is the worst thing he could have done.

"Remember when I tossed you against the wall in Mr. Fleming's office?" Twisden says. "Too bad there are no walls here." And with a roar of fury Twisden grabs Michael from behind and lifts him high off the ground, holds him aloft.

"Alex!" Leslie calls out, fearing the worst.

"Dad!" Adam cries. "Let him alone."

Michael tries to twist free of the grip, but he is held as tightly as a fox in a trap, and a kind of calm begins to settle over him, a passivity perhaps, a recognition of how futile it is to resist. The tops of the trees seem abnormally close; their bare branches form ten thousand cracks in the low gray sky. Across the expanse of clouds, a jet, still in take-off mode from Kennedy, disappears into the clouds, a needle in the haystack of eternity. Michael's only hope is that someone else will intervene.

"Stay back!" he shouts to Adam. "Just get out of here."

"Don't talk to my kid," Twisden all but growls. "He's mine. Mine. Mine mine mine mine."

Over and over, louder and louder, Twisden repeats the word—*mine, mine*—until it becomes a chant, an exercise in self-hypnosis, a battle cry.

Oh my God, Michael thinks. *My life!* Before he can further consider the onrushing darkness that will engulf him, he is tossed into the air by the astonishing force of Twisden's thrust. For a moment, Michael thinks that he is going to fall quickly, and his first instinct is to cover his face, protect his teeth, somehow dampen the thud. He hopes he will hit the grass and not the concrete pavement or one of the benches.

But the odd thing is he is not falling at all, not yet. He is rising, his arms outstretched, his legs too. He turns slightly, sees the bystanders: a couple of skateboarders; a group of Asian tourists, their cameras dangling over their Burberry coats. A fleeting thought: Are these really going to be the last things I ever see?

He reaches the apex of his arc; he can feel the end of his upward surge, a moment of calm while the force of the vile, violent energy that has thrust him upward surrenders its primacy to the omnipotent force of gravity, and Michael begins his inevitable descent. Instinctively, his hands reach out, clawing desperately, as if he were a trapeze artist trying to stop his fall, grasping for a suddenly vanished ring. And yet: his fall does not last more than another instant.

It is fatally interrupted by King Jagiello's raised swords. The bronze point of the south-pointing sword pierces Michael through the thigh of his right leg, and the point of the other sword plunges between his shoulder blades. Driven by his own weight, he slowly sinks down the swords, inch by inch. He feels the pressure of it, the brutal metallic presence of the swords, but, most peculiarly, he feels only mild pain—the insult to his body is so vast that it cannot, at first, be comprehended, and his senses, overwhelmed, cannot perceive what has happened to him. Pain is there to warn us that the body is in danger, but Michael is beyond warning now—just as you would not say "Be careful" to a man who has stepped off a ledge and is plunging into the chasm below; all you can do is watch.

Michael turns his head for a last look at the world. As his eyes dim—it is as if they are filling up with milk—he sees Adam, his rosy lips twisted into a rictus of grief. At least, he thinks it is Adam. It all seems so far away. Michael feels the bronze blades going deeper and deeper. He wonders if there is anything he can do to save or prolong his life, but the possibility seems distant, unlikely—and far too much work. Half his brain is already in darkness, but with what is left he thinks how strange this is, to be dying on this day, and to just be letting it happen. He would have guessed it would be different, he would have guessed that he would struggle more vigorously instead of sinking into his own death like falling slowly slowly slowly to sleep after a long exhausting day.

Gravity moves him another sixteenth of an inch down the length of Jagiello's blades, until the tip of the north-pointing sword touches Michael's heart. He lets out a cry, as if experiencing an electric shock. He hears someone calling his name. *Who is that? Who is that? Xavier?*

Something is next to his face. A ghost. A bird. An angel. No…something else. Someone.

Adam, his face streaked with tears. Oh! The child! The poor child! Michael reaches out, softly touches the boy's hair in that moment of pure imagination, that crack in the dome, that single solitary fissure between the two states, the one that is so fleeting, and the one that is forever. In the final gasp, so much is revealed, and what is shown to Michael is not the secret of eternity or the meaning of life or, really, the meaning of anything, but merely that he was an exceptionally nice man, which may sound like very little but which is actually quite overwhelming, like the sounds of a chorus filling what had been an instant before a silent and empty room.

Never before, never, have Adam and Alice seen their father in a state of fear. He in unhinged, undone. He bends over, his hands on his knees, his head down, panting and trying to catch his breath. Squiggles of saliva hang from his open mouth that, finally, he wipes away with the back of his hand. He stands straight again and surveys the scene with frightened eyes.

Leslie is here, holding her cell phone in front of her, looking at it, showing it to Alex, as if the solution to all their problems might somehow be found in its circuitry. She is crying openly, the tears rushing out of her.

"What did you do?" Alice wails.

"Are you going to leave him there?" Adam shouts.

"You threw him!"

"He's dying. Get him down he's dying get him down."

The whoop of a siren announces that someone has called the police. The first car to arrive must have been close by to begin with, and the second arrives wailing as well and with its headlights flashing, which gives that squad car a panicked look, as if it were trying to escape from a criminal rather than apprehend one.

Alex is suddenly very still. More sirens are on the way. An ambulance, a fire truck, more police. The air shakes with the noise of it. The caw of a million crows could not be more piercing. As the cops come out of their cars—two with Glocks already drawn—passersby gather, including a couple who actually witnessed Alex's throwing Michael onto the king's swords and who, despite their terror, are pointing at Alex, shouting to the police, "He's the one! He killed that guy!"

Leslie gathers her children close to her and they submit to her motherly touch. They have nowhere else to go.

The firefighters are setting up a ladder next to the statue of the Polish king, whose crown and long hair are speckled and streaked with blood.

Rodolfo, arriving from the north, crouches low on his skateboard. Behind him, in a V formation, are two of his buddies, and behind them are three other young folks who call the park home.

Alex feels his blood surging and twisting through him like white water. As his family looks mutely on, he leaps over a bench, with two, now three, now four cops in close pursuit. He goes up the rise, through the dormant foliage, toward the low wall that marks the park's eastern edge. The police don't dare fire; beyond that wall is a busy sidewalk, and Fifth Avenue.

The M1 bus, which runs down Fifth Avenue from Harlem to the East Village, weighs, before the first passenger steps in, over twelve tons, and the drum brakes are capable of stopping these behemoths, but they often must be pumped, and stopping the long, weighty vehicle is not instantaneous, far from it. The M1 that is now on its way, driven by a recent MTA hire named Mariano Gomez, is running four minutes behind schedule, and Gomez, who used to drive a bus in Lima, Peru, tries to make up one of those minutes, maybe even two, simply by getting past the light on Eighty-Sixth Street before it turns red.

His bus is nearly full, though there are still empty seats and no apparent reason why this middle-aged woman with vivid orange hair and a black ski parka is standing on one foot in the aisle, her arms extended like a tightrope walker's. Some new therapy. New exercise. Transcendental loco yoga. New York! He blesses the day he moved here. He notices her fingertips are stained black and he wonders if she is one of the city's multitude of graffiti *brujas* — perhaps it was she and her *compañeras* who defaced the ad for *Blood Sausage,* writing *This de-*

means women across the image of the female corpse hanging from a meat hook.

Gomez glances at his speedometer and sees he is going forty-eight miles an hour. A bit friskier than he had intended. Then he hears sirens, and it's like pressing the bar on his new fridge and having the ice cubes clatter into his glass, only the glass is the pit of his stomach. If he gets stopped for speeding, he's through.

Yet just as he is pressing his foot onto the long brake pedal, he sees something out of the corner of his eye, sees it without seeing it, it's all too sudden, too fast. And the next thing he knows, a rich, once somewhat prominent New Yorker who has slowly faded from public life is running across Fifth Avenue, his route a broken line, a zigzag, like the graph of a volatile stock or the shining path of a lightning crack across the darkened sky.

Gomez hits the brake with all the speed and force he has; the worn pads screech piteously against the drum. The woman on one foot somehow maintains her balance, but others on the bus do not fare as well, and a few of them slide right out of their seats as the M1 swerves, its backside pointing east, its front end veering west. Something— probably a taxi; every other car on Fifth Avenue is a taxi this time of day—hits him from behind, not hard. Some luck there. But the crazy man who has been dashing across Fifth, he's got no luck at all. He looks about fifty, but, man, is he in good shape, with the moves of a superathlete. But he never had a chance, like a dog, like a crazy dog 90 percent instinct, helpless to stop when his legs say go. The guy just ran out and, despite Mariano Gomez's best efforts, there is no avoiding him. He is hit, and hit good. He tried to jump out of the way, but the poor dog of a man just made matters worse. His face is pressed hard against the windshield; half his body too. When the bus comes to a halt, the guy is still stuck there, blood running out of his mouth, his nose. His eyes wide open but dead as rocks. Slowly, ever so slowly, his lifeless body slides down the windshield, falls backward, and hits the street, staring blindly at the cement sky, an odd point of peace and tranquillity in a world of sirens, honking, and the panicked human screams of passersby.

Xavier opens his eyes just enough to see, as if trying to keep his having regained consciousness secret from whoever may be watching him. It has not yet penetrated his beleaguered mind that he is no longer being held captive. He sees strips of lighting on the ceiling, which tells him he is no longer in his cage, which, in turn, causes his heart to race. He closes his eyes again, waiting to settle down. He feels a heaviness covering him, and he opens his eyes ever so slightly again and through the mesh of his eyelashes he sees his chest, his whole torso covered in white. Surreptitiously, he touches what covers him—it's cool, soft. A sheet? Many sheets?

Sounds. The murmur of distant voices. The wobbly squeak of…what? Wheels? Something being carted away? Parts of him? He tenses the muscles of his legs. No: they're still there. *Presente*. A steady gurgling. As if someone has placed a powerful microphone next to the surface of a pot of boiling rice. He moves his tongue around in his mouth. His mouth feels enormous and his tongue feels very small, like a mouse inside a cave. The feverish strangeness of this jolts him and he opens his eyes a little more, tries to sit up. Using his arms to push up. Except he doesn't have arms. He has…arm. He peers over his left shoulder and sees the shoulder itself, a cluster of bandages, and then…a terrible, crushing absence.

It doesn't bother him as much as he would have expected. He knows he is lucky to be alive. He is in a hospital. Never in his wildest imagination would he have thought that the sight of a hospital room would fill him with such relief, waves and waves of relief, one arriving after the other.

At last Xavier dares to fully open his eyes. Pain, like a rain of flaming arrows, beginning in the part of his skull that Alex rammed into the light pole, penetrates him with such sudden vehemence that it makes him moan.

"Xavier?" Someone has called his name, a familiar voice. Some-one...safe. Someone good.

He sees he is connected to a machine. And there are IV tubes going running into him beneath the covers.

"Xavier. Xavier."

His sister is here. Rosalie. Rosalie. She seems to float before him, like a face reflected in a gigantic soap bubble. The sight of her makes him want to weep.

"Don't move, baby," she is saying. "You're okay. You're alive, you're hurt, they fucked you up something good, but you're okay and you're going to make it, baby. You're going to be fine."

He has to think for a moment. Is she speaking English or Spanish?

"Where's my arm?"

"They don't know yet."

"How long have I been here?" His voice is barely a whisper. He has shredded it, screaming for all those hours.

"Shhh, it's okay, Xavier. You've been here just a little while. It's okay."

He wants to say to her *Stop reassuring me and just tell me what the hell is happening,* but it's too many words. *Where have I been? What have they done to me?* He tries to convey it all in a look—she knows him so well, she'd be able to read it in his eyes, but she has gotten up from her chair and is walking toward the squeaking wheels and the murmur-ing voices and the *ding ding ding* of some machine, which sounds like someone has put a stethoscope to the chest of a robot.

"Nurse? Someone?" Rosalie is calling out. "My brother's awake!"

Xavier hears music and he painfully turns his head toward it. He sees now that the room he is in is not a room at all but a piece of hospital real estate in which some of the privacy of an actual room has been created by shelves of medical supplies and stacks of medical equipment on one side of him and a pleated white curtain on the other.

The curtain is only partially drawn, and he sees in the open space the bare, swollen, faintly blue feet of someone in the next bed, someone who is apparently watching a television set that's mounted near the ceiling on a long L-shaped bracket.

Xavier has a clear view of the set. A newsreader, an Asian woman, her dark hair like a swimmer's cap, is looking down at her script, frowning. She looks now at the camera, swallows, takes a deep breath. "Police continue to look for answers in the strange and shocking deaths on the Upper East Side of Manhattan this afternoon, and we're joined now by News Twenty-Two's Carter Davis, in Central Park."

The anchor's face is replaced by that of a local reporter, a rather louche young man wearing a long scarf and a beret, and with a two-day growth of auburn whiskers. "Thank you, Becky. Well, people are still reeling from the events of this afternoon, and we now have positive identifications of both of the dead men in this apparent murder/suicide."

The image changes now to a close shot of the bloodstained tips of King Jagiello's twin swords. City workers have erected a screen to block most of the statue from view, though even now, with the body gone and the initial excitement down from a roar to a hum, there remain two or three dozen people drawn by curiosity and some darker impulse to the sight of the killing, just as once upon a time people would gather at the spot where someone had had a vision or where a miracle had occurred.

"New York City schoolteacher Michael Medoff…" the reporter is saying, and whatever comes after that is lost on Xavier, because a new image now fills the hanging television's screen.

That's Michael's driver's license is Xavier's first thought; his second cannot really be called a thought at all. He starts pulling the tubes out of himself and kicking the covers off. He knows only one thing now and that is he must get to that TV set and take Michael's picture off it.

"Shh. Shh. Xavier, please, *tranquilo*..." Rosalie is at his bedside and she has her warm, soft arms around him and—like home!—is wrestling him down. "Someone?" she calls out. "Help?" And then in a sharper voice, "Please turn that set off. You're disturbing my brother."

Xavier has no strength for the struggle. He falls back onto the bed, pain shooting through him with total violence, the violence of nature, the violence of a volcano. The body—the mind!—cannot survive the onslaught of so much pain....

Though Rosalie tries to cover his eyes with her Lysol-sanitized hand, Xavier can still partially see the set, enough to identify the next picture that comes up. The photograph is of a handsome middle-aged man with a terrific haircut, a white shirt, a striped tie. There is nothing in the picture to remind Xavier of the beast who dragged him out of that taxi—when was that? When? When? His mind gropes for a sense of sequence as a man might flounder for a piece of wreckage to help him survive the explosion of the ship he once sailed. Human beings, he thinks, were not made to endure such pain. Weakly, he tries to remove Rosalie's hand, but he cannot, and now she is joined by someone else.

A nurse is here. Her lined, exhausted face. Her hands. The low hiss of the rayon of her uniform. Her candied breath.

"Okay, Mr. Sardina, can you just relax for me? Please?"

Rosalie removes her hand from his eyes and he stares up at the nurse. African, from the pure blackness of her. Her eyes are dark brown, her expression reserved but kind. The wrinkles on her fingers like little white rings.

"Are you in pain now, Mr. Sardina?" the nurse asks in her up-and-down voice. "Can you put a number value to your pain, with ten being the worst?"

Xavier looks again at his shoulder, and the sad droop of bandages, and the unbelievable emptiness that follows. He remembers: It's where the beast started in. It's where he took the first bite. *Sorry, sorry,* the man had said, staggering away, wiping his chin, breathing quickly, shallowly, like a rapist. *Next time, I'll get something to knock you out.*

"Monster!" Xavier screams. *"Monster!"*

"I need some help here," the nurse says in as calm a voice as she can manage. "Is Nurse Gauthier on the floor?"

"No, Amelie had to leave early," a distant voice answers. "She had some situation at home."

"I knew one day I would see you again. Sometimes I searched for you, just looking at the faces of people when I walked to work. I knew I would recognize you. Even though—and I don't mean this in a bad way—you don't look so much like you used to." Amelie Gauthier is seated with Leslie in a cramped kitchen, the blue Formica kitchen table between them, and she *does* mean it in a bad way. Leslie's skin is like ever-so-slightly-pink clay, her eyes are dark and deeply set and totally without happiness or hope. How can Amelie dislike a person so clearly faltering, so visibly failing to thrive? Yet she does....

There is something hospitable about sitting with someone in your kitchen, but Amelie has brought Leslie into this room because it is the only room in her apartment currently unoccupied. Which must mean the abandoned ones, the wild children of the park, have already cleaned her out, because the kitchen is usually their first stop. Leslie, dazed, limp, has allowed Amelie to lead her to a hard wooden chair. The kitchen reeks of soup and the yeasty redolence of vitamins; Leslie must breathe through her mouth to stop herself from retching. Her hands are folded. She is like a child at her desk in school. Her face is streaked with mascara and tears. She looks as if she has been living in one of the tunnels beneath Pennsylvania Station. Wildness and hopelessness rise off her skin like wet smoke. She squeezes her hands together to try to control her trembling, but the effort only makes everything worse.

"You don't have any idea who I am, do you," Amelie says. She takes a deep breath, folds her arms over her chest, and looks her visitor up and down.

"I'm sorry," Leslie says. She looks past Amelie and into the next room, where her twins have joined Rodolfo and the others. Alice is whispering rapidly, interrupted now and then by Adam, while the others listen, rapt.

"Who are these children?" Leslie murmurs, as much to herself as to Amelie.

"They have something in common with your own children," Amelie says.

Amelie's eyes follow Leslie's gaze and sees how this dark and chaotic apartment must look, its unending dishevelment speaking definitively about the difficulties of Amelie's circumstances and the impossibility of her schedule. Mingled with the profusion of medical supplies she needs to care for Bernard, there are piles of laundry that await folding, stacks of newspapers that await recycling, books that await reshelving, videos that await returning, dishes that await washing.

Leslie blots her eyes with the heels of her hands, takes a deep breath.

"Thank you for letting us into your home," she says.

It is not the first time Amelie has come home to a houseful of the untamable children. She keeps her door open to the kids who live in the park. They are Bernard's friends, his only friends, and she is grateful to them, filthiness and all.

"May I call you Leslie," Amelie asks.

"Of course."

"Do you remember where we met, Leslie?"

Leslie shakes her head uncertainly.

"Well, people like you don't really notice people like me."

Leslie blinks in surprise. "I'm sorry. Do you want us to leave?"

"No, I do not. I'm going to try to help you. But it would have been nice if you had remembered meeting me before. I was one of the nurses in the delivery room with you when you had your *three* children."

"How could I know? I was having a baby. I don't remember anyone from that day. My mind isn't what it once was." She is surprised she has any tears left, but she does.

"Did you hear what I said?"

Leslie cocks her head, tilts her ear toward Amelie.

"I said your *three* children."

"I thought mistake," Leslie murmurs.

"Not my mistake."

Leslie shakes her head. She is not able to process what is being said to her right now. Even under the best of circumstances, she would be confused by what Amelie is saying....

"You didn't have twins," Amelie says. Her voice softens, her shoulders relax.

"Yes, I do. Did. Twins." Leslie has noticed over the past few months that when she is tired or under stress, she makes even more mistakes in her speech, and she has never in her life been more tired and under more stress than she is right now. She thinks for a moment about simply closing her eyes, cushioning her head upon her arm, and letting herself plunge into a deep, obliterating sleep. Yet she does not dare: in the darkness float the excruciating memories of all she has seen today and yesterday and the day before that and the day before that. Darkness is a room where the image of Alex crushed and the image of the pierced body of the young teacher now squeeze themselves into a space that already contains more revulsion and more regret than she ever thought possible. If only she could never ever close her eyes again.

"You delivered three babies, Leslie."

Leslie shakes her head.

"Your doctor?"

"Don't remember. We saw many."

"Yes. From Turtle Bay Obstetrics. Yes?"

"I think so."

"May I ask you how you got here?"

"Here?" Leslie asks.

"Yes, to my apartment."

"We walked across the park. No one was paying attention to us. We just walked. My children. And the other children."

"And they brought you here," Amelie says.

Leslie looks away. An arched entrance separates the kitchen from the shadowy chaos of Gauthier's apartment; her children sit on a sofa with six of the park children. From this distance they just seem like children, hanging out, wasting time. Adam has a video-game controller in his hand, as does Rodolfo, and they are playing a game whose sound track seems to be an unending stream of automatic weapons firing and the wail of police sirens. How can they listen to those sirens and not be reliving what happened right before their eyes? Where do they put their experiences? How do they live?

"Leslie?" Amelie reaches across the table and touches Leslie's arm, causing Leslie to turn toward her with terrifying swiftness, her eyes keen, her lip curled. Amelie puts her hands up.

"Would you like to see your son?" Amelie asks. "Your other son?"

"No. No more. Please. I want everything to stop."

"I have to insist, Leslie." Amelie has a sense of justice, and it must be satisfied. For years, she has tended to Bernard's ever-expanding needs, suffered with him the humiliations of his disfigurement, endured with him the grinding pain of his days. In that time, she never doubted that she was right to have outwitted those who wanted him extinguished— she was willing to defy them all, the doctors, the other nurses, even nature itself. And she never wanted recompense, except for this one thing: she wanted the mother to look at what she had abandoned.

"I have spent ten years taking care of what you were meant to take care of," she says. "And now you are here, in more trouble than you could ever imagine, and you are hiding from—from who? The police? Everyone in the world? Yourself? And you are asking my help. If you want that help, Leslie, you need to take a look at your son."

Amelie pushes her chair back, stands, and gestures commandingly for Leslie to follow her. They walk through the room where the children are parked in front of the TV screen. They all look down, remain silent, which makes the video game sound all the louder.

"Bernard?" Amelie says, rapping a knuckle against his bedroom door. She looks over her shoulder at Leslie. "He may be a bit groggy."

"I have to think," Leslie says. She rubs her forehead.

"If you want to stay here, you need to do what I ask you. It's as simple as that." She raps again on Bernard's door, this time not waiting for an answer before opening it up.

The boy was able to awaken himself enough to call his mother at the hospital, but, still clutching his phone in his two-fingered hand, he has fallen deeply into a vast narcotic sleep. Even from a distance, and even through the darkness of this room, Leslie sees enough of Bernard to make her let out an "oh" of dismay.

"How dare you," snarls Amelie. She goes to Bernard's bedside, takes the phone from him, and holds out his hand for Leslie to see. "You see that?" With her fingertip, she traces the path of Bernard's reddish birthmark, a serpentine squiggle just like the marks on the hands of Leslie's other children.

Leslie does not speak. It is all she can do to nod her head. Calamities collide within her until she cannot tell exactly where one has ended and the next one begun.

Suddenly, she feels something touch her on the back. With a shiver and start, she turns around and sees Alice looking up at her.

"Mom?" she asks. "Are we going to go home?"

Leslie and Amelie are in Fairway Market on Broadway and Seventy-Fourth Street, filling their shopping cart with food for the children. Between Amelie's apartment and the store, they passed two cops conversing in their squad car, a mounted police officer, and two women on foot patrol, and none of them paid Leslie the slightest mind. *Maybe it never happened,* Leslie thinks. Yet memory reacts quickly and decisively to the effrontery of fantasy, and as soon as she imagines that Alex and the teacher are out there, alive, the images of their deaths rush forth to shred her illusions. Now, with everything else, she has a new enemy: the memories that stalk her every step of the way. Her own mind has become a forbidden zone.

Amelie pushes the cart decisively through the thronged aisles, full of people on their way home from work. She fills the cart with plums and apples, orange juice, almonds, rice crackers....

"These kids don't eat anything decent most of the time," Amelie says over her shoulder. "It's the least I can do."

"What about some meat?" Leslie says, in not much more than a whisper.

Amelie stops her cart, turns, and holds Leslie in her gaze for a couple of long moments. "That's the last thing in the world they need."

"Protein," Leslie says, with a shrug.

"Look, Leslie, I know what you've been going through. I know how hard it's been, and it gets harder every year."

"It was just a suggestion."

"I know what to feed these kids. Meat is full of hormones. You know how you feel at night? The temptations? The cravings? Well, that's how some of them start to feel when the hormones really kick in. Right now, they're still basically just kids. But some of them, you have to keep an eye out."

"I have to take care of my kids," Leslie says.

"I know, I know. I've got stuff I can give you back at the apartment. Pills that will take the edge off, pretty much."

"I don't like pills."

"They're not going to turn night into day, but if you take them they might help, for a little while."

"Why just for a little while?"

"You'll get used to them. You'll burn through them, they'll stop making a difference. They might not even make a difference at all. But don't worry. As long as you're with me, I'll keep an eye on you."

"And after that?"

"I'm a nurse," Amelie says. "Mainly nurses just try to alleviate suffering."

A couple of shoppers—a dapper older man and a heavyset younger guy—are listening to Leslie and Amelie with unmitigated curiosity.

"May I help you?" Amelie says to them, her voice as blunt as a kick in the shins.

The two men quickly push their cart away. It is filled with cut flowers, flats of smoked salmon, crackers, grapes, a bottle of olive oil....*Oh, life!* thinks Leslie. The pleasures of life. Whatever happened to the pleasures of life?

A wave of grief buckles her knees. To regain her balance, she grabs hold of the nearest thing, which happens to be a clear-front riser holding a display of oranges. One falls, then another, and in moments dozens of them are bouncing and rolling down the aisle.

Rodolfo and a couple of the others have helped Bernard out of his bed. The effects of the Dilaudid have, for the most part, worn off, and now he is in the apartment's front room, tapping away on his computer. The screen casts its watery glow on what there is of his face. The others wait silently, as if Bernard is cracking open a safe, inside of which is everything they have ever wanted.

Adam takes this opportunity to pull Alice into the kitchen, where he whispers urgently to her.

"We should get out of here."

"Where?"

"I don't know. Where do you think we should go?"

"I'm tired."

"She's going to come back soon."

"She seems like she's better," Alice says.

"It's mad dark. Maybe we should go."

"There's no place left to go, Adam. It's night. Everyone is dead. This is it."

"Someone."

"Someone what?"

"I don't know. Someone will take care of us. What are we going to do? Live in the park? Live here? There's no way."

"At least we're together," Alice says.

Adam nods. He takes his sister's hand, squeezes it. It's like touching a part of himself, another version of himself that has stepped out of a dream. But she's no *dream*. She is the most real thing, the thing he cannot live without.

"Hey, Alice, come in here," Rodolfo shouts from the front room. "Check it out, check it out." His arms are stretched in front of him, and both of his pointer fingers are aimed at Alice. When her eyes meet his, he snaps his fingers, flicks his pelvis, smiles.

A freezing rain is pelting the city, and when Leslie and Amelie come in with the groceries, they are virtually soaked.

"Mom!" both Adam and Alice call out as soon as they see her.

"Come here," Adam says. "You gotta look at this."

Leslie stands behind Bernard, who has brought a video up on his screen. It is Dr. Kis, sitting at a desk, a window full of sunlight behind him.

"Oh my God," Leslie says.

Tentatively, she touches the back of the hoodie that covers Bernard's head. *Son,* she thinks.

The gesture is not lost on Adam or Alice. To see this moment's tenderness in their mother reminds them of the love she has shown them, the love they feel, but most of all it fills them with *hope*. Where does hope come from when it miraculously appears; where does it go when it vanishes? No X-ray, MRI, or CAT scan can locate the wellspring of hope, yet it has been there during every moment of endurance and every triumph, and now that the twins feel it they realize how long they have lived without it, just as you can understand how much pain you have been in only once the agony stops.

Bernard presses the Play arrow, and Kis begins to speak.

"As some of you know, I have been offering fertility treatments for nearly fifteen years. People, many hundreds of them, have come to me, so many without hope. I have not been able to give each and every client a child, but my success rate is unprecedented in modern fertility medicine. There have been articles in *Paris Match* in France, *Der Spiegel* in Germany, *OK!* in Russia, *Town & Country* magazine in the United States, and of course numerous medical journals. There is no question, no question whatsoever, so make no mistake, my friends, I am, in all due modestment, the leading fertility physician in Europe, and the world.

"Have there been errors? Of course there have. Have some been…unfortunate? Yes, without question…"

"He can make it go away," Adam blurts out, unable to stand there in silence while Leslie, her mouth half open, her eyes pinned to the screen, watches and listens as the distant doctor justifies and apologizes for what he has done.

"Mom," Alice says. "Mom…" Her legs feel as if they are made of lead. Her stomach aches, her eyes burn. She knows she is crying now, and it is sort of embarrassing, but it's not too bad. She feels a comforting hand on her shoulder—Rodolfo! "Mom? Mom?"

"Oh, baby," Leslie says, gathering in her daughter and her son. "I am so so so sorry…"

The news stations are filled with reports of the bizarre killing in Central Park, of the murderer who rushed insanely into the traffic on

Fifth Avenue, where he was executed by the M1 bus. The story first appears on local news, though the national cable stations are quick to pick it up, and the major networks are unable to resist it. For the newscasters, the story is a gift that keeps on giving. With one of the dead men a once prominent New York attorney and the other a beloved teacher in a prestigious and pricey Upper East Side private school who was also the teacher of one of the alleged murderer's children, the story creates a kind of porn loop for TV and the Internet. There is a town house, graceful, frightfully expensive, just a touch dishabille. There is the heavyset neighbor rambling on about children climbing out of windows. There is the soaring facade of the publishing company where the mother used to work. There is the plain glass box where Alex Twisden turned the law into a lasso to rope in money for his clients. There is the Gothic facade of Berryman Prep. There is the beautiful office of the headmaster. There are the puzzled faces of the kids in the dead teacher's classes—they look like shell-shocked models in a very sad Ralph Lauren ad.

Meanwhile, Cynthia remains in the precinct's lockup. She has finally made it clear to the officer in charge of her that she does not live in New York, that she had nothing to do with the poor soul locked in that cellar, that she is, in fact, the person who called the police in the first place. As far as she can tell, they have finally gotten the story more or less straight. Yet she remains in custody, and the only reason for this is that it takes a bit of effort to release her, though it may also be the case that they mistakenly believe she knows where Leslie and the children are and that they think if she has to relieve herself one more time in front of another person, she will break down and tell them.

The next afternoon, Leslie, Adam, and Alice are at Newark International Airport, waiting for their flight to Munich, Germany, to be announced—it is already half an hour late, and every moment they are still in the United States, their fragile plan threatens to collapse.

No one can glance in their direction without Leslie feeling a violent lurch in her stomach. Are she and her children being looked for? Is she a person of interest in whatever investigation is taking place into the deaths of Alex and Michael Medoff? Have her children been reported missing? Abducted?

She takes one of the sedatives Amelie gave her, swallows it down without water.

Following Amelie's advice, last night Leslie gave the keys to her house to Rodolfo. His mission was to get her purse with her wallet and her credit cards, which, as best she could remember, was sitting in the kitchen. Next, he was to get the passports, though she wasn't entirely sure where they were. Her best guess was that they were in a desk drawer in the third door to the left (or maybe it was the right—she has become muddled over the difference between the two) on the second floor, which Alex had been using as a kind of home office. In the bedroom, in the night table, was an envelope with several diamonds in it, seven or eight, maybe more, she wasn't sure. They had been pried from various pieces of jewelry, some heirlooms, some more recently purchased, and she and Alex had been selling the diamonds to a Colombian dealer who had a little booth in a jewelry mart on Forty-Seventh Street. Kis was certainly going to want money, and these diamonds were going to have to suffice.

But the most important thing was this: If Rodolfo had the slightest inkling that the house was under surveillance, he was to simply walk by and not make any attempt to get in. If he was to get picked up by the police…It was unbearable to even contemplate the ruination that would follow. Rodolfo chose one other of the wild children, Dylan Shapiro, to accompany him, and before he left he took Alice's hand and kissed it, a gesture that he seemed to have learned from a movie about medieval knights risking all for the good of a lady.

As it happened, it took Rodolfo a full three hours to come back with the triple holy grail of Leslie's credit cards, the envelope with the diamonds, and their passports. He was exhausted, unusually dirty, and he was without Dylan, who he said was hanging out near Bethesda Fountain. When Amelie asked him what had taken so long, he was evasive. Alice noticed there were little gleaming needles of broken glass on his jacket, and she guessed that he had not entered her house through the front door at all, and that even though he had come back with what they needed, it had not gone smoothly or well. When she questioned him with her eyes, he didn't even try to be subtle when he looked away.

That night, no one except Bernard slept. Amelie watched Leslie as she took her Xanax. She was aware that all of the wild children and Amelie, too, wanted to keep an eye on her. For her to tell them that all she felt was crushing sadness and an exhaustion that seemed like a kind of fatal flu and that she was of no more danger to her children or to anyone else than a shadow on the wall would not have put anyone's mind to rest, and so Leslie simply submitted to the indignity of being watched as the night plunged into its darkest hours and then slowly gave way to a weak, drizzling dawn. The twins alternated between playing their video game and sitting next to each other hand in hand, snuffling miserably over all that they had seen, all they had lost.

At one point—Leslie was afraid to look at a clock; knowing the exact time would only lead her to misery—Bernard joined the general wakefulness, and the next thing Leslie knew his chair was next to her. His computer was closed and he laid a plastic hand on its shell. She glanced at him, managed a weak smile, looked away; she had never seen anything quite like him. The genetic misfortune of him was overwhelming.

"Are you really my mom?" he rasped to her through his little hyphen of a mouth.

She shook her head and shrugged. "I don't know," she said to him. But after a few moments of silence, she added, "I guess so."

Leslie, Adam, and Alice sit in a row of chairs in the departures lounge at Newark, exhausted and silent. Adam takes Alice's hand.

Her eyes are half closed; she seems to be looking at the strips of light on the ceiling, almost as if she were in a trance. Yet at the feel of his touch, her hand closes around Adam's. She is remembering this: When they left Amelie's tenement apartment house this afternoon, someone (it was just as she had once dreamed it) opened the window—of course it was Rodolfo, it had to be—and shouted out, "Hey hey hey, I love you. See you when you get back! Okay?"

"Remember when I told you about my dream?" she says to Adam.

"Shh," he says, and indicates with a slight gesture that someone is looking at them.

And someone is. A tall man in his fifties with a reddish face and unruly eyebrows. He cocks his head, like a dog trying to pinpoint the source of a noise.

"Mom?" Adam says.

Leslie looks up at the man and feels a twist of dread, sharp enough to cut through the haze of sedation. He looks like Richard Zolitor, the head of sales at her old publishing house. Has he heard what happened to her husband, does he know that she is missing along with the children, is he putting it all together now that he sees them?

But it turns out that the man's inquisitive gaze has nothing to do with them at all. He is merely looking for the nearest men's room, and now he sees the sign and hurries toward it.

Leslie glances up at the departures board—it's odd to be waiting out here with the majority of the other travelers, in their dastaars and fedoras and yarmulkes and bad perms, not sequestered comfortably in some first-class lounge. She sees that several flights have been canceled. Right now, she asks so little of fate that it makes her feel a little less doomed and, in fact, vaguely fortunate that their flight to Munich is posted as only delayed.

She is ravenously hungry, and there is not an ounce of meat cooking in this entire airport, on a grill, on a stove, in a pot, or in a microwave, that she does not smell with the utmost intensity and avidity. Yet she is worried that any display of appetite will frighten her children. And even as Leslie is pulled emotionally in two directions—a deep, punishing sorrow over the loss of her mate and best friend, and a wild hope that soon she will be released from the biological prison that Dr. Kis condemned her to—the main thing she feels now is a fierce protectiveness toward her beautiful children.

She has always loved them, but sitting there in the departures lounge at Newark International Airport, bound to them by the chains of sorrow and fear, she never felt more attached than she does right now. What will happen to them once they find Dr. Kis and go through whatever it is he will require them to take or do or have done to them to reverse the mutation his treatment triggered—all that remains unknown. Maybe it will never be safe for them to come home to America—what is left of her money, the town house, her sister: all could be lost. Maybe they will have to live like fugitives, maybe in the forest somewhere....No: that's crazy. She shakes her head hard, as if to rearrange her thoughts.

"Hey, guys, stay right here, okay?" Leslie says. "I have to go to the bathroom."

They look worried, but they make no objection, and Leslie, suddenly overcome with a need to relieve herself, hurries toward the ladies' room.

"What if she doesn't come back," Alice whispers to her brother.

"She will."

Alice opens her passport and looks at the little photo inside. It was taken three years ago, when they almost went to Mexico for a winter vacation but didn't. Her hair is parted in the middle and her eyes are open so wide they almost look like circles. She has the jack-o'-lantern smile of a seven-year-old. Above all, she looks happy, and the sight of her own once-upon-a-time grin fills Alice with melancholy. She closes her passport but keeps it in front of her, holding it fast, not letting it out of her sight.

"Seven hours to Munich," Adam says, nodding sagely, as if knowledge of flight times was part of being a male.

"We can sleep."

"From there it's about an hour to..."

"Lufthansa."

"No. That's an airline. Lub...Lub something."

"We can never go back to school again," Alice says.

"I don't even want to."

"You knew him better than me."

"He was my friend," says Adam, in a voice so small that Alice isn't quite sure if he's spoken or if she just knows what he is thinking.

Leslie sits in one of the stalls, her elbows propped on her thighs, her face buried in the warmth of her hands, trying not to make noise as she cries. She feels her tears oozing through her fingers. She sees it all, over and over and over again: the teacher flying through the air, the look on his face as he waited for death, Alex panting, a shimmer of drool hanging from his open mouth, the frantic dash toward Fifth Avenue...

For a moment, she forgets where she is.

For a moment, she forgets her own name.

But all that comes back, though she half wishes it would not. For the first time in her life she thinks she could possibly one day do it: kill herself.

There is a sharp, inquisitive rap against the stall door. She is too frightened to speak.

"Are you okay in there?" a voice asks.

Leslie is not able to answer. She holds her breath, wills herself to complete silence.

Whoever it is out there tries the door. The tongue of the lock rattles in its groove.

"Hello?" the voice says. "Are you quite all right? Would you like me to call someone?"

An elderly woman, by the waver of her voice. *With an accent, a princess-type accent. No, that's not what it's called. What are those kinds of accents called? English. English. An English accent. Come on, Leslie, get it together.* She gets up; the toilet flushes automatically. She looks at her upper legs as she pulls her pants up. Without Alex there to love her and to tell her she is beautiful, there is no one and nothing between her and the disgust she feels for her body.

"I'm almost out of here," she calls through the closed metal door to the stall. She looks down to make sure nothing of her body might be showing through the gap between the door and the floor.

Suddenly, Leslie hears a great commotion. It begins with a scream, followed by another scream, this one even louder, and following that someone shouts, "Oh, for God's sake, that is so gross." There is a scuffling of feet, the sound of valises on their wheels quickly being rolled out of there, and then silence.

When Leslie leaves the stall, however, the bathroom has been deserted. No one is at the sinks; the other stalls are empty, their doors wide open. Someone has left a little plaid suitcase. Where has everybody gone? Looking left and right, moving with caution, Leslie makes her way toward the sinks. And now she sees what has emptied the ladies' room: a rat, at least five inches long, and an alpha rat to judge by its bulk, with long whiskers and a tail the color of wet putty.

The rat makes a run for it—the small opening in the wall from which it emerged is behind Leslie, but she is too quick for the dashing rodent. Without meaning to, without really knowing what she is doing, Leslie stops the rat in its tracks by stomping on the end of its tail. As it turns around to sink its teeth into her foot, she crushes its spine with her other foot. It twitches once or twice; a dark delicate ribbon of blood unfurls from its mouth.

She stands there, swallows, takes a deep breath. What she would really like to do is pop that thing right into her mouth and eat it in big greedy bites. But as famished as she is, she must resist. If she goes back to the kids reeking of rat, it will destroy whatever trust they have in her…She kicks the rat's body under one of the sinks and washes her hands, her face. As she pulls paper towels out to dry herself, a couple of women maintenance workers come in, one pulling a mop and bucket, the other holding a flashlight.

"Under the sink," Leslie says to them as she hurries back to the departures lounge. She sticks her hand in her pocket and jiggles the vial of pills from Amelie. They seem to be working.

The three of them sleep all the way to Munich. They sleep through the takeoff, the safety demonstration, the first movie, the second movie, the several instances of extreme turbulence, the pilot's reassuring patter, and the landing. The smell of the evening meal temporarily awakens Leslie and she eats everything on her tray, and when that is gone she eats everything on the twins' trays as well, because it seems nothing, not even the scent of chicken and chocolate chip cookies, can awaken them, and it also seems to be the case that even three airplane meals cannot satisfy her hunger.

Because of the delay in their first flight, they have little time to get to the plane to Ljubljana. They have but one suitcase between them — and that suitcase is essentially empty, it's more to help them look like normal travelers — but they must go through passport control before proceeding to the gate for Adria Airlines. German efficiency assures a fast-moving line, but as anxious as Leslie is to clear immigration and hurry to their connecting flight, approaching the immigration officers fills her with misgivings. Maybe by now a directive has gone out, and her name and the names of her children are on a…*what is that called? Watch list!* Their names could be on a watch list. After all, two deaths. Two children missing.

And Cynthia!

"Oh my God."

"What is it, Mom?" Adam asks.

"I just remembered something," Leslie says. "It's okay." But the memory of her sister sitting in the kitchen is connected to a second, even more startling memory: the man in the kennel downstairs. She lets out a long, corrugated sigh.

"Mom?" Alice says.

"Here we go," Leslie says as the young uniformed man in the booth gestures for them to step forward. She has a powerful impulse to turn and run. She sees herself racing through the scrubbed hush of the early-morning airport, vaulting over rows of seats, bounding up an escalator. She puts out her hand, and first Adam gives her his passport, then Alice hands hers over, and a moment or two later Leslie slides all three of the passports to the border-control officer, whose eyes are small and unusually close together and whose lips are as plump and round as cocktail franks.

As he types the serial numbers of their passports into his computer, he asks, in English, "You are staying in Germany?"

Leslie tells him they are heading to Ljubljana, in Slovenia, and though it's only an hour away by air, the immigration officer seems to have no idea what she is saying—either he has never heard of the place or he is too absorbed in running the edge of Leslie's passport through his scanner and peering at the information coming up on his console. He furrows his brow, puckers his lips as if to receive a chaste little kiss. A moment passes, followed by another. The man's pursed lips move up and down. He taps something on his keyboard. Waits. Taps something else. Waits.

And just when it feels to Leslie that she cannot bear the uncertainty another moment, he whomps the German stamp onto each passport and slides them all toward her with a brisk nod.

On the flight to Slovenia, Leslie and the twins are asked not to sit together. There are only fourteen passengers, and the stewardess in her dark turquoise jacket spaces them throughout the small jet so that their weight will be evenly distributed. Sitting in the middle of the plane, Leslie looks out and sees the alpine protrusions of the mountains below, jagged and broken, like immense glaciers floating through a sea of snow-covered trees.

Their plane lands far from the gate, and the passengers are herded onto a bus—open-sided, despite the wintry air—which makes its way through a jumble of large jets, some idle, others with their engines warming. Leslie peers into the whirl of a Swissair jet engine, the sides of which look like a beehive; it turns around and around, faster and faster, its heat sending ripples into the cold gray air, the noise rising higher and higher, almost like a human scream.

"Mom?" Adam says, tugging her sleeve.

She looks at him questioningly.

"You all right?" he asks.

She knows it ought to be her asking him, asking them both: Has it really come to this? Are they really now looking after *her*?

"Tired, I guess," she says.

"Do we have money?" Adam asks.

She looks at him blankly. "Some."

"We need euros," Alice says.

"How do you even know that," Leslie says. She is craning her neck, looking back at that whirling Swissair turbine: there is something in it that draws her.

"Mom," Alice says, with a child's sweet exasperation. "I'm ten, not two."

The bus has brought them to the terminal. There are no customs to go through, no passport control either. Leslie almost understands why this is the case—something to do with Slovenia being part of Europe United, or whatever it's called.…Sometimes her mind feels like an old car: she turns the key and the engine almost turns over almost… almost.

"We can get money at one of the money machines," she announces brightly as the three of them walk across the modest airport, with its couple of cafés and its scatter of shops.

"They're called ATMs, Mom," Alice says.

Leslie fishes her bank card out of her purse and hands it to Alice. "Go to the machine and get some of the local money, okay?"

"I need your PIN." She sees the look of confusion on her mother's face. "The numbers. You have to tell them the right numbers or the card doesn't work."

Leslie's face is blank, and she sadly, slowly shakes her head. Over the years, she gradually left more and more of the nuts and bolts of life to Alex. She can't remember the last time she wrote a check, or did anything else regarding their financial life. Dealing with their dwindling investments, opening bank statements, paying taxes, and overseeing the steady stream of heirlooms they have brought to auction were all Alex's responsibility since...actually, she cannot remember when it was that she handed the reins over to him. Nothing was ever said about it, it wasn't a *decision,* it just happened. And now here she is, standing in the Ljubljana airport with her two children, and not only has she no real plan about how they are going to find Dr. Kis, she doesn't even know where they are going to stay for the night or how to pay for a taxi into the city, and she sure as hell does not remember what the secret code is that would allow this piece of dark blue plastic to induce a machine in a foreign country to spit out a wad of cash.

"I don't know," she says softly. Seeing their looks of dismay, she defends herself: "I'm not myself, okay?"

Leslie hands the card to Alice and the twins go off to the ATM to try their luck. The first four numbers they try constitute their birth date, and they are still too young to fully appreciate how amazing it is that it works.

"Ask for five hundred," Adam whispers. "We'll give her one hundred and keep the rest."

Alice agrees with a nod and they move to block their mother's view and stand shoulder to shoulder, shoving bills into their pockets.

"Take us to a very nice hotel, please," Leslie tells the taxi driver, and he brings them to a section of the city that is familiar to her, though not to the hotel where she and Alex stayed nearly eleven years ago. For which she is grateful. Her missing of him is a dull ache that seems to spread—from her heart, to her stomach, to her bowels, to her eyes, to her throat, to her arms and legs. It occupies her as if it were a parasite and she its host.

The driver is a good sort. He wears a brown leather jacket over a T-shirt bearing the picture of Tito. The driver has a round, youthful face, though his short hair is turning gray. His left ear is missing, and in its wake is a little pink ripple of flesh that looks like one of the folds of the labia.

"This is good place," he says, pulling his black Renault in front of the VIP Hotel.

It is the kind of place that Alex would never have stepped foot in— even on his way to bankruptcy, covered in coarse dark hair, and subject to the whip and rattle of unspeakable temptations, he maintained the tastes and sense of entitlement of his forebears and to the end saw himself as a man who simply did not stay in hotels frequented by software salesmen and budget tourists.

"How much?" Leslie asks.

"Forty euros, please," he says. After she pays him, the driver takes a business card from a plastic holder attached to the car's sun visor by rubber bands. "If you need anything, I want you please to call me. Slavoj Bucovec. You need drive. Sights. Maybe go to ski mountains. Slavoj Bucovec is on standby. I am here seven twenty four twelve." He hands her his business card. It shows a cartoonish car with long eyelashes over its headlights and little Valentine hearts pouring out of its exhaust pipe. She reads his name.

"Slavoj?"

"Slave-oh," he says. "The *J* at the end is silent, silent like so much is in this country, where most secrets are taken into the grave."

"Well, if you would wait here while we check in," Leslie says. She looks at her watch. It's a little after 9:00 a.m.; Kis is probably in his office or on the way. "We need to go to a doctor, and you could take us."

"Of course. Do you have the street and the number?"

"That's the problem right there," Leslie says. "But I think I can re-member how to get there. Or maybe you know the way—he's rather well known."

"Slovene medical doctors are among the finest in the world," Slavoj says.

"This doctor, we crossed the bridge with the…what do you call them? Monsters." Leslie spreads her arms and waves them up and down.

"Mom," Alice says, warning, imploring.

"Dragon Bridge," says Slavoj.

"Yes!" Leslie says. Color rushes to her face. She knows now, with a kind of calm certainty, that this is all going to work itself out. "And it was on Castle Street."

"Very close by," Slavoj says. "I can take you."

"Oh, thank you thank you thank you," Leslie says. "Come on, kids, let's get checked in, washed up, and ready." Then to Slavoj she says, "Fifteen minutes, okay?"

"Massive okays to that," Slavoj says.

When they check into the hotel, once again Leslie has to show their passports, and again all goes smoothly. The desk clerk makes it clear there are plenty of rooms available right now—if Ljubljana has a high season, November is not it—and it is no problem at all to give them two rooms right next to each other.

"It might be better if we had a little…space," Leslie says. "Do you have anything maybe one floor up, or down?"

If the clerk finds anything strange in this request, he masks it expertly, and moments later the twins are in room 404, and Leslie is in 511. Her window looks out onto a public square, where a stage and several grandstands have been set up and now stand empty and forlorn in the morning's cold rain. Old posters bearing the face of Gustav Mahler peel gradually from the lampposts.

"Oh, Alex, Alex, Alex," Leslie says, falling to her knees in front of the windows and holding the hem of the long curtain to her face. For the first time since his death, the loss of him exerts its full weight upon her, and it is like being pushed facedown by a giant hand, invisible, implacable, pitiless.

There is still a faint odor of cigarettes, though housekeeping has left the windows open. The room is painted white, with turquoise trim, and there is only one bed for the two of them. A business card advertising a local nightclub and featuring a drawing of dancing girls in elaborate ostrich-feather headgear has been left on top of the television set. Adam picks up the card, looks it over, lets it drop from his fingers, and watches it as it flutters to the floor.

"So, when we become teenagers," he says.

"I know," Alice says. "Or puberty or whatever. I hate that word anyhow. It's like *pee-you*."

"If we turn out like them," Adam says. He opens the minibar and takes out a Toblerone chocolate bar, which he tosses to Alice; he keeps the Three Musketeers for himself. On the inside of the door, there are breath mints, a deck of cards, and a combination corkscrew and bottle opener, which Adam takes and puts in his back pocket.

"Isn't the doctor supposed to have something for us too?" Alice says.

Adam shrugs. "I wish Mr. Medoff was our father."

"He's as dead as Dad."

"Whatever happens, Alice. Us forever." He extends his arm, as if to read a wristwatch, and moves his eyes along the length of it.

"What are you doing?"

"Seeing if it's got a bunch of hair."

"There's something so sick about what happens to people," Alice says. "Even if nothing happens to us, it still sort of makes me nauseous."

There's a knock at the door. "Kids?" Leslie says. "It's time to go."

"I'm scared," Alice says, as softly as possible.

Adam pulls the corkscrew/bottle opener out of his back pocket and shows it to Alice.

"Just let her try something," he whispers.

Slavoj drives the three of them to Castle Trg. It would have been a short walk, but by car they must contend with one-way streets and streets closed to vehicles. Despite the city's attempts to make life easier for pedestrians, Ljubljana feels deserted. Low baguette-shaped gray clouds race from west to east; plump, piebald pigeons hop along the cobblestones unmolested.

"There it is!" Leslie exclaims when they finally reach Castle Trg. There is the stone Art Deco building, the two carved women holding their swords.

The twins stare at the swords, remembering their teacher and the agony that inch by inch ended his life....

"I wait here," Slavoj says.

"It could be a while," Leslie says.

"Everything is very quiet today," he says, gesturing to the empty street. He adds, under his breath, "And every other day." He opens his door and hurries around to the back of the car to open the door for Leslie and the children. "I'll be here," he says with a small salute. He seems a little out of breath. The picture of Marshal Tito swells and shrinks with the rise and fall of his chest.

* * *

It's as if she and Alex were here just a few weeks ago, or yesterday. Over the years, Leslie has done her best not to think about that day when they came to Dr. Kis, but now the memories of it come rushing back, shockingly detailed and eerily vivid. She climbs the stone stairs with her children behind her. She can smell rice cooking. On the third floor, the door to someone's apartment is open. She can hear the TV or the radio, can see an umbrella stand holding six or seven umbrellas, the wooden handles like a bouquet of question marks.

"How you guys holding up?" she asks.

"Is he going to give us shots?" Adam asks.

"We're okay," Alice says quickly.

They hear claws clicking on the stone steps, coming in their direction. A few moments later, a man appears. He is stocky, with the empty left sleeve of his leather jacket pinned to the flap of the pocket. He holds a metal leash, at the end of which is a shaggy, panting Great Pyrenees, a hundred pounds at least, ice white except for a saddle of pale brown fur.

For the moment, it seems likely to Leslie that this man and the giant dog are connected to Dr. Kis — just as that little Englishman was connected to the rottweiler.

"Excuse me," Leslie says to the man once he is in front of her.

He looks warily at her, tightens his grip on the leash.

"Do you know Dr. Kis?" she asks. "Is he still…"

But her question is all but obliterated. The sound of her voice has triggered some guarding instinct in the dog, and his dark eyes flash furiously and he lets out a series of deep booming barks, attempting to lunge at her with each one. Each bark seems to have the power to push her back.

The one-armed man pulls the dog away and continues down the

278 · CHASE NOVAK

stairs. He calls out to them over his shoulder. From the tone, it sounds as if he is apologizing, but they can't be sure.

"I could kill him," Leslie says, wearily. She realizes that the children have heard her. "You okay?" Leslie asks them.

"That dog was scared," Adam says.

"It's just a bad dog," Leslie says. She feels her children's eyes on her, can feel their gaze like little fingers looking for a way into her, a way of prying her open and peering in. It strikes her: *They know everything*. The next flight of stairs awaits them. And the next. And the next. She tells herself that the appearance of that terrible dog was, in fact, a good omen. It means Kis is here....

This much she knows: her mind is not reliable. At this point, half the people in nursing homes can think circles around her. But Leslie is sure that Kis's office was on the top floor of this building, and, indeed, once she is in front of the door that once led to his suite of offices, she is more certain than ever that she has come to the right place. Yet the plaque on the door says something complex in Slovene, and etched into the metal of it is a silhouette of a woman doing yoga. And the smell of incense wafts through the crack at the bottom of the door. Nonetheless, Leslie knocks. Silence. She looks nervously at Adam and Alice. They are holding hands like two urchins who have been left alone on board a ship that is taking on water.

At last, the door is opened by a woman in her thirties with a pixie cut dyed dark orange and wearing a gray sports bra and cargo pants, rolled-up yoga mat in one hand and a mug of something in the other. She looks at Leslie and the twins with unconcealed puzzlement.

"Sorry to bother you," Leslie says. "Do you speak English?"

"Not so good, but yes, I try." The woman's voice is soft, melodious. She smiles.

"I'm looking for Dr. Kis," Leslie says. It sounds too blunt to her ears and she amends it. "We're all three of us looking for him."

"There's no doctor here," the young woman says. "Are you...? Do you need to come in? Rest here for a moment? I can show you the hospital."

"We don't need the hospital," Leslie says.

"But thank you," Alice is quick to say.

"Yeah, thanks, thanks a lot," says Adam.

"Was this a doctor's office before?" Leslie asks.

The woman is silent. Her once mild gaze intensifies as she looks at Leslie and then the children.

"It was empty when we came. We are leaseholders, you understand?"

"I'm looking for a Dr. Kis," Leslie says. "Dr. Slobodan Kis."

"No doctors are here. This is a place for..." The woman gazes upward, as if the correct word might be hanging by a thread directly above her. "Illumination. Mind and *spiritus*. Not invasion of Western so-called medicine."

Leslie smiles—at least she means to smile, though judging from the woman's reaction, Leslie may not have managed more than a simple show of teeth.

"You don't want to fuck with me," Leslie says in a rather soft voice.

"Mom," Alice says.

The woman's eyes widen as she quickly translates what she has just heard.

"Sorry?" the woman says, feeling suddenly burdened by having to hold on to her yoga mat and her cup of tea.

"Yeah, you're sorry," Leslie says. "I know all about sorry."

"Mom," Alice says. She puts her hand on her mother's back, more or less between the shoulder blades.

"Let's go, Mom," Adam says. "The doctor isn't here."

Leslie turns and nods. Her eyes look stunned; her arms hang limply at her side. When she turns again to speak to the orange-haired woman, she sees that the door has been closed. "All right. We can..."

She gestures toward the stairwell, moving her hand in a kind of tumbling circle. "Leave," she says at last.

Slavoj awaits them. He has bought himself a soda and a box of crackers and he is reading a Slovene translation of *The Five People You Meet in Heaven*. When he sees Leslie and the twins approaching his car, he scrambles out to greet them and open the passenger door.

"Very fast," he says.

"He wasn't there," Leslie says.

"He's gone," adds Alice.

"Oh, sorry for this," Slavoj says.

"Maybe you know him," says Adam. "Dr. Kis?"

"Please?" Slavoj says, wrinkling his brow.

"Slobodan Kis," Leslie says. She pronounces it like *kiss*. But then thinks to spell it, at which a look of guarded recognition crosses Slavoj's face.

"Not here," he says, shaking his head sadly. "Very famous." He rubs two fingers against his thumb, the universal sign for money. "But then what? Many problems. The judges don't accept his proofs. And so…" He lets out a low whistle and makes a dipping motion with his hand, signifying someone disappearing underground.

"Fucking hell," Leslie says, and glances at her children. "Sorry."

"We have many good doctors here in Ljubljana," says Slavoj. "You need for…" He pats his heart. "Or for…" He pats his stomach.

"We need Kis," Leslie says.

Alice cringes at the edge in her mother's tone. "How can we find him?" she asks.

Slavoj taps his finger against his chin. "Maybe I can find. My sister works in Municipal Justice Department. Maybe they have records of where he…" Again that low whistle, that dipping hand.

Slavoj needs time to get the information they need, and Leslie, Adam, and Alice go back to the hotel to await word from him. To be safe, Leslie stays in her room, and the twins in theirs, with strict instructions not to open the door to anyone. No matter what.

At about four that afternoon, the phone rings in the twins' room. They have been dozing on the bed and watching music videos on the TV, videos that seem to have been produced in an alternative universe, where the musicians are reminiscent of the current crop of American pop stars but are nonetheless unfamiliar. Adam rolls over on the bed and answers the call. It's Leslie. "Slavoj says he will be here tomorrow morning at...at..." she says, and falls silent.

"When? What time?" Adam says.

"What comes after seven?" Leslie says. "Sorry. I guess I'm really tired."

"Eight," Adam says.

"Right. What's next?"

"Nine."

"Yeah. He said he'll be here at nine."

"All right. That's good."

"Yeah, that's good. So...I'll see you tomorrow. Nine."

"What?" Alice asks, seeing the look on her brother's face.

"She hung up."

Driven by hunger for something beyond what they have pulled from the minibar, the twins venture out of their room. With some trepidation, they first go to their mother's room and knock on her door. There is no answer, but Alice knocks again, after which Adam knocks, too, with both hands.

"Mom?" Alice says.

"We're going to get something to eat," Adam says, cupping his hands on either side of his mouth.

Yet still there is no answer, not the slightest sound from her room. They shrug and make their way to the elevators.

They hope it doesn't make them look like babies, but they can't help holding hands as they walk the cold streets of this unfathomably strange city. They have no idea where they are walking, but they don't want to go too far and forget how to get back to their hotel. The last thing they want to do is ask someone for directions. No, actually the last thing they want to do is meet up with their mother. If she has left her room and is now roaming the city, they would just as soon not see her and they would also rather not have any idea about what she might be up to.

They have plenty of euros, and all they want is to find someplace to eat. They wander in the direction of the Ljubljanica River and find a pizzeria where the outdoor tables are protected by a dark green awning and warmed by large propane-powered heaters. It is easier somehow to sit at one of these tables than to go inside a restaurant. Adam and Alice are relieved that no one questions their presence here. In fact, a waitress comes right over with silverware wrapped in orange paper napkins and two colorful menus in the shape of dragons. To their added relief, she has somehow guessed they are Americans and has given them menus printed in English. They don't want her to regret that kids are at one of her tables so they each order a pizza, a green salad, and a soda, and when she writes it down Adam says to her, "We leave tips."

They remain virtually silent while they wait for their food. They are like people in the middle of a frozen lake who fear that at any moment the ice will start to groan, and twitter, and crack, and that if they dare to make even a step it will be the end of them.

The waitress brings them a basket of bread covered by a red-and-white paper napkin. They reach for the bread at the same instant, and their fingers touch.

"Garlic bread," Adam says, sniffing.

"Like Dad makes."

"Yeah."

"I can't help it," Alice says.

"I know," Adam says. "I miss him too."

"He was nice a lot of the time."

"Yeah, I guess."

"Remember when he—"

Adam covers his ears. "Not now," he says.

"I'm just saying he did a lot of nice stuff too."

"Not now. Okay?" Adam looks away. Though it's not good weather, there are a lot of people walking along the river, families, couples, a skinny white-haired guy dressed in tights and a fur-lined cape and wearing a crown like a crazy old king. Without realizing it, Adam rubs his chest.

"Don't think about that," Alice whispers.

"What's going to happen to us if Mom doesn't get better?" he says.

"She will," Alice says.

"We're supposed to see this doctor? We don't have an appointment; we don't even know where he is."

Alice nods. "You'll see."

Adam looks down at the knife, and, making sure he is not being observed, he slips it into his jacket.

"What are you doing?" Alice whispers.

"Just in case," Adam says.

"That won't do any good. It's a butter knife."

"No, it's not."

"I don't care. It still won't do any good."

"What if I jab her in the throat?" He touches the hollow of his own throat with his fingertip.

Alice looks at him with horror and disgust.

"What are we supposed to do?" Adam says. "Just let it happen?"

"But it's...it's Mom. Then who's going to love us?"

"I said just in case. You think I want to?"

"She won't hurt us."

"She won't want to," Adam says.

Alice is silent. After a few moments, she edges her knife off the end of the table and lets it drop into her lap. As she slips it into her pocket, something catches her attention. A woman is standing on the other side of the narrow river and looking directly at them. For a fleeting fearful moment, Alice thinks it's Leslie, but the woman steps back, away from the light, and disappears into the evening. Before Alice can say something to Adam about it, the waitress comes with their pizzas.

"Two pizzas for you," she says, clattering them onto the table. "Something else?"

"No, thank you," Alice says. "We're good."

"May I ask a question?" the waitress says. "Are you twins?"

"Yes," Adam says.

"My psychic told me I would meet twins today and she said I was to touch you on the tops of your heads and it would bring me the most good fortune." Her hands hover over their heads. "Yes?"

"Okay," they both say.

Her hands are warm, and her touch is gentle.

"Thank you," she says.

"No worries," Adam says.

Either they are hungrier than they have ever been or this is the best pizza they have ever tasted, and for a moment they are happy.

But that moment of happiness is brought up short by the sound of a woman wailing miserably. Her cries grow closer and closer and soon she is on the sidewalk right in front of them. She has dark wavy hair in which the moisture of the night sparkles like diamonds. She wears a red wool coat and knee-high boots, and she holds a leash but has no dog. She begins speaking rapidly, breathlessly, and when she points in the direction from which she came, the twins see that her hand is splattered with blood. Though they do not understand a word she is saying—or anything that those who gather around her are saying ei-ther—they both know from how her face is contorted and the look of disbelief on the faces of everyone around her that someone or something has just done something horrible to her dog.

Back at the hotel, while Alice showers, Adam takes the knife from the pizzeria and the corkscrew from the minibar and stuffs them into his backpack. Next, it's his turn to shower. They are both exhausted. They stagger around the room.

"Is this what it's like to be drunk?" Alice says.

"Why would anyone ever want to feel like this?" Adam wonders.

They wear their towels to bed, and turn on the TV, and watch the first thing in English they find—an old gauzy movie about a black teacher in a tough school in England who wins the trust and admiration of the prejudiced white students. When Alice sees that Adam has covered his eyes with his forearm, she takes the initiative and turns the set off.

"Poor Mr. Medoff," he murmurs.

"He was nice," says Alice.

They feel too tired to sleep, as if they lack the energy needed to close the door to consciousness. Eventually Alice lifts herself up on one elbow and switches off the bedside lamp, and the room jumps down into a well of utter darkness. She follows, breathing smoothly, dreamily, and next to her, Adam's heart begins to pound. Fear has seized him out of sheer malice, like one of those strangers in the night his parents used to warn him about, creatures who grab you just because they can, and because they like it, they like grabbing.

Adam reaches over his sleeping sister and switches the lamp on. The room jumps into view like a jack-in-the-box. He looks around the room. Nothing here, nothing there. Empty. Safe. He switches the lamp off and closes his eyes. He synchronizes his breaths with the inhales and exhales of his sister, until he, too, is sleeping.

But what good is sleep if it only delivers you into the clutches of feverish dreams? He dreams of Mr. Medoff. Impaled on those bronze swords but very much alive, looking at Adam and talking to him as if nothing were the matter. "Have you thought about what you are going to do next semester?" Mr. Medoff asks. And all Adam wants to say is, Are you all right? Are you dying? But if Mr. Medoff wants to pretend that he is not pierced and dying, then Adam will not mention it either. In the dream, Adam looks down and to his amazement he is not wearing any clothes below his waist. And where he has always been delicate and smooth, he is now suddenly large, meaty, and sprouting swirls of dark hair.

He wakes up fighting for breath. He slips his hand beneath the towel and feels his nakedness, smooth and cool. A sense of reprieve, a long pleasurable ripple of relief, but the relief is short-lived. Something is wrong. Does he see something? No. Does he hear something? No.

Nevertheless, he senses someone is in the room...

Alice turns over in her sleep, pulling the blankets with her. Adam lifts himself on his elbows, squeezing his eyes shut and opening them again, trying to decode the darkness. Yet all he sees is...nothing.

"Hello?" he whispers. But there is no answer.

He reaches for the edge of the blanket—his bare shoulders are cold. Very cold. He feels an icy breeze coming through the window though the window itself has been swallowed by the darkness. How did the window open? "Hello?" he says once again, this time a little louder.

He slips out of bed and feels his way to the window. His eyes have adjusted to the darkness and now he can see the shapes of things— the bed, the lamps, the long dresser, the TV set. As he reaches for the window and starts to pull it shut, something touches his skin, and he lets out a little cry of terror.

It's only the curtain, and now that the window is closed the curtain is limp again, having come to rest against the wall. Adam, however, is not at rest. His heart skips and twists, his jaw aches, and his legs tremble. He grips the knot of his towel with one hand. Though he sees no

one here, he is still convinced someone else is in this room, and of all
the people it might be—a robber, a murderer, a kidnapper—there is
one possibility that is even worse…

"Hello?" he says yet again. And now he utters the word: "Mom?
Mommy? Is that you?"

"Adam?"

The call of his name terrifies him, and it takes a long moment for
him to recognize that it isn't his mother's voice.

"Adam, where are you?" Alice cries.

The police, the media, and New York as a whole finally have connected the dots and realize that Xavier Sardina (now fighting infections and raging fevers) is linked to the Berryman Prep teacher and to
Alexander Twisden and that there is not only murder involved here
but cannibalism and, what's more, that half this story is still untold—
the half that involves Twisden's wife and children.

Now the machinery of justice is fully engaged. Now, at last, everyone is looking for Leslie, Adam, and Alice. In every hotel, in every
battered-women's shelter, at every bridge and tunnel, every bus depot,
every train station, every airport. It's really quite amazing how focused
the city can be after it is already many hours too late. Police at all the
metropolitan airports are on alert. Immigration is on alert. And soon,
after checking the manifests of every flight out of New York in the
past forty-eight hours, the police find their names and believe that they
know where they are.

Now it's just a matter of time before they secure the cooperation of
the German police to begin looking for Leslie and the twins in Munich.

No one is there. It is just the two of them.

"What were you doing?" Alice asks.

"I thought the window was open."

"Did you open it?"

"Did you?"

They are silent as their eyes continue to scour the room for a sign that someone is there, or has been there. It all looks perfectly normal.

Alice runs to the door and gives it a shake. It's locked. At the same time, Adam looks under the bed.

There *is* someone there!

No…it's a carpet, rolled up and secured with electrical tape, which the management for some reason has stored under the bed.

"I guess it was part of my dream," Adam says.

"Come on," says Alice. "It's better to be asleep."

Adam allows himself to be led back to the bed. They climb in and Alice turns off the lamp. The darkness spreads its wings, filling the room.

Soon Alice is asleep again, and Adam feels the nearness of sleep, too, the way you can smell the ocean well before you can see it. He feels the heaviness in his legs, the steadying of his heartbeat, the slow dissolution of his thoughts. His eyelids flutter and close.

A terrible thought. They did not look in the bathroom. Whoever he felt was in the room could be hiding in the bathroom.

Room 404 consists of a large rectangular space for sleeping that contains the dresser, the TV, and the entranceway. From the southeast corner of the rectangle there is a little hallway that leads to the bathroom. Adam feels his way along the wall, hoping that nothing will touch him. At last, he feels the closed door of the bathroom, runs his hand along the paneling until he touches the cool metal of the door handle. He turns the handle, opens the door. He reaches into the darkness of the bathroom, saying under his breath, "Don't grab me, don't grab me." He feels along the wall for the light switch until he remembers: the light is above the sink. He must walk into the bathroom, find his way to the sink, and pull the little chain that dangles from the fixture attached to the wall above the sink.

He hesitates at the doorway. "Mom?" he says. "Are you in there?"

Silence. But there are certain silences that betray their own subterfuge, that let you know (even if you would rather not know) that this is not the real silence of absence or emptiness but the false silence of suppression, the tense, quivering silence of someone holding her breath, and that if you switch on the light, or turn around, or feel blindly a foot or two in front of you, you will know for sure that bad dreams do come true.

But Adam does not need to turn on the light. Leslie does it for him.

She stands next to the sink. Her hair is disheveled and hangs in front of her face, masking it. One hand grasps the edge of the sink. The other she has placed on top of her head. Towels, soaking wet, are strewn all over the bathroom. The small, enclosed space reeks of flesh.

"Get out of here," she says, her voice deeper than he has ever heard it.

"Mommy...." Adam's chest heaves; his eyes fill with tears.

"Say go."

"Go."

"Louder..."

"Go! Get out of here!"

Leslie recoils a little, lets go of the sink. She is reeling, and for a moment it looks as if she will collapse.

"Go! Go!" Adam shouts at the top of his lungs while tears course down his face.

"Adam?" Alice's voice comes from the bed.

Leslie claps her hands over her ears. Her grimace shows her teeth. Have they always been so large?

The next moment, Alice is here, standing next to Adam. They hold on to each other, staring with terror at their mother.

"How did you get in here?" Adam says.

"I just wanted to see you. Not to hurt." She slaps her chest with an open hand. "Just to see. And look. Look at you."

"Mom," Alice says. "Please. You're scaring us so bad."

"Oh...dear God," Leslie says, starting to wail. "Oh God, oh God, oh please help me, help me please." She sees her face in the mirror and she rams the heels of her hand into the reflection, sending half the glass into the porcelain sink. A large shard of glass is stuck into her hand, and she looks at it for a moment, with curiosity, as if she doesn't quite know how it got there. She plucks it out, and a bead of blood bubbles up through the puncture.

"Go, Mom," Adam says. "Go away."

Leslie nods and gestures for the children to get out of her way. She slows down as she passes them.

"Go, Mom. Go back to your room."

Leslie is hunched over, but suddenly she draws herself up to her full height. "I heard you, Adam," she says, in her normal voice. "And I must insist that you treat your...*mother*"—she licks the blood off her hand—"with respect."

Adam thinks about the little pizza-place knife in his bag, but he doesn't dare leave his sister to run for it. He looks around the room for something he might use as a weapon. He picks up one of the wet towels, wraps it around his hand, and shakes his fist at his mother.

"You go, okay? You go."

Leslie nods, as if completely prepared to obey his command. She turns toward the door, but at the last instant she lunges at Adam and picks him up with utter ease, as if he weighs but a pound or two. His towel falls away from him, flutters to the tiles, and in his nakedness his arms and legs are rigid with fright as his mother lifts him up toward her mouth and leans slightly forward as if to take a massive bite out of his belly.

"How dare you treat me like...an animal. I'm your mother. You came out of my body. I gave you life. Life! I sacrificed. You have no idea. I ruined myself. We both did, your father and I. We gave everything so you might live."

With every word, she inches closer and closer to his bare tender flesh, and just as it seems she is going to sink her teeth into him, she stops, straightens herself again, and places him, shriveled and shivering, onto his feet.

"I'm your mother," she says, swallowing hard, wiping her mouth with the back of her hand. "I gave you life. I would never hurt you."

She touches his shoulders with her splayed fingers.

"I better take the rest of those damn pills," she says. She smiles weakly, weaving back and forth. "Mother's little helpers."

The next morning at nine the three of them are gathered in the lobby and Slavoj comes in, precisely on time. He is dressed as if for a job interview or church, in gray slacks and a blazer, a dark shirt with a wide collar, and a dark green tie whose knot is the size of an avocado. His hair is slicked back, he is freshly shaved, and he carries a long-stemmed red rose, which he presents to Leslie, much to her confusion.

"Your doctor has left town, but my sister says he is in Idrija, and so…" He claps his hands together, smiles.

"Is it far?" Leslie asks. She glances at the children, who look composed but keep their distance from her. She can't blame them.

"Nothing in Slovenia is far," Slavoj says.

They follow Slavoj out of the hotel and to his car, which he has left in the care of the hotel's towering doorman. Slavoj opens the rear door for Leslie and the twins. Before getting in the car himself, he engages in a bit of conversation with the doorman. The banter suddenly turns serious, judging from the tone and the expressions on their faces. The two men shake hands, and Slavoj runs to his door and slides in behind the wheel.

"To Idrija," he calls out merrily.

As he pulls away from the curb and into the street, the doorman bends his knees and tilts his large head so he can see into the car, and there is no question that he is looking directly at Leslie.

"What did you say to him?" Leslie asks Slavoj. Anger has whittled her voice to a sharp point.

"I thank him for seeing over my car," Slavoj cheerfully reports.

"Right," Leslie mutters, sinking down in her seat.

The back of Slavoj's car is a snug fit for the three of them. Their solitary little suitcase is under their feet; the children keep their backpacks on their laps. Leslie sits in the middle, and both children keep their knees locked together so as not to touch her. She holds on to her purse, with their passports inside it, her wallet, and a small envelope full of loose diamonds. She has a vision of simply pouring them onto Kis's desk. Let him have it all. What difference does it make? She opens her purse, removes the envelope, and sticks it in her front pocket, taking care not to make contact with her kids.

Outside of Ljubljana, they pass by farmhouses and gray wintry fields where enterprising cows manage to find bits of nourishment between the stubbled ruts. The motion of the car as they cruise along the winding roads has lulled Alice to sleep. Her head rests against her mother's shoulder. Her lips are pursed, as if she is about the blow out the candles on a birthday cake.

"You okay?" Leslie says to Adam, daring to pat his knee.

"I'm okay," he says. "Are you?"

She blinks back tears—the sweetness of her boy is almost unbearable.

She takes his hand and he laces his fingers through hers.

The children love her. The beauty and the blindness of the natural order…

Idrija seems like a series of afterthoughts—a petrol station hastily constructed, a little department store, an ice cream shop, a few cafés…No one is outside. You would think the town was completely deserted except for the smoke billowing chalk-white out of the chimneys in the houses along the road.

"Whoops!" Slavoj says as he makes a sudden turn off the main road.

They are now on a road not much wider than the car, with tidy little houses and ever tidier stacks of firewood on either side. Slavoj squints at his phone and announces, "We are near!"

"Is this going to work, Mom?" Adam asks.

"I don't know," Leslie says. "I think so. Or hope." She frowns—the difference between thinking something and hoping something seems quite obscure.

"Are we going to get shots?" Alice asks, waking up.

"I did, when me saw him before," Leslie says.

"Did it hurt?" Alice says.

"Yes. It did."

"This doctor," Slavoj says, looking over his shoulder as he speaks, yet somehow able to follow the narrow road as it unspools before him. "People come here to have child, and you have two. Maybe I don't understand too well. But my sister says one day he will be put in prison. Already he is forbidden to travel. In my country that is the first step, after that…" Slavoj makes a clicking noise such as you would use to urge on an old horse and meant to signify someone's fate being sealed.

Off to the right, a small château sits behind a high iron gate. The stucco walls are enveloped in vines, which, empty now of their foliage, look like a vast network of exposed nerves. A mixture of snow and rain is starting to fall. A weathervane in the shape of a dragon spins and creaks in front of the house. An old Soviet-era Lada, incongruously mounted on gigantic tractor tires, sits in the driveway next to a mountain bike.

Slavoj stops the car, jumps out, and tries to open the gate, but it has been chained shut, and the chain is secured by a heavy lock. Nevertheless, he gives the gate a good shake or two before returning to the car and leaning on the horn.

Leslie rubs her forehead. *Think, think,* she tells herself. She can pose this question: *If he's not here, then what?* But that's as far as she can take it.

Slavoj seems convinced that if he honks his horn for a long enough time, someone will emerge from the house. And his theory is borne out. The door to Kis's house opens, and a man in a bright silver hazmat suit and knee-high black rubber boots comes out of the house and walks quickly toward the gate, waving his arms over his head as if to warn a driver that a bridge has washed out. But Slavoj continues to honk the car's horn, forcing the man to walk down the gravel driveway and come to the gate.

Leslie and the twins sit silently in the back of the car while Slavoj and the hazmat man converse. Soon, their voices rise in volume and intensity, and it is clear they are arguing, though the voice of the man in the hazmat suit is muffled. And it is also clear that of the two, Slavoj is the loudest, and seemingly the most committed to coming out on top in this duel. At last, the man takes off the hood of the hazmat suit. He seems no older than twenty, with platinum hair cut short and combed forward, like a Roman senator's. He speaks more softly now, rapidly, and Slavoj nods.

At last, Slavoj smiles and sticks his hand through the bars of the gate to shake hands, but Hazmat steps back, shaking his head. It doesn't seem unfriendly. He doesn't want to shake hands for Slavoj's own good.

"Not here," Slavoj says, getting back behind the wheel. "Big mess in the house. Everything polluted and…everything bad. Very bad. Dangerous chemicals. This doctor? Very bad. Are you quite sure you want to…"

"We have come a long way to see this doctor," Leslie says.

"The Department of Public Safety closed this house but still no arrest. The doctor has now new house. Not far." Slavoj backs his car up and begins his three-point turn, but once he is aimed in the right direction, he stops. "Lady, please, no offense. I like you. You have great…" He gestures vaguely, looking for the right word. "Energy. This doctor's no damn good. Let's go back to the capital. I can show you all the best places, not touristic, insider stuff."

"How far away is he?" Leslie says in a quiet voice. Her stomach is starting to grumble. She smells the sweet, sweet flesh of her children and the effect it has on her is almost overwhelming, like what it feels like for other people, if famished, to detect the aroma of sizzling butter. She sits up straight, leans forward, putting as much space between the twins and herself as possible. *It's just going to get worse and worse....*

"Please, Slavoj, take us to him."

As Slavoj drives, Adam readjusts his backpack, which he holds on his lap. As secretively as possible, he pulls the zipper down. An inch. And then another. He clears his throat to cover the sound.

"Are you getting a cold?" Leslie asks.

"I'm okay."

His heart races. His mother returns her attention to the passing countryside, but Adam does not dare pull the zipper any farther. But he keeps his fingers on the tab, in case he has to pull it quickly.

Kis is residing in a steep, medieval town called Goce, a half an hour away. Vineyards abound and the winds are so strong that every terra-cotta rooftop has dozens of large stones strategically placed to keep the red tiles from blowing away. Today it is particularly windy and the wind howls up and down Goce's narrow streets. The streets, in fact, are too narrow for Slavoj's car; he parks it at the high end of the little village, and the four of them proceed on foot. The twins hold their ears against the keening wind.

There is not a soul to be seen. There are no shops, no parks, no municipal office, nothing public except a Catholic church in the middle of the village, a church that seems to have been built for five times more people than this little jot of a village could ever contain, and which, today, like everything else here, seems deserted. With Slavoj leading the way, they walk the cobblestoned streets, until Slavoj stops in front of a sand-colored old house, little more than a rectangle with a couple of windows and an old oak door. It is at the end of one of the town's streets. Beyond it lies a vineyard, the thick empty vines forming a long, dark, frozen braid.

"This is the house," Slavoj announces.

An old woman, bundled against the weather, walks by with her dog, an old white terrier of sorts, whose crippled back half is aided by a pair of training wheels. She mutters something at them as she makes her way past them.

"She knows who lives here," Slavoj says.

"What did she say?" Leslie asks.

Slavoj shrugs. "Devil," he says. "The old people are still superstitious."

"Do me a favor, Slavoj," Leslie says. "Bring the kids back to the car and wait for me."

"Mom," Adam cries out.

"I think we better all stay close together, Mom," adds Alice.

Leslie crouches a little so she and the twins are eye to eye. "Listen, you two. You wait for me while I talk to the doctor. He's going to give me something that's going…" She takes a deep breath. "I want to be your mother. I want to be a good mother."

"You are, Mom," Adam says.

"We love you, Mom," says Alice. "We're sorry we ran…."

Leslie's eyes fill with tears. She has not felt like this in years, so tender, so grateful for her children, so calm, so human; it's almost as if Kis has already worked his reverse magic on her.

"But he has to make us better too," Adam says.

"There's nothing wrong with us," Alice says.

"You want to end up like Rodolfo and those others?" Adam says to her, his voice rising.

"I'll go first," Leslie says. "We'll get you two in after that."

Slavoj leads the children back to the car, and Leslie takes a moment to compose herself in front of Kis's door. She is about to knock but thinks better of it and instead tries to let herself in. She notices that a little whatchamacallit camera has been set up above the door and its one glassy ignorant eye is staring down at her. Below the camera is a red light that beats off and on like a tiny heart. As soon as she touches the door it opens an inch or two. Startled, suspicious, Leslie steps back. The surveillance camera peers down at her. The lens catches a bit of sunlight from somewhere and a prism of colors shimmers across its surface, like a trace of oil in a puddle.

Leslie pushes the door open wider and walks in. She is in a small room, damp and dark, and redolent of the centuries. A small sofa is the only furniture, and hanging above it is a medical drawing of the human reproductive system. Opposite the sofa is a rather large aquarium, the water murky, but with no fish in it. At the end of this room there is a door, painted dark blue. Long scratches have scored some of the paint. A thick blanket of silence covers the place; all Leslie can hear is her own breathing. She takes a tentative step forward. The old floorboards creak and she stops, paralyzed for a moment.

Suddenly, she hears footsteps rushing her way, and the scarred blue door flies open, revealing Dr. Kis, very much aged from the last time she saw him. He is wearing shapeless brownish-gray pants held up by suspenders, and a baggy T-shirt. His hair is a thin white tangle. He is unshaven. She can smell the alcohol on him, his breath, his skin. He is holding a walking cane over his head, wagging it back and forth, as if his greatest desire is to strike someone with it. He slurs something at her in Slovene.

"My name is Leslie Kramer, Dr. Kis. I have come a long way because I need your help."

"No more. There is nothing more for you or for me or for any other person. Nothing can be done."

"But you said there was a way back, Doctor. You said you could reverse—"

"Closed for business," Kis says with a cruel, crooked smile. "Everything finished." He looks around, as if to make certain Leslie is alone. "Who let you enter?"

"The door was open. Now listen, please—"

"You tell me to listen? You steal into my house to give me orders?" He takes a wild swing at Leslie with his cane, but her reflexes are very quick and she catches the walking stick mid-arc and wrests it out of his hand.

"You ruined my body," Leslie says, tossing the cane across the room. It rattles its way under the sofa. "And everything else."

"I don't know you," Kis says, trying to regain his dignity. He stands a bit straighter, folds his arms over his chest.

"Please, Dr. Kis, I am begging."

He purses his lips, shakes his head. "Okay, follow."

He turns. The outline of a pint bottle bulges in his back pocket. Leslie follows him into the next room, which is a makeshift examination room. There is a table with stirrups, a glassed-in case holding medical supplies, a scale, a blood pressure cuff. The walls are covered with snapshots, hundreds of them, showing babies, toddlers, children, young teens, some standing, some running, some dressed for church, some for football, some with their proud parents on either side of them, some with their twin, or their two triplets. It could be the cover of a UNESCO pamphlet—children from all over the world, radiating joy, parents beaming, the great symphony of life at its most stirring crescendo.

Lies, lies, thinks Leslie. *Whoever said the camera doesn't lie?*

Kis sits behind at his desk, indicating with a wave for Leslie to sit as well. Before him is an old-fashioned rotary phone, a bottle of water, and a small plastic bottle filled with ovoid white pills. He opens the pill bottle, shakes two of them into his hand, and washes them down with water swigged out of the bottle. The pupils of his brown eyes are smaller than punctuation marks, and the irises themselves swim uneasily in a sea of pale red.

"I remember you," he says, pointing at Leslie. "You are married to the American lawyer. Am I correct?"

"My husband is dead."

Kis does not seem to have heard this, or he simply does not care. "Reggie was with me back then, is that correct?" He takes another drink of water and taps a couple more of the white ovoids into his palm, looks at them for a moment, and puts them in his mouth, swallows them. "And because of me, you had a child. Is that correct?"

"Twins."

"So! Pay me double." He claps his hands and then reaches forward with the right, as if really expecting payment.

"You destroyed me, Doctor. You turned me and…and my husband into…" She shakes her head. "Into something I can't live with."

"What possible difference can it make, we live, we die. I have ceased to worry. My conscience is clear. Clear! You and your husband came here desperate for a child and I gave you the thing you wanted. Double! Don't forget. One for free. How many people in my field can say that? These doctors, they collect millions of euros and still their patients end up going to Africa or Ukraine or the moon for an adoption. I made your body work. I made it give to you the thing it was refusing."

"Many things happened, Dr. Kis. Many things. I think you are aware of all that's gone wrong."

"In some few cases. Why does no one bother to speak of the thousands of successful treatments? What is it about humanity that we only concentrate on things that go wrong?" He taps two more pills out of the bottle and shakes them in his hand, the way men do sitting at bars when they are contemplating the consumption of a couple more peanuts.

"People are dying, Doctor. And monsters are being created."

"Is this what you have come to tell me? Listen to me. We doctors are in a chess match with nature. Nature wants to cripple you, nature wants you to have cardiac failure, nature says you must have small breasts, or wrinkles, or leukemia, or be unable to conceive new life. So we look and we think and we scheme, and then we make our move.

And sometimes we are victorious, and nature backs away, and her plans are forestalled. But she only backs away, yes? She does not *go* away. She returns, stronger than ever. And she always wins in the end." He smiles. "Leave me in peace, miss. There is nothing more I can do."

"You said you had…" Leslie closes her eyes for a moment, tries to muster some sense of composure, while the tireless little demons within disrupt her thoughts, hide the words she means to say. Ah: but one of the little demons has failed to do its mischief and there it is, the word, in fact a whole chain of them, all linked beautifully together. "You said that you have developed some sort of procedure by which the side effects of the treatment could be…" Uh-oh, here come the demons again. Could be…what? What is she trying to say? "Reversed."

"And I said this to whom?"

"And that there were also procedures in place to help the children, so that when they get older…"

"I said these things on advice from counsel. Now everyone is against me. You understand? A cabal of jealous doctors and let's not for a minute forget the pharmaceutical companies all over the EU and in the U.S. too, who were scared little rabbits as they watched me succeed where they had failed." He finally tosses the pills into his mouth, this time not even bothering to take a swallow of water to wash them down. "And so what is to happen to our Dr. Kis? Hmm? All the people who come here shaking and weeping and begging, Please, Dr. Kis, give me a child, please, Dr. Kis, save my marriage, make my life worth living, here is my money, here is my body, please help me. Where are they now when the world turns against Dr. Kis? Have you come here to help me? Is that why you are here in my home? Or are you just one more voice in the chorus, in the great hallelujah chorus that says Down with Dr. Kis, feed Dr. Kis to the wolves, let us all join together and destroy this terrible man who made dreams come true? Is that why you are here, miss?"

"I came here because you said—"

"The authorities were closing in on me, and I did not want to be burned at the stake like a heretic. I was aware of the problems." He opens the desk's bottom drawer and pulls out a sheaf of papers, a mélange of letters and legal documents. He shakes them at Leslie before slamming them onto his desk. "And, yes, I was working on solutions. But was I having success? With no money, no peace, no time. How could I?"

"But you said. I watched you. There was a…" Her heart pounding, Leslie moves her hand around and around, like someone turning the crank on an old movie camera.

"The Internet," says Kis. "It's a storm of lies, with little bits of sunlight here and there."

"You were lying?"

"I was saying what I was told to say. I was playing for time. What else could I do? They wanted to wipe me out so I needed to make a story that I was onto something big, something valuable. And I was trying, believe me, miss, I was trying, night and day. But you can't—what's the phrase?—you can't put shit back into a donkey. Things happen; they can rarely be reversed. The rain falls from the sky, it happens very quickly. But for the moisture to go back up in the air, that is very slow, a gradual process. And unfortunately for everyone involved, the general mood was not to wait for things to develop slowly." Yet again, he reaches for the bottle of pills and then gives it a shake. It rattles like a deadly snake.

Tears slowly roll down Leslie's face, though she is barely aware of them.

"What am I going to do?"

"What am I going to do, lady? You can live your life. Me? They are determined to destroy." He opens the pill bottle, pushing up on the cap with his thumb.

"What are you doing?" Leslie asks, gesturing toward the pills. "Are you sick?"

"Yes. Dr. Kis is sick. Dr. Kis is dying." He lifts the bottle up toward Leslie, as if extending a flute of champagne before a toast.

Leslie leaps out of her chair and grabs for the bottle of pills, but Kis evades her and pours a countless number of them into his mouth. Some he swallows right down, some he chews, showing his long gross teeth, and others dribble out and bounce onto the desk.

"You're killing yourself."

"Too late, it's done," he slurs through the thick white sludge of the half-masticated pills.

Leslie scrambles across the desk and grabs the old doctor. He tries to twist away from her, but she is too quick, and far too strong.

"Spit them out," she says to him.

He presses his lips closed, shakes his head no, furiously.

"You have no right," Leslie says. "You are not going to die, not until you—"

Kis slips from her grasp and falls to the floor. He rolls onto his side, tucks his chin into his chest, and covers his face with her arms. In less than a moment, Leslie is upon him. He is no match for her strength. She uncovers his face and rolls him onto his back.

"Let me die!" he cries to her, and clamps his mouth shut again and continues to swallow the remains of the pills.

Leslie has no plan, no idea of what to do next. All she can think of is getting those pills out of Kis's mouth, and maybe sticking her fingers down his throat, forcing him to vomit up what he has already ingested.

His face has turned a darker shade of gray. Large beads of sweat appear on his scalp, his forehead, the long grooves on either side of his mouth.

"Open your mouth," she commands.

He shakes his head no. And every time she reaches for him, he moves away.

But on the third try she has him. She holds his grizzled chin in one hand. She pries his lips apart and inserts two fingers into his mouth. She attaches her fingernails to his bottom row of teeth and with that small purchase on his mouth she forces it open. He is fighting her off with all that he has, but he is old and the oxycodone tablets are already having their effect.

"Open! Open!" Leslie growls, and with that she gives his mouth an all-out yank. She is angrier than she has ever been, more desperate, more frantic, and she does not know her own strength. She hears the deep dull wet sound of a bone snapping. The bottom half of his jaw breaks off in her grip like a chunk off of a rotted jack-o'-lantern. He cannot even scream. The only sign he gives of the ruin that has come over him is a slight widening of the eyes—they open to their fullest aperture and they stay that way as the light is slowly extinguished from them.

Leslie gets up, still holding the doctor's jaw. Slowly, she relaxes her fingers and the bloody, toothsome thing thuds to the floor.

As she hurries through the little Slovenian town to rejoin her children and Slavoj, Leslie rubs her hands against the sides of the old stone houses to wipe off the blood, but it isn't enough to really clean them. One at a time she puts her fingers in her mouth and sucks them, and when she is finished with that she licks her palms and then dries them against the legs of her pants.

The twins are in the car and Slavoj sits on the hood, smoking a cigarette and reading the newspaper. "Lucky day?" he asks when he sees Leslie approaching the car.

She shakes her head. "I'm all out of lucky days," she says.

"So we wait?" He looks at his watch. "Maybe some lunch. My cousin has a place, not too far."

It's all Leslie can do to shake her head. She opens the door to the backseat. The twins look at her, hopeful that the doctor has helped their mother, fearful that they are next, and even more fearful still that nothing has changed.

"Take us back to the airport, please," Leslie says. "And if you can hurry that would be…" She pauses, steals a look at her hand. It's worse than she thought. "That would be good," she says.

"Now what?" Alice says as Slavoj turns the car around and starts off for the main highway.

"You've never had a chance to know your aunt Cynthia," Leslie says.

"Mom," Alice says, "I mean it. What are we going to do now?"

"Mom?" Adam says insistently. "We've come all this way."

"She'd be a really fun person to live with," Leslie says. "Fun for you, and fun for her."

"Mom, what are we doing?" Alice says.

"I don't think we should be leaving," Adam says. "We came all this way. Maybe the doctor just went out and he's coming back."

"No," Leslie says. "He's not coming back." She forgets there are traces of blood on her hands and she puts her arms around her children and gathers them close. "He's not going to be able to help us. I'm sorry. I know children like to believe that there's always someone out there who's going to rescue them, maybe we all believe that, maybe I do too, or did, but that's not how it works. Not now, not for us. We're on our own."

The children's expressions are grave. She feels their hearts, the rise and fall of their chests as they breathe as one.

"Oh, my darlings," Leslie says.

A thin skin of deep bluish gray spreads over the low-hanging clouds as the oncoming evening paints the first coat of darkness across sky. The airport lights burn bright yellow. Slavoj turns into the departures lane, drumming his fingers nervously against the steering wheel.

"You have tickets, everything you need?"

"We're all set, Slavoj," Leslie says. "Thank you for everything."

"My job and my pleasure," he says. "You are good people and the doctor you have come to visit is a bad man. But don't worry.

Justice in my country sometimes slow, but she arrives, she always arrives."

He pulls up to the curb in front of the international departures and runs around the other side of the car to let them out. With great solemnity, the twins shake his hand and say their good-byes. He can see the fear in their faces, but there's nothing more to do now but smile and pretend that this is just another trip to the airport, another good-bye.

"Here is something for you, Slavoj," Leslie says, reaching into her purse. She takes out the envelope holding the diamonds and sticks her thumb and forefinger into the corner of it. She pinches up three small diamonds. "Open your hand," she says, and when Slavoj does as he is asked, she places the glittering little stones in his palm. "They're valuable, Slavoj. Bring them to any jeweler. You'll see."

Slavoj looks at the diamonds winking in the cadmium airport light. Slowly, his hand closes on the little jewels, and he makes a small nod in Leslie's direction.

"Safe flight," he says.

They are in luck. There is a flight to Munich leaving in half an hour, with a connecting flight to Newark, a night flight, which will mean only an hour and ten minutes' layover in Munich. Despite there being plenty of open seats on both flights, Leslie has to pay a penalty for changing her reservation, but other than that it all goes smoothly. While they were not required to go through immigration on the way in to the country, going out is a different story, and as they wait in line, holding their passports, Leslie grows increasingly anxious. The possibility of catastrophe has doubled—police in America will be looking for them, and perhaps they have put a tag on their passports, and police here in Slovenia by now might have discovered Dr. Kis's body. Step by step, they draw closer to the booths where the immigration officials check documents, the eerie icy light of their laptop computers glowing on their hands.

The immigration officer who looks over their passports has a sad, worried demeanor. He sighs frequently and his eyes are opaque, cloudy, the eyes of a defeated man. He seems barely engaged in checking their passports, going no further than trying to match the pictures in Adam's and Alice's passports with how they look now, three years after. His one vigorous act is to stamp their passports with a kind of controlled violence, and then he brusquely slides them through the slot in the bulletproof glass.

Next, they go through airport security. The two security officers, in bulky uniforms, the material as thick as porridge, stand with their feet wide apart, their hands folded behind them, staring intently at the monitors as the carry-on luggage rides the conveyor belt and is x-rayed.

Their flight is announced and Leslie and the children must make haste.

Leslie places their suitcase on the steel rolling pins that spin in front of the conveyor belt. She gives the valise a little poke with her finger and it begins its journey.

"Backpacks," she tells Adam and Alice.

They do as she says, after which they follow her through the metal detectors. Leslie and Alice walk through without incident, but something on Adam's person sets off the alarm. One of the security workers is roused from his fugue state, and he quickly intercepts Adam and takes him to one side, where he wands him, head to toe. The offending object is not difficult to find. Before leaving the hotel this morning, he put the corkscrew into his back pocket, and though he has been sitting on it all day, he has forgotten it is there. The wand reacts to the corkscrew with a frenzy of clicks. As the guard gestures for Adam to remove the corkscrew, Adam's backpack is being x-rayed, and the other guard is discovering that nestled into the socks and T-shirts are two knives.

Adam is flushed with shame and fear. With one security officer having grabbed him by the arm, and the other emptying his backpack, he wonders if he is going to be taken somewhere, questioned, kept.

Alice's face, as well, scalds with shame. Those knives are as much her fault as his....

"Mom?" Adam says.

Her eyes are filled with tears. "Oh, Adam," she says, her voice barely a whisper. "Oh, baby, poor baby."

The security officers have no interest in detaining Adam. They simply confiscate the corkscrew and the knives and send them all on their way.

"We have to run," Leslie announces, and the three of them hold hands and race down the corridor toward gate 11, where the Adria clerk checks their tickets and tells them in English that the bus to their plane is just about to leave. "Hurry, please, you are the last ones," she tells them.

They go through the terminal gate, through the pedestrian tunnel, and down the movable metal staircase. A stiff wind is blowing now, though the night is clearing up; thin shreds of silvery cloud race past the full moon, which displays its many mountains and craters in a kind of hypervisibility and seems unnaturally close. Leslie, Adam, and Alice are the last ones on the bus, and as soon as they board the driver starts the journey over the tarmac toward the small jet that awaits them. On their way, they pass a Swissair jet, a Lufthansa, and a Federal Express jet, all of them 757s, warming their engines for takeoff.

There are still empty seats on the bus but the three of them stand, holding on to a single pole for balance. Adam is staring at his mother's fingers on the cold silver pole. She feels the intensity of his stare and she knows without checking that he must see the little wisps and spatters of the doctor's blood that she has been unable to wash off.

"It's okay," she murmurs to him.

"I love you, Mom," he says.

"I love you too, Adam. I love you both."

"We'll find a way," Alice says.

"I know you will," Leslie says.

"She means all of us," Adam says.

Leslie gazes at the other passengers on the transit bus. Businessmen, students, a pensive short-haired girl holding a French horn case. There are a couple of nuns sitting side by side and talking excitedly to each other, and for a moment Leslie is sure they are the same sisters she and Alex saw leaving Ljubljana ten years before. But how could they be? They are young, and those two nuns from the past were old, and now would be very old, possibly dead. Yes, nuns die too, and the thought of dying nuns fills Leslie with an unutterable sadness. Everyone dies, schoolteachers, husbands, everyone.

"Are we sitting together?" Alice asks.

Leslie looks at her.

"On the plane," Alice says. "On our tickets."

"I think so," Leslie says. She pulls their boarding passes out of her purse and hands them to Alice.

"You worry so much," Leslie says. "You worry about everything."

"Not really," Alice says, nervously.

"Mom," Adam says. He gestures with his eyes and Leslie follows his gaze and sees a police car racing silently across the runways, its light bar a frenzy of blue and white.

"Listen to me," Leslie says.

They stare at her, afraid to speak.

"Kids have a way of blaming themselves for things that are not their fault. Can you just remember this? You never did anything wrong. You were always really good kids, I mean, really, really good. Everything that turned so awful, it was never your fault. You understand me? It was never your fault. Ever."

"Mom..." Adam's voice cracks.

"Whose fault was it?" Leslie asks. "I want you to tell me. I want you to say. Whose fault was it?"

"It doesn't matter, Mom. We just want to stay together."

It's Adam who says this. Or is it Alice? Suddenly, Leslie cannot be sure. Her mind is starting to break into pieces. Anyhow, it doesn't matter. One of them said it, and it's not going to happen, they are not going to stay together.

She thinks of it. The corkscrew. The pathetic little knives. It might be the worst thing yet. Yet they point a way. They do, they do....

"Don't forget your aunt Cynthia," she tells the children.

They look at her, confused. But they won't be for long....

The police car has made a sharp turn and now it is heading directly toward the bus. Every thought in Leslie's mind is eclipsed by the overwhelming imperatives of freedom and escape. The bus is starting to slow as they approach the Adria flight to Munich, but before it comes to a full stop Leslie hops off it. Waving her last good-bye to her children with her back to them, she starts to run.

For a few moments she runs with no one chasing her. But when the police car sees the figure of a woman racing between the idling jets, it sets off in pursuit of her, and a moment or two after that a mechanic, and after the mechanic a baggage handler, and then a security guard are also chasing after her.

There really is no possibility of escape. There are simply too many people in this airport whose primary job is to protect the integrity of the airport. But there are more ways of eluding your pursuers than outrunning them. You can also disappear. But how to disappear? Can you clap your hands and become invisible? Can you chant a magic spell and turn into a bird and fly away? Leslie cannot do these things.

But she has another idea, one that has been with her since the hour they arrived in Ljubljana and the bus brought them past the whirling turbine engines of the jumbo jets, with their lethal titanium honeycombs.

When she is beneath the engine attached to the right wing of the Delta 757 she is at first surprised and discouraged by how much higher off the ground it is than she had realized. From a distance, it had looked as if you could just reach up and touch the engine, but now that she is right next to it, it looks to be fifty feet above her. The plane itself seems immense, impossibly so. Fumes of burning fuel ripple through the air. She looks up, and through the smudgy glass of the cockpit she sees a pilot with headphones over his ears. He seems to be looking down at her.

She hears voices behind her, shouts. She imagines they are crying out for her to stop, to turn around, to give herself up....

She feels strong. She feels the tension in her legs. She takes a deep breath. Air fills her lungs like helium, and she leaps. It is almost as if she has taken flight. She rises up and up and when she can rise no farther she reaches out and clasps the lip of the turbine's wide-open mouth. She can feel it wanting to suck her in, to consume her. Her hair is streaming toward it. The noise is deafening. It feels as if her eyes want to pop right out of their sockets. With one more burst of energy, she hoists herself up, and that is all it takes. In less time than it takes for her heart to contract and expand, she is sucked into the jet, like a goose, like debris, like something of no account, and the engine has its way with her. It eats her as if it were ravenous, and in moments there is nothing recognizable left of her.

Everyone on the bus taking the passengers to the Adria flight to Munich sees what happens to Leslie. There are no screams, no shouts, no words. Every last person just stares in a complete stunned silence, and the silence persists until it is broken by a strange keening noise. The passengers look to the left and to the right, trying to locate the source of those long, lonesome howls. The winds have blown the last of the clouds out of the cold night sky, and it really does sound as if a wolf—no, it's two wolves!—two wolves baying brokenheartedly at the big orange moon, so close, so bright and round that it looks as if someone has punched a hole out of heaven.

ABOUT THE AUTHOR

Chase Novak is the pseudonym for Scott Spencer. Spencer is the author of ten novels, including *Endless Love,* which has sold over two million copies to date, and the National Book Award finalist *A Ship Made of Paper.* He has written for *Rolling Stone,* the *New York Times, The New Yorker, GQ,* and *Harper's. Breed* is his debut novel as Chase Novak.

BREED

a novel by

Chase Novak

CHASE NOVAK'S THOUGHTS ABOUT HORROR

I don't think it will be too surprising to learn that I am very taken with *Rosemary's Baby*. Ira Levin's novel is a model of economy and understatement, with the added pleasure that it lends itself to multiple interpretations. I appreciate the care (and ease!) with which the everyday world of New York City is presented in this novel—no haunted castles, no super powers. Here evil is conjured by rather sad, nosy neighbors and a husband driven by actorly ambitions. In his film adaptation of Levin's novel, Roman Polanski barely deviated from the narrative strategies of the novel. Often, movies suffer when the filmmakers adhere too closely to the source material, but in the movie version of *Rosemary's Baby* everything is done just right—the actors are brilliant and Polanski's work is imbued with the hard-won knowledge that catastrophe lurks around every corner.

Roman Polanski made another truly terrifying film, aptly titled *Repulsion,* in 1965. Here Catherine Deneuve plays a manicurist who lives with her sister and her sister's boyfriend. The Deneuve character is repulsed by sex, and because she is so beautiful men are naturally drawn to her, which plunges her constantly into states of madness. The torments inflicted on her by her own mind are so powerful that the audience actually feels a bit of *relief* when some poor guy wanders in close enough to be brutally slain. The control of the filmmaker is so masterful here that an apparition in a mirror or a sudden crack in a wall is as startling and upsetting as being suddenly grabbed in the dark.

I don't think of novels as belonging to one genre or another. (Genre is about categorizing books, not writing or reading them.) But here are a few of the ones that are normally filed under Horror that grabbed me and would not let go: *The Stand,* by Stephen King; *Dracula,* by Bram Stoker; *The Island of Dr. Moreau,* by H. G. Wells; and *The Other,* by Tom Tryon. I suppose it could be said that I am a fan of "literary horror" novels, though Henry James's *The Turn of the Screw,* routinely cited as a perfect example of how to blend high style with mounting fear and unease, leaves me restless and dissatisfied, and frankly a bit bored. Compare Henry James to, say, Edgar Allan Poe, and you realize that what makes tales of monsters, ghosts, hauntings, and curses great is the writer's ability to venture as deeply into the darkness as humanly possible, and to go there without protection, without reservation, without hope.

A CONVERSATION WITH THE AUTHOR OF *BREED*

How did you come up with the name Chase Novak?

I know someone whose first name is Chase and I always liked that name and I just seized upon it. And Novak is my mother's maiden name, from back in the day when people had maiden names.

It's almost an androgynous-sounding name. It could also be a woman's name, right?

Yes, it could. And that was in the back of my mind as well. Because when I first conceived of having this book come out, I thought my identity would remain much more secret than it turned out to be. I didn't think there would be a picture, I didn't think that my name would be anywhere near it, so I thought Chase Novak would have much more of an independent life than he's turned out to have.

Did you write Breed *as Scott Spencer or as Chase Novak?*

I wrote it as Chase Novak. I moved away from Scott Spencer's desk. Chase didn't even use Scott Spencer's computer for this. He went to a separate part of the house and did it on his own. I really felt right off the bat that Scott Spencer couldn't write that book. And I'm not sure why I thought that, except that it didn't really fit in with any of my other books and I didn't want it to. And I just wanted to be free of that and free of myself and do something completely different.

What are the advantages to writing under a pseudonym?

I think the dream of having a second identity is not that uncommon, and this was an opportunity to grab a little piece of that dream without giving up my primary identity. Just walk away from that for a little while and do something completely different. And I must say, it was extremely liberating and very entertaining to just take on another persona and write a different kind of book with different kinds of goals for the book, and just have a lot of fun telling a classic story.

Is Chase Novak a faster writer than Scott Spencer?

One of the goals I had for the book is that it would move quickly. I'm not asking someone to sit down with the book for a week and make that sort of commitment. I wanted the book to go and go and go, not unlike the experience of seeing a movie. So in order to create that sort of momentum, I felt I should write with that sort of momentum. I think it got written in about a third of the time I would spend with Scott Spencer's novels.

Speaking of movies, you've also written screenplays. Was that a help in writing this novel?

It was more influenced by my experience of horror movies. My nostalgia for a certain kind of horror movie that you don't see much anymore. Obviously, there's a lot of *Rosemary's Baby* here, in the New York sociology of it. And I'm a great fan of those old Hammer films in which there is a kind of operatic sense of evil and doom. What I have very little interest in is these sort of slasher/serial-killer movies. When the body count gets up high, my interest starts going low.

Are there any common threads linking Breed *to your other novels?*

It's probably more like my other novels than even I realize. If there's one thing I can think of that connects this to Scott Spencer's novels, it's that sense of the fatal decision, the fatal act that the action turns on and that leaves the lives of the characters inalterably changed. When David starts the fire in *Endless Love,* or in *Waking the Dead* when the main character's lover is killed (in an explosion). I'm drawn toward that moment. But I suppose it's not all that uncommon in fiction, how stories are built. In John O'Hara's *Appointment in Samarra,* someone just throws a drink in someone's face.

You went to Comic Con in San Diego on behalf of Breed. *How did you find it?*

It was an overwhelming experience. It's massive. There are like 150,000 people there. And a large percentage of them are in costume of one sort or another. I got communication from the Comic Con people telling me what the parameters were of the costume I could wear. What kind of sword I could have. What sort of sword would not be allowed. So I had never gone to a literary conference in which it would be assumed that I might be carrying a sword.

Will Chase Novak be heard from again?

Yes, the story in *Breed* is going to continue. The next book will pick up with the lives of the children a few years later. I'm also working on a Scott Spencer book now, so we'll see who gets there first.

This interview was conducted by Ken Salikof, the author of *Spy In a Little Black Dress* and *Paris to Die For.* He can be followed on twitter at @kensalikof. This interview first appeared on *NY Daily News*'s Page Views blog. Reprinted with permission.

QUESTIONS AND TOPICS FOR DISCUSSION

1. On their way to meet with Dr. Kis, Leslie tells Alex that sometimes she believes life would be easier if they had less money. Why does she say this? Do you agree with her?

2. Leslie and Alex undergo the fertility treatment in Slovenia as a sort of last resort. When in life have you wanted something desperately? Did you put yourself in a less than desirable or risky situation to come closer to your goal? Would you have done the same as Leslie and Alex?

3. In Part Two, we learn that the Twisden residence is falling apart and many family heirlooms have been sold off. Recall that Alex had insisted on not adopting because he felt he owed it to his lineage to have a child by blood. What does the derelict state of the house say about his decision? Has he managed to preserve his heritage? What has he lost or gained?

4. Adam's parents tried to instill in him a fear of what can befall a child at night, but instead they made him more terrified of the click of his bedroom door's lock each evening. Did your parents tell you cautionary tales as a child? Which scared you the most? What dangers do you think they were trying to shield you from? If you have children, what warnings do you dispense to keep them safe?

5. Alex believes it is language and memory that make us human. Do you agree? Why or why not? What faculty would you have to lose to make you feel less human?

6. Safe in Amelie's apartment after the incident in the park, Leslie observes Adam and Alice playing video games, carefree, and wonders, "How can they listen to those sirens and not be reliving what happened right before their eyes? Where do they put their experiences? How do they live?" Do you feel Adam and Alice fully grasped what happened to Michael and their father's crime? What do you think enables children to compartmentalize experiences?

7. The last scene in the book is powerful and gruesome. Was it what you expected? Did it make for a satisfying ending?

8. *Breed* is gory and shocking, but it's also darkly humorous. How did the humor affect your reading? Imagine the book without any of its comedic elements. How would your reading experience have been different?

9. The author is hard at work on *Brood,* a sequel to the book. What lingering questions do you hope it will answer for you?

10. What message did you take away from *Breed*? If this book is a commentary on modern parenting, what do you think the author is trying to say about it?

**If you liked *Breed* then we think you'll like
Stephen Leather's supernatural thriller *Nightshade***

In Jack Nightingale's world – where reality and the
occult collide – sometimes the only way to fight evil is
with evil.

A farmer walks into a school and shoots eight children
dead before turning the gun on himself. It's a harrowing
but straightforward case – until police search the man's
farm and unearth evidence of dark Satanic practices.
When the perpetrator's brother approaches Nightingale,
adamant that his brother was set up, it's clear that
something even more sinister lurks at the heart of the case.

And there are dark forces elsewhere. A young girl
miraculously returns to life, claiming she's spoken to
those from beyond the grave. Those in contact with her
are dying hideous deaths . . . forcing Jack Nightingale to
make the hardest decision he's ever faced.

'Written with panache, and a fine ear for dialogue,
Leather manages the collision between the real and the
occult with exceptional skill' *Daily Mail*

Turn the page to read a gripping extract . . .

Out now

NIGHTSHADE

Nightingale shivered as he stared at the house. It was a neat semi-detached with a low wall around the garden and a wrought iron gate that opened onto a path leading to the front door. There was no garage, but half of the front lawn had been paved over as a parking space for a five-year-old Hyundai. Beyond the car was a path leading to the rear garden, which was how he planned to get into the house. It was after midnight and the streets were deserted. It was a cloudy night with only occasional glimpses of the moon overhead and the lights were off in pretty much all the houses in the street.

Nightingale eased open the gate, slipped inside and closed it behind him, then walked carefully down the path and around the side of the house. He stopped and peered through the kitchen window until he was sure that there was no one there, then walked to the kitchen door. He tried the handle and wasn't surprised to find that it was locked. He'd brought a makeshift burglary kit with him including tape, a glass cutter and a screwdriver but he didn't want to start breaking glass unless he had no choice.

There was a large glass sliding door that led into the

sitting room. The curtains were drawn but there was enough of a gap to see that the room was in darkness. He pulled on a pair of grey surgical gloves, checked the lock at the side of the door and smiled to himself as he took out the screwdriver. It took him only seconds to force the screwdriver into the gap between the door and the wall and pop the lock.

He gently slid the door open, pushed the curtain aside and stepped into the room. He stopped and listened for a full minute, then slowly slid the door closed. There was a sofa and an armchair and a glass and chrome coffee table facing a 42-inch LCD television. He went over to the TV and pressed the back of his hand against the screen. It was cold, so the family had been in bed for some time. In his pocket was a small can of starting fluid that he'd bought from a garage in south London. He'd turned up in his MGB and the mechanic who'd sold him the fluid had assumed that Nightingale was having trouble getting the old car started on the cold mornings and suggested he bring it in for a service. Nightingale said he would have a go himself but that if the problem continued he'd book it in. It was premium starting fluid, which meant that it was sixty per cent diethyl ether, perfect for giving a boost to a reluctant engine, but also a very efficient way of putting someone into a deep sleep.

He tiptoed across the sitting room and into the hallway, listened again and then headed up the stairs, keeping close to the wall to minimise any squeaking boards. When he reached the landing he stopped and listened again. There were four doors. There was one to the rear of the house that he assumed was the little girl's bedroom. The door immediately to his left was open. The bathroom.

He guessed that the bedroom facing the street would be the master bedroom where her parents were sleeping. The door was open slightly and Nightingale tiptoed over to it, breathing shallowly.

He pushed it open. The woman was closest to him, sleeping on her side. Her husband was on his back, snoring softly. Nightingale took a handkerchief from his pocket, twisted the top off the can and soaked the material with the fluid. He tiptoed across the carpet and held the ether-soaked handkerchief under the woman's nose for the best part of a minute, then draped it over her face.

He prepared a second handkerchief and did the same to the husband.

When he was satisfied that they were both unconscious, he tiptoed out of the room and pulled the door closed behind him. His heart was racing and he stood where he was for a full minute, composing himself, before soaking a third handkerchief with ether and pushing open the door to the little girl's bedroom.

She was lying on her back, her blonde hair spreading out across the pillow like a golden halo, breathing slowly and evenly. Nightingale closed the door quietly, wincing as the wood brushed against the carpet. When he turned back to the bed, her eyes were open and she was staring right at him.

'You're Jack Nightingale, aren't you?' she said.

Nightingale said nothing.

'You've come to kill me, haven't you?'

I

THREE WEEKS EARLIER

Jack Nightingale woke up, stretched, and lit a Marlboro. As he lay on his back and blew smoke rings up at his ceiling, he ran through what lay ahead of him that day. He had to explain to a middle-aged woman that the father of her two children had a second family up in Birmingham and that on the nights he told her he was away on business he was actually with them. He had to spend the afternoon in a pub, watching a barmaid who a brewery was convinced was ripping them off to the tune of a grand a week by serving sandwiches she had made herself and not the ones the brewery provided, and in the evening he had to follow an unfaithful wife. Nightingale knew the woman was being unfaithful because he'd already followed her to a hotel where she'd spent two hours in a room with a co-worker. The cuckolded husband had read Nightingale's report but now he wanted photographs. So far as Nightingale was concerned photographs would just be rubbing salt into the wound, but if that's what the client wanted Nightingale was happy enough to provide them – at a price.

He finished the cigarette, stubbed it out in a crystal

ashtray on his bedside table and looked at his watch. It was just after eight o'clock. He had set his mobile to silent, so he checked the screen to see if he'd received any calls. He hadn't. He put down the phone and considered lighting another cigarette, but he decided to shave and shower instead. He padded to the bathroom. So far as Nightingale was concerned it was going to be a typical day, business as usual. It was only in the movies that private detectives got involved in car chases and shoot-outs or met steely-eyed blondes packing heat. Most of Nightingale's work involved following sad, lonely and embittered people on behalf of sad, lonely and embittered clients. But it paid the bills and kept him off the streets. Actually that wasn't true – much of what he did involved being in the street, which is why he favoured comfortable Hush Puppies as his footwear and generally wore a raincoat.

He looked at himself in the bathroom mirror as he shaved. He bared his teeth and wondered how much teeth-whitening would cost. Nightingale was a smoker and coffee-drinker and both addictions played havoc with his enamel.

As he climbed into the shower he had no idea that eight children were going to die that day, nor that their deaths were going to change his life for ever. The man who would kill the children was sitting at his kitchen table cleaning his shotgun as Nightingale rinsed the shampoo from his hair. His name was Jimmy McBride and he was a farmer with a smallholding near Berwick-upon-Tweed, the most northern town in England.

McBride had made himself a cup of Nescafé and two slices of toast and he kept breaking off from cleaning the shotgun to drink and eat. McBride had a few hundred cattle, a decent number of chickens and almost fifty acres that supplied new potatoes to the Morrisons supermarket chain. McBride lived alone on the farm. He'd never married, and once he'd reached the age of forty he had resigned himself to living a solitary life. He did most of the work on the farm himself, though when the potatoes needed harvesting he bought in a team of Polish contractors. They worked hard, the Poles, and they never complained about the weather or the long hours.

McBride had owned the gun since he was a teenager and used it to keep the rabbit population down. Like most farmers, McBride hated rabbits. They weren't cuddly cartoon characters, they were parasites that needed to be kept under control, and the best way to do that was a blast from a shotgun followed by several hours in a casserole with onions, carrots, served with new potatoes pulled straight from the ground.

There was a box of shotgun shells on the table next to his toast. There had originally been 250 in the box but he'd bought them two years previously and there were only about a hundred left. That would be more than enough. On the chair by his side was the canvas bag he always took with him when he went out rabbit-shooting. It was big enough to hold fifty cartridges, a flask of whisky-laced coffee and a pack of sandwiches.

McBride filled the bag with cartridges, let himself out of his farmhouse, and walked across a ploughed field, whistling softly to himself.

It took him less than half an hour to reach the school. There was a large sign at the entrance that said 'Welcome' in a dozen languages. The wrought iron gate was closed but not locked and McBride pushed it open. He already had two cartridges in the breech and as he walked across the playground he snapped the twin barrels into place.

A bald man in a grey suit opened the door that led to the main school offices. The deputy headmaster. Simon Etchells. Etchells frowned as he saw the shotgun in McBride's hands. 'Excuse me, can I help you?' he called.

McBride continued to walk across the playground.

'You can't bring a gun onto school premises!' shouted the deputy headmaster. 'I really must ask you to leave!'

McBride shot the man in the face without breaking stride. The man fell to the ground, his face and chest a bloody mess. Three pigeons that had been sitting on the roof scattered in a flurry of wings.

He walked into the main school building. The administration offices were to the left, and beyond them was the canteen. McBride turned to the right. There were classrooms leading off both sides of the corridor. There were posters and artwork on the walls, including photographs of all the pupils with their names handwritten underneath, and above the doors in multicoloured capital letters were the names of the teachers.

McBride ignored the first two classrooms. He was humming quietly to himself. Mozart. He seized the handle of the door to his left and opened it slowly. As he stepped into the room the teacher turned to look at him. He frowned and lowered the book he was holding. There were thirty-two boys and girls sitting at tables, sharing textbooks. A few of the children were frowning but most of them were more quizzical than worried.

Grace Campbell was sitting at the table on the left of the room, between a red-haired boy and a plump girl with pigtails. McBride swung the gun up and pulled the trigger. Grace took the full force of the blast in her chest and she fell back as blood sprayed across the wall behind her.

The sound was deafening and the air was thick with acrid, choking cordite, but no one said anything. The children stared open-mouthed at McBride, unable to believe what they'd seen. The teacher, a middle-aged man with a receding hairline and a greying moustache, backed away, his hands up as if hoping to ward off the next shot.

McBride turned on his heel and walked out of the classroom. As he reloaded and headed across the corridor the screams began.

As McBride opened the door to the second classroom, the teacher was standing facing his class and shouting at them to be quiet. The children were talking among themselves but they immediately fell silent when they saw McBride and his shotgun. The teacher held up a hand, palm outward, as if he was a policeman stopping traffic. 'You can't come in here,' said the teacher firmly, in the voice that he used to keep unruly pupils in order.

McBride brought his gun to bear on a girl sitting by the window. Her name was Ruth Glazebrook and she had arrived at school that day with invitations to her eleventh birthday party. She was only inviting girls because she still thought that boys were yucky and besides, her mother had said that she could only invite six friends because they were going to go to McDonald's and money was tight. McBride pulled the trigger and Ruth's face disintegrated and she slammed against the wall.

The teacher staggered backwards and he tripped over a desk and fell to the floor before scrambling on all fours and hiding behind his desk.

The children sitting at Ruth's table stared at McBride in horror but the rest of the pupils ran to the back of the room. McBride raised the shotgun to his shoulder again, sighted on another girl and pulled the trigger. The girl's name was Emily Smith and she died clutching the invitation that Ruth had given her just minutes earlier. McBride walked out of the classroom, ejecting the two spent cartridges. He slotted in two fresh ones as he walked to the next classroom.

2

Phillippa Pritchard had heard the first shot but it had been in the playground and she'd assumed that it had been a car backfiring. The second shot had been closer but she still hadn't realised what it was until the screaming had started. The third and fourth shots followed in quick succession and the thirty-four children in her class all looked at her fearfully, waiting to be told what to do. The problem was, Phillippa had absolutely no idea what to tell them. She had been a teacher for almost twenty years, but nothing had prepared her for the sound of gunshots and the screaming of terrified children.

There was only one way out of the classroom and that was through the door that led to the corridor. Phillippa looked at the windows. They led out to the playing fields at the rear of the school. 'Everyone over to the windows, quickly!' she said. The children looked at her, too shocked to move. She clapped her hands. 'Come on, this is a fire drill. Let's pretend that the corridor is filled with smoke and that we have to escape through the windows.' She walked quickly over to the nearest window. It was the sash type with a catch. She took a chair from one of the boys and stood on it. She had to stand on tiptoe to reach the catch and it was stiff but she pushed hard and forced it to the side. She stepped down off the chair and pushed the lower pane up. 'Right, come on!' she said, pushing a table close to the window. 'Onto the chair and then onto the table and through the window. Come on, quickly!'

She heard a metallic click in the corridor and her stomach lurched as she realised what it was. The shotgun had been reloaded.

'Come on everybody, let's do this as quickly as possible!' shouted Phillippa, fighting to keep the fear out of her voice. The first pupil was on the table, looking nervously out of the window. It was Jacob Gray, a timid boy who had a tendency to blush when spoken to. 'Jeremy, jump, go on.'

'It's too high, miss,' he said, his voice trembling.

'Just do it, Jacob, you're holding everyone up.' The door handle turned slowly. Phillippa turned to look at the door, her heart in her mouth. The door opened and she saw the twin barrels of a shotgun followed by a green Wellington boot.

'Miss, I'm scared,' said Jacob.

'Just jump, now!' shouted Phillippa.

Phillippa gasped as the middle-aged man stepped into the classroom and raised the shotgun. He was grey-haired and ruddy-cheeked, as if he spent a lot of time outdoors. It was his eyes that chilled Phillippa. They were blank, almost lifeless. There was no tension in the man, no anger, no emotion at all. He just stood in the doorway looking slowly around the room, his finger on the trigger.

Phillippa took a step towards the man. She was more terrified than she'd ever been in her whole life but she knew that she had to protect the children. She put up her hands the way she'd try to calm a spooked horse and tried to maintain eye contact. 'You need to leave,' she said as calmly as she could. 'You need to go now. You're frightening the children.'

The man didn't look at her. He continued to scan the room, the twin barrels of his shotgun matching his gaze.

'You have to go,' said Phillippa, more forcibly this time, but still the man paid her no attention.

Jacob fell through the open window and yelped as he hit the ground outside. Phillippa took a quick look over her shoulder. Two girls were on the table and a third stood on the chair, looking anxiously at the man with the gun. Phillippa made a shooing motion with her hand then turned to look at the gunman.

He had raised his shotgun to his shoulder and Phillippa gasped as she saw his finger tighten on the trigger. He was aiming it at Paul Tomkinson, one of her favourite pupils, always eager to please and one of the first to put up his hand, no matter what the question being asked. She opened her mouth to scream but before the sound could leave her lips there was a deafening bang and the shotgun kicked in his hand. The children screamed and scattered like sheep to the back of the classroom. Phillippa realised that there was a child lying on the ground, what was left of his head touching the wall. Blood and gobs of brain were dripping down the wall.

Phillippa covered her mouth with trembling hands. The two girls on the table threw themselves through the window, screaming.

The man swung the shotgun in Phillippa's direction and her stomach turned liquid. She felt her bladder open and a warm wetness spread around her groin but she was barely aware of it. Her legs began to shake uncontrollably and she mentally began to run through the Lord's Prayer, Our Father, who art in Heaven, and then the shotgun swung away from her and roared again. A girl fell, her chest and face a bloody mess. Phillippa realised it was Brianna Foster, one of the quietest girls in the class, so passive that Phillippa had to constantly keep an eye on her to make sure that she wasn't being bullied.

Brianna lay on the floor like a broken doll as blood pooled around her. The gunman turned back to look at Phillippa and for the first time they had eye contact. He broke the shotgun and ejected the two cartridges. They flew through the air and clattered onto the floor.

The man groped in his haversack with his right hand, slotted in two fresh cartridges and snapped the weapon closed, all the time keeping his eyes fixed on Phillippa. He brought the shotgun up so that it was pointing at her chest and the breath caught in her throat. She was sure that she was going to die there in the classroom, in front of her pupils. Time seemed to freeze and all she could think of was that she would never see her husband again. Her dear darling Clive. She'd kissed him on the cheek when he'd left the house that morning and she'd said that she loved him and it gave her a small feeling of satisfaction that if they were her last words to him then at least he would know that he was loved. For the first time she saw something approaching emotion in his eyes. Not anger, not hatred, not contempt, but something approaching regret. She saw him swallow and then he turned around and walked out of the classroom.